Kamila KNOWS BEST

PRAISE FOR FARAH HERON

KAMILA KNOWS BEST

"Both Austenites and movie fans who fondly remember *Clueless* will be delighted."
—*Publishers Weekly*

"A sweet, slow-burn story."
—*Kirkus*

ACCIDENTALLY ENGAGED

A BEST BOOK OF THE YEAR FROM NPR, VULTURE, AND THE CBC!

"Reena and Nadim have electric chemistry, buoyed by Heron's crackling banter. But it's their tenderness, for each other and the food they adore, that lends the comedy some beautiful heft…*Accidentally Engaged* is voraciously readable…fresh, warm, soft in all the right places…both its comedic and emotional moments sing. We dare readers not to devour it. Grade: A."
—*Entertainment Weekly*

"*Accidentally Engaged* is an engaging read with authentic characters who continue to surprise you."
—*USA Today*

"Farah Heron spins a delectable tale brimming with wit, emotion, and deliciously sexy banter that will leave readers hungry for more." —Farrah Rochon, author of *The Boyfriend Project*

"A mouthwatering romantic comedy...This book is undoubtedly what Heron would pull out during the Showstopper Challenge on a literary version of *The Great British Bake Off*." —*BookPage*

"Equally sweet and spicy, this is sure to leave readers smiling." —*Publishers Weekly*

"Heron writes a compelling story...[that] will appeal to readers looking for complex family dramas and sumptuous descriptions of food and cooking." —*Kirkus*

"Full of heart and humor...Farah Heron balances the ingredients for a charming romance: a heroine finding her way, a swoonworthy love, a complicated but loving family, and a happily ever after." —Shelf Awareness

"Heron delivers an engaging romantic comedy that explores culture, family expectations, and personal growth." —*Library Journal*

"*Accidentally Engaged* has an optimism that I couldn't help but carry with me past the end of the book." —Smart Bitches Trashy Books

FARAH HERON

FOREVER

New York Boston

Forever
Hachette Book Group
1290 Avenue of the Americas, New York, NY 10104
read-forever.com
twitter.com/readforeverpub

First Edition: March 2022

Forever is an imprint of Grand Central Publishing. The Forever name and logo are trademarks of Hachette Book Group, Inc.

The publisher is not responsible for websites (or their content) that are not owned by the publisher.

The Hachette Speakers Bureau provides a wide range of authors for speaking events. To find out more, go to www.hachettespeakersbureau.com or call (866) 376-6591.

Library of Congress Cataloging-in-Publication Data

Names: Heron, Farah, author.
Title: Kamila knows best / Farah Heron.
Description: First Edition. | New York : Forever, 2022.
Identifiers: LCCN 2021041686 | ISBN 9781538735008 (trade paperback) | ISBN 9781538734995 (ebook)
Classification: LCC PR9199.4.H4695 K36 2022 | DDC 813/.6--dc23
LC record available at https://lccn.loc.gov/2021041686

ISBNs: 9781538735008 (trade paperback), 9781538734995 (ebook)

Printed in the United States of America

LSC-C

Printing 1, 2021

*To my family, who always let me unleash
my inner extra-ness.*

I do not know whether it ought to be so, but certain silly things cease to be silly if done by sensible people in an imprudent way.

—Jane Austen, *Emma*

Kamila

KNOWS

BEST

CHAPTER 1

Kamila Hussain didn't have a lot to complain about in her life. She realized self-loathing was all the rage among her millennial peers, but in her opinion, she didn't have much to loathe. She was blessed with a steady income as an accountant at Emerald, her father's accounting firm. She loved her job and had recently redesigned the office with soothing pastels and stress-relieving greenery, so it was a joy to be there. She had no shortage of friends, and if she wanted a little something more, she had no problem finding dates or hookups. She adored her living situation—a quaint brownstone in Toronto's east side that had also been recently redone. And of course, she had Darcy, her adorable bichon frise. Darcy was arguably the cutest dog east of Yonge Street, with more Instagram followers than many reality stars, and who had gone full-on viral on TikTok five times.

But in her own eyes, the most significant of Kamila's blessings was her father. Dad was easily the sweetest, kindest, most supportive parent in existence. Being a daddy's girl was such a cliché, but Kamila had no shame in telling anyone that she happily lived and worked with her father. He wouldn't do well alone, and Dad deserved to be healthy and happy more than anyone in the world.

In fact, it was for him that she was awake at eight on a Saturday morning, even after she was muddling fruit for virgin caipirinhas pretty late last night. Dad's annual physical was in a few days, and she intended to do whatever she could to make sure his blood pressure and cholesterol were in line. She couldn't leave the men to fend for themselves for breakfast this time. Nope. No eggs fried in ghee and boiled chai on her watch.

She smoothed her robin's-egg blue apron over her red floral full-skirted dress and admired her kitchen prep. The toast toppings she'd mashed, diced, and sliced were in colorful handmade Portuguese bowls that glowed against her white marble countertops. She snapped a pic and uploaded it. #dreamkitchen. #blessed. #homecooking.

"Kamila is cooking," Rohan said from the stairs. "Isn't this the third sign of the apocalypse?"

She glared at him. "Shush, you, or you don't get any."

He was still in his pajamas—a matched buttoned-up set. Did he dress like this even alone at home? His hair needed to be combed, and his chin needed a shave, but somehow Rohan still managed to exude the air of the powerful corporate executive he was. Hearing his voice, Darcy's ears perked up and she rushed to him. Because of course she did—the only human Darcy loved as much as Kamila and Dad was Rohan, despite Rohan's usual indifference to her. Kamila really needed to have a girl-to-girl with her dog about when to ease off if your affections weren't returned.

Rohan chuckled at the dog while rubbing his fingers over the scruff on his own chin.

Kamila put her hands on her hips. "No snark from you

today, mister. Dad needs to eat better. Every weekend he fries eggs in ghee."

"I'm looking forward to trying something new," Dad said from behind Rohan on the stairs. "Kamila takes such good care of me. Can I help you, beti?"

Kamila looked carefully at her father's eyes as he reached the bottom step. They looked a little tired, which was expected for early on a Saturday. But there was a hint of amusement and contentedness there. Good. Kamila spent a great deal of time studying her father's eyes. It helped that they were so expressive. Some people wore their heart on their sleeve, but Kassim Hussain showed it in his eyes.

"I got it, Dad. Go ahead and sit. I'll pour your tea."

He smiled and planted himself at the dining table, then opened his iPad to read the news. "You always take such good care of everyone, Kamila. Rohan, did she tell you she's in charge of the puppy prom for the animal shelter this year? That's the last event at Dogapalooza, right, beti?"

"That's right, Dad."

The Dogapalooza was an annual fundraiser for the animal shelter where Kamila had volunteered for years. This year, she and her friend Tim were in charge of planning the festival's final event—the Sunday-night puppy prom.

Rohan looked sideways at Kamila. "Can't say I'm surprised Kam would volunteer for a party. She's a consummate host."

"Did you just compliment me?" she asked playfully as Rohan joined her in the kitchen.

"That's up for interpretation." He looked at the spread of dishes Kamila had already prepared. "You know, when I said yesterday that your Uber Eats account might see more action than your Tinder account, I wasn't hinting for you to cook. Chai and toast are fine." He swiped a cherry tomato from the colander and ate it. "Are those sweet potatoes? For breakfast?"

"They're high in potassium to lower Dad's blood pressure. I got hibiscus tea, too. It's good for both blood pressure and blood sugar. He's going to nail his physical."

He leaned back against the marble counter. "Food to manage his blood pressure? Wow, Kam, I'm impressed."

"Why are you impressed? I can google."

"Clearly." He looked again at the spread laid out on the counter, then at the new canvas print she'd hung on the kitchen wall. It was Darcy's head photoshopped onto a French chef's body, standing outside a Paris bistro. Rohan shook his head, laughing at the print. "At least you're cooking and not Darcy. Actually, you have more cooking ability than I realized. Or at least"—he looked into the bowls again—"mashing-black-stuff ability. What is that sludge, anyway?"

"Crushed black beans."

He raised a brow, skeptical, then looked at the clear glass teapot where vibrant red hibiscus flowers were steeping in hot water. "Can I have regular chai instead?"

"You know where it is."

He filled a pot for his chai. Normally, Kamila would never expect a guest to make their own tea, but Rohan was hardly a stranger in this house. He spent most Friday nights in her spare room after her Bollywood-and-biryani party instead of driving back to his downtown condo, so he and Dad could talk business after breakfast. "I don't get why you go through all this trouble, Kam. After last night's spectacle—"

"Last night's party was *not* a spectacle. It was low-key. I didn't even serve a signature mocktail."

"Then what were those Brazilian things you all were drinking?"

"Virgin caipirinhas! Ernesto brought them. Wasn't that sweet of him? He brought the makings for alcoholic ones, too."

Kamila *did* drink, but not very often. And she never drank at her own parties—she preferred to be alert and sober when hosting her friends. She went back to quartering bright cherry tomatoes for the pico de gallo. Kamila accepted that *low-key* by her standards was a pretty swank party to most, but since she hosted her friends for dinner and a movie every week, the party wasn't that much exertion for her anymore. She may have sourced a special Kashmiri biryani last night to match the old Kashmiri movie Rohan had picked, but the charcuterie board didn't have any single-origin dark chocolate on it this time. She hadn't even put out her special party throw cushions and candles.

"Besides," she said, dropping the tomatoes in a bowl, "considering you've never missed one of my movie parties, I'm surprised you're complaining."

"I'm not complaining. But I'd be here even if you served potato chips from a bag."

Probably true. Rohan loved old Hindi movies more than the average tax lawyer. "Maybe next week we can get you to join in the postmovie sing-along."

Rohan snorted. "Who taught you to play Bollywood hits on the ukulele anyway?"

"I'm taking lessons over video conference." She adjusted the tomatoes in the bowl a bit, then clapped her hands together. The tomatoes looked like glimmering rubies with the bright pot lights reflecting on them. "Look at all this color." She snapped a picture with her phone.

"Ah. Your true motivation. Your precious Instagram."

"We eat with our eyes first." She took a short video clip of the spread of food.

"You eat with your camera even before that." He hopped out of the sight line of the camera. "Hey, leave me out of this. I don't want to turn up on your tick-tack-toe thing."

"It's TikTok. You don't have to participate in social media, but unless you want to further solidify this boomer rep of yours, at least learn what the platforms are called."

"Eh. What's the point if I don't use them? And unlike everyone else in the world, I don't need the clicks to know my worth."

Kamila laughed. "I don't use social media to tell me my worth. I already know I'm fabulous. That's why I have a duty to share all this with the world." She swept her hands over her dress with flourish. "Now, go wait with Dad, old man," she said, throwing in the nickname to annoy him. "You're making me nervous. Nerves combined with newly sharpened knives are a disaster in the making."

Kamila knew Rohan's snarky comments were just teasing, and she usually liked to volley right back. She'd known him literally her whole life, and they both knew exactly which buttons to press without going too far. Still, she wasn't exactly an experienced cook, and she'd prefer to finish the job without a running commentary.

He snorted. "Fine. If only to spare your flawless skin." He smirked as he took the tray with his masala chai and Dad's hibiscus tea to the dining room. Kamila picked up the next vegetable to cut.

As if on cue, disaster chose that moment to strike. The honed steel knife slipped in her hand and sliced her finger instead of the organic sweet potato. No problem. Barely a scrape. As she rustled in the drawer looking for a bandage, several crimson drops of blood spilled onto a bag of rubber bands. She took a breath as she reflexively wrapped her hand in her apron, and cringed as a red stain grew on the pale-blue fabric.

Her beautiful new apron. "Siri, what gets out blood stains?"

"Oh dear, beti, what happened?" Dad rushed to her side while Siri was detailing the wonders of hydrogen peroxide and enzyme soap. He unwrapped the apron from her finger, his gentle touch and concerned expression grounding her. "Oh no. I'll get the first-aid kit." He smiled and lovingly patted Kamila's arm. "Everything is okay, Kamila. Do your breathing. I'll be right back."

Dad rewrapped the finger in her now probably ruined apron and disappeared up the stairs. She pressed on the cut to stop the blood as she leaned against the fridge, feeling light-headed. Even after all these years, she couldn't cope with the sight of her own blood.

She closed her eyes and heard her therapist's voice in her ears. *Breathe.* The apron—maybe it could be saved? *Count to ten.* She had plenty of peroxide from a misguided attempt to go blond a few years back. Actually, this was a much better use for that peroxide. She opened her eyes and focused on a point on the wall. *One, two...*

Rohan stepped back into the kitchen.

"Don't say it," she warned.

"Don't say what?"

"Any comment at all about my ineptitude in the kitchen."

Shockingly, his smirk was nowhere to be found. He took her apron-wrapped finger in his hand and applied firm pressure as he looked into her eyes. "You're shaking, Kam."

Was she shaking? *Three, four...* "I don't like blood." She shivered, looking down. The room was spinning a bit. Not much, really. She was fine.

"Kamila, breathe deeply. Talk to me. Tell me what you're doing for the rest of the day."

Five, six... "I have a meeting with a prospective client, and then I'm taking Darcy to the dog park for a photo shoot." Her voice was shaky.

"A client meeting in that dress?"

She tried to smile and even tease him back, but her voice was too brittle and her words weren't working.

"Look at me, Kam."

She did. His eyes were so familiar. Deep and dark. And *here.*

Seven, eight, nine... Whenever disaster struck—and she reluctantly agreed it struck this family often—Rohan was here.

Still holding her hand, Rohan spoke with a soothing voice. "Look at all this you've done here. It's exquisite. You've even got the June Cleaver dress on. With matching shoes."

Ten. She let out a breath, grounding herself in his face. Focusing on it. Studying it, mostly so she wouldn't pass out. But also, she noticed something.

"That's more than a day's worth of stubble on your face," she said weakly.

He chuckled, still holding her hand. "I'm considering growing a beard. What do you think?"

She narrowed her eyes. "It will suit you."

This Rohan, the one in pajamas in her house every Saturday morning, wasn't the Rohan the rest of the world saw. He was usually in suits and ties so high-end and perfectly tailored that any facial-hair situation would complement them, so long as it was neat and tidy. He'd probably look even *more* dignified with a beard. She nodded, letting a smile sneak onto her face.

The room had stopped spinning. She pulled her hand back from his and wrapped the apron tighter around it. She felt weird about Rohan seeing her freak out there, but it was fine. They were friends.

The landline phone rang, and she heard Dad answering it upstairs.

Kamila turned back to the food so she wouldn't break down again. She lined up the uncut sweet potatoes on the board. "You're ordering the biryani for next week's movie night, right?"

"Yep." He plunked another cherry tomato into his mouth. "I scoped out a new place. We will be feasting on Burmese biryani."

She raised one eyebrow. "Burmese? Trying to one-up me for the Kashmiri?"

"It looked interesting. The biryani is served with a dried shrimp topping."

Kamila was skeptical. "At least it's my turn to choose the movie. Enough of your epic oldies. I have the perfect film picked out for next week. *Jab We Met*. It's about a buttoned-up business-man and the free-spirited woman who makes him want to live again." Kamila wrinkled her nose. "Now that I think about it, that's really sexist. Like, the only purpose for the quirky woman is to be an object that teaches the uptight man to enjoy life? But anyway, the scenery in it is supposed to be amazing. And I checked—the lead actress dances soaking wet in the rain. I know you're not happy unless you see at least one dancing-in-the-rain scene in an Indian movie."

He blinked, blank faced.

"You know it's true, Rohan. I swear, if I ever find a man who looks at me the way you look at a woman in a wet sari, I'll be set for life."

He laughed, turning to look at the food on the counter. "Is there an issue with how that child you're dating looks at you?"

"Ernesto is *twenty-three*. And we were *hooking up*, not dating. It was an FWB situation."

"FWB?"

"Friends with benefits. But the benefit period has now ended. His internship is done and he's heading back to Brazil today. That's why he left before the movie last night."

Rohan's head tilted in what looked like genuine concern. "Oh, I'm sorry. I didn't know. You okay?"

Kamila shrugged. "We had fun, but like I said, casual." She frowned when she remembered Ernesto's goodbye last night. "It's probably for the best he's leaving now—the guy was growing a little too . . . enamored. I would have had to have broken it off anyway."

"Honestly, Kam, I don't get how you can only want casual. You don't want people feeling things for you?"

She rolled her eyes. "Of course I want people *feeling* things for me. Just not, like, permanent commitment-type feelings. Casual is the new exclusive." She exaggeratedly looked around the empty room before lowering her voice and stepping closer to him. "It's pretty great to only have shiny new-relationship sex and never boring routine sex. Nothing like that new man smell." She licked her lips, watching a cute shade of pink rise up Rohan's cheeks.

This was fun. "Although . . ." she continued. "I *am* going to miss Ernesto. We had a *private* final date on Thursday, and let me tell you, that man is talented. He could do this thing with his fingers and his tongue in sync—"

Rohan slapped her hip with a tea towel to stop her. Probably best. She loved knowing she could unravel Mr. Buttoned-Up like that, but she knew he wasn't getting much action. It was cruel to rub it in. "Anyway," she said. "You *know* why I only do casual. I have no intention of abandoning Dad, and that's what a serious relationship would do. All a girl needs are friends, companionship, and sex. I have plenty of the first two, and I always know exactly where to find the third."

Her father wasn't over Kamila's best friend, Asha, who'd lived just around the corner, moving four kilometers away into her new wife's McMansion. Bad enough that Kamila's sister, Shelina, and her husband, Zayan, who happened to be Rohan's brother, moved two hours away to London, Ontario, with their sons a few years ago.

Rohan was still a touch pink, so she decided to see how frazzled a CEO could get. "You should think about having casual sex sometime, old man. You've been divorced for what—a year now? I saw an ad for a seniors mixer at the community center. Want me to get the deets for you?"

He looked comically affronted and almost said something before shaking his head, smiling. "Kamila Hussain, you are *trouble*. Capital T. I have no idea why I put up with you."

She smiled her sweetest smile and ran her finger over that scruff on his cheek. "Because I make you feel young again."

At thirty-two, Rohan was only five years older than her twenty-seven, so hardly an old man. With his rock-climber's body, chiseled jaw, and seriously intimidating demeanor, he was the perfect example of a high-powered King Street executive. Except, of course, on Saturday mornings when he was in his pajamas and swatting Kamila with tea towels. Rohan would have a lineup of women happy to be casual, committed, or anything in between if he wanted it. But he didn't seem to be interested after his wife left him.

Dad reappeared then, a small box of bandages in his hand. "Sorry, beti, I had a phone call."

Kamila took the box from him. "Go, sit, drink your tea." She could handle this. Her blood thing was usually only a problem at the first sight of her own blood. Rohan looked back at her, concerned. "I got this. Go sit," she told him.

"Okay, but I'll be right here if you need me to put out any fires."

After bandaging her own hand, she finished slicing the sweet potatoes and put two slices in the toaster.

"That was Rashida on the phone," Dad said to Rohan. "Jana Suleiman is returning from Tajikistan soon."

What? No. Kamila must have misheard. Jana Suleiman's fancy contract at an international aid agency was supposed to go on for a few more months.

"Her contract is over already?" Rohan asked.

"Apparently she's left her post early," Dad said.

They continued talking about Jana the Great, while Kamila's mind was reeling. *Fudge.* Kamila did not like Jana Suleiman.

She took a breath. This wasn't a big deal. Her focus should only be on Dad's health and growing her client list at Emerald. So what if her secret nemesis was moving back to town? She felt a throbbing in her finger, a reminder that she'd already had one mishap here and didn't need another. But it was fine. One cut finger was hardly a fire to be put out.

Dad suddenly stood, knocking his chair to the floor. "Kamila! The toaster's on fire! You need to put it out!"

Damn it.

CHAPTER 2

K amila put that little kitchen inferno out of her mind because her client meeting today was beyond important. It *had* to go well—this was a dream client. It was exactly the type of large, complicated account Kamila needed to prove to Dad that she could manage things fine if he went down to part-time at Emerald. But if there was one thing Kamila prided herself on, it was her ability to brush off setbacks and forge ahead, usually with impeccable style. And style was something she'd need to wow this client—Nirvana Lotus Day Spa was a buzz-worthy establishment whose soothing bamboo and vibrant lotus flower decor was so Insta-worthy the place had risen to the top of Toronto spots to be photographed in. That was why Kamila hadn't changed out of the full-skirted floral dress and matching heels.

After arriving at the posh building, she gave her name to the receptionist and waited for one of the spa owners to meet her.

Five minutes later, a woman appeared in the waiting room. "Ah! Kamila! Fabulous! Thank you so much for meeting me on a Saturday! I'm sorry I had to cancel yesterday. Can I offer you a manicure to make up for it? I was just about to get my weekly polish change."

This was Kacey McKinley, one of the owners of the spa. Kamila wasn't about to say no to the manicure, as she'd discovered that business owners were easier to please when immersed in the services they provided. She'd signed a hairstylist client while getting her color done, and she'd secured Ink Girls, a chain of tattoo shops, while a watercolor-style peony was tattooed to the side of her right rib cage just last week.

"So, tell me more about your company itself," Kacey asked as the technician soaked off Kamila's polish. "I'm always looking to support women-owned businesses."

"Well, we're not woman-owned per se. My father owns Emerald. Dad is all about gender equality, though!" Kamila cringed, well aware that she sounded amateurish. She sat up straighter as a woman wearing a dust mask clipped her cuticles. "We each keep our own clients. He works mainly in the health-care sector, while I'm moving toward providing freelance CPA and financial-analyst services for small- to medium-sized service-industry businesses."

"You don't look anything like any of the other accountants I've met with."

Kamila grinned. She knew she didn't look or dress like most accountants. For some, that might be a negative, but for a client like Kacey McKinley, it was a strike in Kamila's favor.

"I'll be honest with you, Kamila. I'm meeting with other accountants this week," Kacey continued. "Bigger firms that have experience working with businesses at our level. We are planning to expand significantly in the near future, and the finance piece of it will get complicated. Plus, a conscientious accountant is important to us. We value sustainability and ethical commerce above all else. Did you know we work with a women's collective in the Congo to make the herbal soaks in our vitality ponds?"

The nail tech held out a tray of gel polishes, and Kamila picked a nude similar to the one Kacey was having applied. Not Kamila's usual vibrant hues, but maybe she needed to play the part here. "I've done a lot of research on your business." Kamila would normally have brought out a file folder with a full proposal for the client at this point, but her hands were, of course, occupied. Good thing she had a stellar memory. "On the phone you mentioned looking for new capital. Well, I found several grants for women-owned businesses in Ontario you can apply for. You can also leverage your work with the local college to get funding from the Ministry of Education. And there are opportunities if you register as a sustainable business. Another of my clients was able to get—"

Kacey interrupted her. "I'm interviewing an intellectual collective next—a group of women who provide business services cooperatively. Every summer they pack up their business and work remotely while planting trees in the North."

Kacey continued talking about this collective, which progressed to her telling Kamila about her mind-opening trip to Thailand where the Buddhist Eightfold Path had enlightened her brain to the possibilities of conscious business, and how compassion and sustainability were driving the momentum forward in her spa.

Kamila smiled and nodded, realizing that signing this client seemed unlikely at this point. She wished she'd gone with the red polish.

☂

After first nearly burning down her house and having her unsustainable and inexperienced accounting practice rejected by a Buddhist white lady in palazzo pants and a headwrap, Kamila desperately needed a boost to her self-image. Thankfully, she had plans with her friend Asha that afternoon. The Norwegian colorwork sweaters she'd ordered for Darcy and Asha's dog, Lizzy, had finally come in, so it was time for a photo shoot of the two dogs frolicking in the fall leaves wearing their Nordic attire. Darcy's fans were clamoring for new glamour shots, and with any luck, she'd go viral again. After rushing home to change and get the dog and her sweater, Kamila drove to her neighborhood dog park.

"You look...autumnal," Asha said as Kamila got out of her car. Kamila had changed into a full-skirted cream shirtdress covered with huge orange-and-yellow blooms. She'd paired the dress with an open mustard cardigan and knee-high boots in the softest brown leather imaginable.

Kamila kissed her friend on both cheeks. "I'm so stoked it's finally sweater weather. That septum ring new?"

Asha grinned, tilting forward so Kamila could get a closer look at her ornate new nose ring. "Another gift from Nicole. She likes to adorn me like a Christmas tree, and I'm loving every second of it."

Asha looked effortlessly luminous, as she always did. Her riot of curls was barely held back with a yellow scarf today, and she was wearing her standard black-leggings-and-dress combo with a red lipstick that looked amazing against her rich brown skin. Kamila had known Asha for about four years, since Kamila had started volunteering at the nearby animal shelter where Asha was the operations manager. They'd chatted while Kamila cleaned up after puppies and cut carrots for rabbits, and Kamila was delighted to learn that Asha lived in the condo on the other side of the dog park. When Asha adopted a one-year-old corgi that had been surrendered to the shelter with the unfortunate name of Lizard-Monster, Kamila acknowledged that as the owner of a dog named Darcy, she had no choice but to be good friends with someone who had a dog named Lizzy. Their friendship had only deepened in the last couple of years.

Kamila looked down at the sweater stretched over Lizzy's back. "The sweater is a bit..."

Asha frowned. "Tight—yeah, I know. Lizzy's also getting spoiled these days. Two moms, double the treats. Twice last week he tricked Nicole into giving him a second dinner. We need to figure out a system."

Kamila patted the dog's head with amusement, then looped her arm through Asha's. "C'mon, let's get some pictures by the trees before going to the off-leash area. If we get good shots, I want to photoshop them into this Norwegian Christmas market picture I found."

It was supremely basic to wax poetic about fall, but Kamila was happy to own her basic-girl status, because September was so excessively idyllic. The warm sun. The hollow hum of cicadas and laughing children excited to be reunited with their friends after summer holidays. Foliage transforming to the exact tones that best complemented Darcy's pale-beige and white fur and brown eyes. These pictures would be epic, even unphotoshopped into Norway.

But the moment Kamila unclipped Darcy's leash for pictures, the dog jumped headfirst into a pile of leaves. Lizzy looked on, head cocked, knowing his mom wouldn't approve of him joining his free-spirited friend. Lizzy might have had the fine eyes of Elizabeth Bennet, but they were paired with the dignified stoicism of Fitzwilliam Darcy. Kamila had often wondered if the two dogs should trade names.

"Take pictures quickly. Darcy's sweater will be caked in leaves in about three seconds. I'm not sure wool is best for active dogs," Asha said, gently urging Lizzy to play with his friend.

Kamila hurriedly took some pictures with her phone.

"How did your client meeting go today?" Asha said as she picked up a suspicious Lizzy and attempted to deposit him in the leaves.

"Terribly. Look at this profoundly drab manicure." Kamila held up one hand to show off her nails. "I think this is all I'll be getting from Nirvana Lotus Day Spa. Certainly not a freelance accountant retainer."

"Oh no! Why not?"

Kamila sighed. "She didn't seem that impressed with me. It's fine. I'm not sure I want to work with a born-again Buddhist vegan anyway. I'm feeling a little wounded that she didn't think I was *righteous* enough, though."

"Righteous? Is that what she said?"

"She implied it. And she implied I couldn't possibly have the experience needed to work with them on an expansion. It's frustrating. I have loads of new clients, but they're all pretty small. If I got a big client like this, maybe I could convince Dad to go part-time."

"Didn't your dad's client refer someone to you last week? How did that pan out?"

Kamila snorted. "Even worse than the spa. He's like this sixty-eight-year-old who owns a chain of medical walk-in clinics. I agreed to meet him so Dad wouldn't take the new client, but that dude's not going to hire me. I'm learning that I lack a certain something many of Dad's older clients prefer in an accountant."

"A penis, I assume."

"Yep. Or at least glasses and sensible slacks."

Asha laughed. "Glasses might look cute on you, though."

"Of course they'd look cute on me." Kamila snapped some more pictures as Lizzy sniffed Darcy's nose.

"If it's any consolation, Nicole is technically one of your dad's older clients, and she adores you. She'd switch to you in a second if he retired."

"Yeah, I don't see that happening, anyway. Dad retiring, I mean. Honestly, if he'd just agree to go part-time, I'd worry less." She put her phone down and grinned at Asha. "And of course Nicole loves me. I introduced her to the love of her life."

"And you'll never let any of us forget it."

"Nope. I'm a matchmaking *artiste*. I'm very proud of my work."

Kamila had always enjoyed playing matchmaker for her friends, but she was particularly proud of Asha and Nicole. They were different races, religions, and tax brackets and had a ten-year age difference, and yet the moment that Asha told Kamila she was looking for something long-term, Kamila knew Dad's client Nicole was for her. A quiet, Black, plant-loving ob-gyn and a self-proclaimed social-justice-focused Indian dog lover weren't an obvious match, but as expected, it was practically love at first sight. It was their complementary dry and sometimes absurdist senses of humor. Plus, their love of cheesy movies and romance novels.

Kamila snapped another picture of Lizzy. Darcy was still digging in the leaves, but Kamila at least managed to capture Darcy's rear end in the shot.

Asha's text tone rang then. She glanced at her phone. "It's Maricel. She's bringing some shelter dogs here for a walk in a bit."

"Oh, good." Kamila grinned. "I found some possible spaces for her puppy academy." Maricel was one of Asha's employees at the shelter, and Kamila was helping her launch a dog-training business. "I was totally going to call her earlier, but it slipped my mind after the calamity at breakfast."

"What calamity at breakfast? Your dad didn't like the sweet potatoes?"

"He'd have liked them fine if he'd actually eaten any." She managed to get a few more pictures, some miraculously with both dogs' faces in the frame. "The toaster went up in flames before I could serve anything."

"Holy shit, Kamila! Fire? How did that happen?"

Kamila put her hands on her hips. "It wasn't my fault. I'm pretty sure Mercury is in retrograde or something. It would explain a lot about my day. I was following the recipe and suddenly the sweet potatoes were on fire."

"The sweet potatoes were in the toaster?"

She'd already put up with Rohan's incredulous rant about why she'd put vegetables in the toaster—she didn't need to hear it from her best friend. "Asha, it was sweet potato toast—how else was I supposed to toast them?"

Asha shook her head, clearly straining not to laugh, so Kamila went back to photographing the dogs.

"You should have at least kept an eye on them in the toaster," Asha said.

"I know. I was distracted. I'd just heard Jana Suleiman is coming back to town."

Kamila was fully aware that pettiness wasn't an attractive character trait, so she'd kept her father's best friend's daughter's status as her secret nemesis to herself. Asha had only met Jana a few times and barely knew her.

"Oh. It'll be great to have your old friend back in the neighborhood."

Kamila shrugged. Old friend? Hardly. Not when Jana had always been smug about clearly being a better daughter to her parents than Kamila was. But there was more to Kamila's dislike of Jana. When Kamila and Jana were both in their last year of high school, the nosy aunties in their circle told Kamila's parents that they saw Kamila in a parked car outside Jana's house with the neighborhood bad boy, Bronx Bennet, when she was supposed to be at school. That was bad, because Kamila had been forbidden to see Bronx since the last time she'd been caught in a parked car with him.

But the thing was, even though Kamila *had* skipped school that day, and even though she and Bronx *had* still been secretly hooking up, she hadn't actually been with him that day. Kamila had spent the whole day at the mall. But of course, Kamila's mother hadn't believed her.

Mom used to throw these massive parties back then...and she'd hosted a huge one for Shelina a few years earlier for her high school graduation. Kamila didn't really want a graduation party, but Dad (bless him) insisted that Kamila deserved a party, too. But after the Bronx-in-the-backseat accusation, Mom deleted Kamila from her party. Deleted Kamila, not canceled the party, because she'd already hired the caterer and rented a hall. She proclaimed the celebration was now in honor of Jana's fancy scholarships. When Kamila confronted Bronx about the incident, he told her it had been Jana in the car with him. Jana had known Kamila had lost her graduation party because of this accusation, and she hadn't come forward to admit it was really her steaming up Bronx's old Toyota's windows.

But even though Kamila lost the hookup buddy, and any respect she had for Jana Suleiman, she decided not to tell anyone the truth about it. Jana was heading to Oxford in the fall, and the last thing Kamila wanted was for something to jeopardize her nemesis's school admission. Kamila preferred Jana on another continent.

Kamila didn't want to talk or think about Jana anymore. She shook her head while mounding the leaves in a pile. It wasn't working; Darcy was diving in and destroying her progress the moment she had more than three leaves assembled. "Darcy! Can you not?"

"How is your kitchen?" Asha asked.

"The kitchen's fine. The toaster is . . . toast. Rohan put the fire out before any other damage."

"Thank goodness Rohan was there."

"Yes, yes." She waved her hand. "Super Rohan saving the day, like always," she said with plenty of sarcasm in her voice. "I could have dealt with it. I know where the fire extinguisher is. But whatevs. Anyway, a new toaster will be delivered tomorrow. I got a turquoise one this time. Do you think it will work with the brass fixtures? Or should I—"

"He's over a lot lately," Asha interrupted.

Kamila gave up and lifted Darcy out of the leaves. "Who?"

"Rohan."

"Yeah, of course he is. He loves Bollywood, and he and Dad talk business after breakfast every Saturday." Dad pretty much ran the show at Emerald, but it was technically a subsidiary of Rohan's company. And Dad still had a minority share in that company.

"I just hope it's not because he's lonely, but yeah, I think that man is into Bollywood even more than Nicole. Did I tell you I caught her reading the *Times of India* gossip pages?"

Kamila flashed a satisfied smile. "You two have the perfect marriage. I did really well there."

"Do I get any credit for the success of my marriage?"

Kamila beamed, shaking her head. "Nope. It's all on me. I have a gift, you know."

Asha laughed, reaching to pull Lizzy out of the leaves. "You should set up Rohan with someone next."

What? That was an utterly ridiculous idea. Kamila picked more leaves off Darcy's sweater. "Why would I set Rohan up with anyone?"

"C'mon. All alone in his gilded cage? He's clearly craving company. He should at least get a dog."

"Rohan's not a dog person. He had a cat, but his ex-wife took it in their divorce settlement." Kamila clipped Darcy's designer leash to her purple studded leather collar. "And a King Street penthouse is hardly a gilded cage. Although..." She frowned. "I haven't actually seen his condo. Holy cheese crackers, do you think his place is actually gold? I mean...he *is* an uptight finance lawyerly type. Oh my god, do you think it's all like Trump Towers–esque?"

"Hold your tongue, Kamila. You're technically a finance type, too."

"I'm a glorified bookkeeper in a small tax office over a coffee shop."

"Kamila. You're a CPA who is trying to expand her business."

"Yes, and Rohan is one of the city's top tax lawyers and owns one of the province's largest financial service providers, with offices in Toronto, Ottawa, and London, Ontario. You do see the difference, right?"

Asha shrugged. "You're both capitalist money crunchers, as far as I'm concerned. And you have an awful lot of brass fixtures in your house, so maybe you shouldn't talk about *gilded* homes?"

Kamila's nose wrinkled. She didn't much like being called a capitalistic money cruncher, but it was technically true. "So, *do* you think Rohan's place is all nouveau riche? I mean, it's strange he's never invited us over, right? Maybe that's why."

"Doubt it. Probably standard dude decorating. I'd put money on a black leather chair somewhere. Maybe a recliner. A whiskey decanter with those rocks that you freeze to chill your drink. He's been alone for how long—three years?"

"Only two-ish years since he and Lisa separated. Divorce finalized a year this month."

Asha's eyes sparkled with mischief. "He's totally ready for someone new. Who can we find for Rohan? Aren't you still looking for someone for Maricel, too?"

Kamila's head shook vigorously. "I just said no!" The entire thought was preposterous. "Yes, I'm looking for a man for Maricel, but I am *not* setting up Rohan. With anyone. We've got a happy balance in the family right now. Equilibrium. You know I'm not looking for a serious relationship for Dad's sake, and Rohan in a relationship again would be worse, right? He's supposed to take Dad to the doctor this week!" Kamila loved her father, but he was a bit...old-school. After Kamila and her sister noticed that he avoided the doctor when either of them offered to take him, they realized he'd prefer a male escorting him to his medical appointments. Since Kamila's brother-in-law moved away, that job fell to Rohan.

"Yeah, I guess it's a bit more complicated to play matchmaker with someone you're related to."

"We are *not* related." Well, not technically, at least. Rohan was Kamila's sister's brother-in-law, not hers. "Rohan is my..." She frowned. *Friend* didn't seem right. Tim was a friend. Maricel and Asha were friends. "He's...my *Rohan*. I've known him *forever*. And if he finds another relationship, he won't help with Dad. We barely saw him when he was with Lisa. What Rohan needs is to get laid, not a girlfriend. But he doesn't believe in casual."

"Ah. So, it's selfishness. It's not Rohan's happiness you're thinking of here."

"Really, Asha? How is it selfish if I'm putting Dad's well-being first?" Kamila sighed. Rohan knew better than anyone how fragile Dad's health was. Besides, if he actually wanted a relationship, he would date. He wouldn't need Kamila to help him find someone.

And yeah, she'd only this morning suggested he find someone to hook up with, but a hookup wasn't the same thing as a relationship, and Kamila's matchmaking endeavors were only for relationships. Sex, as she'd told him, was easy to come by. Apps were perfectly sufficient. Rohan could find his own darn bedroom playmate if he wanted one. Her nose wrinkled. "I'm not getting any good pictures here. May as well let the dogs play in the off-leash." Kamila gave Darcy a scratch behind the ear and guided her dog to the off-leash area of the park.

"Hey, there's Dane," Asha said, waving to a twentysomething man with a medium-sized dog as they walked into the fenced-in off-leash area. He waved back at them. Dane was the husky owner who had rented Asha's condo when she moved into Nicole's house. Kamila had first met him at the dog park last week. He was a bit of a tech bro and was white, with medium-brown hair and a nice smile. And more importantly, he was single. His dog, Byte, was a bit of a nightmare obedience-wise, though. What Dane needed was a dog-training girlfriend. And Kamila had the perfect candidate.

She squealed under her breath as they made their way to him. "This is amazing. Maricel's on her way."

Asha's eyes narrowed. "You're not thinking Dane and Maricel, are you?"

"Of course I am." Kamila beamed. "They're an ideal match. Maricel loves dogs but doesn't have one, so she needs a boyfriend with one. And only a dog lover would put up with Byte."

"Are you more concerned with the dog's happiness or the humans'?"

"C'mon, Asha. Dane's nice to look at. And Maricel is a total catch. Hey, there she is!"

Maricel had the leashes of four excited dogs in one hand, and was unlocking the gate to the off-leash area with the other. Kamila winced when she noticed who one of those dogs was.

Maricel Aquino was sweet, good-natured, and beautiful, the type one would expect to be followed by woodland creatures serenading her, not by an absolute hound of hell. But that was the best way to describe the shelter dog Maricel was currently unclipping from her leash to run free in the enclosure.

"Oh my god." Kamila's hand was on her mouth. "They're letting *Xena* visit the dog park?"

"Yeah, apparently her socialization has been going well, so

they've added dog-park trips to her training. I'm skeptical." Lizzy looked skeptical, too, and gave Asha a short bark, warning that something chaotic was about to go down.

Kamila decided to heed Lizzy's warning. She was plucking Darcy into her arms just as Xena ran by at a speed that made Kamila wonder if there was a little greyhound in her beagle mix. At least five other dogs were chasing Xena, including Dane's Byte, followed by their owners, while a crowd of onlooking dogs erupted into a cacophony of barking. Lizzy was watching the chaos with concern, while Darcy was, of course, doing her best to jump out of Kamila's arms to join in the fun. Kamila handed Darcy to Asha. Maricel clearly needed help. "Xena! Heel!" Kamila yelled, running after the dogs.

Maricel finally caught Xena by the collar and held firmly while a poodle and two golden retrievers attempted to climb over Maricel to get at their beagle pied piper. Overbalanced, Maricel tumbled to the ground, barely hanging on to Xena while one of the golden retrievers started licking her face. Behind the golden, Dane's Byte looked ready to...well, bite Maricel.

This all happened so fast, and by the time Kamila reached Maricel, Dane was pulling a growling Byte away. Kamila grabbed Xena by the collar and waved off the poodle trying to jump on top of her.

"I got you, Xena. Heel. Heel..." Kamila said, repeating the commands they used in the shelter. Not that she expected Xena to listen. She'd never met a dog so resistant to training.

"Here. Let me," Maricel said, brushing off the handful of dogs still jumping at her with glee. She scooted in front of Xena with both hands on the dog's collar and started talking softly. Somehow, even with her jeans covered in white gravel and her hair barely contained in its low ponytail, Maricel was still stunning. Small, with soft curves, long jet-black wavy hair, and smooth tawny-brown skin. She did have room for improvement, though. Her jeans were at least two sizes too big. Kamila made a mental note to take her friend shopping, and soon.

In record time, Xena put her head down in a submissive stance. Maricel clipped a leash on her. "Kamila, oh my god, thank you."

"No problem. You okay?"

Maricel nodded as she tried to smooth her hair with one hand. "That didn't work."

Kamila laughed as she put her free arm around Maricel and guided her and the demon hound out of the enclosure. Asha was waiting on the other side of the gate. Kamila could see Dane pulling his angry husky out of the park.

"I should just take Xena back to the shelter," Maricel said, still looking a little shaken.

Asha nodded. "Go ahead. I'll bring the others back."

Kamila smiled at her friend. "I need to talk to you, but I'll call you later."

Maricel nodded and headed across the park to the shelter.

"Maricel is a bit of a hot mess," Kamila said as they walked back over to the benches at the other end of the enclosure.

Asha chuckled. "It'll be good for her to get her obedience school up and running. She's so excellent with dogs. Did you see how quickly Xena calmed right down? She's a total dog whisperer."

Kamila smiled. "Imagine what she could do with Byte."

Asha laughed. "Okay, I couldn't see Maricel and Dane before, but now...I see your point. Do your matchmaking magic. Hey, is the puppy prom committee meeting this week?"

Kamila checked her phone. "I think Tim canceled it. Next week."

"Your dad's physical is Monday, right?"

Kamila nodded. "Yeah. I'm worried. If the news isn't good...I just don't want a setback, you know? Mental health–wise, I mean."

Asha patted Kamila's arm. "Whatever happens, you're not alone. All of us are here for you and for your dad. Call me whenever you need me, okay?"

Kamila nodded. She was very lucky to have such great friends. She wouldn't have survived without Asha the last time her father went through a depressive episode. Asha was right. Kamila had no shortage of people looking out for her family. But the thing was, the Hussains had always had a strong support network. And it hadn't helped much the last time things got bad for Dad.

But there was no point in worrying until Dad met with the doctor.

Darcy showed up at her feet then. "C'mon, Darcy," Kamila said, clipping on the dog's leash. "Let's go sit with Dad. Make sure he's happy."

Because making sure her father was happy and healthy was always Kamila's first priority. Everything else came second.

CHAPTER 3

On the drive home from work on Monday, all Kamila could think about was how desperately she wanted to take off her black-and-white gingham dress and matching heels and put her feet up on the coffee table. She was pretty sure there was pumpkin-pie ice cream in the freezer, and after a busy day at Emerald, she was all over the idea of Netflixing and chilling for the rest of the evening.

But Dad's physical was today. She'd of course called him earlier to see how it went, but she couldn't get much out of him. She planned to interrogate him now...and if he wouldn't talk, she'd call Rohan, who'd taken Dad to the appointment.

She did not expect to see Dad's chauffeur himself sitting on her couch with his feet on her coffee table, watching TV when she opened the door. "What are you doing here?"

Rohan glanced at her, then back to the TV. He was wearing dark dress pants with a dark-gray dress shirt and light-gray tie and watching an old Hindi film he'd probably seen a thousand times. Darcy was sleeping, pressed up against Rohan's leg. "Did you forget I was taking your father to the doctor today? He got dinner for you two on the way back here."

"Of course I didn't forget. Hopefully something healthy?"

"Salads."

Kamila sat on the armchair and peeled off her shoes. Ah. Relief. She wiggled her toes, letting the circulation back in. "Oh, that feels good. Where's Dad?"

"Napping."

Kamila sat up straight. Why was he napping at this hour? That wasn't a sign of trouble, was it? "Is he okay?" she asked. "What did the doctor say?"

Rohan shrugged. "He seemed fine. A little worn-out. I just drove him to the doctor, though—I didn't go in. I assume he'll have to wait for the results from the blood work, anyway."

Kamila bit her lip. If the news was bad, he would have told Rohan, right? She wanted to talk to Dad so she could see how he really was herself, but she also wanted to let him rest if he was tired.

Rohan paused the movie and turned to look at Kamila. "We stopped in at Emerald to get some papers after the appointment. The place looks nothing like the last time I was there."

"I'm going to take that as a compliment, because it used to look like an eighties basement."

Rohan snorted.

She relaxed in her seat. She still wanted to take her dress off and put on some sweats, but she loved the way it looked with the lavender cardigan she was wearing with it, so it seemed a shame to change when there was company here. Even if it was just Rohan. She curled her feet under her, spreading her skirt over her knees. "Tell me honestly. Did he seem upset after the appointment?"

He shrugged. "Not really. We talked business on the way home. HNS and Emerald are both doing well, so your father is happy."

HNS—or Hussain, Nasser, and Suleiman, as Dad still called it—was Dad's first baby. He'd started the tax firm over thirty years ago with his two closest friends, Rohan's father and Jana Suleiman's father. Today, the firm was owned and operated by Rohan and his brother, Zayan, but Dad still owned 30 percent. Even though Dad was no longer involved with operations, he was still emotionally invested, and he counted on regular updates from Rohan on everything going on there. Emerald was technically a subsidiary of HNS, but Rohan and Zayan were completely hands-off with the smaller firm.

Kamila had wondered if Rohan was only humoring Dad with his HNS updates, since Rohan wasn't exactly a young ingenue needing a mentor when he took over operations—he had come from a busy law firm where he'd been a tax lawyer for years. But after Kamila sat in on some of these meetings, she could clearly see that Rohan actually wanted Dad to know what was going on with the company that still carried his name. Kamila was eternally grateful for that. No one—not Dad's old friends, not even Zayan—was as patient with Dad as Rohan. He made Dad feel valued.

"Good," Kamila said. "If Dad is happy, I'm happy." She stretched her legs and rested her feet on the coffee table. "Darcy, you didn't even get up when I came in."

Rohan chuckled, then looked down at Darcy. "I have a feeling this sweater she's wearing cost more than yours."

"Marginally, yes, it did. Why exactly are you still here, Rohan?" She remembered what Asha had said—was Rohan lonely?

He leaned forward, his relaxed pose disappearing. "I wanted to make sure you were okay. I'd planned to go to the climbing gym, but...you were so worried about this physical."

Had she told him she was worried? She had told Asha, but not Rohan. But then again, Rohan knew, maybe more than anyone, why Kamila should be scared. "If he doesn't pass his blood tests..." Her voice trailed.

"You're worried it could trigger another depressive episode."

"It could." Bad news...*unexpected* news, was always a little bit harder for Dad to cope with. And since both his wife and his best friend had died of heart disease, health-related bad news was extra tricky. Last year's physical had needed a few extra cognitive behavioral therapy sessions for his anxiety, and his test results had all been fine. But the readings on his home blood pressure monitor had been high for the last few months. He'd tried taking Darcy for long walks and enthusiastically enjoying the heart-healthy food Kamila prepared for him, when it wasn't charred to a crisp, that is. But was that enough?

"I think he'll be fine," Rohan said. "He seems to be in a good place. Emerald is growing. He's even updated the office."

She grinned proudly. "The growth at Emerald? That's all me, not him. And the redesign, too. I'm trying to convince him that I can handle things alone if he goes part-time." Dad was still resistant, though. Ugh...she wished she'd secured the Nirvana Lotus account. That would have convinced Dad to reduce his hours.

Rohan nodded. "I've seen your client list. You've done well. I'm impressed."

Kamila raised her hands in the air. "It's an autumn miracle— Rohan Nasser complimented me! Praise be to our queen Beyoncé!"

He smirked as he leaned back on the sofa.

"Anyway," she continued, "it's not all sunshine and popsicles. I didn't get two potential big clients this past week. Maybe if I had, Dad would agree to reduce his hours." She told him about the old doctor and the white hippie lady, and how she didn't seem to have the experience, or the penis, they wanted in an accountant.

"Ah, I'm sorry." He looked at her with an expression that Kamila couldn't decipher. "You know...you're always welcome to come work at HNS, if big-financial-institution experience is something you want."

She raised a brow. "Really? You're offering me a job?"

"Sure. You're a CPA, and your father started the firm—his name is still on the door."

She shook her head. "Well, I don't want mine there. I tried working at HNS, remember?" Rohan hadn't been working there at the time, but he knew why she left. "I have no interest in going back to that sterile, emotion-sucking pit of mundaneness. I mean, did you see my new desk at Emerald? Why would I give that up? Plus"—she dipped her chin and batted her lashes—"don't you think I'd be too much of a distraction in your corporate jungle?"

He laughed, shaking his head. "True. You'd fit in like an arctic penguin in that jungle."

"Who are you calling a penguin? My legs are longer than average for a South Asian woman." She lifted one high to prove her point, then rubbed her foot briefly on his on the coffee table.

He chuckled. "Kam, there is no way I'd ever forget about your positive traits since you're always reminding me of them. By the way, it still stinks of melted plastic toaster in here."

Kamila rolled her eyes and got up to light a scented candle. Then she sat next to him on the sofa.

"That'll work," Rohan said. "Fire to mask the smell of fire. Anyway, I'm sure your father is fine. He seems to be making clearheaded decisions right now."

"Why'd you say it like that? Has he been making other big decisions lately?" She wouldn't put it past Dad to tell Rohan things he didn't tell her. Dad still felt the need to protect his precious daughters from big issues.

Rohan shrugged. "He's been talking about planning for the future—that's all."

Ah. Estate planning. Since Rohan was the executor of Dad's estate, it was good he wanted to make sure Dad was of a clear mind and all that if he was working on his will. She wished Dad would talk to her about it, but he probably thought talking about his death would upset her. Which it would.

"Well, even if I didn't get those big clients," Kamila said, "Dad has to see that I can take on more at Emerald. I have signed three new clients recently, got two comped shellac manicures, and a stunning balayage hair treatment in the last month alone." She pulled her long hair from behind her back and ran her fingers through it. Kamila's hair was one of her best features and she loved to show it off since she worked so hard on it. Past halfway down her back, it had a natural wave she could coax into a curl if she used a diffuser, and it was a deep, rich brown that lightened to golden chestnut at the ends.

"I have no idea what those things are, Kam."

"That's fine. You don't need to keep up with nail and hair-color trends. One of my new clients is a tattoo studio who is looking to open a new location. I got a tattoo."

That seemed to interest him. "Really? Where?"

She pulled her hair into a messy bun on the top of her head. "That's a personal question, Mr. Nasser." She leaned closer to him to inspect the new scruff on his face again. "Speaking of hair, I think your beard is growing in salt-and-pepper. You really are embracing the old-man vibe, aren't you?"

He chuckled, running his hand over his chin. In actuality, Kamila saw it as a good thing that he'd have a heavy dose of salt in his black-pepper facial hair. She loved a silver fox and had no doubt the gray would suit him.

"Do you still approve?" he asked.

"I do," Kamila said, smiling. "Very distinguished. So, you still going to go climb walls for no real reason?"

"You trying to get rid of me, Kam?"

She settled in next to him, curling her legs under herself. "Nope. Stay here and veg with me on the couch. We can split my salad."

"We got one for me, too."

"Good." She plucked the TV remote from him and restarted the movie. "I'll even watch this movie with you. I don't think I've seen it."

"You should show it this week for Bollywood night."

"I told you, I already picked the next movie. I need to stay with a romance. I'm hoping to inspire love for some friends." She intended to invite Dane this week, so she needed to set the stage for his perfect meet-cute with Maricel, to wash away the memory of Byte trying to bite her butt.

Kamila was in the mood to make others fall in love.

After they ate their salads (which turned out to be fancy
ones with grilled ahi tuna and sesame dressing—totally Rohan's
doing), Rohan left for his downtown condo. Kamila finally was
able to talk to Dad about the doctor's appointment while they
were having hibiscus tea after dinner.

"So tell me the truth. What did Dr. Anchali say?"

Dad waved his hand. "I told you—it's fine. Nothing to
worry about."

"Dad…" Kamila gave him the look. When her mother had
used that look, it had always worked better on her dad than
Kamila.

"Kamila, beti, there is nothing we can do until we get the
blood test results. You worry about me too much."

"What did she say about your blood pressure?"

Dad put his tea down. "It was a little too high. She gave me
a higher dose of the blood pressure medication. And she would
like me to exercise more. But I have to wait for the blood tests
to know more."

"Did she mention anything about you working less?"

"Kamila, I can't yet. My clients count on me. I told you I
just signed on to help Anil Malek launch his new nonprofit.
If it goes well, they'll put Emerald on retainer for all their
finance needs."

"Dad, I can take your clients! I'm used to bigger accounts
now. This new tattoo shop has an annual revenue of—"

He shook his head. "Nah, beti. You have your work at the
shelter, and your parties, and your own clients."

"But remember what Dr. Piersanti said! You need to minimize your stress!" Dr. Piersanti was Dad's last psychotherapist. The one he refused to see anymore, claiming the man didn't understand how Indian families worked. Which, granted, was true.

Dad patted Kamila's hand. "There is no need to have this argument now. The test results will be ready in a week. Let's talk about that then. Would you like me to take Darcy out before bed?"

Kamila exhaled. "Okay. Thanks, Dad. I'm going to turn in."

While Kamila finally took off the lovely, but frankly not very comfortable, dress, she thought about how to convince Dad to take better care of himself. He was so frustratingly stubborn when it came to work. Kamila didn't know how much of it was patriarchal whatever from their culture, or if it was because he thought he owed the family after everything that happened after Mom died.

But everything that happened after Mom died was exactly why he deserved to be healthy and happy, maybe more than anyone Kamila knew. He saved Kamila then. And she owed him the world and more for that. But all she could do now was hope those test results were fine. Then all would be good until next year's physical.

🌂

On Thursday night Kamila had dinner plans with Maricel so they could work on her business proposal for her puppy academy. Kamila was worried Dad would eat junk if she wasn't home, though, so she dropped suggestions to Dad that he eat at the home of his closest friend, Rashida Aunty, who Kamila had called to make sure she was cooking a healthy meal that night.

Maricel had chosen a new boba tea place that had just opened on Queen East and was waiting outside the restaurant when Kamila arrived. After taking in her unflattering jeans, T-shirt, and oversized cardigan, Kamila made a mental note to lend her clothes for the next night's biryani party. Dane had agreed to come, so Maricel needed to shine.

The restaurant, Boba Noodle, was a dark storefront with a minimalistic sign, but Kamila had seen it on just about every "what's new and hot" list recently. Still, Kamila full-on squealed with delight when she walked in. The interior was pale pink, with huge ferns and palm trees everywhere and a bold floral wallpaper on one wall. It contrasted so well with the golden wood tables and chairs. The whimsy crossed with sophistication was utterly perfect and weirdly matched well with the chic, pink French maid outfit the hostess was wearing.

After they were seated, a cute waiter—sadly, not dressed like Victorian household staff—gave them menus and said he'd be back in five to take their orders.

"So, there's someone I want you to meet at tomorrow's party," Kamila said. "Dane. He's really good looking and friendly. He loves dogs. I don't know him too well, but Asha had a background check done before she rented him her condo, and his credit rating is good. He's a bit of a tech bro but really smart..." She didn't mention that Dane was the owner of the husky that had tried to eat Maricel when Xena was having her freak-out at the dog park. She was pretty sure Maricel didn't notice the husky, anyway—she was focused on the hound of hell.

Maricel, who was studying the list of teas like there would be a test later, suddenly frowned. "Tech bro?"

"Yeah. But he owns his own company. Did I mention he loves dogs?"

"Do you know if they have Earl Grey here?"

"Dunno. So, you're interested, then?"

"I mean, yeah. I love Earl Grey."

"No, in meeting Dane."

The cute waiter returned to the table then. "Hi! What can I get for y'all?" he said as he pulled a small notebook from his back pocket.

Kamila hadn't even opened the menu. "What tea do you recommend"—she looked at his name tag—"Kevin?"

He smiled, rogue dimples appearing on his cheeks. "Well, what do you like?"

Kamila shrugged. "I like green tea."

"Matcha?"

She nodded. He smiled widely. "Do you like creamy, milky drinks, or fruity ones?"

After discussing her preferences with Kevin, he recommended a mango-matcha smoothie with tapioca pearls. He then grinned at Maricel. "What about you? Same?"

"No. Um," Maricel stammered. "Um, do you have Earl Grey?"

He looked crushed at that question. "I've been trying to source a good one. You know how so many Earl Greys taste really fake? Like the bergamot is like, wow, holy *too much*. I'm looking for an all-natural one. We do have a rad oolong, though."

"Okay," Maricel said. "I'll have a milk oolong with grass jelly. Half-sweet, please."

"Awesome choice. You'll love the oolong. I'll get these made and will be back for your food order in a few." He grinned again and left the table. Maricel's eyes were glued to him, specifically to his backside, as he walked away.

"He's adorable," Kamila said.

"What? Oh." Maricel quickly looked back at Kamila, blushing. "Yes. And um...friendly."

"I didn't realize you were so into tea."

"Oh, I'm not really. I just don't like supersweet drinks. My lola said I'm the only Filipino she knows who doesn't like sugary drinks. My cousin brought me this Earl Grey from England last year, and I've been trying to find one as good here."

They talked about tea for a while before Kamila steered the conversation back where it belonged. "So, about Dane. Are you interested in meeting him?"

Maricel frowned. "Of course! I mean, I always like to meet your friends. I had such a nice time at your movie night last week. Thank—"

"Maricel, I'm asking if you want me to set you up with him."

"With who?"

This was frustrating. "Dane."

Maricel smiled widely. "Oh! That's why you wanted me to meet him! I understand now!"

Kevin showed up with their teas then. "Here you go, ladies," he said, sliding the two cold glasses toward them.

Kamila took a sip of hers. It was delicious. "Wow, you guys *do* make awesome tea!"

"Of course! I told you we were the best. How's the oolong?"

Maricel took a sip, and a look of surprise transformed her face. "It's good! Perfect sweetness."

"That's what I love about oolong," Kevin said. "It's so delicate that you don't need a lot of sugar. My family is convinced I'm not actually related to them because I don't like supersweet stuff."

Maricel laughed. "My family, too!"

Kevin leaned in to Maricel subtly. "Do they secretly put more sugar in your coffee when you're not looking?"

"Yes!"

He laughed. "Are you two ordering from the food menu?"

Kamila picked it up. It was also extensive. "What do you recommend?"

"Oh, that's easy," Kevin said. "We're famous for our beef noodle soup."

Kamila closed her menu. "Perfect. I'll take that."

"Me too," Maricel said.

After Kevin was gone from the table, Kamila decided to put Operation Maricel and Dane Equals True Love on ice for a bit. They were here to discuss Maricel's business plan. Kamila pulled a binder out of her tote.

"Okay. I did some market research, and I think this plan is competitive. Your overhead isn't much, since dog training doesn't need a lot of special equipment, but rent is going to be high in most neighborhoods that have a lot of dogs. Did your aunt agree to come on board to sew dog clothes to sell, too?"

Maricel nodded. "Oh yes—I forgot! I have some samples for Darcy." She handed Kamila a plastic bag. Kamila opened it to see a tiny doggie jean jacket and a Hawaiian print shirt.

"Eeee!" Kamila squealed. "These are amazing. Yes, you have to sell these. I'll help boost them on my socials... They'll be flying off the shelves. For locations, any interest in going farther east? There is a grant you can apply for for new businesses by women of color in Scarborough. Also, I was thinking—this might be premature—but if this goes well, we should approach venture capitalists to expand. Pet services are such a growing market."

This was fun. Kamila always felt energized when strategizing business plans with a client, and it was extra special when that client was a friend. If everything went well when she introduced Maricel to Dane, even better. Kamila was using her magic as a business consultant and accountant and as a matchmaker for such a good cause—to make her friend happy. They talked more about the financial needs of the start-up while eating what turned out to be excellent beef noodle soup. She made a mental note to bring Rohan here one day—this dish was right up his alley.

☂

Kamila worked from home on Friday, and after immersing herself in spreadsheets for half the day, she started preparing for Bollywood-and-biryani night. She cleaned her whole house until it smelled acrid lemony. Then she lit some incense to get rid of the acrid smell, resulting in a patchouli-citrus scent. She put out some Indian-print throw cushions she'd found while clothes shopping with Maricel after their dinner and scattered some candles about. Finally, she put out big golden bowls of huge magenta gerbera daisies.

Along with Asha, Nicole, Dane, and Maricel, she was also expecting Tim and his husband, Jerome, Brit from the dog park (but alas, not her husband, Justin, since the baby was teething), the woman who colored Kamila's hair last week, and two friends from her former book club. And, of course, Rohan.

Dad came down the stairs as she was putting jewel-toned coasters on every horizontal surface in the room. He was in a suit, jacket draped over his arm and tie hanging over his neck. Dressed for Friday-night prayers at Jamatkhana, the Ismaili Muslim place of worship.

"It looks lovely in here, Kamila. New pillows?"

"Yeah. I got them at a store that makes home decor out of saris."

"Your mother used to do all this work for parties, too."

Kamila frowned. Why had he said that? If Mom were here, she'd have listed thirty things Kamila was doing wrong planning this party. She set down the box of coasters, walked over to her father, and started tying his tie so she could sneak a peek into his eyes. They looked fine—no sign of despair. "You sure you won't stay for dinner, at least? I know you want to try Rohan's Burmese biryani." So long as it wasn't too greasy. Dad hadn't received his test results yet, but he'd been so positive all week. And so good! Exercising daily, eating all the fruits and veggies Kamila put in front of him. A tiny bit of biryani couldn't hurt.

"I don't want to miss prayers," he said. "I'm going to Rashida's for a card party after. You can save me some biryani." Dad frowned as he put his jacket on. "What kind of biryani do Burmese people eat?"

She shrugged. "I guess I'll find out soon enough." She adjusted the pocket square in his jacket. Dad was so dapper and always wore a pocket square. She patted his chest and went back to putting out coasters.

"So why all the extra decorating tonight?"

"A couple of new friends are coming." She told Dad about Dane and her hope that one day he and Maricel would be as happy as Asha and Nicole.

Dad smiled warmly. "You're generous with your friends, but

I wish you wouldn't make so many matches. We rarely see Asha anymore—she used to be here helping you set up every Friday."

"Yeah, but Asha is *glowing* these days...I can sacrifice her help with parties for that kind of happiness."

"You're too good, Kamila. I wish..." He sighed. "I was looking at some old pictures today...You've come so far. I know things were hard, and I wasn't there for you when you were young, but you've grown into—"

Kamila tensed again. "Don't say it, Dad. You *were* there for me. More than anyone else. Remember the doctor said not to dwell on things you can't change?"

This was troubling. Dad should *not* be thinking about the past so much. Kamila went to the kitchen and opened the box of appetizers she'd picked up earlier.

"Hakka?" Dad asked.

She nodded and started plating the appetizers onto a large platter. She'd actually entertained the idea of making appetizers herself this week—or at least with Asha's help, since she didn't want to risk destroying any more kitchen appliances. She even found time to duck into the library a few days ago to look at a Burmese cookbook. But after skimming the table of contents, she learned that spring rolls featured in the cuisine of Burma. Or technically, Myanmar, as it was now called. She'd actually gotten caught in a research tangent that night prompted by the cookbook and ended up reading a lot about the fragile politics of the region and the devastating plight of the Rohingya people there. After a quick donation to an aid agency working with refugees from the region, she placed an order at her local Indo-Chinese Hakka restaurant, which made the best spring rolls in Toronto. Asha wouldn't have had the time, anyway.

She frowned at the overladen platter of samosas, pakoras, and spring rolls. "I ordered too much. I'll send some to Rashida's for your card party later. But go easy—you're only allowed three, okay?"

Dad chuckled as he headed toward the hall mirror. "You're so good...taking care of a troublesome old man."

"Nonsense, Dad. You *aren't* troublesome." She looked into his eyes. He seemed okay. But mentioning Mom and the past, and then calling himself troublesome? Self-loathing wasn't a good sign.

"Dad, when do you think you'll hear—"

There was a knock on the door followed by Darcy tearing down the stairs and barking. Dad answered it while Kamila held Darcy's harness so she didn't bolt. It was Rohan, a huge aluminum foil tray in one hand and an overloaded tote bag in the other.

"Speaking of troublesome old men," Kamila said, grinning, while she released Darcy. No way the dog would be going anywhere now that her favorite human was here. Darcy immediately jumped up onto Rohan's legs.

He chuckled, placing the foil tray on the kitchen counter. "They had an interesting-looking coconut cake at the restaurant, too, so I got one." He bent to scratch Darcy's head. "Hey, girl."

Kamila peeked at the foil tray. "This is huge! This looks like biryani for fifty, not twelve."

He shrugged. "So you'll have leftovers to eat later," he said. "This way you won't try to cook again. I have a busy week—not sure I can be here to put out any fires."

"First of all, ha ha. Second of all, firefighters exist. In fact, a strapping fireman might be a welcome addition to my life. Remind me how I started that fire again?"

"You know you prefer me any day," Rohan said, eyes narrowed suggestively. Huh. Last week he'd stammered indignantly when she threw anything remotely flirty his way. Seems he finally decided to play along. Kamila giggled and turned back to the platter of food.

"Look how beautiful everything is tonight," Dad said. "And without Asha's help! Kamila, you're a gifted hostess."

"Yes, she is." Rohan nodded. "But Kam knows her strengths. If we remind her of them, her head will grow bigger than it already is."

"My head is *not* big," Kamila said, patting her hair. "This volume is thanks to very expensive hair products and my diffuser." She squeezed Rohan's arm. He was in a suit again. He always wore a suit to her parties. He said it was because he came straight from work, but Kamila suspected he preferred to look like the most powerful person in the room. And he claimed *she* had a big head.

Today's suit was dark charcoal, perfectly tailored, and looked expensive. It went well with the new beard—which had grown in mostly rich black, but with delightful silvery bits near his ears and on his chin.

Kamila smiled. "The facial-hair situation is looking good. Very imposing. I'm glad I was right about it. I have excellent taste."

He chuckled, rubbing his chin. "See? Kamila doesn't need us praising her. She does a great job of it herself. Where'd you get that dress, Kam? The costume department for a sixties TV show?"

Kamila frowned at her dress. Another vintage-style, full-skirted floral, this one was deep teal with flowers in fall colors and wide off-the-shoulder straps. "You showing up to parties in a suit is very midcentury, too. I feel like I should be handing you a martini after work." She headed toward the kitchen, running her hand over Rohan's beard as she passed him. "I should introduce you to my ukulele teacher—he's got the most epic red beard I've ever seen. He can give you grooming tips."

Dad laughed, then looked at his watch. "I really should be going. Oh, Rohan, I was meaning to talk to you—I heard you're volunteering with Anil Malek's incubator project? He's contracted Emerald for the nonprofit start-up administration."

Rohan nodded as he took some jars of chutney out of his bag. "He's asked me to sit on the board. It's an excellent cause. I didn't know he was looking for an accountant."

Dad and Rohan continued to talk about this project while Kamila uploaded some pictures of Darcy she'd taken earlier. Her attention was pulled back to them, however, once she realized what—or specifically, *who*—they were talking about.

"...I'm surprised she backed out," Rohan was saying. "But she says she won't have the time."

"I can understand that. It's a shame for Anil, though. It would be a major boon to this foundation to get someone of Jana's caliber."

Jeepers Carmichael, were they talking about Jana *again*? Kamila had tried—and succeeded for the most part—to put Jana Suleiman out of her head this week. Clearly, almost burning down her house was proof that letting that woman into her mind wasn't healthy for her, or for her kitchen. But of course, someone had to bring up that name again. "What are you talking about?"

Dad smiled. "Anil's nonprofit start-up that Rohan is volunteering on...Jana was supposed to be involved."

Kamila frowned. If Jana was due back soon, why wasn't she doing this thing? Not that Kamila wanted Jana working with Rohan, though.

Rohan swiped a pakora from the platter Kamila had painstakingly arranged. "It would have been a good role for her. This kind of nonprofit work is exactly her area of expertise and talent." He popped the pakora into his mouth. "Where are these from? Don't tell me you cooked, Kam."

"Hakka Empire." Irritated, she took a pakora out of the box to replace the one on the tray. She smiled at Dad. "It's too bad you're missing the movie tonight. We're watching a rom-com with Shahid Kapoor."

Dad pulled out his dress shoes from the closet. "You don't need an old man here. You young people enjoy yourself."

"But we have an old man. Rohan is always here." She patted his arm again. Wow. All that rock climbing was paying off.

"Shahid Kapoor…Isn't he the one you call Hottie Pants?" Dad asked.

Rohan snorted. "Ranveer Singh is Hottie McHottie Pants. Shahid Kapoor is Honey Bunches of Oats, because, and I'm quoting here, 'he's both delicious and wholesome.'"

Dad slipped on his shoes, laughing. "Okay, I'm really leaving now. Have a good night, kids."

Once Dad left, Kamila glared at Rohan. "You shouldn't talk about me drooling over leading men," she said. "I swear you only watch these movies for the actresses. Your jaw drops the moment a wet sari plasters itself to a cropped sari blouse." Kamila paused, assessing the amount of pakoras on the platter.

"I'm not going to deny I like to look at attractive women."

"Why are you here so early, anyway?"

"I was meeting someone in the area and I thought you might need help setting up. And..." He picked up Darcy.

"And what?"

He nuzzled his face in Darcy's fur. "I had a bad day. Wanted to see if you could make it better." He lifted his head toward the ceiling and inhaled. "It still smells like burnt sweet potatoes in here."

She sighed and filled up her aroma diffuser with lavender essential oil.

"Trouble on Bay Street?" Kamila asked as she plugged the unit in.

"Nah. How's your finger?"

She held up her fully healed index finger. "I'm once again flawless. Just how you like me."

He snorted before swiping another pakora from her perfect platter and sharing it with Darcy. Great—now the dog would be following him around all night. Which, to be honest, she'd probably be doing anyway. Darcy had taste.

CHAPTER 4

Helping Maricel buy a new outfit for the party had clearly been a brilliant idea, because Kamila's young friend turned every head in the room at Bollywood-and-biryani night. Especially, to Kamila's utter delight, Dane's. In high-waisted navy trousers, a soft floral silk T-shirt, and hair in cascading curling-iron waves, it was no wonder Maricel had the tech bro's undivided attention during dinner. Kamila kept an eye on the budding lovebirds while making sure everyone's plates were full of biryani, samosas, pakoras, and spring rolls.

She was spooning more biryani from the foil tray onto her magenta platter when Rohan, followed closely by Darcy, came to get seconds.

"Are you giving my dog fried food again?" Kamila asked.

"What? No. She's still following me, though."

"Of course she is. You're her one true love forever. Having a good time?"

"Always."

"You didn't take any fish pakoras. They're your favorite." She placed two on his plate.

"I know. I ate six before anyone else got here." He nodded toward Maricel on the sofa. "I like what you did with Maricel. You've turned her into a young Kamila."

"Hardly. I'm short waisted. I could never pull off those pants. Anyway, she's not that young. She's going to be a pet obedience-school tycoon, you know. If her business takes off, I'll need you to introduce us to your venture capitalist friends." Kamila put the spoon down and reached up to smooth the lapels on his jacket. "You know, my parties don't have a jacket-required dress code. I should take you shopping. You need some new casual wear."

"I have plenty of casual wear."

"Then why aren't you wearing it?" She moved to straightening his tie.

He swayed forward a bit and lifted his chin, letting Kamila work. On a whim, instead of adjusting the crooked knot, she pulled it open, slowly sliding the silk through the high thread-count shirt collar. He said nothing, but one corner of his lip upturned. Eyes never leaving his, she slowly folded the tie and placed it on the nearby end table. Biting her lip, she inspected him without it. Better, but not there yet. Slowly, she unbuttoned the top button on his shirt. A small shudder escaped his lips as her hands came into contact with the skin on his neck. Was Rohan ticklish? She smiled widely. "There," she said.

His chin dipped. "I meet your exacting standards, now?"

She patted his shoulder. "You weren't that far off, but I only want the best for my friends. Come, you should get to know Dane." She pulled Rohan toward the sofa, where Dane and Maricel were looking at something in Maricel's hand.

"Hey, you two. Dane, did you meet Rohan? He's an old family friend."

Dane stood quickly. "Yes, Rohan Nasser." He shot his hand out. "I read your profile in *Toronto Business* magazine. The branding you've done with your firm is impressive."

"Um, thank you."

"I'm a small-business owner myself. I'm launching a technology start-up. We should talk. I'd love to pick your brain on how—"

"What do you have there?" Kamila interrupted as she perched on the armrest and looked at what turned out to be a photograph in Maricel's hand. "Oh! It's from the dog park!"

It was clearly taken last week, when Maricel had been struggling to contain Xena's antics. Kamila's head was tilted down in the picture, looking at Maricel with concern, while Maricel was focused completely on the demon dog. The sun illuminating Maricel's face highlighted her cheekbones, and her hair had escaped her ponytail in loose wisps framing her face. Even Xena looked a bit less satanic in the picture. It was a striking shot.

"I didn't realize you took this," Kamila said. Had he been snapping a picture while his dog was snarling at Maricel?

"I *had* to pull out my camera when all that chaos started. I was hoping to get a viral-worthy video but got this picture instead. I printed two copies, one for you and one for your friend, but then she turned out to be here!" He smiled at Maricel, making her blush.

This setup was going altogether too well. He was absolutely captivated by Maricel.

"I didn't realize you were into photography, too," Dane continued. "Maricel said you had that made?" He pointed to the printed canvas on the wall. It was another one of Kamila's photoshopped jobs—Darcy's and Lizzy's heads on a regency couple's bodies to resemble their literary counterparts.

"I make the pet portraits myself! I put Tim and Jerome's

Afghans on a Pre-Raphaelite painting last month." She took Dane's photo from Maricel. "This is an amazing shot."

"I think it's one of the best photos I've taken. Of course, when the subjects are so easy on the eyes…" He grinned at Kamila.

Rohan leaned over and looked at the picture. "It looks overexposed. Kamila is washed out."

Kamila waved Rohan off. "Shush, you. It's stunning." Grinning, she propped up the print next to a framed photo of Shelina, Zayan, Rohan, and her from Shelina's wedding.

"These samosas are delicious," Dane said. "You're a talented cook."

Rohan laughed at that. Loud. Because of course he did. Kamila pinched his side before he could reveal her root-vegetable inferno shame. But the pinch turned Rohan's laugh into a yelp and made Kamila wonder how many ab days he did each week. Also, he was *definitely* ticklish.

"It's takeout," Kamila said. "Do people even make samosas from scratch anymore?"

"Rashida Aunty does. I saw some at her house," Rohan said, rubbing his side where she'd pinched him.

Kamila stood. "That reminds me—I promised to bring the extra pakoras over to her. I'll be back." She smiled at Dane and Maricel and went to the kitchen to grab the tray. Rohan came up behind her and took it from her hands.

"I'll go," he said. "You stay."

"No, you're a guest. Give it back."

"I'm not a guest—they are," he said, indicating toward the others in the room. "I'll be back in a few minutes." He took the tray and headed to the front door. Kamila picked up Darcy so she wouldn't follow Rohan out.

"When are we starting the movie?" Tim asked, coming into the kitchen as Kamila put Darcy down. Darcy, of course, immediately made a beeline to wait by the front door.

"When Rohan gets back, I guess. He's dropping something off at a neighbor's. Hey, Tim, do you think I'm turning Maricel into me?" She peeked out the kitchen doorway to look at Maricel, who was now sitting alone on the sofa. Dane was across the room talking to Brit.

Tim tilted his head and looked carefully at Maricel. "Yes, I suppose she does look like a small Kamila today. Get her to cut her bangs like yours next—they'd look good on her. By the way, my glass is empty."

"I'm working to set her up with Dane."

Tim chuckled. "I'm glad I met you *after* meeting Jerome, because otherwise I'd end up in your scrapbook of couples."

"And what's wrong with that? I'm very good at this. Look how happy Asha and Nicole are."

Asha joined them then, an empty glass in her hand. "Is there any more of this . . . What is this anyway, Kamila?"

Kamila laughed, heading out to the dining room where the signature drink ingredients were on the sideboard. Her friends followed her. "Gotcha. Two more Starry Fuzzy Fizzes. Do you want prosecco or soda water in yours?"

"You're a gift to humanity, Kamila," Tim said, tapping the bottle of prosecco. "Why is Darcy watching the door forlornly?"

Kamila poured peach nectar from a crystal pitcher into Tim and Asha's glasses. "She's waiting for Rohan to get back."

Asha laughed. "Just like a bichon. A fool in love."

"It's because Rohan spoils her with fried food," Kamila said.

Asha shook her head at Darcy. "The way to a woman's heart. It worked with Nicole. You told me Rohan didn't like dogs."

"Nah, he likes dogs. He's just not really a dog *person*, like, say, you or me. He gets it from his parents—they call Darcy the Gujarati term for overgrown rodent." She added star anise simple syrup to the glasses.

"Jerome's mother calls Luke and Leia Wookiees," Tim said. Luke and Leia were Tim and Jerome's matching Afghan hounds.

Kamila finished the drinks and garnished them with mint leaves and whole star anise. "I'm going to put the movie snacks out soon, so if you want more biryani, take it now." She handed her friends their glasses.

"How long will Rohan be gone?" Tim asked.

"He'll be back soon. He's only at Rashida's down the street to drop off pakoras."

He smirked. "See? Fried foods. Delivering pakoras must be the Indian version of borrowing a cup of sugar."

"What are you talking about, Tim?" Asha asked.

"You know, 'borrowing a cup of sugar...'" He winked suggestively. "An excuse to visit a hot neighbor."

Kamila scrunched her nose. "*Ew*, Tim. I don't think Rohan is looking to make Rashida Suleiman his Mrs. Robinson. You do realize we call her Aunty, don't you?"

"Kamila!" Tim laughed loud. "Oh my god, I was talking about her *daughter!*"

Damn it. She'd been hoping for no more mentions of Jana today.

"Jana's in Tajikistan. She'll be back soon, though, right, Kamila?" Asha said.

"She's here. I met her at the park today."

Kamila nearly dropped her drink. "What did you say?"

"I met Jana. She was walking at the park with her mother."

Impossible. "No, you didn't."

He nodded. "I did. She introduced herself as Jana Suleiman. Tiny girl, right? Really pretty. Speaks very formally—almost like she has a British accent or something?"

An advanced degree at Oxford would do that.

Poop nuggets. This was bad. Did Rohan already know Jana was back? She put her hand on the table to steady herself.

Was his meeting in the area with *Jana*? Was he actually *borrowing a cup of sugar*, after all?

"Tim, do you think Rohan could be..." She made a sour face. She couldn't say it...It seemed too inexplicable. "*Attracted* to Jana?"

Tim shrugged. "I don't really know what Rohan's into, but Jana is objectively a beautiful woman. Highly educated, too, right? She's fancy, like Rohan. Doctors, lawyers, and...what is it Jana does?"

Kamila's shoulders slumped. "She has a PhD in comparative development and a master's in nonprofit management."

Tim nodded. "See? Fancy people. You're the excellent matchmaker—they could be good together. Make your magic."

Kamila shook her head. That would be a disaster of dizzying proportions. "If Rohan gets into a relationship again, we can say goodbye to all he does for Dad."

And Jana? She was always taking off for far-flung places for one illustrious assignment after another. What if she took Rohan with her? And even if they stayed put in town, what—he'd start bringing Jana to Bollywood night? And, *shudder*, would Jana spend the night with him in the guest room so Rohan could have his meeting with Dad the next morning? Would Jana join Rohan in his criticism of Kamila's cooking?

Forget Dad's mental health—this could destroy Kamila's own.

But Dad's was, of course, more important. Those signs earlier—him putting himself down, alluding to the abuse Kamila had endured from her mother...Dad might be on the edge of a depressive episode. Kamila couldn't risk anything upsetting him. Not now.

"Your family is strange, Kamila," Tim said. "You guys take *codependent* to the next level."

Asha laughed loudly. "You don't know a lot of Indians, do you?"

Kamila could think of nothing intelligent to say, so she emphasized her previous point. "Rohan can't be *into Jana*."

"You're probably right," Tim said. "You said you all grew up together? He probably thinks of her like a sister. Like he thinks of you."

"Rohan does *not* think of me as a sister." Kamila frowned.

Asha shook her head. "No, he's in his own category. He's her *Rohan*."

Kamila rubbed her temples. She was getting a headache. She was seriously wondering if this whole entertaining-friends hobby of hers was good for her self-care.

Darcy started barking then—loudly. "Darcy! What are you freaking out about?"

The door opened. Rohan was back. And he wasn't alone.

Jana Suleiman *was* back in town. She was in Kamila's house.

And Kamila's dog was barking and growling at her as if the Antichrist herself had walked in.

See? Kamila's dog had impeccable taste.

CHAPTER 5

Why. Was. Jana. Suleiman. Here.

A month early, or a week early, or whatever. She wasn't supposed to be in Toronto. And she *really* wasn't supposed to be at Kamila's party.

And most of all, Rohan wasn't supposed to have been the one who brought her here.

The golden child, returning to the world of mere mortals. The warmth and admiration on Rohan's face made Kamila want to puke. Everyone's faces—all her closest friends—basking in the glow of that flawless, dewy skin. Ugh. What kind of toner did Jana even use? The tears of sirens or something?

But Kamila needed to play along, too. This was a *secret* nemesis.

"Jana! What a surprise! You're here!" She kissed both of Jana's cheeks, ignoring the scent of honeysuckle and jasmine wafting from Jana the Great's invisible pores. "How wonderful to see you. Come, let's get you some biryani."

Jana didn't say much as Kamila loaded her plate with biryani, pakoras, and coconut cake. But then, Jana rarely said much to Kamila. Ever. It was strange. Like Rohan, Jana had been in

Kamila's life literally since she was born, and yet with Rohan, Kamila felt familiarity, warmth, and comfort. With Jana? Always coolness, even before the Bronx Bennet episode. She was like a stranger. No one else seemed to have noticed, but it was clear to Kamila that Jana disliked her as much as Kamila disliked Jana.

"Shall we start the movie?" Kamila said loudly over everyone's chattering, all looking for details about Jana's work in Central Asia. Even Tim, who minutes ago was so impatient to get the movie started, was hovering around the newcomer in the room. After a bit more wrangling, Kamila finally managed to get everyone to sit for the darn movie.

But still, even after she'd pressed Play on Netflix, Jerome, who was an anesthesiologist, asked, "So, does Doctors Without Borders have an outpost in Tajikistan?"

Kamila cranked the volume up.

But the movie was completely ruined. Even the adorable Shahid Kapoor scolding the sari-clad Kareena Kapoor couldn't sweeten Kamila's sour mood. Also, the actors' matching last names were suddenly giving Kamila uncomfortable brother/sister vibes. After trying valiantly to pay attention, she finally gave up and watched Jana instead of the subtitles on the film.

Her thick, silky hair was now almost shoulder-length instead of in the no-nonsense pixie she'd had the last time Kamila saw her. Her cheekbones were more pronounced—what did they feed her in Central Asia anyway? But she looked healthy enough—if a little tired. She was wearing loose cream trousers paired with a blush-pink oversized cable-knit sweater and a wide gray headband pushing her hair off her face. Minimal makeup and striking dark-red glasses frames. Tiny, composed, perfect. Kamila felt like an Amazon clown in her floral dress. She patted her hair that she'd spent an hour drying into tousled curls. Even it felt like too much. Maybe she should cut her hair short like that. How long would it take to grow out her bangs?

There was no logical reason why Kamila and Jana shouldn't have grown up the best of friends. They were the same age. Their parents had been tight since forever, and Dad still saw Jana's mom several times a week. But Jana had always been a combination of reserved and studious, which clashed profoundly with Kamila's childhood reputation as a foul-mouthed trouble-maker. After so many years of every adult in Kamila's life saying things like "Why can't you be more like Jana! Did you hear she won a fellowship?" it was no wonder Kamila deeply resented Jana the Great.

The movie finally ended, and Kamila tried to herd her guests out so she could clean and wallow in her newly reemerged inadequacies, but her friends were feeling chatty. Well, at least some of them. Most left, but Asha, Nicole, and Rohan stuck around to "help clean up." And Jana. Jana stayed. Jana should really have gone home.

"It must feel weird to be back after so long. If you need any-thing to help settle in, let me know," Asha said warmly. Because of course. Asha was warm. It was her thing. Even when her best friend was mid existential crisis.

"It will take time for me to reacclimate, but I'll be fine. I'm used to traveling." Jana still spoke with that posh accent. Everyone assumed it was from years of studying in the UK, but Kamila could swear that Jana talked fancy like that before Oxford. Jana started collecting glasses scattered throughout the living room.

"Please, Jana," Kamila said, laying it on probably too thick.

"You're a guest—you don't need to clean. You must be exhausted. Here, let me get you some spring rolls. Food always helps me with jet lag."

"Oh no, I couldn't. My mother made samosas today and I ate much too many. And actually..." She paused, looking down. "I only arrived in Toronto today, but I've been at my former employer's head office in Washington, D.C., for the last week. My jet-lag has long passed."

Kamila squeezed the glass in her hand. Rohan saw home-made samosas at Rashida's—today. He *had* gone there before Kamila's.

"D.C.? Really?" Asha said. "What—"

"Rohan," Kamila interrupted. "What do you want me to do with the rest of the biryani? I'll put it in a container. Hey, Asha, tell them about that massive Tupperware store we found down by the waterfront. So weird!"

The front door opened. Dad was home.

"Oh good, you're all still here!" He passed around hugs and kisses on cheeks before smiling at Jana. "Your mother is waiting up, Jana. Kamila, were you surprised to see her? I didn't expect it! And when Rohan came with the pakoras, he convinced her to join you for the movie!"

Kamila smiled blandly and resumed spooning biryani into a container while everyone talked.

"It's been a long night," Dad said. "I saw Anil Malek in Jamatkhana, and we went over some of the plans for his incubator project."

Rohan turned to Jana. "I heard you know Anil?"

Jana made a snooty face. "Yes, a little. Our paths crossed in Washington a few times. I was required to be there every few months as part of my position. I believe Anil was looking for American donors for his project then, but I was also meeting with investors for my own initiative."

"Oooh, you have an initiative?" Tim asked. "Anything you can tell us about?"

"I've been working on a start-up for software servicing the nonprofit sector."

Kamila looked at Jana. "A do-gooding software start-up?"

She nodded. "It's like a job-search interface, except it's to connect volunteers to volunteer opportunities."

"What a brilliant idea. I'm sure it will be successful," Dad said.

Kamila didn't doubt it would be. Jana touched it, so her venture would turn to gold.

Jana nodded. "I think it's a viable opportunity. I am confident I can acquire the skills I need outside my areas of expertise. I feel it's important for me to challenge myself so I don't grow stagnant in my field."

"Yes," Rohan said. "There is nothing I respect more than someone willing to expand their mind in new and innovative ways."

Vomit.

Jana nodded. "I'd like to stay close to home for a while, but imagination and innovation are muscles that can atrophy like any others. And I must use my energy to make a positive impact on the world. When I see people wrapped up in the exploits of the Kardashians or whoever the hottest Bollywood actor has been seen with, I wonder if those mental resources could be used for the greater good instead."

God. Kamila *really* disliked this woman.

"You're absolutely right," Asha said, nodding. "I can connect you with some classmates of mine in nonprofit management. Even the volunteer coordinator at the shelter. They might be able to help you with a needs assessment for your project."

Ugh. Her best friend, too? Kamila tuned them out as they talked, picking up the snack bowls from around the room.

"What's this incubator project about anyway?" Nicole asked.

Rohan smiled. "It's the brainchild of an old college friend of mine, Anil. It's to help business start-ups get off the ground, focusing specifically on new immigrants and refugees. He has an innovative partnership structure for companies to donate both time and money to the project."

Jana loudly dropped a glass, but since this was Jana the Great, it didn't break. Why was she still cleaning? Probably to make herself look perfect. Kamila took the glasses from Jana's hands.

"Oh, interesting," Asha said.

Rohan nodded. "The initial committee is only fundraising now, though." He looked at Jana. "Sorry to hear you won't be working with us. I'd love to have an old friend on the team with me."

"I am not able to work with Anil on this," Jana said curtly. "I cannot risk extinguishing the growth on my project now."

Too bad Dane was gone, because he'd feel right at home with Jana's pretentious jargon.

"Hey, Kamila, why don't you volunteer for this incubator!" Asha said suddenly. "You'd be so perfect for it."

Kamila's head shot around to her so-called best friend. "What?"

"Sure—you're great at fundraising." Asha looked at the others in the room. "She's chairing the puppy prom this year."

Asha gave Kamila a pointed look—one Kamila understood. Helping businesses get off the ground was exactly the kind of thing Kamila loved—and volunteering for this incubator could give Kamila the cachet she needed to get bigger clients and more credibility.

Jana raised one eyebrow. "But are refugees glamorous enough for Kamila? I don't think there will be any fluffy dogs involved."

Rohan snorted a laugh at Jana's dig.

Kamila's head shot to look at Rohan. That hurt. Jana's comment wasn't really a surprise. But Rohan laughed. Did he really think she cared only about glamour and fluffy dogs? Volunteering at the shelter was the furthest thing from glamorous. Until she ended up on the prom committee, she spent most of her time there cleaning up poo.

Asha, a peacemaker down to her bones, tried to defuse the tension in the room. "Uncle," she said to Dad. "Did you try this Burmese coconut cake Rohan brought? Come, let me get you a slice."

"That's probably not a good idea," Jana said. "It's very sweet. Uncle, you said your blood sugar test was high this week. You should watch your carbohydrate intake."

Kamila's head shot to Dad. He had his test results already? And he'd told *Jana*, but not her? "Dad, when did you get your test results?"

He gave Kamila a reassuring pat on the arm. "Today, beti. I didn't want to worry you before your party."

But he was fine with worrying Jana?

There were too many people around to scold Dad now. Not to mention Jana still had that smug expression. But Kamila had every intention of giving her father a much-deserved piece of her mind later. In the meantime, though, she needed to wipe that look off Jana's face.

"I'd love to learn more about the incubator," Kamila said. "I could totally volunteer. Helping refugees is such a great cause."

"Are you sure, Kam?" Rohan asked. "It's not really your scene."

Jana frowned. Was her expression smug?

"Of course I'm sure," Kamila said. "I love fundraising! And I'm good at it."

Rohan still looked skeptical but nodded. "I suppose I can ask Anil if he has use for you."

"I'm pretty sure they won't be needing anyone to lead a ukulele sing-along," Jana said.

How did Jana even know about her ukulele? Kamila hadn't been in the mood for a sing-along tonight and hadn't brought it out. Kamila didn't care who saw her and gave Jana a death glare. But everyone was too busy chuckling at Jana's comment to notice.

Dad didn't laugh, at least, but he didn't look convinced. Did no one have faith in Kamila?

"Volunteering is so important," Kamila said. "It sounds like a worthy cause. And it would be great to be on this committee with Rohan. We always have a good time together, right?"

Jana finally lost that smug look on her ice queen face. It was wonderfully replaced with...irritation.

This idea was getting better and better. A worthy cause, indeed.

CHAPTER 6

Dad excused himself to bed even before the others left, so Kamila couldn't talk to him about the test results he hadn't told her about. And of course, Rohan spent the night in the guest room. He always slept over on Fridays, and Kamila usually didn't mind the slightest bit. But when she woke early Saturday morning, she was decidedly less than thrilled that she'd see him at breakfast. She dreaded the thought of talking to Dad about this in front of someone who thought all she cared about was fun, glamour, and fluffy dogs.

It was raining heavily outside her bedroom window, which, frankly, matched her mood a little too well. She checked her Instagram, but her head started pounding after responding to only a few comments. Tossing her phone on her bed made Darcy stir as the dog noticed her human was awake. She jumped onto Kamila's chest and started licking her face. So much for sleeping in.

"I know, I know. You want outside." She picked up Darcy and scratched below her ears.

Coffee. Kamila desperately needed coffee. She could let Darcy out in the yard for a few minutes, then grab a mug, and take it back to bed to maybe get a little more sleep. Dad wouldn't be up yet anyway. Not bothering to change or even take her sleep bonnet off her head, she made her way straight to the back door and let Darcy out.

"Good, you're up," Rohan said from the kitchen.

"Not really. Need caffeine." She passed him on the way to the cabinet to get a mug. He'd at least made a pot.

"Nice hat. You look like the sultan from *Aladdin*."

She pulled the purple satin cap off her head, releasing hair probably frizzy from sleep.

He raised a brow, looking at her face. "Rough night?"

She ignored him as she poured her coffee. It *had* been a rough night. She'd taken so long to fall asleep after that terrible bout of self-loathing triggered by Jana and, partially, by this man, too. She considered skipping her usual Saturday morning of doting over the men by making sure they were fed and happy. She could talk to Dad after Rohan left. But...her stomach gurgled. Something smelled good. Rohan was cooking? A cutting board was drying in the dish rack, and a container of feta cheese sat on the counter. She turned to the stove.

Rohan was cracking eggs into a bubbling red sauce. She watched him awhile, the scent of the coffee in her hand soothing her sour mood. Or maybe it was the smell of the rich, spiced tomato sauce. Was this a peace offering? Did he know her self-esteem had been fed through a wood chipper last night?

"What are you making?"

"Shakshuka," Rohan said.

"Bless you," she responded.

"It's a Tunisian breakfast dish. Not a sneeze."

Kamila rolled her eyes. "I know what shakshuka is. I was making a joke."

"Oh. Can you slice the bread? It's on the table."

She fetched the loaf and grabbed her bread knife. The bread was high-quality multigrain, with a crisp crust and tender crumb.

"Where did this come from?" she asked.

"I ran out to the bakery early. It's whole grain, so, good for your father. We can show your dad that healthy breakfasts can be full of flavor. And not on fire."

She decided not to take the bait of his teasing. "Did you know he got his test results yesterday?" she asked.

He shook his head. "Not until Jana mentioned it. I figured we could ambush him together with this meal."

Kamila looked over at him as he covered his pot of sauce. He was the same. Kind, caring, and teasing her. Acting as a united front in caring for Dad. This breakfast was Rohan being Rohan. Taking care of them.

Was that why he'd gone to see Jana before the movie? Just Rohan being kind to another old friend? Or was Tim's suspicion true, and Rohan had caught feelings for the most flawless person in their families' social circle? It made sense—Jana was beautiful, brilliant, and (puke) accomplished. Rohan was smart, hand-some, and successful. And now legally single—which he hadn't been the last time Jana was here.

Fancy people, as Tim put it. As a person with a matchmaking hobby, the potential match was undeniable.

But Jana was cold. Reserved. Kamila couldn't imagine her *intensely* into anyone. And despite Rohan's cool-as-a-cucumber corporate persona, Kamila happened to know he had a bit of a wild side. There was some serious passion under those designer suits. He liked his movies steamy, and he could make someone's toes curl with one touch. And he kissed with his whole body. Kamila had seen that side of him once. But that was a long time ago, and she didn't like to think about it too much. For reasons.

No. Rohan would be wasted on someone like Jana.

"Don't bother toasting the bread," he said, smirking. "Let's not risk your shiny new toaster, eh?"

"Smart bum."

He snorted. "Your dad's not even here. You're allowed to swear in front of me."

She gave him a pointed look. "You realize I don't swear in front of *anyone*, right?"

He laughed as he crumbled feta with his hands. "It's sometimes hard to believe you're the same person as the kid I grew up with," he said. "I'm five years older than you, and I think you *taught* me my most colorful profanity. So, you've had shakshuka, then? I haven't wowed you with something new?"

She pulled down her wood baguette platter board and put the now-sliced bread on it. "Did you really think you could find anything I've never experienced? I've had shakshuka at that North African brunch place downtown. I didn't know you could make it, though, or I would have come to your place instead. For some reason I seem to enjoy your flavor of patronizing hipster better than most."

"I'm not patronizing. And hardly a hipster."

Kamila leaned over to pat his shoulder. "Yeah, you're patronizing. You are more stuck-up preppy than hipster, though." She eyed him head to toe exaggeratedly. "Although, *look at you* today. Mr. Buttoned-Up is in a hoodie, and are those *blue jeans*? Dressing like the proletariat?"

He shook his head, laughing.

"Where's Dad?" she asked.

"Still sleeping, I assume."

Darcy started scratching at the back door, ready to be brought in, so Kamila opened the door and dried off her dog with a towel. "I wish it would stop raining," she said. It was so gloomy, and her headache wasn't easing. She sat on the floor and hugged her dog close. Even while smelling like wet dog, Darcy was a comfort.

Dad came down the stairs at that moment. "It's raining hard out there. I hope the roof holds. Maybe we should call the townhouse board?"

"It will be fine, Dad. The roof was done six months ago, remember?"

"Yes, but I think they did it wrong. With so many vents and peaks—it's so easy to overlap the shingles backward. I'll—"

"Dad." She got up and led him to the dining table. "Don't worry so much. Come, sit. Rohan made breakfast. It looks delicious."

Kamila was still annoyed at Rohan, but after sitting down to eat, she reluctantly admitted to herself that his shakshuka was very good.

"This is tasty, right, Dad?" Kamila asked. "Healthy breakfasts can be satisfying, too."

"Especially when they're not burnt," Rohan added. Unnecessarily.

Dad scooped some tomatoes and egg with his bread. "I could eat like this every day."

"Good. Because you might have to." She arched an eyebrow at Dad. "Are you ready to tell us your test results now?"

Dad sighed and put down his toast. "I didn't want to worry you, beti. You had your party yesterday."

"Blood sugar was high. What else?" she asked.

Dad sighed. "Cholesterol. And blood pressure, but you knew that. And apparently, my heart is stressed. According to my EKG."

Kamila dropped her fork. "Dad! You didn't even tell me you had an EKG! Did you talk to Dr. Anchali? What did she say?"

"She says it's not too bad…I don't have to worry. Yet."

Kamila shook her head. "When does she expect us to worry, then? When you're dead?" She couldn't believe he'd kept this from her.

Dad blinked.

Great. Now she was upsetting him. Right after he'd told her that his heart was stressed. Kamila rubbed her temple. She was really bad at this.

Rohan put his hand on her arm. "What did the doctor advise?" he asked.

Dad glanced to the window before looking back at them, resigned. "Same thing everyone advises. Lower my stress. But I can't stop working. I tried before. I can't bear it." Kamila could see the despair sneaking into his eyes.

Kamila watched him closely. He was right. It hadn't been good the last time Dad didn't work. After his first major mental health episode not long after Mom died, everyone told him to rest. Take time off. To not worry about HNS, that they had it covered. But resting didn't work for Dad. He only sank deeper into his depression. He wasn't the kind of man who could be idle. He needed to feel useful to feel valued. But going back to HNS wasn't good for him back then, either. It had already grown huge by that point, and it wasn't the small, quiet tax office Dad preferred.

So, Rohan's father had helped Dad open Emerald as a subsidiary of HNS. A small tax office, like what Hussain, Nasser, and Suleiman had been when it first opened. Dad called it Emerald, after Mom's birthstone. And he thrived there. When Kamila got her CPA, she first joined HNS, but when that didn't work out, she came to Emerald, too.

Kamila gave Dad a sympathetic look. "Dad, you don't have to retire completely. Try part-time for now. I can take some of your clients."

He shook his head. "You can't, Kamila. My clients aren't like the salons you work with."

"That's ridiculous, Dad. My clients' businesses aren't easier because they're not white-collar professionals, or doctors, or whatever. That's sexist. You don't agree with that, Rohan, do you?"

Rohan frowned. "Well, I don't think that type of business necessarily makes it easier or harder, but your clients are smaller than your father's. And...younger."

"You don't think I can work with older people? That's ageism."

Dad patted her arm. "But seriously, beti. I know you like to be casual with your clients. And you're so...stylish. That's fine for them, but my clients are old-fashioned. Do you think Dr. Johansson will want you coming in with your big dresses and that dog purse?"

Kamila didn't even bring Darcy in her designer dog carrier to client meetings. Anymore, at least. Kamila wrinkled her nose. Dad might be right, though—Dr. Johansson was an octogenarian gastroenterologist who owned a few colonoscopy clinics in the city. He would not trust an accountant in bold florals or red lipstick. Heck, she didn't think he'd trust an accountant with breasts. Despite him being quite fond of staring at Kamila's whenever she saw him.

"I know you say you're happier when working," Kamila said. "But your therapist said you need balance. Why don't you try it…for a month, at least? Let me take some of your clients and you can reduce your hours as a trial run."

"And HNS can take a couple, too. Then you'll have a part-time workload," Rohan said.

"But, Kamila, you have your own clients. And, you said you wanted to volunteer for Anil Malek, too."

"Leave that to me. I can handle it. And actually, this Anil guy—why don't you also give me his actual accounting work? I can do all the nonprofit start-up paperwork."

Rohan shook his head. "I don't know, Kamila. Volunteering with them for fundraising is one thing, but also acting as their financial consultant? The nonprofit world is quite traditional, and Anil is very…corporate. I think HNS would be a better fit for their needs. It's going to be a complicated case. I'll speak to him."

Kamila balled her fists. "Do you two seriously have no faith in me? I can be corporate fancy if I need to be! All I need is a pantsuit! And don't give me this hogwaddle that I can't handle a complicated case. Give me a month with this stuffy suit Anil Malek, and I guarantee he'll put Emerald on retainer for all their financial needs."

"Insulting clients isn't the place to start here," Rohan said, frowning.

"Calling someone a stuffy suit isn't an insult. I call you that all the time." She looked at Dad, pleading. "Let me try this, Dad.

If it goes well, then I can take on more of your 'conservative' clients and you can stay part-time."

Dad sighed weakly. "Fine. Okay, beti. Maybe I don't have a choice. I will go part-time for one month. I'll call Anil."

"No need. I have a meeting with him this afternoon anyway." Rohan turned to Kamila. "Kam, if you're serious about this, you can join me."

"Perfect." She'd have liked to have gone to J.Crew first to get new "professional" clothes before meeting the man, but she was pretty sure she still had that pencil skirt from a few years ago when she was a sexy dead flight attendant for Halloween. Wait…the Dogapalooza meeting. "Oh, I just remembered—I have a meeting at the shelter at noon. Tim's taking us to see a new venue for the puppy prom. Apparently, it's a former church."

Rohan, who was scooping shakshuka and egg with his bread, shook his head disparagingly. "If you're going to take this client and volunteer for the incubator, it will be a major time commitment."

"Yeah, so everyone said. You clearly think a formal ball for dogs isn't a good use of my time. I hear you. You think I'm ridiculous."

"I don't think you're ridiculous, Kam. I just want to make sure you know what you're signing up for. It's serious."

Kamila pushed her hair behind her ears. She would have ceremoniously taken her earrings off if she were wearing any. "When have I ever half done anything? Have you seen my parties? My work at the shelter is important. My work at Emerald is important. I'm fully committed to both. I can handle this client, and I wouldn't have offered to volunteer if I didn't think I could do it. I know what serious means."

"I never said you couldn't be serious. All I meant was—"

"Enough, kids," Dad said, his voice shaky. "Kamila is so generous. Both of you. Such big hearts. All this because of me...I'm nothing but trouble for all of you."

Great. Now Dad was upset. She shook her head. "Dad, it's okay. Rohan's just teasing me. We don't mean it. That's just how our friendship is. Give me Anil's number, and I'll call him myself to set up a time to meet." She'd hopefully covered up her annoyance—okay, probably more like anger—at Rohan there. She didn't want Dad worrying even more. But yeah, her blood was boiling. Kamila pushed her chair out. "And actually, I remembered I need to check some things with Asha at the shelter before the meeting. I should get dressed." She needed her best friend. Asha would be on her side.

As Kamila climbed the stairs, she wondered what she had gotten herself into. She talked a good game, but could she actually be the respectable, corporate-type accountant that Dad's clients expected? She had to try. Because nothing was more important than Dad—and if this was the way to get him to reduce his hours, she'd happily buy a blazer and sensible shoes.

She could do this. She had no choice.

CHAPTER 7

S he called Asha as soon as she was in her room.

"Sorry, Kamila, I'll see you at the meeting with Tim later, but I can't hang out right now. I've got my hands full at the moment," Asha said.

"What are your hands full with?"

"Puppies."

"What? What puppies?"

"A litter was left in a cardboard box outside this morning. Literally puppies in a box like this is a sitcom or something. Believe it or not, their medical records were left in the box, too. One of them peed on them. Or maybe all of them did. There was a lot of pee. Like, holy shit, a *lot* of pee. Obviously, these dogs weren't dehydrated."

This was unconscionable. "There are new puppies at the shelter and you didn't call me right away?"

"There are no other managers here. I needed to get them examined and processed."

"How are they?"

"Four are in perfect health. I'll give the fifth to the vet to examine if you get off the phone. He's the runt but—"

"I'm on my way."

A supportive friend was what Kamila'd *thought* she needed after that breakfast. But instead, the universe gave her what she *actually* needed. Puppies. She changed in record time.

Twenty minutes later, Kamila was on the floor of the largest enclosure in the animal shelter in a calf-length magenta corduroy skirt and a black fitted mohair sweater, sitting on old bedsheets with three tiny black puppies wriggling on her lap.

"I suspect someone was giving backyard breeding a try," Asha said, "then realized how much work it is. The medical records say they're Lab mixes. It's nice to see healthy puppies surrendered for a change. They're about four weeks old now. We'll probably wait until they're eight weeks before we adopt them out. Give or take."

Kamila laughed as one of them stood on the head of another to lick her face. A fourth puppy was chewing on the toe of Kamila's boot (which was fine—she'd specifically bought these Hunter rubber boots to wear at the shelter). Asha was holding the fifth puppy, the only beige one in the otherwise all-black litter.

"I want them all," Kamila said.

"You don't have time for a puppy."

"I know, I know. I just want them." She buried her face in the fur of the one closest to her. Ah, that new-puppy smell. "Let me see that one." She put out her arms to take the beige puppy from Asha's hands. Holding him out in front of her, she looked at his sweet face. "Aw, this one's the runt, isn't it?"

Asha nodded. "Yup. Smallest, and the only brown one. He's got some catching up to do, but he's healthy enough."

Kamila cuddled the soft puppy in her arms. He was calm compared to the others and seemed to love being close to her. He was probably cold. She snuggled him into her sweater and leaned back against the wall. "This one is my favorite. He's like a perfect little potato." She stroked his ear. "I was in a spectacularly bad mood before I called you. But this little potato healed everything."

Asha laughed as she picked up one of the others. "I'll never understand why people pay for therapy. They need to hang out in animal shelters."

"I've spent thousands on therapy, and I agree—puppies work just as well. Better, actually."

"Why were you in a bad mood?"

"Ah, you know. Family. Mind-numbing feelings of inadequacy." She picked up another puppy to snuggle along with Potato. Because why snuggle one puppy when there was an abundance of puppies available? "By the way, Asha, what was that all about yesterday? Telling everyone I'd be perfect for that volunteer thing?"

"Ugh. Yes, sorry about that. I shouldn't have volunteered you. It's just... *Jana*. She was getting under my skin."

Kamila nearly dropped the puppies. But she didn't, because they were puppies and puppies should be protected at all costs.

"Did you say *Jana* got under your skin?" Was it possible Kamila wasn't the only one who didn't drink the unicorn tears and honeysuckle Kool-Aid of Jana Suleiman?

"Yeah, I'm sorry. I know you two are tight."

Kamila blinked. Maybe it was time to come clean... to at least one person. "We are not tight. In fact, I've considered Jana my secret nemesis for most of my life."

Asha's eyes widened. "Oh, thank god. So, it's okay if I say I'm pretty sure she's the type to turn around quickly after she farts so she can inhale her own special aroma?"

Kamila fell to the floor laughing, which resulted in four puppies attacking her face with puppy kisses. Sweet, wonderful torture.

After Kamila managed to get herself to a sitting position again with no puppy tongues on her face, she sighed. "But seriously, why did Jana have to come home early? And then come to my party? I had no time to prepare my defenses. Then you went and said she'd be a good match for Rohan..."

Asha cringed. "Yeah, that was before she started on her 'but imagination and innovation are muscles that can atrophy' business. Sorry if I made everything worse. Were you able to get out of volunteering for that incubator thing?"

"No, I'm going to try to do it. And I'm also going to be taking the guy's accounting work so Dad won't do it."

"Why?"

Kamila buried her face in Potato's neck. "I'm worried about Dad. His test results weren't good. He said he'd go part-time for a month, so I'm taking some of his clients. If I can convince this stuffy-suit that I'm a real accountant in that time, and if he puts Emerald on retainer for all the incubator's financial needs, then maybe Dad will stay part-time after the month. But...ugh. I don't know what I was thinking. How am I supposed to be all...accountant-y?" She frowned but then looked down at Potato's nose, which was delightfully sort of heart shaped. She booped it.

"Kamila, you are actually an accountant, remember?"

Kamila waved her hand. "Technicality."

"So why are you still bothering to volunteer for the thing, too? Just impress him with your stuffy accountant ways."

"I'm scared if I don't volunteer, Rohan will try to convince Jana to do it."

"You only want to do it so Jana won't? That's enormously petty."

Kamila exhaled. "Okay, yeah. Maybe...But also, it's a good cause, isn't it? It sounds like a more dignified volunteer role than organizing a puppy prom. It's better for Emerald."

"I don't like the idea of you feeling as if you need to change who you are just to impress your dad's clients."

"It's not just them." Kamila sighed. "If getting some power suits and sensible shoes and being less...unconventional is what I need to do to save Emerald, then I feel like I should give it a shot."

"Save Emerald...Is it at risk?"

"I mean, yeah, it is. Emerald is technically a subsidiary of HNS. If Dad can't work anymore because he's sick, or even if he retires, then Emerald and its clients will just fold into HNS."

"You wouldn't be out of a job, though. You could work at HNS, too."

"I know. Rohan offered me a job there earlier this week. But I love Emerald. I worked at HNS before and I hated it. There is too much...testosterone there. A whole office full of suits who don't believe a girl wearing mascara could possibly understand complex tax deductions." She smiled as she noticed two puppies had fallen asleep in front of her.

"I've always thought you were the most unlikely accountant around, but I know you are dedicated. You're good at your job."

"Thanks." She watched Potato sleep for a while before asking a question that had been bugging her since last night. "Asha, do you think Rohan *is* into Jana?"

"Dunno. Did he say he was into her?"

"No. But he was at her house before he came over for movie night."

"So? Holy crap, do *you* have a thing for Rohan?"

"No, oh my god, no. It's just...Tim said Rohan and Jana are both, you know, fancy."

"But I'm pretty sure you're fancy enough for Rohan Nasser."

"I'm the wrong kind of fancy for him. And I'm not talking about me here."

"Are you sure?"

Potato did a little twitch in his sleep. This *was* better than any therapy. "Fine," she finally said. "I admit it. Rohan and I are getting closer these days. *As friends.* With you married...I can't risk losing his friendship, especially to Jana Suleiman. I like teasing him, and I like it when he teases me." Most of the time. Last night, however, his teasing crossed a line. This morning, too. And the only thing different was Jana was now in town. She frowned.

"You won't lose him, Kamila. And I'm still your friend, aren't I?"

"Yeah, you are. But unlike Nicole, Jana doesn't like me. Rohan with Jana means the end of my friendship with him. She'd totally sour him to me."

Asha tilted her head. "Kamila, that wouldn't happen. Rohan is better than that. And who knows? Maybe Ms. Perfect will chill a bit once she's been here longer. Maybe you two will be friends."

"I doubt that. It's not only her insufferable smugness...I have other nonpetty reasons for disliking her." Kamila told Asha the story of Bronx Bennet and his popular backseat.

"Holy crap, *Bronx Bennet*? Tell me that wasn't his real name."

Kamila giggled. It had been a while since she'd considered how ridiculous her high school hookup's given name was. "It was. He really had no choice but to be a bad boy or a country music star with that name. I didn't care too much about losing Bronx—dude was white and wore an om necklace and smelled like incense. But there's more..." She told Asha about Mom giving Jana Kamila's grad party.

"Holy shit, she just let your mother give her your party when she *knew* she was the one in the car? That's low...I don't think I like Jana Suleiman, either."

Potato squirmed a bit, so Kamila gently rocked him until he was calm again. "I didn't want a grad party, anyway."

"I thought you'd dropped out of university?" Asha asked.

"This was before that. The party was supposed to be my *high school* graduation party. I dropped out of university two years later when I was twenty." And then she'd re-enrolled after Mom died a year later.

"I'm sorry about your mother," Asha continued. "I knew she wasn't great to you. I don't think I realized it was that bad."

Kamila shrugged. She really didn't want to talk about her mother right now.

She absently rubbed Potato's soft puppy fur. "The past is the past. I just don't want things to change *now*. Jana was more than willing to throw me under the bus back then, and I have no doubt she'd do it again. If doing this incubator thing is the way to keep Rohan away from Jana Suleiman, then I think it's a worthy cause."

"Helping refugees and newcomers is already a worthy cause."

"Yep. That too."

Asha laughed. "Well, I have to say, this is a new one. I've

known you for years, Kamila. You've been constantly match-making for your friends. And now? Match-breaking. Isn't that against some sort of matchmaking oath?"

"I'm not breaking anything. I'm match-preventing."

"Semantics, my friend."

CHAPTER 8

Once they'd extracted themselves from the puppy room and cleaned off the drool, Kamila and Asha met Tim in the lobby so they could check out the new prom venue he'd sourced. They'd already reserved the space they used last year—the gym in a local community center—but Tim had been grumbling that it wasn't *memorable* enough for weeks.

The venue was very close to the shelter, so they walked there for the tour. It was a former church, and had interesting mid-century modern geometric stained glass, and blond wood floors and walls. Tim oohed and aahed about the vaulted ceiling and natural light. The aesthetic would make for amazing pictures and the raised stage area was big enough for Kamila's canine freestyle performance, but she worried untrained dogs would pee on the pulpit. After leaving the church, the three of them went to a nearby Japanese/French patisserie to discuss.

"Such a stroke of luck getting that place," Tim said, stirring lemon into his tea. "The social media team will love it." Tim was positively giddy about this.

He seemed to forget Kamila *was* the entire social media team.

"I don't know. Could be a lot of work to change everything. The prom is in four weeks."

"Nonsense. Everything is online—it's easy to make changes. Raj is giving the shelter the space for free as a donation. And it's walking distance from the shelter, so people can come after leaving the Dogapalooza."

"I'll have to rework the decor plan. What do you think, Asha?"

"The place is stunning. But you two will have the most work if we change the venue now."

And more work was exactly what Kamila didn't need. Not now that she was potentially taking on extra work at Emerald.

"Imagine it," Tim said. "A red carpet down the aisle. Photo booth in that old confessional. We need to let Raj know soon if we want it. I think it's perfect, so my vote is to change the venue."

"Fine. I'll look into what needs to be done to move everything." She took an angry bite of her matcha croissant, which was irritatingly perfect. She was in a mildly foul mood again now that she wasn't in contact with puppies anymore. The buttery croissant should have cheered her up, though.

"Oh, Kamila," Asha said, "did Danielle talk to you about the Dogapalooza fashion show? She wants you to emcee."

Danielle was one of the other shelter volunteers. "When is that?" Kamila asked.

"Saturday afternoon, I think. I haven't seen the finalized schedule."

Kamila blew out a puff of air. People sure loved to volunteer her for things. "Sure. Whatever."

"Someone's grumpy today," Tim said. "Distraught over the departure of your little boy toy?"

"What? No." Kamila quite honestly hadn't thought of Ernesto once since he'd left last week. She'd assumed she wouldn't miss his presence in her life, and thankfully, she'd been right. "He wasn't a boy toy, and no, that's not why I'm grumpy. It's a work thing. I need to learn how to be a boring finance type for that incubator client of Dad's."

"What are you talking about?" Tim asked.

Of course, Tim had left the Bollywood party before they'd talked about Anil. She and Asha filled him in on the events that occurred after he left, and on her morning convo with Rohan and Dad.

"So, what's the problem?" Tim asked. "You're good at your job. You can help this guy Anil get his business off the ground."

She sighed. "I'm second-guessing myself. Nonprofit people are apparently...conservative." Jana was a nonprofit person, and she was uptight. That was like conservative times twenty.

Asha snorted. "I work for a nonprofit. I'm hardly conservative."

"That's different," Kamila said. "You work with animals, not people."

Asha rolled her eyes and pulled out her phone. "What's his full name?"

"Anil Malek."

"Wow," Asha said. "Check out his resume...He's been involved in some major projects. Sits on some impressive boards, too. Talk about fancy people."

"Ugh." Of course. Someone even more perfect than Jana. Why was everyone testing Kamila's self-worth these days?

"He's bald! But he's actually pretty nice to look at." Asha put her phone in the middle of the table and started a video. It was a fundraising plea for the project. Anil was talking directly into the camera about the inspiration behind it and what he was hoping to accomplish.

And yup, he was kind of hot, even without a single strand of hair on his head. Dark eyes, chiseled jaw, and a wide smile. His dark suit had a conservative cut, and he had the same dignified air as Rohan but with the charming smile and generous look of someone who started a company to help refugees. Kamila liked his face.

"Single?" Asha asked.

"No ring," Tim said when Anil was being particularity animated with his hands. Tim pulled out his phone. "I'll search up his socials." After a few minutes, he grinned. "Bingo. He mentioned separating from his wife in an Instagram comment a few months ago." He kept scrolling Anil's Instagram. "Doesn't sound too distraught about it. He's talking about living his authentic self. He's new in Toronto. Did you know that?"

Kamila shook her head. She couldn't keep her eyes off the video. Anil Malek was mesmerizing. He had an open, compassionate demeanor. Friendly. He was talking about his project, specifically about lifting up immigrant communities by helping women launch small businesses. Another plus. The guy sounded pretty feminist. He was centering women in his incubator.

Maybe...maybe Kamila should be more enthusiastic about working with this project? Anil's mandate seemed to align with hers—helping women-owned businesses. He was extremely easy on the eyes. He didn't seem uptight at all. Plus, single.

Impressing this man meant Dad would go part-time, which would keep him healthy and help her keep Emerald. And also? Keep Rohan from spending too much time with Jana Suleiman.

She'd been determined to take over Dad's work for this man's project, but honestly, Kamila had been kind of dreading it. But now...she was intrigued. It could be fun to spend time with this accomplished, handsome man. Kamila was suddenly eager to meet Anil Malek. Even if it meant getting a briefcase.

She emailed Anil that night, telling him that she was taking over his nonprofit incorporation paperwork because Dad needed to take some time off. She suggested they meet to go over any other business needs he had. And she asked if he had room for a new volunteer on his fundraising committee. He wrote back Monday, saying he'd love to get together and discuss all of that. Somehow, the man was able to exude as much charm in his email as he had in the video clip. He suggested Wednesday or Friday to get together. Wednesday was no good—Dad was going to London to spend a few days with Shelina and the kids, and Kamila promised to drive him to the train station. And of course, Friday was Bollywood night. On a whim, she invited Anil to join her then, saying they could get to know each other at her dinner party, and then talk one-on-one later. He agreed.

It meant Bollywood night would have to be a little more... respectable this week. No ukulele sing-alongs. Probably no signature drink. But Kamila could be elegant and sophisticated. She was up for the challenge.

CHAPTER 9

After dropping Dad off at the train station Wednesday night for his visit with Shelina, Kamila found some time to do some research on Anil so she'd be ready to wow him on Friday.

Even though his project was only starting, it was impressive. The donors that had already signed on were pretty big deals—real estate companies, law firms, big tech companies. And HNS, of course. Emerald's name attached to this project in any capacity would be fantastic for business.

Bollywood night needed to be utterly perfect. This time there was no room for cut fingers, kitchen fires, or anything else that could go wrong.

She tapped her gel manicure on her computer desk, thinking. Where was there opportunity to class up this party? Maybe the tableware? Her normal plates were very good, very bright Kate Spade, but she could get something more elegant. And she could kick up the food a bit. She already had the biryani ordered (Mumbai style this week). Maybe plate it in a fancier serving dish? Could she add elaborate appetizers? She pulled down an

Indian snack cookbook that some generous soul had given her as a hostess gift and thumbed through it.

She wanted to make her favorite—kachori chaat. But it looked much too complicated, and she was low-key afraid of starting a grease fire if she deep-fried anything. Not to mention it was messy. She considered bhel puri, but it seemed too simple. And even messier.

She needed wow factor, while being secretly foolproof and tidy. And flame resistant. She finally settled on chili-paneer kebobs and vegetable momo dumplings with chili-ginger chutney. The momos looked a bit tricky to wrap, but nothing a YouTube momo-watching marathon couldn't solve. The best part? They were steamed—and thus, nearly impossible to ignite into flames.

Of course, she wasn't serving any alcohol at all this time. She had no idea if Anil was a religious enough Muslim to refrain from drinking himself, or if he would be judgy about others imbibing. Kamila herself wasn't really religious, but she knew others might be uncomfortable with the normal drinking at her parties, even if she didn't normally participate. Apple cider simmered with whole cinnamon and cardamom would be lovely.

She left the office a little early on Thursday to visit an outlet mall where she bought classy matte black dinner plates, small pink rose-printed luncheon plates, and brushed-gold flatware. She also picked up a black tiered serving plate that the momos would look amazing on, along with some large clear globe-shaped bowls for fresh flowers. And she got new clothes. Fancy, sophisticated party clothes. No flared skirts or bold prints to be seen.

It was after eight by the time she got home and started

cooking. She needed to make the food tonight since she had client meetings tomorrow and couldn't work from home. The paneer was easy—she cubed the cheese and tossed it in a simple marinade of yogurt, ginger, garlic, and spices, then parked it in the fridge. She'd thread the pieces onto skewers and roast them tomorrow.

The momos were less accommodating. The dough for the wrappers was a nightmare to knead smooth, and she couldn't seem to roll it thin enough. And even after all those YouTube videos, her pleating technique left a lot to be desired. Still, they ended up looking mostly cute, and they miraculously stayed together during steaming. She knew with a bit of garnish they'd be fine. The chili-ginger chutney was utterly perfect.

It was after two a.m. when she finally cleaned up the kitchen. Her first client meeting was at ten, which meant waking at seven to wash and blow-dry her hair straight. It was fine. It would be worth it to see everyone's face when she brought out a platter of handmade momos.

Kamila was exhausted the next day, but she managed. Her meetings went well, and just as importantly, her blowout was perfectly on point. She left work at four and changed into her new black shift dress with three-quarter-length sleeves and straight below-the-knee skirt and had just rolled her hair into a respectable updo when there was a knock on the door. She added white pearls and put her sensible shoes near the stairs so she'd remember to put them on when the guests arrived.

It was Rohan at the door. In dark jeans and a gray knit cardigan. A big bouquet of vibrant-yellow sunflowers in one hand and a reusable liquor-store bag in the other.

"What are you doing here?" Kamila asked. She probably

should have said hello, but Darcy had that covered. She was jumping and yelping for attention at Rohan's feet.

He leaned down and patted the dog's head. "It's Bollywood night." He frowned at Kamila. "What are you wearing? Is there a costume theme tonight?"

"I'm wearing a perfectly respectable dress."

"I know. That's why I'm confused."

She rolled her eyes. "You're early. Bollywood night starts at seven."

"I always come early."

"Two and a half hours early? Last week you were an hour early." Was he gradually moving up the party time just for himself? Not that she was complaining. It was too quiet in the house with Dad gone the last few days.

He walked in, smirking. "I heard Anil was coming and that you're cooking. I came to make sure disaster doesn't strike." He handed Kamila the flowers and a bottle of sparkling wine and slipped off his shoes. He then opened the cabinet under the sink and pulled out the fire extinguisher, placing it ceremoniously on the counter. He smiled. "Put me to work, Kamila. I'm here to help."

Kamila rolled her eyes while tying her most subdued apron, a pale-green linen, over her dress. "I'm pretty much done cooking. But since you're here, you can wash the new dishes. Then set the table." She gave him a once-over. "You're looking good. I like the sweater. That's almost a color." His beard was growing in well—and the chunky charcoal knitwear was a nice change from his suits, even though the whole look was still pretty preppy. More intellectual academic preppy instead of finance-guy preppy, though. "Did you go shopping just for me?"

He smiled. "What, this old thing? Show me the dishes that need washing, boss."

Kamila put on a playlist on her stereo, and they worked silently for a while—Rohan unboxing the new dishes and giving them a quick wash, while Kamila cut the stems of the flowers and arranged them in the bowls. Rohan's sunflowers would be the brightest thing on the table, but they went well with the white lilies she'd picked up.

"Did you work today?" she asked. The rest of the HNS team might do casual on a Friday, but not Rohan.

"Worked from home. Did you buy all these plates just for tonight?"

"Yup." She pulled out the bamboo skewers and set them to soak in cool water.

"Seems overkill."

"It's to set the mood. Create an air of sophistication."

"But why? You're already pretty...urbane."

She preened before taking one of the bowls of flowers to the dining table. "Look at you! That's almost a compliment. I'm so happy you came early to shower me with praise."

He chuckled, shaking his head. "It's my duty, isn't it? Honestly, though, Kam, I came early because...I wanted to apologize. I'm sorry I was discouraging you from taking on Anil's nonprofit. I didn't mean to upset you."

She looked at him, head tilted. She *had* been upset with him. She'd actually been pretty furious on Saturday. The puppies had helped. But also...it was hard to be mad at Rohan. Kamila had never been good at holding grudges—except, of course, when it came to Jana. But still. "Do you still think I'm not capable or qualified for this incubator thing?"

He shook his head. "No. I never thought that at all. I just wanted to make sure you knew what you were signing up for. But I may have gone too far. I am sorry for that. People underestimate you, Kam, but I *do* see how hard you work. You'd be an asset to any team. I spoke to Anil and told him his project would be in good hands with you. I think this will give you the credibility you were looking for without torturing yourself by working with me at HNS."

She touched his arm. "Aw, you told Anil how awesome I am? Thank you. And *you* wouldn't be the torture at HNS. You, I like. Boardrooms and people who say, 'Let's circle back to that,' or, 'We need to leverage our position,' is what I want to avoid."

He laughed. "So, still friends?"

"You can't get rid of me that easy. Of course—still friends." She pulled him in for a quick hug, then squeezed his arm. "Now, back to work, friend."

Now that their Hallmark moment was behind them, they worked together to finish setting up the party. It was nice to have someone to help her since Asha didn't come over as much anymore. Rohan let her lead with minimal snarking—obeying her on where to move the tables and chairs, which throw cushions to put where, and how to set up the dining table. After lighting some cream scented candles, it was time to start on the food. First, she set the cider with the spices on the stove to simmer, then she pulled out the paneer and started threading the marinated cheese cubes on skewers.

"Wow, you really did cook. No takeout at all today?"

"The biryani is takeout. DoorDash will deliver in one hour."

"Well, this stuff looks impressive. Let me help."

He rolled up his sleeves and helped her thread the paneer

along with some cubed vegetables onto the sticks. Soon, the skewers were roasting gently in the oven, adding a creamy, spicy aroma to the apple-cider-and-cardamom scent that was already permeating the room. The table looked perfect—the pink and black plates popped against her wood table. The golden sunflowers were the perfect contrast to her white lilies. This party was going to be amazing.

Smiling smugly to herself, she took the momos out of the fridge. She figured re-steaming them for a few minutes was the best way to heat them, so she might as well load them up in the steamer now so they would be ready to go when the guests arrived.

"Who made that? Actually, what is that?" Rohan asked, looking over her shoulder.

"Momos. I'll have you know I made these completely myself. From scratch. Including the wrapper dough."

"I'm impressed, Kam. They look a little…" He frowned. "Are they supposed to look like used Kleenexes?"

"Shush, you. They're perfect. Wait till you taste one." She grabbed a pair of chopsticks to feed Rohan a momo. Even though they were fridge-cold, she knew he'd be impressed.

But when she tried to lift the momo from the top of the stack, the whole container, and the three dozen momos in it, came with it. She dropped the chopsticks and the container fell back to the counter.

"No problem." She smiled. "A little stuck."

She took out a spoon and tried to gently pry the steamed dumpling from the others. It resisted. A lot. She stopped with the gentle and pulled a little harder. The momo finally budged…sort of. It tore right in half, revealing the vegetable filling stained purple from the red cabbage.

"Fudge," Kamila whispered.

"That wasn't supposed to happen, was it?"

She glared at him and he wisely stopped speaking. He took the spoon from her hand and pulled on another one. But it also tore in half when he tried to dislodge it from the ball of momos.

"Did you grease the container before putting these in?" he asked.

She shook her head. "No."

"Maybe putting hot steamed dough in contact with itself while cooling wasn't a good idea?"

She pouted, peering into the container. Now it looked like a giant wad of wet tissues with gobs of purple snot peeking through. Nasty. What the hell was she thinking, making food herself? True, nothing was on fire, but what was she going to serve Anil?

"What's that smell?" Rohan asked.

Of course. The paneer was burning.

The paneer, thankfully, wasn't burnt. Well, not *very* burnt, at least. Just a little charred. Rohan took the gold pen and black note cards still on the dining table and rewrote the food label—*Blackened Paneer Kebobs.*

"They're fine," he said.

But the momos—they were *not* fine. Kamila had no idea how to salvage the doughy, gummy mass stuck to the bottom of her largest container. She eyed the mound, hoping inspiration would strike. Would steaming them again dislodge them from each other? Maybe freezing them and taking a chisel to them?

She could throw the whole mass in the food processor and call it "deconstructed momo soup."

"How do we save these?" she asked.

Rohan shook his head. "Glue is made from cooked flour. They're permanently stuck." He poked at them again with a chopstick.

Her shoulders fell. She was a *disaster*. Why did she think she could do this? She sighed as she scraped the blob out of the container, mutilating it even further, and tossed it into the compost bin.

Now all she had was some overcooked cheese on sticks and a pot of hot apple juice. Hardly sophisticated party food. Everyone would rave about the store-bought biryani, and no doubt someone would ask why the house smelled like burnt cheese. With a lingering flaming-sweet-potato undertone.

"Let's make more," Rohan said.

She looked at him, blinking. "More what?"

"Momos. There's"—he checked his watch—"an hour and a half before everyone gets here. Do you still have ingredients?"

She nodded. She'd only used half the red cabbage, and there were plenty of carrots, green onions, and flour.

He pulled another apron from the hook beside the door.

And there he was. *Rohan* being Rohan. Her suit-wearing, stiff, tax-lawyer CEO friend was wearing her red polka-dot apron so he could help fix *her* mistake. This was why she could never stay mad at him. Also…the apron looked adorable on him. "What do you know about making momos?"

"Nothing. But I can cook. Lisa's grandmother taught us to make har gow once. I'm sure I can handle this."

Turns out, he *could* handle this. It shouldn't have been

a surprise—Rohan excelled at anything he did, so of course making a wheat dough was one of his many talents.

She watched his hands as he rolled a ball into a circle. "How are you doing that so well?"

"Didn't your mother teach you to make rotli? Zayan and I had to learn to roll a perfect circle before she would teach us to drive."

Kamila's mother had not taught her to cook. She'd taught Shelina. "My mom decided I wasn't capable of cooking."

He took another ball of dough and started rolling it out. "That's ridiculous. Anyone can cook."

Kamila sighed. "Let's just say she thought teaching me wasn't worth the trouble."

Rohan stopped rolling and looked at her.

He, of course, had known her mother. He'd grown up with her, just like she'd grown up with his mother. But he didn't really *know* Mom. Most people saw the stylish woman with the impeccable house who threw lavish parties. Most didn't see the criticisms, the comparisons, the complete disappointment in anything her youngest daughter did. Kamila was mostly over the verbal abuse she'd endured from her mother, thanks to years of therapy, great friends, a loving father, and of course, Darcy. But even healed wounds left scars.

He had to know some of what her mother was really like, though, right? How could he not? His brother was literally married to her sister. He'd seen slivers of her mother's passive aggression when they were kids. He'd been present when Mom led the others in a rousing round of "let's talk about everything wrong with Kamila." But he didn't know about the last fight she'd had with her mother.

He was still watching her, sympathy in his eyes. Kamila's

breath hitched... His stare was so intense. Maybe he *did* know. Mom could have told his parents. Expressed her shame over her harpy of a daughter's loose morals. Apologized for Kamila throwing herself at someone as upstanding as Rohan Nasser.

His stare bored into her, and for a moment it felt like he was going to touch her. A huge part of her wanted to touch *him*—to rub his arm reassuringly. Tell him it was fine. That he shouldn't worry—she was okay. Not traumatized. Not hurting anymore. Just the fun, quirky Kamila who he never underestimated.

Finally, he tilted his head. "I'm sorry," he said softly. He turned back to the dough and started rolling another ball. "I knew your mother was rough on you back then. But I... I didn't know how to support you."

"Rohan, you were a kid. There was nothing you could have done." She grabbed her own ball of dough and rolled it out into a warped amoeba shape. "I'm okay. I've accepted my mother wasn't good at being a mom, and it wasn't my fault. That one statement is worth thousands of dollars of therapy, by the way. Anyway, I had your mom and Rashida Aunty. They were great. Dad was always there for me, too. He protected me from so much..." Dad shouldn't have had to, though. Trying to keep Kamila safe had taken such a toll on him.

Rohan touched her arm for a second. "I know I'm hard on you, too, Kam. Maybe I'm too critical. Tell me if I go too far, okay?"

Kamila nodded, biting her lip. She didn't want things to change between them. That was the whole point of keeping Jana away from him. "I like how things are with us." She smiled. "I can take it, old man. Anything you throw at me. That's why we're great friends."

He chuckled as he filled his perfectly rolled circle with filling and pleated the edges, creating something so much nicer than her wet-tissue momos. "My mom only insisted my brother and I learn to cook so we'd find better wives. She claimed her mother taught her to make round rotlis to snag a husband, and it was her duty to do the same for us, even if we were boys. I think it was really because she was afraid she'd be making our rotlis for the rest of our lives."

Kamila watched as his strong, firm arms rolled another perfect circle of dough. She'd never seen a man roll rotlis before. Rohan and Zayan's mother had clearly been on to something. She made a mental note to ask her sister if her husband's rotli-rolling skills had anything to do with their relationship.

"Did Lisa appreciate your cooking skills?" Kamila couldn't believe she asked that. He rarely talked about his marriage, and she never asked him about it. She didn't even know why they'd split. Rohan had a wall—a boundary he didn't cross with Kamila. As close as they had become lately, and as much as Kamila detailed her sex life to him all the time, he didn't talk about his own relationships. He wasn't a kiss-and-tell kind of guy.

"Lisa didn't care. I don't mean that in a bad way." He shrugged. "I didn't really cook much when we were together. We rarely ate at home. I think that was the main problem in our marriage."

"What? You divorced because you didn't cook?"

He didn't look at Kamila but kept making momos as he spoke. "No, not the cooking, specifically—more the not spending time at home. We met at work. We worked together. She was at the office even longer hours than I was, and then we would meet somewhere for dinner. Almost every night."

"Sounds like you spent too much time together." Kamila

would never set up a friend with someone they worked with. Couples needed space.

"Ah, yes and no. We were together all the time, but we were never alone. Work isn't living, you know? We weren't really *together*. I don't remember ever feeling like I wanted or needed to spend every waking moment with her. I thought that was because we saw so much of each other, so there was no urgency to be alone." He sighed. "I'm never getting involved with a colleague again. It distorts the relationship. That's one of the reasons why I left the law firm and finally started full-time at HNS—I'd hoped not working together would fix us. But . . . we weren't really suited. That became clear when we stopped seeing so much of each other."

So that was why they'd split. Kamila had resented Lisa after their separation because she assumed Lisa had hurt Rohan in more ways than just taking his cat. But it sounded like it wasn't one of them hurting the other, but two people at the wrong place and time, caught up in what they thought they were supposed to do.

Kamila wanted to know more—had he *ever* felt that urgency to spend time alone with Lisa? Before things went stale? But that felt like prying.

But she was still curious. "Have you ever felt that for anyone at all?"

"What?"

"That urgency. Desperation, *craving* . . . to be alone with someone. Not just for sex."

"Have you?"

She snorted. "Always a lawyer. Answering a question with a question. No, I've never felt that. I'm not sure I'm capable. Which is fine for me. I'm happy with casual, remember?"

He looked at her, lip upturned. "I think you're capable, Kam. Maybe you're not ready yet."

She laughed. "Oh? And how would you know that?"

"I'm older and wiser. I know."

She laughed as she pinched the seal on another momo. She was getting the hang of this, but Rohan's were still better. She couldn't believe Lisa didn't care that he could cook. Watching him was mesmerizing, even in the polka-dot apron. Sweater and shirtsleeves rolled up (because, even if no suit, he had a dress shirt under the sweater). Biceps flexing as he worked the rolling pin. Large hands surprisingly delicate while pleating the tops of the perfect dumplings. And dear lord, those forearms. She wasn't sure she'd seen them before—well, not in a long time, at least. Strong. Solid. Those capable forearms made momo-making seem effortless, but the bare hint of sheen at his hairline proved he was putting effort into this.

Would anyone else have done this for her? Roll up his sleeves and make dozens of dumplings only an hour before a party? Yes, probably. Ernesto would have done it. Definitely Asha. Even Dad would have tried his hands at momo-making, if he were home. Not Tim, but Jerome might do it.

It wasn't really all that special that Rohan was doing this for her. But it *felt* like it was. This felt precious.

"Okay, old man, show me how you're doing those pleats. Clearly, you're the momo expert in the room, and I want to absorb some of that brilliance."

He grinned as he peeled a wrapper off the counter and filled it. He moved nearer to show her close-up how he pleated the tops. It took several tries, but with his hands under hers, she was able to make dumplings that looked almost as good as his.

"Hey," Kamila said as she carefully measured a teaspoon of filling into another wrapper. "Did you know momos were almost banned in Delhi a few years ago?"

He raised his brow. "That's absurd. Why?"

"They claimed it was because of the monosodium glutamate. But instead of banning the ingredient, this whacky politician decided to try to ban the entire food." She pleated the dough over the little mound of filling. "MSG is in fried chicken and Doritos, but they decided to go after this one Tibetan dish that had recently become ridiculously popular in India. It's totally xenophobia. Fear of the unknown and nationalism is the root of it, as usual." She put the completed momo on the parchment-paper-lined tray, ensuring it didn't touch any of the surrounding dumplings. Kamila was determined that no momo should ever touch another momo again, lest they get stuck together, forever. They would live solitary, lonely lives until they met in her stomach.

"It's weird," she continued as she pinched off a piece of dough for the next dumpling. "I'm, like, super happy to be Indian, and the food and culture are awesome, but we're Muslim, too. With the nationalistic sentiments getting stronger, at some point we may have to examine our obsession with Bollywood and question what we are supporting. That's why I picked the movie *Amar, Akbar, Anthony* this week. I wanted to see if it really does celebrate religious tolerance like I remember it does. Also, that scene with Amitabh jumping out of an egg and dancing is epic. Too bad we couldn't have done a seventies theme again for tonight. Remember? Asha made the best pineapple upside-down cake the last time we watched a swank seventies movie." She couldn't do a theme party on the week she was trying to be *sophisticated* to impress Anil.

Kamila then noticed Rohan was no longer making momos and was looking at her, a curious expression on his face.

"What? Did I do something wrong?" she asked, looking at the momo in her hand.

His eyes were wide, and his expression was a new one. The slightest hint of...admiration. "No. It's what you said about India. This is what I mean when I say people underestimate you. I think they're making a big mistake."

"Nonsense. I'm exactly who I appear to be." She turned on the stove to heat the water in the steamer. "Now, are you ready to get all hot and steamy with me?" She winked.

He chuckled, shaking his head. "There's my Kam. Trouble to the core. You going to tell me where your tattoo is yet?"

She smiled impishly. "Nope. You'll just have to use your imagination. You can thank me for that later, because that daydream is going to be life changing."

CHAPTER 10

By some stroke of divine luck, most of the momos were steamed and on the tiered platter by the time Asha and Nicole arrived at the brownstone.

"Yay!" Asha said as Kamila spooned chutney into gold bowls. "Momo Hut!"

Kamila beamed with pride. "Nope. Hussain Hut! We made these. Rohan and I."

"Really?" Asha pulled a spoon out of the drawer and tasted the chutney. She frowned. "This is good." She looked at Rohan. "I'm going to need the recipe."

Rohan grinned. "Ask Kam. She made the chutney and the paneer kebobs. I only helped with the momos."

"Did anything catch fire?"

Kamila crossed her arms and glared at her so-called friend.

"Don't listen to her, Kam," Rohan said. "You were awesome. Very competent in the kitchen today."

He hadn't mentioned the wet-tissue momos or pointed out that the paneer wasn't supposed to be blackened, so she gave him a smile. "Thanks to you. If the finance thing ever grows stale, we should give it all up and open a momo cart on Queen West."

"Deal." They shook on it.

"Kamila, what exactly are you wearing?" Asha asked. "Shit. Was there supposed to be a *Breakfast at Tiffany's* theme tonight?"

Kamila ignored her and took out the next batch of momos from the steamer. The rest of the guests—but not Anil—arrived in quick succession, and soon all were huddled around the dining table holding fancy plates and munching on paneer kebobs and momos. Everyone agreed the food was incredible. When the biryani arrived, people cheered.

Kamila was spooning the biryani onto a platter when she noticed Dane was talking to Maricel. Excellent. She joined them when she was done, hoping to get a feel for how their true love was progressing.

Dane grinned at Kamila after she said hello. "Maricel was just telling me about the movie we're watching tonight."

"Yes, *Amar, Akbar, Anthony*. It's an old-school bonkers Bollywood classic. Do you follow Bollywood?"

"I've been doing some research since you first invited me. I haven't heard of this title, though."

"It's fab. I used to watch it once a week when I was a kid but haven't seen it in ages. Have you seen it, Maricel?"

"No. I've only seen—"

"Maricel?" Asha called out. She was across the room with Tim and Jerome. "What was it you told me about that organic baker selling cupcakes at the Dogapalooza? They needed an extra table or something? Tim's putting in the order for the rentals tomorrow."

"Wasn't it that they needed shorter tables?" Kamila asked.

Maricel had spoken to the vendor, and Kamila didn't know details.

"Higher, actually," Maricel said. "Bar height. I'll talk to Tim." She smiled apologetically before excusing herself.

"She looks gorgeous tonight, doesn't she?" Kamila said. "I love that dress. Pink is so her color."

"She does look great. You have great taste."

"So how are you settling in? Is Byte getting comfortable with the neighborhood?"

Dane sighed. "Not yet. He's a nightmare at home. Ruined the backs of three dining chairs. He's lonely. Byte is always happier when I have a girlfriend to spoil him."

Kamila's eyes widened. "Ah, did you know Maricel is a dog trainer? I'm helping her open her own dog school soon." She glanced at Maricel, still talking to Tim.

Dane followed Kamila's gaze and smiled. "You have such great friends. These parties are a great way to get to know so many great people."

First, holy wow, Dane said the word *great* a lot. Second, squee! He was so into Maricel and he wanted to get to know her better. As Dane would say, this was all great.

There was a knock at the door. Kamila excused herself, but Rohan beat her to open it.

"Anil, my friend!" Rohan did that manly bro-pat-on-the-back thing, then brought the man of the hour in to meet Kamila.

"Kam, this is Anil Malek. Anil, my old friend Kamila Hussain."

"Kamila, it's a pleasure to meet you finally!" Anil put his hand out for Kamila to shake.

Kamila smiled, taking his hand. "Likewise! I'm so happy you could join us tonight! Can I pour you a hot cider?"

Anil flashed that million-dollar smile she'd seen in his video. In person, he looked younger than Rohan and a little less...stuffy. Easy good looks combined with dark eyes and full lips. And yes, not a strand of hair on his head. It was the sexy kind of bald, though. More Jason Statham than her Shiroz Uncle. Anil had a solid build—like he spent more time on free weights than the treadmill at the gym. Overall, he was captivating.

"I'd love a cider," he said. "I was thrilled to get an invitation to one of your famous parties. Your reputation precedes you. This is an amazing space." He looked around. "That print on the wall...that's a Raqib Shaw, right?"

Kamila had, of course, removed all her pet photoshopped prints. But she'd hung this art print on the dining room wall even though she'd been worried it was too colorful and not very...professional. It was the only thing big enough for the space, though, other than the print of Darcy, Lizzy, Luke, and Leia photoshopped onto the original *Star Wars* poster. Kamila beamed and handed him a clear mug. "It is! I love his work. So detailed and layered. I think the colors really complement the neutrals in the room."

"Well, I don't know much about interior design, but clearly you do. I actually saw a Shaw exhibit in England a few months ago. His works were shown side by side with classical pieces. It was a fascinating juxtaposition. I bought the guidebook from the exhibit. I'll bring it by to show you one day."

"I would love that!"

"I hear they're bringing in a famous neoclassical collection on loan at the Art Gallery of Ontario. We should go together."

"That would be wonderful! I love art galleries!"

"Anil," Rohan asked, "I'm surprised your wife hasn't joined you in town. How is she?"

Kamila cringed. True, Rohan wasn't exactly a social media kind of guy, but he should have known the wife wasn't in the picture anymore.

Anil, seemingly unfazed, shook his head. "I hear she's fine. Probably counting down the seconds to when she can finally sign those divorce papers. But you know what that's like, right, old friend?"

Kamila squeezed her lips together. *Awkward.*

"I didn't know you'd separated. Sorry to hear that," Rohan said.

Anil chuckled. "We grew apart. No regrets. She's still in D.C. Are those momos?"

"Yes," Kamila said. "Come, let's get you some food." She led Anil toward the dining table, quickly tossing a pair of Darcy's rainbow sunglasses that were on an end table behind the couch. And the digital tuner for her ukulele. She must have missed them in the cleanup.

The doorbell rang. "I'll get it," Rohan said.

Kamila handed Anil a plate. "This all looks delicious," he said, eyes sweeping over the food.

"I can't take the credit for all of it. The biryani is from this amazing Indian place—they have over fifteen types of biryani, and in the restaurant they serve it with naan crust on the bowl. But I did make the momos and the paneer kebobs."

"Well, I can't complain about takeout when it's this good." He spooned rice onto his plate. "The Indian restaurants in this city are blowing my mind. I haven't had food this good since I was in India."

"Are you planning to be in Toronto long-term?" Kamila asked.

He looked around the room a second, then smiled at Kamila. "That's the plan."

"I'm excited to learn more about the project. Launching a nonprofit is a big undertaking…administratively," she said. "Not that I'm not up for the challenge!"

He smiled roguishly as he rubbed his hand over his chin. "I did a great deal of research on your little firm—your father has a strong financial background and is very respected in the community. I'm confident my project is in good hands with him, once he's over his concerns."

Kamila frowned. Little firm? That was a bit condescending. "You'll be in good hands with me, too. I'll just put this out there now, but I'm hoping I'll have the opportunity to work with your organization long-term." He looked skeptical, so she added, "I'm a CPA, too."

"Oh, are you? I wasn't aware." He chuckled. "I'm surprised someone with as high a reputation for fabulousness as the great Kamila Hussain is something as mundane as an accountant."

"Fabulousness! Well…" She giggled. He was forgiven for the condescension. "Flattery will get you everywhere. But don't you worry—I am well versed in nonprofit financials and fully capable of drawing up the articles of incorporation. And I'm open to helping with fundraising, too. I've been working with a local animal shelter for years, and this year I'm chairing their biggest benefit event."

"Clearly you have many talents." He tilted his head down ever so slightly and looked at her with a panty-dropping smile. She actually hated the term *panty-dropping*, but honestly, there was no other way to describe the look on Anil's face.

Then he laughed, the flirty look instantly replaced with pure mischief.

He was a total flirt. Unexpected. And actually? Completely

delightful. "I have a feeling you and I are going to get along very well," Kamila said. "Let me introduce you to some friends."

He looked around. "I think I already know some. Rohan, of course."

"How well do you two know each other?" She'd never heard Rohan mention Anil until recently.

"We did our undergraduate degrees together. My wife—well, soon-to-be ex-wife—was in his program. She was closer to him than I was."

Ah. That explains why Rohan asked about her.

"And," Anil said, "looking around, I see someone else I know. Jana Suleiman. I've known her professionally for years."

Jana was here? That was probably who was at the door when Rohan answered it. Who invited her?

"Yes, she mentioned she saw you in Washington recently," Kamila said.

"Yes, and in Tajikistan, too."

Kamila raised a brow. That, she didn't know. Why wouldn't Jana have mentioned it? "Really?"

"I wasn't there long, just visiting an old friend." He glanced toward Jana. "My friend was going through a rough time—his marriage was ending. I swung by on my way back from England. Since I had recent experience with that particular hardship."

"Tajikistan isn't on the way from England."

He laughed. "Details, details. Anyway, my friend was Jana's boss, so I saw her a few times."

"Interesting." Kamila wondered if Anil knew the reason why Jana had left her post early.

"Tell me." He leaned closer to Kamila. "How well do you know Jana? Are you close?"

Kamila forced an elegant chuckle instead of a snort. "No. I mean, I've known her all my life. She's an old family friend. But..." She glanced over to Jana, who was talking to Tim and Jerome and looking as detached and distant as always. "We've never been close."

"She has never struck me as the type of person to have a lot of close friends," Anil said. "She's a hard nut to crack."

Kamila laughed, relieved Anil was on her wavelength. "Yes, that's it exactly. She's so reserved!"

"She was popular enough in Central Asia," Anil said. "Although, I'd say she left her glow behind when she came here. She looks...tired."

"No, that I will *not* accept. Jana may not be the warmest person, but her skin is luminous." Even scowling, Jana was incandescent.

"All the same, I should say hello...I mean, it's only polite, right?" He grinned back at Kamila, flashing those gleaming white teeth. "But then, I want to hear more about your work at the animal shelter. And I want to hear what's in this chutney." After another charming grin, Anil went to Jana. Kamila smiled to herself, so pleased at how well this was going.

"What are you smirking about?" Rohan said, joining her.

"I wasn't smirking. I was smiling. I'm at a party. I'm supposed to have fun."

He snorted, then popped a momo in his mouth. "These things are really good."

"They're not just good. They're superb." She took the last momo from Rohan's plate and ate it. "You and me, old man. We're going to retire on these momos. No need to have a nest egg—we'll just make dumplings on our little cart all day."

He laughed. "Looking forward to it."

She looked over to watch Anil talking to Jana. He was animated, charming, and personable, while Jana looked annoyed. Actually, quite miserable. Why did she come to a party if she didn't want to talk to people?

Rohan gestured toward them, frowning. "Don't tell me you're doing your matchmaking thing with those two, are you? Because you shouldn't."

Good lord, no! Matching anyone with Jana Suleiman? "No, of course not. Anil and Jana? That's a terrible match."

Also, why was Rohan so opposed to the prospect of seeing Jana with someone?

"Anyway," Kamila said. "I got the impression Anil isn't very fond of Jana. Did you know they saw each other in Central Asia, not just in Washington? I wonder if he knows the reason she left her contract early."

Rohan's jaw clenched. "I'm *not* gossiping about my friends. You shouldn't, either. And I'm glad you're not matchmaking anymore—you should leave your friends be."

Kamila frowned. "Of course I'm still matchmaking! Just not with those two. Things are going so well between Dane and Maricel. You saw that picture he took. I mean, who even prints pictures anymore? Hey, is Jana leaving?" Jana was at the front door, putting her shoes on. She wasn't going to say goodbye to the host of the party? Or hello, for that matter? Actually, Kamila hadn't said anything to Jana, either, so she couldn't exactly be offended.

"The picture of you," Rohan said.

"What?"

"Dane printed a picture of you."

"Of Maricel," Kamila corrected. She looked over to Dane and Maricel talking on the couch. "Look how cozy they are. Say it, old man. I have a gift."

He rolled his eyes.

"I know what you're going to say, that my gift is for getting into trouble, but it's a gift all the same."

Someone tapped her on the arm. It was Anil.

"I'm so sorry, but I won't be able to stay for the movie," he said. "I have an early meeting with a donor I've been trying to nail down for weeks. I'll need my beauty sleep to impress them." He winked. The man's expressive face was just so appealing.

"Totally understand. Thank you so much for coming." She put out her hand for him to shake.

He took her hand, but instead of shaking it, he lifted it and kissed the back gallantly. She giggled. He was the perfect mix of professional and playful.

"I'll be in touch soon to talk about the project. Good to see you, Rohan. Enjoy the movie."

Yay! There was no question in her mind that she nailed that informal job interview.

Asha joined them near the table. "Hottie Mr. Clean is leaving?"

Rohan snorted . . . loudly.

Kamila glared at him. "I happen to find bald men sexy."

"Can we start the movie?" Asha asked. "Jerome and Nicole's conversation is heading toward pain management during childbirth and Brit's turning a bit green."

Kamila winced. "Say no more, Asha." She walked to the center of the room. "I'm starting the movie in five minutes. Grab your snacks and find your seats."

Kamila ran upstairs to change out of her boring dress first—

she put on her sunflower sundress to match Rohan's sunflowers, then headed down to corral everyone to their seats and refill their munchies and cider. She pulled out her ukulele in case anyone wanted a sing-along and poured herself a warm cider. Kamila was left with few options on where to sit and ended up squeezing in next to Dane, who, to Kamila's delight, had Maricel on the other side of him. Asha, Nicole, Brit, Tim, and Jerome crowded on the bigger couch, and Rohan took the armchair.

Dane leaned close once the movie started. "I saved you that seat. Even with the subtitles, I was confused last week. I need you to translate for me."

Kamila frowned. "I don't speak Hindi. Asha does, but I'll be reading the subtitles, too."

"Shhh!" Tim hissed, annoyed. "No talking. I want to listen. I'm up to level ten on Duolingo Hindi."

Kamila laughed, settling in to watch the movie. Tonight had gone spectacularly well. Better than she could have ever imagined. Now it was time to breathe and relax. She pulled out the decorative cushion digging into her back, curled her feet under her, and enjoyed the movie.

The room was dark, and all Kamila could hear was a low rumble—a deep voice speaking gently. A comforting, familiar voice but closer than she was used to hearing it.

"She was up cooking late last night," the voice said. It was Rohan. Kamila was too tired to open her eyes, but she could tell her head was on his chest. How had that happened? He was warm and comfortable and she was so tired, so she decided to stay there.

"And she had client meetings this morning." That was Dad, speaking softly. He must have just gotten back from the train station. "Sometimes I think she only stops moving when she sleeps. She's a remarkable girl, that one."

Kamila decided to let them think she was asleep a little longer—she wanted to hear what Rohan would say.

He chuckled, the low rumble reverberating through her. "There is no one like Kam."

"She has always been like this," Dad said. "Three hundred percent, go, go, go all day, then crash. I used to carry her up to bed almost every night when she was a girl." He paused. "She looks so much like her mother. I sometimes wonder if that's hard for her." He sighed sadly. "She's so beautiful, though."

"She's always been beautiful," Rohan said. His voice was almost a whisper. "A complete handful, though."

"Nonsense," Dad said. "What would I do without Kamila?"

Both were silent for a while. Kamila knew she should really open her eyes. She was about to stretch her arms out, when Rohan spoke again. "I don't like keeping things from her. I have reservations."

"This will make her happy," Dad said. "This is all for *her*, before anyone else."

What? What were they talking about?

They were probably estate planning again. Or maybe Dad was agreeing to go part-time permanently even before the month was over. If so, why would they keep it from her?

"And for you," Rohan said. "This will help your health problems. You need a break." Oooh, maybe they were all going on a surprise trip. Kamila didn't have time to speculate more, because Rohan was still talking. "How are you doing this week? Sleeping better?"

Dad's voice was even quieter. "Some. It was good to see Shelina and the boys. They make me feel grounded."

"More balance will be good for you."

Dad snorted. "Balance. That's what that shrink said to me. I need *coping strategies*, *self-care*, and *acceptance*. But there is no balance. It's not possible. It's all or nothing, this life, isn't it? Be careful, Rohan. Don't become me."

No one said anything. Finally, Rohan spoke. "You know, Kamila was the first person to ever fall asleep on me."

Kamila smiled as she slowly opened her eyes, stretching and yawning and sitting upright next to Rohan. "Aw, everyone left? I missed the final song of the movie. When did you get home, Dad?"

"Not long ago. You were asleep. I took a taxi."

"Did you have a good trip?"

"Yes." He stood and kissed her forehead. "I had a wonderful time. Your sister sends her love. I'm very tired now. Good night, beti."

After Dad left, Rohan started to get up from the couch. Before he could leave, Kamila put her hand on his chest. "I slept through everyone leaving?"

"You were dead to the world."

"Yeah, I was making the disaster momos until two. Was I really the first person to fall asleep on you?"

"You heard that? I thought you were asleep."

"I heard that part."

He looked at her with skeptical eyes for a few seconds, then nodded. "Yes. You fell asleep on me the first time I held you. It was the day your parents brought you home from the hospital. I was five years old. You drooled on my arm."

A smile spread on Kamila's face. "And now I'm the last person to fall asleep on you." She leaned up to kiss him on the cheek, above that lovely new beard. "Thank you for being there for Dad," she whispered into his ear. She didn't know exactly what they were talking about, but Dad was certainly not confiding in her. At least he had Rohan. She pulled away from him and grinned with mischief. "Did you like me then as much as you do now?"

He chuckled. "I prefer you now, actually. You're still trouble and a complete handful, but at least you sleep with your mouth closed these days. Less drooling. Good night, Kam." He kissed her quickly on the forehead, then got up and climbed the stairs to the guest room. Kamila laughed to herself as she put her glass in the kitchen then followed him upstairs to her own bedroom.

CHAPTER 11

Kamila met with Anil at the Emerald office the next day to talk about the incubator project, or Aim High, as it was called. After they went through his needs, the conversation shifted to his travels, her work at the shelter, his love of art, and Emerald.

"You're a fascinating person," he said. "You still don't seem the finance type, but clearly you're passionate about your work. This office is impressive, too."

She was in a gray pantsuit with a white silk blouse today . . . not her usual style at all. But it was worth it—no question she was continuing to impress Anil. "Thank you! I really love my job. It's so rewarding. It's nice to take the financial stuff off business owners' plates, you know? My absolute favorite is helping start-ups. It feels so good to help people figure out how to make their dream come true." She leaned close. "And problem solving is so much fun!"

"What kind of clients do you have at Emerald?"

"Dad's clients are mostly doctors and other medical practitioners, but I've been expanding into other industries—mostly personal-care services. You know, small salons, spas, aestheticians. A lot of women-owned businesses." She suddenly remembered that the point of this meeting was to convince Anil that she could work with Aim High permanently. "And I love to work with nonprofits."

"Oh! I didn't know you were focusing on women-owned businesses. Aim High isn't only planning to help women, but we do want to focus on women-identifying and LGBTQ+ people. We hope to address some of the barriers that have held these members of the community back in their homelands. Women-run businesses are shown to better improve the health of the family and the whole community."

Kamila smiled. She liked Anil—a lot. This incubator sounded like a fabulous initiative to help people who really needed it. Kamila discovered that she wanted to work on the project as much as she needed to work on it.

"Any chance you'd let me join the training team, too? I can teach small-business finance."

He laughed. "We haven't really started compiling that team yet, but I'll keep you in mind. For now, we'll get you started working on our opening financial statements and the articles of incorporation. Then, in a month or so, the board can vote on retaining your firm for all our financial needs going forward. How does that sound?"

"Amazing. I'm excited to get started."

"Finance really is your passion, isn't it? I would have thought you would be more into marketing or PR—more people-oriented business fields."

"God no. I'm all about the numbers. There's something so meditative about dealing with rows of figures. I love people, but sometimes they're too much. Numbers are predictable. Although..." She smiled. "I love to let my creative-freak flag fly in my volunteer work. Like planning the puppy prom."

He laughed. "Well, if you were serious about helping with our fundraising effort, too, I have a creative, people-y assignment for you. After seeing your famous Bollywood party, you're the perfect person for this job. I'll send you a meeting invite for our next fundraising meeting."

Kamila smiled. "Yay! I'm looking forward to it!"

"Welcome to Aim High. I have a good feeling about you, Kamila Hussain."

Kamila beamed. She had a good feeling about Anil and this project, too.

☂

When she got the invite for the three p.m. Aim High meeting on Monday, Kamila's first thought was what kind of volunteer committee met in the middle of the afternoon on a weekday? But after arriving at the downtown shared-office-space boardroom, she realized the answer to her question: a committee made up of corporate bigwigs who could leave work whenever they wanted, and underemployed social philanthropists. Unfortunately, it was blatantly obvious to everyone that Kamila didn't fit into either of those categories.

She'd dressed professionally again—straightening her hair and pinning it up, wearing a very business-y outfit, even carrying a briefcase-type bag instead of the orange designer tote she usually took to client meetings. But the strangers sitting around the boardroom table made Rohan's normal workday attire look like casual wear. Even Rohan himself, who was sitting near the end of the table, looked extra buttoned-up today. Had he slicked his hair back? Kamila's blue pantsuit was brighter than everyone else's, and she immediately regretted the teal blouse with the oversized bow at the neck. She'd thought it would be fine since Anil hadn't seemed too conservatively dressed when he'd come to Emerald. But the look she got from the suits around the boardroom reminded her of when she'd shown up to Model UN in high school in sweatpants and a Spice Girls T-shirt. She did *not* fit in here.

Also, she probably should have been on time, but there was traffic. Smiling apologetically, Kamila took the empty seat next to Rohan.

Anil was standing at the head of the table and beamed at her. "Kamila, great. You're here. Let me introduce you. This is the Aim High board of directors: Ayesha, Derrick, Rajesh, Marlene, Shayla, Robert, and of course, you know Rohan. I'll let them tell you their areas of expertise on their own time. Kamila's firm is handling the start-up financial administration...and Kamila herself is a fundraising maven, so she agreed to come on board as a volunteer, too." Rohan nodded at Kamila and poured her a glass of water.

Anil and the others started discussing their fundraising needs, which evolved into talking about the dearth of funding in rural versus urban ventures to coaching and resiliency after significant trauma so fast that Kamila would have had significant trauma if she had tried to keep up. For the second time since she walked in, she was sure she was in way over her head.

She peeked at Rohan. He was participating in the discussion actively along with the others, talking about the psychological impact of escaping a war zone as if he were an expert on the subject. Huh. He'd said Kamila shouldn't be underestimated, but clearly Rohan was more than the average tax lawyer. Maybe because she spent so much time with him in his albeit very fancy pajamas, she often forgot how brilliant, knowledgeable, and accomplished Rohan was. Why exactly were they such good friends? He leaned close after the topic shifted yet again. "Everything okay, Kam?"

She nodded.

He smiled in return. But this wasn't a normal Rohan Kam-you're-incorrigible smile, but a completely different one. Weirdly...professional. Was this his corporate-self smile?

Was it a touch condescending, or was she imagining it?

This wouldn't have been the smile he'd have given Jana Suleiman if she had been here instead. Jana would have gotten a smile of admiration. Of respect.

Would it have had affection in it? Or...heat? Attraction?

Kamila shuddered. *Stop thinking about that.* Jana wasn't here. Kamila was doing this committee thing so Rohan wouldn't give Jana this hypothetical smile.

Kamila cocked her head and winked at Rohan.

And he laughed, and it was the Kamila-is-incorrigible laugh. There. Better.

Finally, after a good twenty minutes of conversation that flew high over Kamila's head, Anil smiled. "Well, before any of these ideas can be implemented, we need the money to do it. As we discussed last week, the plan is to kick off the fundraising efforts with a launch party. Kamila, this is the assignment I thought you would be best suited for." He looked at the others. "Kamila here is a stellar party planner. You should see her weekly parties, and she's running a huge event for an animal shelter. Kamila, how would you like to plan the Aim High fundraising launch party?"

Okay. Wow. That was what he wanted her to do? Plan a party? She'd been worried she was out of her league, but party planning she could do. "Um, what do you mean by *fundraising launch party*?"

"Right. I forgot you weren't here last week. We're envisioning launching the fundraising effort with an event where the sponsors can invite high-profile potential donors instead of individually going cap in hand to them." He grinned at her with playful eyes.

"What kind of party?" Kamila asked.

"Marlene, tell her what we discussed."

The blond woman with suburban mom hair smiled a not-genuine smile. "Carmela, right? That's certainly an interesting blouse. What do they call those? Pussy bows? Anyway, we're thinking a fun, informal kickoff to set the tone for the whole project. Put the *fun* in *fundraising*, you know? Hey! I invented a new word! *Fun-raising*! Do you think you can handle that, Carmen?"

"It's Kamila. I've been on the planning committee for an animal shelter's major fundraiser for three years. *Morning Sunrise* called the Dogapalooza easily the most enjoyable charity benefit in Toronto last year. This year I'm chairing the final event—the puppy prom. It's been sold out for weeks." She knew a thing or two about *fun*-raising, even though it was a terrible word that should die a thousand fiery deaths.

Somehow Marlene managed to frown with her nose high in the air. "Well, I've already booked the event room here at this shared workspace," she said, not even acknowledging what Kamila had said. "I'm imagining a cocktail reception, but I concede to you to iron out details. You'll need someone to work with from the committee. Most of us here have specific skills that I think would be underused in party planning. I suppose I could partner with you on this while I'm also looking at real estate—"

"I'll work with Kamila," Rohan said.

Marlene frowned. "Oh, Mr. Nasser, I already have you down to spearhead the organizational bylaws. With your legal expertise, you—"

"I can do both." He looked at Kamila. "Kamila and I know each other well. We're a good team."

It was a little disconcerting that he was calling her Kamila instead of Kam, and she was pretty sure he only volunteered to save her from Marlene and didn't actually *want* to plan a cocktail party with her, but Kamila was still delighted he volunteered. Rohan was the only one in this crowd she wanted to spend more time with (except maybe Anil). This was perfect. She loved making momos with him the other night, and this could be just as fun.

"Okay, then, Mr. Nasser is on the launch-party team. I'll send you the contact for the venue. Three weeks should—"

"Wait," Kamila interrupted. "Three weeks? When exactly is this party?"

Marlene gave a bothered huff. "I just said, in three weeks. The room is booked for Saturday evening." She named the date.

"Oh fudge. I can't, then." Kamila cringed and looked at Rohan. "The Dogapalooza is that weekend. I'll be busiest on that Sunday for the prom, but I'm going to have stuff on that Saturday, too."

She started listing the events on her fingers. "The canine couture show, the dog-and-car wash, the corgi high tea—"

"So, you can't do it?" Marlene said. "Why did you volunteer, then?"

"I never actually told Kamila the date of the event," Anil said. He looked at Kamila apologetically. "I should have asked first. But your main event is on Sunday, right? And you have a committee helping you there?"

"Well, yes—technically," Kamila said. Tim was the co-chair of the prom. But still, it was a lot for one weekend.

"It's your call—but I have faith you can manage both," Anil said. His voice was full of trust. It was strange. She really didn't know Anil that well yet, but there was something respectful about the way he spoke to her. Unlike Marlene.

Rohan said on Friday that many people underestimated her. Well, Anil was someone who didn't.

"It's too much to put on Kamila's plate," Rohan said. "She has other clients, too."

"Well," Marlene said. She looked at Kamila, then quickly turned to Anil. "What about that friend of yours, the fund-raising expert you knew from Pakistan? Maybe she'll work with Mr. Nasser on this event."

"Tajikistan, actually," Anil said.

Damn it. No, not Jana.

"I'll do it," Kamila said.

Rohan shook his head. "You don't have to, Kam."

"I want to. It will be fun." She smiled at Anil. "I can plan a party with my eyes closed. Plus, I have Rohan to help." She elbowed him gently. "We're a great pair. We're planning to retire together to run a street-side momo cart, you know."

After the meeting, Anil showed Rohan and Kamila the event space where the cocktail party would be. It was completely devoid of personality, but Kamila could work with it.

"I'm so pleased you're joining us," Anil said to Kamila at a moment when Rohan had stepped away to take a work call. "Why don't I take you to lunch or dinner sometime soon? A nonworking meal. I think I owe you an apology for putting you on the spot there."

"Oh!" Kamila said. "Apology completely unnecessary, but thank you. Lunch would be great."

"Excellent. I'll call you to set something up. And I'll email you those figures you needed for the incorporation papers. Feel free to contact me with any questions about any of this. Our next fundraising meeting is in two weeks. See you then!"

CHAPTER 12

I'm sorry, Kam. I feel like you were ambushed there," Rohan said as they made their way into the cool evening. "I can talk to Anil if planning this party is too much for you."

Kamila sighed as she wrapped her scarf around her neck. "It's fine. I'll make it work. Ugh—I might stop movie nights until these parties are done. Everyone will be annoyed. Although..." She grinned. "I'm happy I get to work with you. Should we set up a date to discuss our party?"

A smile spread across his face. "We're together now. Why don't we discuss over an early dinner? Or do you need to go home to your dad?"

Kamila preferred to be at home for dinner when Dad was home so she could keep an eye on his mood and make sure he ate well. But one night couldn't hurt. "Let me call him."

Dad of course insisted she have dinner with Rohan, saying he would happily eat salad and biryani and would take Darcy for a walk. He sounded upbeat on the phone, so Kamila figured he'd be okay.

"Looks like we're on a date. Dad's fine." She looped her arm through Rohan's. "Where are you taking me?"

"Where would you like to go?"

She thought about it. The night was cool and she could use some comfort food. She grinned widely as an idea came to her. "I know a perfect place. To make up for putting me in front of those lions, you're going to take me to the girliest, most extravagant-looking tea-and-noodle shop you've ever seen. It's aggressively pink, with lots of plants and floral wallpaper, and the hostess dresses like a French maid, so you might feel uncomfortable in your pants." She hugged his arm tighter. "You'll make fun of me for loving this place until you try their tea and their mind-blowing beef noodle soup. At which point you'll thank me profusely and promise me your undying love forever." She guided him to the sidewalk and started walking toward the subway station.

"Oh, is that what's going to happen?" He laughed.

"Yes. Exactly like that. We'll both end the day better than it started."

He grinned. "Sold. Let's go."

And like she knew would happen, Rohan absolutely loved Boba Noodle.

"Honestly, I can't get over how good this is," he said, taking another sip through the wide boba straw. "This has to be high-end Assam tea."

"Best boba tea you've had, right?"

"First boba tea I've had. I always assumed it would be too sweet for me. I didn't know you could get it with half the sugar."

"See? You need to accept that I know what's best for you in all areas of your life." She untied the now frankly annoying oversized bow on her blouse so she wouldn't get soup on it. "I love the wallpaper in here. Hey, I just realized these peonies look like my tattoo."

"Ah, so your tattoo is flowers. You going to tell me where it is yet?"

Kamila shook her head impishly. "What, and deprive you of the mystery that's been giving you life?" She had no idea why she didn't want to tell him where it was—the side of her rib cage was no big deal. He'd for sure see it next summer if Nicole had another pool party. "You have to try my tea." She held up the mango-matcha smoothie with brown sugar boba.

"That looks like too much. How can you have so much sugar with your dinner?"

"It's spectacular. Try it, Rohan."

He leaned forward and took a tentative sip, eyes widening as he drank. "Holy crap. That's good, too. I would never have thought—mango and matcha."

"See? Kamila knows best. The soup is good, too, right?"

"Yes, Kam, it's excellent." He smirked. "Thank you, brilliant one. What would I do without you?"

"Well, I can guarantee your life wouldn't be as interesting without me." She couldn't help grinning ear to ear. She knew he'd love this place. After slurping another chopstick full of thick wheat noodles into her mouth, she groaned with pleasure. "Mmm...I really needed this."

"So, you're feeling better, then?"

She nodded. "That Marlene woman got under my skin. But I'm not bothered about being asked to plan the party. I mean, I volunteered for the committee—how can I expect not to be put to work, right?"

"But the same weekend as the shelter event?"

"It's fine. Tim's doing a lot at this point, and I can delegate more if I need to. I will need to make the time to practice

Darcy's dance number on Saturday before our performance on Sunday at the prom."

"I still can't believe you're dancing with your dog. In public." He shook his head.

"I know you think I'm ridiculous, but it took a lot of focus and determination to train Darcy to do that. Musical canine freestyle is really just extreme obedience." Maricel had helped her a lot with training—she really was a genius trainer.

"I don't think you're ridiculous."

She put her chopsticks down. "You think I'm trouble."

"You love being trouble," he said, then paused. "But you're right about one thing. You do make my life interesting. Actually, you make my life . . . better."

Kamila slapped both palms on the table. "Oh my god, what's in this soup? Whatever it is I should bottle it, because it made Rohan Nasser admit his life is better with me in it. Excuse me, miss? I need the recipe—"

Rohan barked a laugh. "Kamila, you're incorrigible. Great, now a waiter is actually coming."

She clapped her hands together. "Oh good. The French maid is going to flirt with you some more!"

To Kamila's surprise, it wasn't the French maid that turned up at the table, but Kevin, the boba tea guy who'd recommended the beef noodle soup last time. Kamila hadn't seen him at the counter when they walked into the shop.

"Oh, hi!" Kevin said. "I remember you! Mango-matcha with tapioca!" He grinned.

"Yes! Wow, Kevin, you're good."

"Ah, you know. It's the only job I got. Whatcha need?"

Rohan shook his head. "Nothing. We're fine. Kamila was—"

"I was telling my friend here how delicious this soup is. You must tell me the chef's secret."

"It's *sick*, right? Star anise and white pepper, and the broth is simmered for twelve hours."

"*Twelve* hours!" Kamila said. "No wonder it's so good. Our compliments to the chef."

Kevin beamed. "I'll tell her." He leaned close, a conspiratorial grin on his face. "The chef is actually my aunt. It's an old family recipe she brought from Taiwan."

"Well, tell her this soup is so magically good that it's made my fancy lawyer friend here realize how much he needs me in his life," Kamila said.

Kevin laughed. "That's the magic of Taiwanese food. Hey, how's your other friend, half-sweet oolong iced latte with grass jelly?"

"Wow, you remember her, too? Maricel is fine."

"Say hello to her for me, will you? Tell her I sourced an Earl Grey for her that's up to our standards. I'd love to hear what she thinks of it."

"Will do!" Kamila said.

"All right, peace out. Holler if you need me again." He grinned happily as he walked away.

"He's a lively young man," Rohan said.

"Yeah, he's great."

"Sounds like he has a bit of a crush on Maricel. Some possible matchmaking material there?"

"Of course, who wouldn't crush on Maricel? She's a doll. She and Dane are progressing well, though, so no need for me to do any more matchmaking with her."

"You're not going to tell her that this guy bought tea specifically for her?"

"What's the point? Dane's *really* into Maricel. I think it's best if I don't make it more complicated for her by introducing another potential admirer."

"That's ridiculous, Kam. Let her make her own choice!"

"I'm doing this to make her happy. She can do better than a skater-boy boba waiter—even if they're both into tea. Dane has his own software company."

Rohan shook his head. "That's awfully elitist. I never pegged you for a snob. Even if it were necessary to match his career status to hers, she's an attendant in an animal shelter."

"Who is starting her own business, remember? I'm telling you, this obedience school is going to be huge. Trust me—Dane and Maricel are perfect for each other."

Rohan shook his head. "I don't get it, Kam. I know you love matchmaking, but there is a line between what you're doing now and meddling. Plus, something about Dane rubs me the wrong way. He's an ass kisser."

"Of course he's a butt kisser to you! You're *Rohan Nasser*!"

His eyes widened. "What's that supposed to mean?"

"Rohan. You head one of the biggest personal and corporate finance firms in the country. You've been cited in *Financial Times* as one of Canada's top executives to watch. You wear a suit and tie to a movie party. Of course mere mortals would love to lay their lips on your very fine rear end."

He actually blushed. Rohan Nasser turned a shade reminiscent of the wallpaper behind him and ran his hand through his hair. "Don't be absurd, Kam."

"People want to know you. People want to bask in your glory."

"So, everyone who's nice to me only wants something?"

"All relationships are because someone wants something.

Companionship, support, sexual release, whatever. Anyway, Dane's a bit awkward. I think it's charming that he was intimidated by meeting the great Rohan Nasser and wasn't as subtle as everyone else with their kissing up to you."

"Not everyone. I'm not sure you're capable of subtle, and you never kiss my ass."

Kamila cocked her head and chuckled. "You and me." She reached out and ran her finger across his bearded cheek. "We're beyond fake butt kissing. When we kiss each other's rear ends, it's completely honest. That's why we're such great friends."

He shook his head, laughing. "Yes, Kam, you're right. And that's why you keep my life interesting."

CHAPTER 13

Dad was in front of the TV when Kamila got home, watching a food reality show.

"What show is this?" she asked, picking up Darcy and scratching her ear.

"*Home Cooking Showdown.*" His eyes didn't leave the screen. "Where were you? You missed dinner. There is so much biryani left."

"Yeah, I told you. I ate with Rohan." She stood watching the show for a few minutes. "Is the show any good?"

"My old friend told me about it—his daughter won the finals last year. He won't stop talking about how proud he is. He says he has the most talented daughters in the world, but he's wrong. Mine are."

Kamila stood watching his eyes as he watched the show. This was troubling—she *told* Dad she was eating with Rohan. Dad was absentminded the last time he had a mental health episode. She should have come home for dinner. But his eyes looked okay. He was completely focused on the woman on the screen making what looked like cabbage soup. "I'm going to the basement to do a run-through of Darcy's routine for the puppy prom. But then do you want to go though some recipe books to figure out what to eat for the rest of the week?"

"Sounds fine," Dad said.

Kamila went downstairs to practice with Darcy.

Her dog was in one of her rare accommodating moods, so Kamila got three rounds of the routine in before a tennis ball proved to be infinitely more interesting. After making a heart-healthy meal plan with Dad, taking a shower, blow-drying her hair, and completing her seven-step skin-care routine, it was past eleven thirty. She quickly edited and uploaded a video of Darcy dancing on TikTok and cross-posted to Instagram, then put away her phone and turned on her e-reader.

Kamila's text tone rang a few minutes later. She glanced at her phone, fully intending to not respond until tomorrow.

But it was Rohan. The text on the screen said, I have the answer to your problem. I could . . . And then the text cut off.

Ha, *problem*. Kamila had way more than just one problem right now. She unlocked her phone.

The rest of the text continued, I could host this week's Bollywood night.

That was not at all what she'd expected. Bollywood night was her thing—no one else hosted it. Rohan didn't have people over to his place. She immediately texted back.

Kamila: What do you mean? And why are you texting me so late? I could have been sleeping.

Rohan: You just posted a video of Darcy dancing on Instagram. I knew you were up.

Kamila: You follow Darcy's Instagram?

He didn't answer that question.

Rohan: I went to my condo gym after we had dinner. It overlooks the building's party room. It's on the rooftop terrace. There are heaters, lots of seating, and they just got a screen and projector. I already checked—it's available this Friday night.

Kamila didn't know what to write back. Bollywood night at a posh King Street rooftop terrace instead of the living room of her brownstone? Rohan hosting a party?

Kamila: Seriously? You'd do that?

Rohan: It's not a big deal. You do it every week. I'd like to take some pressure off you.

Kamila: What about Dad? I don't like leaving him at dinnertime.

Rohan: Got it covered. Rashida Aunty is hosting a dinner before her card party.

Kamila: Wow. You thought of everything. I'll have to bring my ukulele and serenade you with "Wind beneath My Wings."

She frowned at her phone. If Anil was invited, she'd have to be the new "sophisticated accountant" Kamila. No ukulele. Actually, having the party at Rohan's fancy condo could help her. It would definitely be posh and sophisticated.

Rohan: Kam, I take back what I said earlier. You are ridiculous.

Kamila: And you're generous. Thank you. I appreciate it. You won't have to do this alone—we'll host together. As practice for the Aim High party. I can get the biryani. Do you want me to make appetizers?

Rohan: I'm not taking something off your plate if you're still doing the work. You can send out an email letting everyone know about the location change, but leave everything else to me.

Kamila: At least let me come help you set up the space. I assume it's pretty bare, right? I'll come and tzhuj it up a bit.

Rohan: I'm sorry, what? Tsh...

Kamila: Tzhuj. You know, kick up the glamour a bit. Except, elegantly.

Rohan: Did you make up that word?

Kamila: No.

Seconds later, an incoming video call from Rohan showed up on her screen. She hesitated a moment—she wasn't really fit for a video chat. Her hair was in that bonnet he said made her look like a sultan, and her pajamas were not the cute ones. But this was Rohan—hardly company. She opened the call.

"I think I need to hear you say that word with your mouth," he said, voice laced with amusement. From the looks of it, he was also in bed. Wearing…a long-sleeve navy tee? What happened to his plaid pajamas set? Surrounding him was a gray duvet, gray pillows, and a dark wood headboard.

"I can't believe you FaceTimed me at this hour. From bed," Kamila said.

"Say it, Kam." His voice was full of playful challenge.

"Say what?"

"You know. Say the word." He smirked. How the heck did anyone find this man intimidating?

She grinned. "I want to *tzhuj* up the party space a bit." She enunciated the word slowly, puckering her lips as she said *tzhuj*. "Actually…" She put the phone closer to her face to look at his surroundings. "From the looks of it, your bedroom could use some tzhujing up, too."

"*Jooje?*" he said slowly.

"Yes, tzhuj."

He shook his head, smiling. "Well, whatever it is, if it results in my bedroom looking like yours, I'll pass. Are those tassels on your pillows?"

"It's a throw pillow. You're welcome to borrow it." She grabbed the bright-fuchsia raw-silk pillow from behind her head and held it up for the camera.

"I'm afraid those tassels would end up in my mouth when I'm sleeping."

"I don't actually sleep with it." She tossed it aside and laid her head down on the deep-purple satin pillow she actually slept on. "It's decorative. So, this is a new development in our friendship, right?"

"What is?"

"Late-night video calls. Me getting to see your bedroom. But of course, I *am* the first person to ever fall asleep on you. And the last."

He chuckled low as he settled back against his headboard, his hair on his plush-looking, high-quality pillow. "Kam, we've known each other literally forever."

Kamila suddenly sat up straight. "Wait—I am, aren't I?"

"You are what?"

"The last person who fell asleep on you. I mean, that was only a few days ago...but...are you secretly getting some action?" She wasn't about to entertain the possibility that this action was with Jana Suleiman, but what if there was someone else in his life that she didn't know about? Maybe that's why he was so private about his home. What if all the work she was doing keeping him from Jana was moot, and he had another person in his bed? She wasn't sure how she felt about that.

"Kam, I'm hanging up now."

"Does that mean you have a secret paramour?"

He snorted. "Really? *Paramour*?"

"Lover? Flame? Mistress? Hookup?"

"Kam, good night..."

She crossed her legs, sitting in the middle of her bed. "I mean, if you did, it would be okay. Like I said before, celibacy is way overrated. Casual sex is great." She frowned. "It's been weeks for me. I hope I'm not getting sexually frustrated."

"Kam, this is too much information."

"No, it's not. We're close friends. Anyway, you'd tell me if you were seeing someone, right? Or if you were hooking up?"

It wouldn't bother her if it was just a hookup. Because this hypothetical hookup wasn't getting in the way of her friendship with him. Or his relationship with her father.

So, it was fine—100 percent.

"Kamila," Rohan said firmly, "if I was dating someone, do you think she'd be okay with me sleeping over at your house once a week, texting you several times a day, and now video calling you at almost midnight?"

"I should hope she'd be okay with it. We're friends! We need to talk about your hypothetical paramours, Rohan. This one seems a little insecure. You can do better."

"*Good night*, Kam."

She smiled, stretching her legs out and resting her head back on her pillow. "Good night, Rohan. I'll talk to you soon about the tzhujing efforts."

He chuckled. "Looking forward to it."

"Excellent," she said, but she didn't disconnect the call. He didn't, either. They watched each other for a few seconds.

"And Kam," he finally said, "you were the first and the last. Sleep well." He finally disconnected.

Kamila smiled to herself as she put her phone on her nightstand and turned off the light.

She read her book for maybe five minutes when she sat up

with a start. How exactly did Rohan know Rashida was having a dinner party on Friday? Dad would have mentioned it if he'd known while they were meal planning. There was only one explanation—Rohan was still secretly talking to Jana.

Fuddle butt.

Kamila stopped in at the shelter after work on Wednesday to drop off some grant applications for Maricel to sign. She waited in the puppy room for her friend to finish her shift.

The puppies were growing well and were very popular with the shelter staff and volunteers. Potato wasn't nearly as timid as he used to be, and while he still wasn't as lively as the other puppies, his affectionate, sweet personality made up for it in spades. He was small but silly, with a plump little round belly. The name Potato was utterly perfect for him. Kamila was kissing his ears when the door to the enclosure opened.

"Maricel!" Kamila said when her friend entered. "Did you see Potato's new belly?"

"He's always stealing food from the others."

"That's my boy." Kamila kissed Potato's nose. "I can't believe how much he's grown in just a few weeks."

"They're doing well," Maricel said. She picked up one of the black puppies. "This one is a biter, though. We think she needs to spend more time with people." Maricel sat on the floor of the enclosure and gently scolded the puppy for biting her fingers.

They talked through the details of the business grants Kamila had found while Maricel gently corrected the biting puppy's behavior. She was so good with dogs.

"Are you coming to Bollywood night at Rohan's this week?" Kamila asked after they were finished going through the grants.

"Yes! I'm excited. But I hope it's not cold on the roof of his building."

"Nah, there are space heaters up there. You should wear that pink-and-gray sweater we bought together. Dane couldn't keep his eyes off you when you had that pink dress on."

Maricel blushed. "You think so?"

"Of course! You do see how much he's into you, don't you? He's always talking to you at my parties."

"That's just because he doesn't know anyone else."

"He's into you. Believe me. I know. He even printed that picture of you. I've barely done anything to encourage him." Despite what Rohan seemed to think, Kamila didn't consider putting two people in the same place at the same time as *meddling*. "You're into him, too, aren't you? Or...am I over-stepping?"

"No, I...He's nice." Maricel blushed deeper. "And I don't think you're overstepping. I'm happy you introduced us."

Kamila grinned. Maricel was as smitten as Dane was. To prove she was letting her friends live their own lives, she decided to give Maricel the message from Boba-guy Kevin. "Oh, by the way, I was at Boba Noodle, and that cute waiter said he has an Earl Grey for you to try. He found one that meets his high standards."

Maricel's face brightened. "I'll go after work!"

Kamila grinned. See? Not meddling at all.

CHAPTER 14

True to his word, Rohan took care of everything, and Kamila had little to prepare for movie night that week. Her normal eighteen-point list was reduced to four items: email the Bollywood party guests, telling them about the amazing new one-time-only venue; ensure Rashida Aunty's dinner fit with Dad's new dietary restrictions; get a gift for Rohan; and finally, select a mature and accountant-y rooftop-patio outfit to match the movie. Rohan didn't even let her come early for the much-discussed tzhujing, claiming tzhujing was unnecessary for a casual movie night with friends, and the space was perfectly presentable.

Picking the outfit was the most challenging part of her pre-party duties. After spending time with Anil, she didn't think she needed to worry too much about how she dressed around him. But at the same time, she needed him to trust she was mature and responsible enough to manage his organization's financials. She ended up picking a pair of slightly glossy slim black ankle pants, with a loose sleeveless white blouse, and black patent heels. And a shiny black trench coat. Plus, nude polish on her nails and neutral lip color. She pulled her straightened hair back in a slick ponytail trailing halfway down her back.

It was even harder to exercise the necessary restraint with Darcy's outfit. In the end, she put the dog in a simple fall shearling coat. Darcy looked better in bold colors, but that would just clash with Kamila's look. She swiped both her and Darcy's bangs to the side to complete the professional chic look. Perfect.

Kamila hated driving downtown, but she drove to Rohan's since she didn't want to navigate the subway with the rather large and awkward gift, plus a hyper dog. After parking in the visitor parking outside the building, she walked up the stairs to the condo entrance.

Although she'd never actually been to Rohan's place, she'd seen the exterior before. It was an old redbrick building that had been completely gutted and modernized with a glass extension taking it from six stories to twenty. Kamila took Darcy's leash in one hand and her purse plus the large paper shopping bag in the other and headed straight up the elevator to the penthouse party room as instructed. She wasn't exactly fashionably late but hardly perfectly punctual, either. She intended to make an entrance.

The elevator opened to a short hallway. At the end of the hallway on the right was a small indoor lounge with black leather couches, a bar, and huge windows. She could see straight to the outdoor space, and it was also perfectly presentable. Actually, quite striking—upscale black-and-gray patio furniture, large potted palm trees, and another bar where the food was laid out. Kamila reluctantly agreed to herself that the orange haze from the setting sun hitting the abundance of green plants more than made up for any lack of colorful decor out. No tzhujing required—it was already quite atmospheric. And very elegant. Almost magical.

Her friends were gathered in the seating area, including Asha and Nicole, Tim and Jerome, Maricel, Dane, and Anil, as well as Asha's and Tim's dogs. And Jana, of course. Always Jana.

Darcy was eager to run out and see her dog friends and was pulling on her leash, so Kamila lifted the dog in her hand. Not knowing where to leave her bag and Rohan's gift, she headed back down the small hallway, hoping there was a coatroom past the elevator. But instead of finding a coatroom, she walked right into a hard wall.

Wait, not a wall. A person. *Rohan.* When did he become so solid? Strong. She wavered, losing balance.

"Kam!" he yelped, putting his hands out to steady her. One hand landed on her upper arm and the other on her waist. He held her firmly until the risk of falling on her butt passed. Darcy took advantage of Kamila's wobbles and hopped to the floor, jumping up and down at Rohan's feet, probably assuming he had a samosa or a pakora in his pocket for her.

Once steady, Kamila laughed and stepped back out of Rohan's grip. She looked at him. Actually, she did a double take. He looked so...different. Not his clothes—although he was dressed a bit more casual than normal. His slim black pants were a touch shorter than ones he normally wore, showing off naked ankles and casual loafers. His fitted plum-colored dress shirt had two buttons open and no tie to be seen, and the sleeves were rolled up his forearms. But really, a dress shirt with dark pants was what he always wore, so why would this look so different today? Maybe his hair? Nope. Trimmed tight and close to his head on the sides and back, with more length highlighting his natural wave on top. Plus, of course, that appealing graying at the temples and on his beard. She grinned when she realized what was different. He was smiling hugely, all the way to his eyes. He had a lightness to his posture. She wasn't sure she'd ever seen him this relaxed.

"Whoops. Thanks, Rohan," Kamila said, flipping her ponytail behind her shoulder and standing straight.

He gave her a kiss on each cheek. Very fancy.

"Mm..." she said, smiling. "You smell good." She pointed outside. "It looks fabulous out there."

"It's no Kamila Hussain party. But I do what I can." He frowned at her. "What are you wearing? Didn't I say no theme?"

She looked down at herself. "I don't look good?"

"You look great. It's just...out of character. I was just getting some drinks. What would you like?" He headed behind the bar.

"What do you have?"

"Italian sodas, juice, beer. Red and white wine."

She wasn't hosting, so why not? "Red wine, please."

He pulled out a bottle and came around to the front of the bar to pour it into a large red-wine glass. And just like when they'd made momos together, she found herself entranced by his forearms. For a slim man, they looked so solid. Must be all that rock climbing he did. The skin there was paler brown than his hands, and soft, probably because they were usually hidden behind layers of silk and fine wool. Would the skin on his chest be that soft, too?

Also, what the heck was going on with her? Why was she

reacting to Rohan this way? Maybe it was because she usually saw him in a suit jacket? This felt like an intoxicating peek into the taboo. She shivered.

"What?" he asked, putting the bottle down. "Is something wrong with the wine?"

She shook her head. "No. Looks good."

"You're staring at my hands."

She squeezed her lips together, eyes wide. "Oh…um, sorry. Um, it was actually your forearms I was staring at."

He raised one brow. "My forearms?"

She put on her teasing smile. "Putting them on full display like that…You're giving me the vapors. Not to mention those ankles. What's next—thigh-revealing short shorts?"

He shook his head, laughing. "Kam, I don't know what to do with that." He handed her the glass.

She took a sip. It was delicious wine—full-bodied and rich. Expensive. "Keep feeding me this and you can do whatever you want with me. Oh! I forgot. I brought you a present! Like a hostess gift to thank you for having me. A host gift. Here." She held out the bag.

He chuckled. "I'm touched, Kam." He took it and removed the tissue paper–wrapped gift.

"Pillows?" he asked, eyes narrowed. "With tassels?"

"Pom-pom tassels! They're decorative throw pillows! For your bed. These are called bolsters and they'll give you back and arm support if you're sitting up in bed…so they're not just for show on your bed. They're functional!"

Kamila clamped her mouth shut to stop the rambling. How many times had she just said *bed*?

She'd looked long and hard to find the perfect accessory for

Rohan's bedroom, even after seeing it for only a few minutes on her phone screen. These pillows were mostly gray, so that went with his bedding. But they had deep emerald green and gold piping, and green pom-pom tassels to add a touch of whimsy. The gift hadn't seemed inappropriate when she'd bought it.

But that was before she'd had a near religious experience admiring the man's forearms. Maybe buying him things for his bed was crossing a line.

He laughed, rubbing his hand on his beard. "Actually, *shockingly*, I really like these. Thank you, Kam." He put the pillows back in the bag and hugged her for a second. She resisted the urge to inhale deeply again. What was that soap? Also, what was in this wine?

"Now, let's get you some biryani before it gets cold." He grabbed a tray of drinks and led Kamila and Darcy outside to the party. He pointed her in the direction of the food before leaving to deliver the drinks for the others.

Kamila was impressed with the spread. The shrimp biryani looked light, with fluffy mounds of fragrant basmati rice and plump pink shrimp dotted throughout. There were also pickled onions, cucumber raita with whole cumin seeds, and chana in a rich tomato gravy. And movie snacks, too, of course. Big bowls of chips, popcorn, and Indian snacks, along with a healthier crudités-and-fruit platter, with chaat masala to sprinkle on top. The table was decorated with large tropical leaves and fern fronds arranged around black paper plates and cutlery. There were even floral arrangements, mostly greenery, with a few striking white tropical flowers. Apparently, Rohan could tzhuj after all.

Asha joined her at the food and kissed her cheek. "It's amazing up here, right?" she said as Kamila piled biryani on her plate.

Kamila nodded. "To be honest, I didn't know Rohan had this in him. I'm a little worried he did all this to upstage my parties."

Asha tilted her head in a knowing gesture. "Seriously, Kamila? He did all this to *impress* you, not upstage you." She frowned. "What are you wearing?"

Kamila waved her friend's question off. "Well, color me impressed. This is a wonderful new side to Rohan. Being all social and gracious. He'll be competing with Anil for who can be the most charming tonight."

"Nah, I think Anil will win that one. He was all gallant rescuing prince before you got here. Maricel nearly face-planted tripping on the projector cable, and Anil caught her in less than a second."

"Really?" She looked at Maricel—who was standing near the projector, animatedly talking to Dane. She was wearing the pink-and-gray sweater Kamila had suggested. "How long has she been talking to Dane? He looks entranced."

Asha shrugged. "Not long. But speaking of entranced, Anil's been asking when you'd get here."

Kamila grinned. "Has he? Well, let's not leave my adoring fans waiting, then, shall we?"

Kamila took her plate and headed to the seating area and squeezed in next to Anil, who greeted her warmly. He was also looking good tonight—in dark jeans and a gray Henley that perfectly showed off that impressive physique.

She'd been working for the last week on the Aim High paperwork and had already started drafting the business license and incorporation papers. She didn't know why anyone doubted she could do this job, because it was pretty straightforward and uncomplicated. And Anil had been available whenever she had a question or needed clarification on something. They'd also started texting regularly—fun little messages and jokes. He'd called her yesterday while she was at the shelter visiting Potato, so she'd sent him a picture of her favorite puppy, and they chatted about dogs and pets and life in general. Overall, they were getting along well and Kamila was happy to have a new friend/client.

"So, what did I miss?" Kamila asked.

Tim, then Jerome, were sitting on the other side of Kamila, and Asha squeezed in next to Nicole on a massive outdoor armchair. On the opposite couch, Dane, Rohan, Maricel, and Jana were sitting in that order. Kamila was disappointed to see that Dane and Maricel did not sit together when they moved to the couch, but at least Jana and Rohan weren't sitting together either.

"Well, Maricel nearly took out the whole projector system," Tim said. "Then Jerome and I tried to get the others to play a drinking game, but we caught a lot of resistance. Asha dropped a bombshell that she played spin the bottle with a Bollywood actor when she was fifteen and living in Mumbai, and I realized my friends are all way more interesting than I am. I mean, even this new guy you've brought into the fold, Kamila." He smiled at Anil. "His accomplishments make me seem like a hermit who spends his weekends brushing his dogs, which, to be fair, I am."

Anil laughed. "I'm not really that accomplished. I'm just a working stiff lucky enough to get assignments in some pretty amazing places."

"This project of yours is impressive, though," Jerome said. "It's a great concept."

"It is. I think it has real potential to make a difference. I've wanted to do something like this for a while, but the timing was never right. I'm glad I have such a great team to work for the incubator." He squeezed Kamila's knee fondly.

"I'm so happy to be involved!" Kamila said. "But do you think the word *incubator* is weird for this? Sounds like you're hatching babies or something." She paused. "Oh, I just realized that's what Aim High will be doing—hatching small businesses. Duh!" She turned and looked at Anil. "I can't wait to be a proud parent with you. And Rohan! Lucky little babies."

Jana made a disparaging sound. "If nothing else, the businesses will be covered when it comes to hairstyling and head-shaving expertise, plus all the celebrity gossip they want."

Rude. Kamila raised a brow at her. Ms. Grumpy was extra irritated tonight. Why add the crack at Anil's minimalistic hair?

Kamila wasn't in the mood for Jana's patronizing now. Honestly, she was never in the mood for it. Who kept inviting Jana to Bollywood night anyway? Rohan, of course.

"What's the drinking game?" Kamila said. "That might be fun."

"Yeah, we should play," Anil said. "Kamila, now that you're here, insist they all join in with us."

"Insist?" Jana said, narrowing her eyes at them. "Should *you* be insisting anyone do anything? Not everyone drinks."

"There's a bottle of soda in your hand," Anil said. "No one said it was going to be an *alcoholic* drinking game. A round of Never Have I Ever is a great way for me to get to know all of you better."

Kamila beamed. "I love Never Have I Ever! That's it. I'm going to have to go ahead and *insist*." She turned to Anil. "I want to learn all your deepest secrets."

Rohan cleared his throat and Nicole whispered something into Asha's ear.

"I'll play," Maricel said, picking up her glass from the table. "I played this in school."

"Rohan, you'll play, too, right?" Kamila asked.

"Course he will," Anil said. "Right, old friend?"

Rohan didn't look enthused. Actually, he looked as annoyed as Jana. This was what Kamila had been afraid of—Jana's sour mood was contagious.

"C'mon, old man." Kamila said. "Loosen up a bit."

"Fine," Rohan said. "But let's keep this surface level. No personal questions that people might not want to admit. And anyone is allowed to bow out at any point with no pressure to keep playing." He may have glanced at Jana there, but Kamila couldn't be sure.

"Of course," Kamila said. "This is supposed to be fun."

"Okay," Maricel said, "I can go first."

Kamila grinned. "Remember, everyone, take a sip of your drink if you *have* done the thing Maricel says she's never done."

"Never have I ever"—Maricel bit her lip—"been in a limousine?"

Pretty much everyone took a sip of their drink.

Kamila groaned. "My turn. I'll think of something more daring than that." Rohan narrowed his eyes at her, but she ignored him. She tapped her fingernails on her wineglass while thinking of something to say.

"Difficult to find something you've never done?" Asha asked, teasing.

Kamila giggled, then turned to Anil. "Don't listen to her. There are plenty of things I haven't done." She narrowed her eyes and quirked her lip. "But plenty I'm thoroughly experienced at, too."

"I know something Kamila has never done," Jana said. "Refrained from flirting with every man in a three-meter radius."

Wow. Jana was really *not* playing nice anymore. Why was she suddenly taking their secret feud public? Kamila opened her mouth with a retort when Maricel interrupted.

"I think that's a double negative. Are we allowed to do that?"

"No, we're not," Kamila said, glaring at Jana. "Okay. Never have I ever…" She looked at Rohan, smiling. "Shared a passionate kiss in the rain."

There. Success. Rohan turned pink. Asha and Nicole each took sips of their drinks. As did Maricel and Jerome, but not Tim. Kamila herself didn't take a sip—there wasn't much that would make her go out in the rain, let alone kiss in it. Not when she spent so much time on her hair.

Rohan didn't drink, either. Such a shame. That was a little heartbreaking.

"My turn," Anil said quickly. "Never have I ever… hmmm…What can I really challenge you with?" He winked at Kamila. "Never have I ever…been involved with someone already in a relationship with someone else."

Wow. Kamila's head turned sharply to Anil. That was *personal.* Clearly, he wasn't following Rohan's rules.

But Kamila was curious…Who here had been in a relationship with someone already taken? Kamila had never—not knowingly, at least. She looked to see if anyone took a sip of their drink.

Anil smirked but didn't drink. Neither did Rohan, Dane, or Maricel. Tim and Jerome smiled knowingly at each other and sipped their drinks. Weirdly, Nicole also sipped her wine, which made Asha laugh. Kamila made a mental note to get her friends to spill the tea on those sordid details another time. Jana had an expression that was even more irritated than normal. In fact, almost... pained. Anil was watching her.

Holy seersucker. *That* is what had happened in Tajikistan. Jana had an affair with a married man, and Anil knew about it. Maybe that close friend going through a divorce Anil spoke about—Jana's boss? Was it possible that her fling with Bronx Bennet wasn't a one-off and Jana the Great was still fond of other people's men?

Kamila snorted, eyeing Jana's obvious anger at Anil's statement. She hadn't said anything after Jana's hair, gossip, or flirting comments, and after what had happened when they were teenagers, she was entitled to a slight dig here. "Really, Jana? Still playing the other woman? I figured you would have grown out of that since high school."

Jana blinked at Kamila, then stood suddenly and put her drink on the table. "I'm leaving. Sudden indigestion."

"But, Jana." Anil smirked. "You haven't had your turn yet."

"Let her go," Rohan said, voice clipped.

Jana shot a dagger-eye look at Anil.

"Jana," Nicole said, standing. "Can I help? If you're not feeling well."

Jana shook her head and headed to the glass sliding door. "No, I'll be fine. Rohan, I left my bag in your condo when I was there earlier."

Jana had been in Rohan's condo? Why?

Rohan sprang to his feet. "Yeah, I'll take you down to get it. Be right back."

Kamila's hand tightened on her wineglass. He specifically said he didn't want Kamila to come early to help set up, and he invited Jana instead?

Add this to him knowing about Rashida's dinner party and not defending Kamila when Jana was rude earlier, and it was clear. There *was* something going on between him and Jana.

Fudge. This was bad.

Asha gave Kamila a concerned look.

"So, whose turn is it now?" Tim asked.

Kamila stood. "Play without me. I'm not feeling it anymore. I'm getting more wine."

She went inside, left her wineglass on the bar, and went straight to the bathroom.

She looked at herself in the mirror. What was wrong with her tonight? Why did she care if Jana had been in Rohan's condo? Jana and Rohan were free and consenting adults allowed to do what they wanted with their lives. This wasn't a repeat of the Bronx Bennet situation. Kamila rubbed her temples. If a thing was starting between Jana and Rohan, it certainly hadn't stopped Rohan from being there for Dad. He was even planning to come for breakfast at the house tomorrow—despite not spending the night this time.

But still. Jana didn't like Kamila. Rohan spending so much time, innocent or not, with the person who always made Kamila feel smaller and less capable would change the way *he* saw her. Because really, how could someone be close to both Jana and Kamila?

And what *fancy* person would want a *Kamila Hussain* in his life when he could have a *Jana Suleiman*?

She squeezed her fists. *No.* It had been so long since Kamila felt like this. She hated that her feelings of inadequacy had resurfaced since Jana came back. Kamila pulled out her phone and sent an email to her therapist, asking if she could schedule an appointment for a tune-up on her self-esteem sometime after the Dogapalooza. She could not allow Jana Suleiman to derail all her hard work.

When she came out of the bathroom, Asha was waiting for her at the bar.

"You okay, Kamila?"

"Yeah, fine. Sudden headache. Probably the red wine. I'm switching to white."

Asha nodded toward the others, still sitting on the patio, presumably still playing Never Have I Ever. "What do you think that was about? There seems to be something Anil knows about Jana that the rest of us don't know."

"Anil told me he's close friends with Jana's old boss in Tajikistan, and that his marriage just ended."

"Oh wow. Because of Jana?"

Kamila shrugged. "I don't know. Asha, why was Jana in Rohan's apartment before the party? This was what I was worried about—I don't want some home-wrecker going after my friend."

"Seriously, Kamila? I'm thinking we shouldn't call her a home-wrecker without knowing what exactly happened."

"What about Bronx Bennet?"

Asha snorted. "Sorry, I still can't get over that name. I'm not going to hold something she did as a teenager against her now. *Home-wrecker* is such a sexist term anyway— it takes two to end a marriage. I'm sure no one is calling this dude anything nearly as nasty for not keeping his dick in his pants. If that is what happened, which I'm not speculating, because *we don't know*."

Kamila sighed. She knew Asha was right. Kamila didn't like Jana, but she liked sexist double standards even less. She opened the bottle of white wine and poured herself some. Poured herself a lot, actually.

"Kamila," Asha said, "maybe it's time to ask Rohan what's going on between him and Jana. Tell him you're obsessing over him possibly neglecting you and your dad. If he knew how much you depended on him, then he would assure you he'll always be there for you. Because he *will*. Also...I'm not sure if I should say this part."

"Say what part?"

"You don't actually need Rohan. You are capable of managing your life and caring for your father without him. Maybe it's time to look at why you seem to think you can't."

That was all ridiculous. Asha was her friend, but she didn't know how hard it was to manage Dad when he was in a depressive episode. Maybe Kamila *could* handle him on her own, but she didn't want to. Rohan made Dad feel valued, and Dad deserved that. Back when no one made Kamila feel valued at all, Dad was the *only* one who fought for her. She had to keep fighting for him, too.

The elevator opened. Rohan was back.

Asha walked toward the door outside. "I'm heading back. Take your time—I'll manage the crowd. See if Rohan wants some wine, too." Asha left.

Kamila held out the bottle of wine for him, and he nodded. She poured him a glass.

"So, Jana was in your condo?" Kamila said, not meeting his eyes.

"Yes."

"Why?"

"Why are you asking?"

"Just curious." She handed him the glass of wine.

"It was personal." He took the glass and sipped from it.

Kamila's stomach soured. *Personal*...what exactly did *personal* mean here?

She must have looked as miserable as she felt, because he clarified. "We talked."

See? He wasn't going to tell her anyway. Because that would cross the goddamn wall he kept up between them. This friendship was completely one-sided. She told him everything, and he just humored her. Kamila was a fool.

Rohan nodded toward the others outside. "You know anything about why Anil was being an ass to her there?"

"He wasn't being a...you know. He was just teasing her. And she wasn't exactly being kind to me—saying that thing about me flirting with everyone."

"Is it rude if it's the truth?"

Kamila put her glass down. That was low. "Seriously, Rohan?"

"Look, I don't know the extent of the relationship between those two, but clearly—"

"I know *some*. Anil is good friends with her former boss. Sounds like maybe Jana had a fling with the guy. She's never mentioned any of this to you?"

Rohan paused. Maybe he did know something. "I'm not about to betray her confidence or gossip about my friends. But I will say that it was completely out of line for you to make that crack about her."

Kamila gritted her teeth. "Of course *you* would take her side. Everyone thinks she's Ms. Perfect and can't possibly do anything wrong. And everyone thinks that I'm nothing but trouble and a disaster waiting to happen. You, just like everyone else, are completely blinded by Jana's shine, and there is nothing you wouldn't do for Jana the Great."

His eyes flashed with anger. "What the hell is that supposed to mean? She's my friend, and I support my friends. Just like I support you all the time. It's no different. Why are you so bent out of shape that I'm helping Jana?"

"I don't know. Maybe because once again I have to deal with her upstaging me?"

"How is she upstaging you by just showing up?"

"Oh, come on, Rohan. She thinks I'm a frivolous waste of space who only cares about Bollywood, my Instagram, and my hair. You say you're there for me, but did you defend me when she made that crack about me? Or before when she claimed I'm too hollow brained for the incubator? Nope. Because you feel the same way about me. You claim we're friends, but this friendship is nothing but your obligation to Dad, right? You *humor* me. You find me amusing. You put up with me in a fond-uncle kind of way. That's not a friendship. I think you get off on scolding me. It makes you feel superior."

Rohan stared at her. Now he was very angry. There was even a vein throbbing on his forehead. Good. "Jesus Christ, Kam. Do you even listen to yourself? God forbid someone take you down a peg from that high mountain you imagine yourself on. You'll only accept fawning and adoration from us all, nothing else. You know what? Maybe it's good Jana makes you insecure. Maybe you'll learn to be more like her. When Jana's going through a rough time, she doesn't take it out on her *friends*. And she lets them live their own lives. Not you—you only allow your friends to be who *you* want us to be. To act the way you want, dress the way you want, to date who you want. I can't even be friends with people you don't approve of. We're all your toy soldiers to play with, here to entertain the whims of Kamila the Exalted One. You don't care about anyone but yourself, Kam."

He took a long gulp of his wine. Kamila didn't know what to say. She looked down, blinking. Is that really what he thought of her? Was it all true?

"I don't need this." She wiped a tear. "Not from *you*." She walked past him and went back outside.

Rohan started the movie when he came back out, but he didn't say anything. It was near impossible for Kamila to enjoy the film, though. Even watching a delightful comedy while Anil made hilarious commentary in her ear didn't help her forget what Rohan had said.

You don't care about anyone but yourself, Kam.

This should have been an amazing night—all her friends gathered, watching a movie on a rooftop patio under the stars. But instead, it was soured because of Jana again.

About a half hour into the movie, Kamila's phone rang. She checked the call display.

It was Jana Suleiman.

Absolutely not. Hadn't Jana already done enough tonight? Why was she calling Kamila?

But curiosity got the better of her and she answered the phone.

"Kamila," Jana said, sounding like she was in a car. "When I got home, your dad was complaining about chest pains. I'm taking him to the hospital."

CHAPTER 15

Kamila closed her eyes as her phone dropped out of her hands.

Chest pains. Hospital.

Suddenly there was someone at her feet. Taking the phone off her lap.

"This is Rohan," he said into the phone. "What happened?"

Kamila didn't hear what Jana said. Because that's how phones worked. Someone was rubbing her back. Anil.

Dad is on his way to the hospital. That's what Jana had told her.

Kamila's hand went to her face, scrubbing away the sharp pain she felt over her whole self. She needed to pull herself together. She had to get there. She stood. "I need to be at the hospital."

"They're on their way to Sunnybrook. I'll take you right now," Rohan said, disconnecting the call.

"Rohan, you can't take her," Asha said. "We've all been drinking. Call an Uber."

Kamila didn't want an Uber. She looked at Rohan. *Fix this,* she wanted to say. *Put out this fire.*

But he couldn't. It might be too late to fix anything.

Anil stood. "I've only had soda. I'll take her."

Rohan looked like he wanted to be the one to sweep in and save Kamila—because that was what he did. He was there for his friends. Whether it was because he felt obligated to or whatever, he was still there.

But Asha was right. Kamila had just watched Rohan practically down a glass of wine in one sip.

"I'm coming with you," Rohan said.

"No, it's fine," Kamila said. His words from earlier hadn't lost their sting. He said she only cared about herself. Maybe Asha was right—she *could* do this without him. She held his eyes for a minute. "Call my sister. Tell Shelina what's going on."

Rohan sighed. "Okay, but promise you'll call me as soon as you know how he is."

Kamila nodded and went inside with Anil. Asha followed them to the elevator. "I'll take Darcy home with me," Asha said. "Call me when you know anything. I can be at the hospital in twenty minutes if you need your best friend."

"Thank you." She hugged Asha, then stepped into the elevator.

On the ride to the hospital in Anil's Lexus, Kamila clutched the armrest tightly. Dad had to be okay. She'd accept nothing else.

"I'll say a prayer for your father," Anil said. "I really hope he's fine."

Kamila nodded, saying a silent prayer herself.

"It was lucky Jana went home, although this must be hard for her," Anil said. "She knew what to do. She once mentioned she was there when her father took ill. He died of heart failure, didn't he?"

"Yes. And my mother died of a heart attack."

"I didn't know that. I'm so sorry, Kamila." He squeezed her knee. "Hang in there. I'll get you there soon."

They pulled up to the hospital ten minutes later. She texted Jana that they were there and got a quick response that she was in the emergency department, but Dad had been taken back for an EKG.

"I'll leave you to be with your family," Anil said as he pulled up next to the door. "If there is anything I can do, please don't hesitate to call me."

"Thank you, Anil. I appreciate the ride."

He paused, eyeing her intently. "You know, Kamila, I hope this doesn't come out wrong, but I've never met a family with such a loyal support system as you and your father. People fight over each other to help you. And you're both so loyal to your friends. Anyone in your circle is lucky to be there. You are blessed."

She sure didn't feel blessed right now.

Kamila found Jana almost folded into herself in one of those terrible metal chairs in the ER waiting room.

As worried as Kamila was about her father, and as much as Jana was the furthest from her favorite person right now, she conceded Anil's point—this *had* to be hard for Jana, too. Jana's father had died two years before Kamila's mother. Kamila knew only a handful of people who had been through this experience, and maybe it was good that one of them had been there for Dad tonight.

Jana stood. "Kamila. The doctor hasn't come out to see me yet, but they took him in for tests a while ago."

Kamila sat in the empty chair next to Jana. Jana sat back down.

"What exactly happened?" Kamila asked.

"He was obviously in pain when I got home. He kept saying it was just heartburn. But he was sweaty and pale...I wanted to be safe." Her voice cracked. "And then he got really worked up on the way here."

He was probably terrified. Kamila should have been with him. "He has a panic disorder."

Jana lifted her head to look at Kamila. "Oh. I didn't know that."

Most people didn't know. Mental illness, especially affecting grown, respected men, wasn't exactly something people talked about in their community. Kamila closed her eyes for a moment, then rubbed her temples. "How's your mother?"

"She's worried. She texted eight times since I got here. She's not alone, though. Some friends stayed with her at home. Your father is her closest friend. She'd be lost without him."

Dad felt the same way about Rashida Aunty. It was funny—last year Kamila wondered if the two of them should consider taking their friendship to the next level. They were both widowed and were closer than most male/female unrelated people of their age in their community. Dad put Kamila in her place immediately, though. "She's my best friend's wife. She is my sister."

Now it made Kamila wonder what their lives would have been like if things had been different. What if Kamila had had a mother who supported her the way Rashida Aunty supported Jana? Would Kamila have been more of a high achiever? More respectable?

What would have happened if Kamila and Jana had been friendlier growing up? What if they had been sisters?

But it was a waste of time to entertain what-ifs. There were so many variables, and it was impossible to change the past, anyway. The one thing she was glad for right now was that Jana cared about Dad. Enough to be sitting here in the emergency room, so worried she was tapping her leg furiously on the linoleum floor.

"Thank you," Kamila said. "For getting him to the hospital. For looking out for him."

"Your father is my favorite uncle. Always has been."

Kamila smiled sadly. "Your father was my favorite." It was true—of the three men who'd started HNS, Jana's father and Kamila's father were the most similar. Sweet, kind, generous souls. Rohan's father was more like Rohan. Buttoned-up corporate shark but with a heart of gold under that perfect tie. Kamila's chest tightened.

They sat quietly for a while. Waiting. Bearing witness to each other's pain.

The wait was a hair long enough to get awkward when a nurse called out, "Hussein? Hussein family?"

Kamila stood quickly. "That's us."

"You can come back. The doctor will speak to you."

"C'mon," Kamila said, motioning for Jana to join her.

The nurse pointed them to a Black woman in scrubs.

"I'm Doctor Matheson," she said. "Are you Mr. Hussein's daughters?"

"Yes. I mean, I am," Kamila said. "She's my…friend." Did she just call Jana her friend?

The doctor looked at Kamila. "Okay. First of all, your father didn't have a heart attack."

Kamila exhaled as Jana took her hand and squeezed it.

"I think the chest pains started as heartburn. He told me he's been eating well lately but fell off the wagon today and had taco samosas."

Kamila frowned. "Taco samosas?"

Jana winced. "I got my mom a Mexican cookbook for her birthday. She's been putting garam masala in her picadillo. Sorry."

"The chest pain seems to have triggered a significant panic attack," the doctor said. "I understand his wife passed from a heart attack?"

"And his best friend died of heart failure," Jana said.

"Ah. The poor man. His blood pressure is very high. I'm worried. I've given him a strong antacid and am running some blood work. Can you tell me all the medications he's on?"

Kamila listed his blood pressure and cholesterol meds, then looked at Jana. It was one thing to admit to Dad's panic disorder but another to mention the drugs he took. But screw it—why should she keep hiding this? "Plus, antidepressants. He has clinical depression and anxiety." She listed the specific meds.

The doctor nodded. "Yeah, those he did *not* tell me about. We've given him something to calm him, so he's pretty relaxed now. I'd like to keep him overnight so I can see the test results. He didn't have a heart episode today, but his heart is *stressed*. We're getting him moved to a room. Then you can go in to see him for a little while, but let's see if he can get some sleep after that. I'll tell the nurse to let you know when he's been moved. And…" The doctor smiled. "He'll be fine. I'm being extra cautious here. You have a lovely father. He reminds me of my own…and now I want to call him."

Kamila's eyes welled with tears, overcome with emotions. Worry, fear. *Relief.* She took in a shaky breath and felt Jana squeeze her hand again.

"He's okay, Kamila," Jana said.

Kamila nodded and pulled her phone out. "I guess I have calls to make."

She headed back to the waiting room and phoned her sister first, telling her everything the doctor had said. Shelina was relieved and told Kamila to let her know when she could call Dad. Kamila texted Rohan next.

Kamila: It wasn't his heart—he had bad heartburn from Rashida's desi taco experiment.

Kamila frowned. Saying it like that kind of diminished the issue here.

Rohan: Oh thank god it's nothing. I'll pick you and him up.

Kamila: It's not nothing. The chest pains triggered a panic attack, which has put stress on his heart. His blood pressure is very high. They are running a bunch of tests and gave him a sedative. They want to keep him overnight. Jana can bring me home.

Rohan: I only had two glasses of wine, and that was hours ago. I'm coming.

She didn't want him coming to get her. She wasn't over their argument and felt this fragile support she was getting from Jana would shatter if she brought anyone else into their fold. Especially Rohan.

Kamila: It's fine. We'll see Dad for five minutes, and then she'll drive me home. I'll talk to you later.

Dad was almost asleep when Kamila and Jana were finally allowed to see him. He mumbled twice about missing his cooking show, called Jana Shelina, then fell asleep. But he looked well. Alive. Kamila kissed his forehead before they left.

The ride home with Jana was understandably pretty quiet. They'd never been friends, but Kamila liked to think they'd reached some sort of truce tonight. She didn't expect it to last—in fact, she fully expected Jana would do something so nauseatingly perfect or condescending tomorrow that it would bring her right back to her previously held spot as secret nemesis in Kamila's life. Only not really a secret anymore.

"I know it's a weird thing to say, but I'm glad you left the party so you could be there for Dad. Thanks," Kamila said.

"Thanking me is not necessary. You would have done the same for my family." Jana's voice was clipped. It seemed she was back to being annoyed and irritated with Kamila.

Ah well. Perhaps it was better to stay on familiar ground. "Well, I know you're quite busy with that company you're starting, and all those *personal* talks with Rohan—"

"How do you know I spoke to Rohan?"

"Jana, *you told us*. When you left the game in a huff, you said you left your purse in his condo. Plus, he mentioned it."

"He told you why I went to see him? I can't believe this. I'll never understand how you manage to get everyone wrapped around your—"

"No, he didn't tell me what you talked about. Rohan wouldn't betray your confidence. All he said was that you two talked."

Jana pulled up in front of Kamila's door. "Look, I'm going to say one thing—don't believe everything that man says."

"Rohan wouldn't lie to me." Scold her, yell at her, call her selfish, yes. But not lie.

"Not Rohan. *Anil*. He can't be trusted. Let's say he's a wolf in sheep's clothing."

"Sounds like he knows the real reason you left Tajikistan and you're afraid of it becoming known."

Jana looked at Kamila, blinking, then turned and looked straight in front of her. "Goodbye, Kamila. Let me know if your father needs anything from me."

CHAPTER 16

Kamila's limbs felt heavy as she climbed the stairs to her front door. She finally checked the time. Past two a.m. The moon was bright in the sky—although only a sliver of a crescent illuminating the mist surrounding it. It seemed fitting somehow—a new moon.

In her religion, new-moon nights were considered especially holy. She wasn't really much of a praying person, or really religious at all, but after a night like tonight, she needed all the help the universe was willing to give her. So, she said a prayer that Dad would be a little better tomorrow. And a little better the day after that. She said a second prayer, that she would be strong enough to handle whatever came after that.

She knew her intense mental and physical exhaustion was amplifying her emotions. She'd probably have more hope and optimism about this situation tomorrow. But right now, she felt monumentally sad. Sad her father had suffered, and she hadn't been there with him. Sad he had to sleep alone in a hospital room. And sad she had to be alone in her house tonight. Not even her dog was here to greet her. She was even sad about Jana, that their mutual support of each other hadn't lasted. And she was sad that even after everything she had done to keep him, she'd still lost Rohan.

But this is what she signed up for, right? She deserved this loneliness. Just like Rohan said. She'd rested her own happiness on her ability to control others, and when they didn't do what she wanted, she was left with nothing.

Kamila needed to stop this line of thinking. She had no desire to let existential dread take hold now. She had to stay strong for Dad. He was in a hospital bed right now, probably in the early stages of a major depressive episode, and Kamila was only thinking about her own loneliness. Rohan was right—she *was* selfish.

As she walked into her house, she noticed the kitchen light was on. Strange. She never forgot to turn off the lights. When she looked at the stairs, she saw a coat hanging off the banister. A familiar charcoal overcoat.

Rohan's. She looked back at the shoe mat near the door, and sure enough, the leather loafers he'd been wearing at his party were there. She went into the kitchen to look out the window. Her own car was there—not Rohan's. He'd brought her car home. Then stayed?

Kamila took the stairs up two at a time and went straight to the guest room. It was, of course, dark, but with the light from the hallway, she could clearly make out his sleeping form. Remarkable. After everything she had said and everything he had said, he was here. Why?

He didn't stir as she watched him sleep. It was slightly voyeuristic to watch the normally solid and starched Rohan softened by sleep, but if he was going to let himself into her house to sleep like some sort of corporate executive Goldilocks, then she figured she was allowed to look. But not for too long—that was creepy. She snuck out and changed into flannel pants and a T-shirt, brushed her teeth, and washed her face.

And then returned to the guest room instead of her own room. He was like a siren calling to her—she was drawn almost against her will. Certainly against her better judgment. She sat on the edge of the bed.

She didn't know why he was here, but she did know it was for *her*. Not for Dad—he wasn't even home. Not for obligation, either. He was here only because he cared about Kamila.

She was the first and last person to ever fall asleep on him. While she knew others, presumably his ex-wife, had shared his warmth while sleeping between those two times, as of this moment, their connection was a circle. He was a constant in her life, as she was in his.

She'd told him off fiercely earlier. He had said even worse things to her. But he always came back. She'd do something silly—burn his breakfast or shamelessly flirt with him—and he'd scold her or tease her, and she'd be upset, and maybe they would argue. And then they'd be right back again. They'd known each other forever, but this cycle had only intensified in the last year.

He stirred. She watched as he shifted, stretched, and finally opened his eyes. He blinked a few times. "Kam." He sat up. "Kam, you're here. I was waiting for you. I fell asleep."

"I see that."

He looked around, clearly confused after his abrupt wake-up. He scratched his chin and frowned. "What time is it?"

"Two thirty."

"Your father—how is he?"

"Resting. He was pretty dopey on meds. Test results will be ready tomorrow. He should be able to come home then."

"How is he *really*?"

"As well as can be expected. Sedatives are nice."

"And...how are you?"

"I don't get why you're here."

"I brought your car back. And...I thought maybe you wouldn't want to come home to an empty house. But I can go..." He started to get up.

"No, wait." She put her hand on his forearm to hold him in place. "Why do you care if I come home to an empty house?"

He shrugged. "I know I don't like coming home to an empty apartment."

"Then why do you live alone?"

He exhaled. "Kam, we're both tired and not making sense. I'm here because I wanted to make sure my friend is okay. I'll go if you want me to."

"No." Kamila tightened her hand on his arm. "Stay."

He nodded. Their eyes locked for a few seconds. Kamila didn't really think about what she did next. The surge of emotions from her day overwhelmed her, and she couldn't bear climbing into her cold bed, alone. Very slowly, she shifted her body, swinging her legs up into the bed and under his covers. He slid over to make room for her, and she lay next to him.

She watched his face, and when there was no sign of objection, she rested her head on his shoulder. His arms immediately came around her. He fitted her next to him.

"I'm sorry about what I said," he whispered. She could feel, rather than hear, the words.

"So am I," she said. "Should we talk about it?"

He sighed, tightening his arms around her. "Yes, but not now. Get some sleep, Kam."

She closed her eyes as her own heartbeat fell into sync with his slow breathing, and they both fell asleep.

The room was still dark when she stirred but less dark than it had been before. Rohan was still wrapped around her. But she'd slept—something she hadn't thought she'd be able to do tonight. She checked her watch—five a.m. She stretched her neck a bit, shaking out the crick from the tight position. He stirred from her movement.

"You okay, Kam?" he asked, voice soft from sleep.

She nodded and shifted so her head was next to his, instead of on him. She said what she should have said before. "Thank you for being here for me. Even after I yelled at you."

"S'okay. You were upset. And I yelled at you, too."

"I don't really deserve you."

He smiled a sleepy smile. "Maybe, but you're stuck with me anyway. Get some more sleep."

She smiled. Yeah, that's what she should do. His hand swung around and landed on her waist, and he closed his eyes. She knew this was weird, and probably wrong. She knew friends didn't sleep wrapped in each other's arms, no matter how terrible their days had been. But everything in her—her mind, her body, her soul—wanted to stay right here, with only this person.

Besides, it was barely dusk—the magical hour. No one was awake. No one was here. No one but the person who maybe saw more of her than anyone ever had. She didn't feel she had control over her hand as it reached out and touched Rohan's cheek, her palm flattening half over his soft beard and half over the smooth skin of his cheekbone. She felt him gasp softly with surprise. His eyes opened. He stared at her a few seconds. Finally, he whispered, "Kamila."

She slid over and kissed him.

Right there on the lips... she kissed Rohan Nasser. He didn't pull away. He only flexed the hand on her waist. She kissed him gently, slowly. Exploratively. It seemed so strange—this was Rohan. It shouldn't have felt so... normal. True, kissing him wasn't entirely new, but it had been over seven years since their lips had touched. Nothing was the same as it was then.

Even this kiss was different. More restrained, sadder. But still not unfamiliar. She kept kissing him, exploring those soft lips like it was the most natural thing for her to do. She wrapped her hands around his neck, discovering skin still warm from sleep, and strong. So strong. He pulled back a few inches and searched her face.

"Kam... what are we doing?"

She shrugged. She didn't really know the answer to that question. All she knew was this was what she needed right now. "Just... be here for me?" she asked.

He reached out and took her face in one hand, lightly stroking her cheek with his thumb. She could feel the calluses on his hand, from rock climbing probably.

"You're sure you're okay with this, Kamila?" he whispered.

And this was why she was okay. Because Rohan would always make sure she was safe and protected first. He would always put out her fires. Putting out her fire right now meant staying as close as physically possible. She smiled softly and nodded, tilting her head to kiss his hand on her face. "Please," she whispered.

And then he devoured her in a deep, all-consuming kiss. Holy heck, Kamila was reminded that he was a thoroughly excellent kisser. She shouldn't have been surprised; he was exceptional at everything he did. She pressed herself closer against him, loving how their bodies molded together. Fit together.

He'd always been her friend—this was just that. Friendship—reinvented. Leveled up. She moaned quietly as she ran her fingers through his hair. His hands on her waist searched until they came into contact with her skin. He lifted her shirt a bit, a question in his eyes. She grinned and sat up, pulling the shirt over her head, then watched while he did the same with his own. Then they were chest to chest, and Kamila couldn't believe how good it felt. She shivered as she felt his warmth envelop her. She closed her eyes and turned off her brain, because his skin against hers and his hands on her body were too perfect and she didn't want to break this spell with reality. His head dipped to explore her chest with his mouth.

"Found it," he whispered, and then he traced her tattoo with his tongue. She had a full body shudder, having no idea that her rib cage was such an erogenous zone. He moved back to her breasts and then up her neck. She clutched him tightly, feeling like Rohan had both thrown her overboard and was the only thing that could save her from drowning.

"Kam," he whispered, before coming in for another devouring kiss. He still called her Kam, the name she'd preferred when she was younger. Even that day seven years ago, in her parents' living room, he'd called her Kam and laughed as she'd straddled his lap. She'd never forgotten the feel of his body under hers. Of his strength, of his hands all over her.

Another night, another house, same man. That memory from the past was intertwined with another memory—the argument with her mother the next day. Mom saying Kamila was *using* Rohan. That he was too good for her. That he was only humoring her, and he'd never take someone like her seriously.

Then Dad standing up for her. Fighting with Mom. The accident.

Kamila put her hand on Rohan's chest, stopping him. And she rolled out from beneath him.

Maybe nothing had changed since then. Maybe she was still using Rohan. She closed her eyes and rested her head back on the pillow.

That kiss seven years ago probably meant nothing except two horny friends taking advantage of an empty house. But the hours and hours of teasing through her feelings about the aftermath weren't nothing. But this time was different, right? Her mother wasn't here anymore. Kamila had changed.

But her father was in a hospital. Scared and sedated. And here was Kamila, making out with Rohan Nasser again.

She whispered, "I'm sorry. I shouldn't have done that. I'm . . . This—" She located her shirt and fumbled it back on.

He put a hand on her cheek and looked at her tenderly. "Don't apologize, Kam. We're both tired and emotional."

See? It didn't mean anything. For either of them. "Okay." Her voice cracked.

He pulled her close so her head was on his chest again, but this time it was bare. "Sleep, Kamila. We'll deal with this later." He kissed the top of her head.

She didn't sleep. Not for a while. Instead, she focused on his heartbeat under hers and tried to figure out how to move on from this day.

She really didn't know how.

CHAPTER 17

Kamila managed to get a few more hours of sleep but woke up shivering in the guest room. It was no wonder she was cold—Darcy wasn't in her usual sleeping spot pressed against her legs. Also, the comforter in the spare room wasn't nearly as cozy as her own down and high-thread-count duvet. And of course, the man she should definitely not be sleeping with, but was pretty sure she spent most of the night wrapped around, was no longer in bed with her, and he'd taken all his body heat with him.

She checked her phone. It was ten a.m. and she'd missed a call from her sister. She called her.

"Kam, good—you're up. I'm at the hospital with Dad," Shelina said.

Kamila frowned. "What? You came all the way from London?"

"It's not like I live in London, England! London, Ontario, isn't that far—of course we came. We had the nanny come early so Zayan and I could get on the road."

Kamila sat up. "Okay, lemme get dressed. I'll be there in a bit."

"No, don't worry about it. Dad's doing fine, but they're only letting in two guests per patient in the building. Zayan and Rohan are in there now. I'm in the parking lot."

Ah. That's where Rohan had gone. "What did the test results say?"

"Results aren't in yet. They said we could bring him home when we have them. Dad's spirits are good. I know you were here late last night, so rest up. You're on Dad duty alone once we head back home, so let us take this shift."

Okay, then. It was great to hear Dad was fine, and she supposed it was good that her sister was helping, but it felt a little weird to be told not to bother coming to the hospital. Then again, Rohan was there. Maybe he didn't want to see her.

"Okay. I need to go get Darcy, anyway." Kamila swung her feet to the floor. "Call me if you need me to pick anyone up, or if Dad needs anything, or—"

"Don't worry, Kam. We got this covered. Talk soon." Shelina disconnected the call.

Kamila got up. After a stop in the bathroom, she headed downstairs in her socked feet. The house felt so weird for a Saturday morning. Quiet. No dog jumping on her. No Dad reading his news sites and drinking chai. No Rohan criticizing her cooking. She peeked out a window—her car was still here. He must have taken the subway or an Uber.

He'd left without saying anything. Not really much of a surprise, as he'd clearly (or at least hopefully) realized that sharing a bed with his brother's wife's sister whose father had been hospitalized with a panic attack wasn't the wisest move. Kissing her was probably an even worse idea.

After making coffee, she texted Asha to let her know she'd be over in half an hour to get Darcy, and then headed to her bedroom.

While she was dressing, she thought about what to do about the Rohan situation. She didn't want to ignore what happened—namely, because she didn't like the implication that she felt any shame over locking lips with him. That was the furthest thing from the truth.

Kamila was long past any shame for her lifestyle, and that included her sexual activities. Mom wasn't around to call Kamila a harlot anymore, and Mom was wrong anyway. Kamila played safe and consensual, and she wasn't really all that promiscuous anyway, not that there would be anything wrong with it if she were. She just knew what she liked and wasn't shy about it. She realized she talked a good game and could be a bit of a flirt, but she liked to think she didn't cross any lines or lead anyone on.

And at any rate, who the heck would feel shame about making out with Rohan Nasser? He was a top-tier catch. A ten in just about anyone's books.

They'd just have to get over any awkwardness and actually discuss what had happened in the dim guest room while they were both dopey with sleep, feeling emotional and fragile after fighting. They would have to talk about the fact that they kissed and were on their way to doing a lot more than just kissing.

It was the right thing to do. She needed to salvage their friendship, and this was the only way. Problem was, Kamila had no idea how she was going to do it.

She was dressed by the time she finished her internal post-mortem on the events of five hours ago. Wearing a vintage pale-yellow day dress, she threw on a burgundy cardigan and headed to Asha's to get her dog.

Darcy attacked Kamila with jumps and kisses the moment

she walked in the door. Kamila reached down and picked up her baby, snuggling her close.

"Darcy! I missed you. Did you have a nice sleepover with Lizzy?" At the mention of her BFF, Darcy squirmed to get free of Kamila's grasp and go play with her friend.

"How's your dad?" Asha asked, as she closed the door behind Kamila. Asha knew he hadn't had a heart attack since Kamila had texted her last night.

"Apparently pretty good. Or so Shelina says. She's with Rohan and Zayan at the hospital. I've been relieved of Dad duty for now."

"Nicole's at the hospital today—I told her to look in on him. You look exhausted. You haven't had breakfast, have you? Want avocado toast?"

Kamila smiled. Asha knew Kamila didn't eat when stressed. "That would be amazing."

Crusty bread from Kamila's favorite bakery smeared with ripe avocado, sprinkled with flecks of sea salt and black pepper, and garnished with a squiggle of vibrant sriracha hot sauce really hit the spot. The tension in Kamila's shoulders fell by the second bite. She moaned in appreciation. "God, I needed this. I barely slept last night."

"I can imagine. How was your dad when you saw him last night? Mood-wise."

Kamila shrugged. "He was doped up. Shelina says he's in good spirits now, but…" She exhaled. "I know his depression will be back with a vengeance after this."

"Yeah. You going to try to get him a new psychiatrist?"

"Only Rohan can get him to see a doctor. And who knows if Rohan will do anything for me right now."

"Of course Rohan will help if you need him! You know you can depend on him."

Kamila exhaled. "Yeah, well, maybe before. Things have changed."

"Why, because of that fight yesterday? Or is this because of Jana? Oh my god, did you find out there *is* something going on between them? Holy shit—"

"No!" Kamila interrupted. "There is nothing going on between them." That was one thing Kamila didn't need to worry about anymore. His spare-room antics wouldn't have happened if he were involved with someone else. Hell, if he had a secret thing with Jana or any other woman, for that matter, he wouldn't have let Kamila into his bed in the first place. He wouldn't have pulled her close so their heartbeats were in sync as they slept.

And holy sweet mother of dragons, it really hit her that she'd actually *slept* with Rohan. Not figuratively "slept with him," which Kamila knew wasn't always as intimate an experience as actually sleeping all night wrapped around someone. There was no way things could go back to the way they were before.

"I screwed up last night," Kamila said. "Well, this morning. I've made things awkward. I don't know if I can save our friendship."

"What did you say to him?" Asha said with a scolding tone.

Kamila exhaled and rested her chin in her hand. "It wasn't something I said. More like…something I did. Sort of." She closed her eyes. "I kissed him again."

Asha didn't say anything. She was quiet so long that Kamila opened her eyes to see if her friend was still there. Asha's mouth was wide open. Her eyes looked a few sizes larger than normal.

"Say something, Asha."

"Kissed? Like on the cheek?"

Kamila shook her head.

"Forehead? Top of the head? Back of the hand? Help me out here, Kamila."

"I kissed his lips. A kiss kiss. A real one. He drove my car home and was sleeping in the spare room when I got home."

"This kiss happened in a bed?"

Kamila pressed her lips together, nodding.

"Holy shit, you had sex with him."

"No! Just a kiss...Plus, we also..." Kamila's voice trailed off.

Asha was silent a few moments before speaking. "Kamila, I don't think I've ever heard you be prudish about spilling bedroom details."

"Yes, well, I'm not exactly used to getting to second base with a friend, am I?"

"Oh my god, you've been to all the bases with friends before! You're the friends-with-benefits queen!"

Okay, yeah, maybe that was true, but this felt so much more complicated than any friends-with-benefits situation she'd been in. Probably because the stakes were higher—she simply couldn't lose Rohan.

"I can't believe this," Asha said. "I mean, I know you said that you don't think of him as a brother, but I didn't in a million years think...And holy shit, you said *again*. This is a regular occurrence? Wait—what's second base again?" She picked up her phone, presumably to find a definition.

"Of course it's not a regular thing. It's only happened once before. Seven years ago."

Asha stared, blinking a few times, then read from a search on her phone. "Second base is groping. Maybe on the breasts. There seems to be some debate about manual stimula—"

"Asha, can we not right now?"

"Okay, okay." She put her phone down. "Tell me everything. Start with the seven-years-ago part, then the now part." Asha stood up and turned on her kettle. "I'm making tea. Spill, Kamila."

"Okay, so last night—"

"No. Start from the beginning, Kamila. Seven years ago, when this sporadic kissing affair started." Asha sat across from Kamila.

Kamila winced. "Fine. Back when Shelina and Zayan came home after university, Mom used to insist they have a chaperone so they weren't alone, even though they practically lived together at school and had been going at it for years. So, either me or Rohan, or both of us, was forced to go with them wherever they went. We didn't really hang out much before then—he's five years older than me, but he used to look out for me when I was little."

"Like he still does."

"Yeah. But that summer we were alone a lot. That's when we started watching Bollywood together. While our siblings were banging nonstop in Shelina's room, we went through all the comedies in my parents' collection. We would all go out sometimes, too. This one time at Canada's Wonderland, Rohan and I lined up for the biggest roller coaster six times. An hour each. I had so much fun with him—I don't think I'd laughed that hard in months."

"So that summer you became friends."

"Yeah. He was about to start at that law firm, but he had the summer off." Rohan had always been so driven and ambitious, and that was the first time she saw him unbuttoned. "We pretty much spent two months together."

"And you started hooking up while your siblings were going at it?"

"No. But..." She paused. "But I did actually develop a little crush on him."

"And he on you?"

"I doubt it. I wasn't... That was the old me. Remember, I was the bad kid back then. This was right after I dropped out of university. I was with my sister and her boyfriend all summer because my mother was always grounding me."

"How old were you?"

"Twenty. Rohan was twenty-five."

Asha shook her head. "Typical desi parents. Who grounds a twenty-year-old? I know you told me you were a wild child, but I honestly can't see it. You're nothing but the hustle now."

"I was a hot mess. I used to swear like a sailor and sneak out to meet men in parking lots. I was not the good Indian daughter Mom wanted."

"I can't see it."

"Everyone thought I was a delinquent. Shelina, Zayan, Mom, my parents' friends... but not Dad, of course. But that summer I thought Rohan saw more of me, too." She chuckled. "Plus, he was so hot back then. He was way out of my league."

"He's still hot, and not out of your league. When did you kiss?"

"My parents weren't home, and Shelina and Zayan were in her bedroom, of course, and I thanked Rohan for actually, you know, not treating me like I was a worthless kid. I don't know—there was something in his look after I said that... so I jumped him."

"And he let you."

"I think he froze a second—but then he most definitely kissed me back. Hard…" Kamila blushed, the memory of that night warming her core. It was so vivid…that moment. The way he kissed her. It was nowhere near her first kiss, but it had felt so electric. It had felt like it meant something. "We kissed for a long time."

"Second base?"

She shuddered. "No. Thank god, no. Mom and Dad walked in on us."

"Shit."

Kamila nodded. "We separated quickly, and Rohan went home. My parents didn't say anything that night. But the next day we were in the car—Mom, Dad, and I—and Mom started yelling at me. That wasn't new—she was always laying into me about something, but she was extra vicious that day. She said I couldn't *ruin* Rohan—he was good. Smart. Going to be a big success. I was a slut. A seductress tempting him." Her voice lowered to a whisper. "Rohan was a lawyer…The last thing he needed was a run-in with a girl like me. I told them it didn't mean anything, that we were fooling around, but she kept calling me names."

"And your dad?"

"Dad stood up for me. He *always* stood up for me. He told Mom that maybe if she'd treated me better, I wouldn't rebel like this. He told her *she'd* ruined me. They had a huge argument."

"You were in the car for this?"

"Yes. Mom was driving. Yelling at me and Dad. Then we got into a car accident."

Asha sat up straight. "Holy shit—was that when…"

Asha knew that Mom's heart attack had been a week after they had been in a serious car accident. Mom's side of the car was hit head-on. The car was completely wrecked, and airbags and seat belts had saved their lives. Mom walked away without a scratch but died of an unrelated heart attack a week later. Dad told the story many times as a cautionary "you never know what life will bring you" tale. Kamila herself rarely spoke about it though.

"Yup. Mom wasn't watching the road. Dad broke his wrist. I cut my arm." She showed Asha the scar. "Which pissed Mom off even more. She said, 'I can't handle the drama all the time, Kamila,' when she saw the blood. Mom basically stopped speaking to me after that. Until..."

"Her heart attack."

"The next time I saw Rohan after that kiss was at Mom's funeral," Kamila said. "We've never talked about what happened. He doesn't know the accident was because of a fight about him. And he met Lisa when he started working at the law firm."

"After your mom died, that's when your dad got sick, right?"

"No. He'd obviously had depression before that, but it got a lot worse. Mom had been helping to hide it from everyone. He finally got a diagnosis and meds then."

They were quiet for a while, then Asha put her hands over Kamila's. "You aren't to blame for your mother's death. Or your dad's mental health."

Kamila nodded. "I know." She did—and she had therapy to thank for that. She knew her mother didn't take care of herself. She knew there was a history of heart disease in Mom's family. She knew Dad's depression was an illness and not caused by his difficult child. And Kamila knew she herself had more value than her mother had believed.

But she'd spent enough time blaming herself that the scars were still there. Just like the scar on her arm.

Asha squeezed Kamila's hands. "I didn't know you then, but

Kamila, what your mother said, that you would have ruined Rohan's life, that's also not true. He *did* see you back then, like he does now."

"We had one innocent make-out session on the couch. Neither of us wanted more."

"But what about now?"

"Now we're friends again."

"Just friends?"

"I was very upset last night. And really, really lonely. I didn't want to sleep by myself, so I went to him. We're adults and we're close. Something like this was bound to happen. It honestly didn't mean more to me. I needed to feel something…and he was there."

"You slept in the same bed all night?"

She nodded.

"You say you don't feel that way about him anymore, but are you sure that he doesn't feel that way about you?"

"What? No. He even admitted right away it was only because we were tired and emotional. Rohan does *not* have feelings for me. He was just…too polite to push me away."

"Oh, of course, Kamila. Sticking his tongue down your throat is just the good manners his mother taught him. You're delusional."

"Gee, it's so great to be able to talk to my supportive best friend about my problems."

"Seriously, Kamila. Rohan is objectively quite a catch. A lawyer, a partner in a successful accounting firm. Responsible, educated, smart. No gambling habit or toxic masculinity to be seen. His only flaw seems to be that he's a workaholic, and yet he's always, and I do mean *always*, with you."

"So?"

"Why wouldn't you want to try for something here? You two drip with chemistry—everyone can see that. I had no idea it was sexual chemistry. I thought you were just utterly perfect as good friends, or pseudo-siblings. Think about all the things he does for you...making momos with you, driving your car home in the middle of the night, volunteering to plan this charity party with you. You've spent the last month tripping over yourself to make sure he doesn't date anyone else. Just fuck already—put each other out of your misery and live happily ever after."

"Jesus, Asha! He's...he's Rohan! He's way too good—"

"Don't you dare say he's too good for you. You know it's not true."

She shrugged. Kamila wasn't big on self-loathing, but this was ridiculous. There was no way Rohan took her seriously enough to want more than a few kisses. And she didn't want more, either—Kamila didn't do relationships.

"Honestly, Asha. I want things to stay the same between us. I need him as a friend. The last thing Dad needs now is change, and starting a relationship with Rohan would be change." There was no way they could keep this friendship when the relationship went sour. Which it probably would because they were way too different.

Asha sighed. "So what are you going to do?"

"I don't know. I need to think..." She checked her watch. "But actually, I should probably get going. I don't know when Shelina will be bringing Dad home, but I should be there. Thanks for breakfast. And for keeping Darcy last night."

"Any time. And...before you go...I'm going to say one thing. I don't have kids, but I can imagine how frustrating it is when your kids don't meet your expectations for them. But your mother, she should have adjusted her expectations and realized that even if you weren't who she expected you to be, you were— you *are*—still an amazing person who is worth knowing. She missed out on knowing you, and that was on her, not you. I'm not surprised Rohan could see how great you were, but I wish your mother had, too."

So did Kamila. But it was too late for that. Kamila smiled and hugged Asha before taking her dog home.

CHAPTER 18

Shelina, Zayan, and Dad turned up at the house around two, after Kamila had nervously cleaned Dad's room, the kitchen, both bathrooms, and the living room. She didn't enter the guest room—she wasn't ready for that yet. But she did want all the areas Dad would see to be as spotless as possible when he got home. Anything to keep his stress down.

But weirdly, he looked far from stressed when he walked in. In fact, the only word Kamila would use to describe her father's mood was...giddy.

"Kamila! Beti!" He gave her a big grinning hug, then patted her cheek. "You must have been so worried! Imagine, everyone thinking I had a heart attack when it was just heartburn! It sounds like a *Fawlty Towers* joke."

"It wasn't *just* heartburn, Dad," Shelina said as she took off her shoes. "You had a panic attack."

"Well, who wouldn't?" He waved his hand. "Being rushed to the hospital like that. But how great for me that Jana was there! Such a good girl. I'm lucky I have all you girls to look out for me. Who needs sons!" He chuckled as he glanced at the

TV. "I can stream my show now, right? I missed the semifinals yesterday. You know, Shelina, my friend's daughter won this competition last year. Kamila, you should enter next year with Rohan. Kamila has become quite the cook. You should have seen the perfect momos she made. She made some bad ones first, but then Rohan saved the day! They were better than—"

"Dad," Kamila interrupted, "sit. Watch your show." She turned on the TV and switched to the FoodTV streaming service.

He nodded as he sat in his chair. "Yes. Thank you."

Kamila looked at Shelina with an expression she knew her sister would understand as *What the heck is going on with Dad?*

Shelina shook her head and pulled Kamila into the kitchen, where hopefully Dad wouldn't hear them. Zayan followed.

"First of all," Shelina said, pulling Kamila into a hug, "it's good to see you, Sis."

Kamila hugged her back. Kamila wasn't super close with her sister—it was hard to be when for years Kamila thought Shelina believed her little sister was a disgrace to the family. But they'd talked it out and Shelina had apologized in family therapy. Apparently, Shelina had coped with the tension in the family by staying out of it as much as possible.

Kamila would have preferred her older sister had stood up for her instead, but she forgave her and assumed if they lived closer together now, they would be friends. But even if they weren't really tight, Kamila loved her sister and was happy to see her. Zayan, too, who was a great guy and a loyal brother-in-law.

She hugged him, trying not to think about what she'd been doing with the man's brother only hours ago.

Another reason to tread carefully with this issue with Rohan. She didn't think of Rohan as a brother. Obviously. But he *was* a part of her family, and that was one more reason why a relationship was impossible. All Kamila could think about were the people who would get hurt when things went belly-up between them.

Kamila squared her shoulders and switched her mind back to what was important here—Dad. Not her feelings for Rohan. She looked pointedly at her sister. "Okay, what the heck is Dad on?"

"A new antianxiety medication." Shelina chuckled. "It might be working a bit too well. He'll probably have his dosage tweaked when he sees the new psychiatrist."

Kamila shook her head, smiling. "Maybe I should get some of this stuff myself. How'd you get him to agree to see a psychiatrist again?"

"Rohan convinced him."

Figured. "How were his test results?"

"Nothing significant. He still needs to work on his cholesterol and blood pressure, but we knew that. His heart is okay. In fact, all things considered, he's well enough. The doctor said we can treat this whole episode as an early warning. She recommended he take some time off work and reduce his stress for a few weeks. He needs to learn better self-care and mood monitoring. The doctor suggested yoga."

Kamila nodded, but her mind was racing. Time off work? This messed up their whole plan. He was supposed to be part-time for a month while Kamila proved she could manage the more complicated Emerald clients. But if he stopped working altogether, who would take the rest of his clients? Could she? She still had her own. Plus, the puppy prom and the Aim High party. How could she impress Anil Malek if she was spread even thinner?

"I hear you've already taken some of his clients. Rohan's agreed to take the rest for a few weeks," Zayan said.

"That's not necessary," Kamila said quickly. "I can take them. Rohan is too busy." She couldn't ask him to take on even more for Dad.

Shelina shook her head. "How are you going to do that, Kam? You have your own clients."

Zayan snorted. "Rohan's not going to be taking the clients himself, anyway. He'll divide the cases among the team at Toronto HNS."

Well, that was a relief. Of course, it made sense—Rohan wouldn't do this himself. He was in a delegating role at his company, not a doing role.

"He might come by for dinner so we can discuss details," Zayan said, taking an apple out of the fruit bowl and rubbing it on his sweatshirt. He took a hearty bite.

Fudge nuggets. Rohan was coming here? Today? She *did* want to speak to him, but she wasn't thinking right away.

"By the way," Zayan said, chewing the apple with his mouth open. Zayan wasn't nearly as...polished as his brother. He was the hoodie-and-jeans sort of executive, instead of the suit-and-tie type. "I can't believe what you did yesterday."

Kamila's eyes widened. *Crap crap crap*. It hadn't occurred to her that Rohan might be the kiss-and-tell type. He certainly wasn't seven years ago.

She tried to look nonchalant. "Oh, I—"

"Zayan, don't tease Kamila. So what if she brought him throw pillows?"

"Hell, I'm not complaining," Zayan said, laughing. "Someone has to try to breathe some life into my brother. He was even wearing a color this morning."

Phew. But also, Rohan told them about the cushions she bought him?

"Kamila!" Dad called out. "I'm hungry. You should have seen the lunch they gave me in the hospital. They called it soup...but broth with two carrots isn't soup. Is there any more of the bean stew you made? With some crackers. The ones the hospital gave me were salted...Can you imagine! I have high blood pressure!"

"Okay, Dad, relax. I got this..."

And Kamila didn't have time to worry about Rohan, or anything else. She only needed to take care of Dad.

Kamila spent the weekend mostly on the couch with Dad, watching cooking shows and working with him to come up with a meal plan for the week. His mood was the same—almost too happy and enthusiastic about everything. While she was glad to see him in a good mood, the fact that it was chemically induced didn't do much to put her at ease. Tomorrow, he could be back to how he was before. Or worse.

She heard from most of her friends at some point, checking in to see how Dad was doing. Asha, Nicole, Tim, Anil, and surprisingly, even a (very brief) phone call from Jana. Shelina had called about eight times after heading home Saturday night. But nothing at all from Rohan.

She did get an email from his assistant though—to her Emerald email address asking her to send them a list of the Emerald clients that HNS would be taking over temporarily. And Rohan called Dad to briefly check in and discuss the cases. But still.

Rohan used to check in on *Kamila* when he knew Dad was in a bad way. Not this time.

Maybe she should contact him? She almost sent a text—even drafted a light and breezy message telling him about the new Malaysian noodle recipe she was planning to cook this week.

But she couldn't pretend what had happened hadn't happened, and she didn't know how to talk about it. So, she did nothing. Which was so completely outside of her comfort zone she didn't know how to feel about it. Thankfully, she was almost too busy with Dad to worry about it too much. Almost.

She stayed busy for the next few days. Client meetings, plus the Aim High paperwork. She'd had to hit three different stores to get the ingredients for the Malaysian noodles. Wednesday, she worked from home so she could keep an eye on Dad, but she was steadily busy until five, when she tag-teamed with Rashida Aunty to keep Dad company so she could rush to the shelter for a puppy prom meeting. Thankfully, Asha brought the puppies to the meeting, so that alleviated a lot of Kamila's stress.

"Potato!" Kamila squealed. She pulled him into her arms. "Look how big you are!" She buried her face in Potato's soft neck while he squirmed in her arms, trying to lick her face.

Asha laughed. "I figured you needed some puppy time." She unclipped the leashes from the rest of them. They all promptly ran straight for Kamila, jumping up to her lap to join their brother.

Kamila laughed. "I did. I totally did need these guys."

"Oh, sweet mother of Alanis Morissette—*puppies!*" Tim said

from the doorway. Which made the puppies leave Kamila and attack the new person in the room.

It took them a while to get settled, of course. But eventually, the three of them were able to get some work done, each with a puppy or two in hand. Soon they had the final list of sponsors, the itinerary, and the menu for the prom sorted out. Kamila wished all charity committees were like this. Puppies might even make the Aim High meetings pleasant. After wrapping up, they headed to Boba Noodle for dinner, since Rashida Aunty was still with Dad.

"Hey! Look who's here!" Tim said as he opened the door to the noodle shop. Kamila was behind him so she didn't see who he was talking about, but she assumed it would be Maricel, finally coming to try Kevin's Earl Grey.

She was three steps from the table when she saw it wasn't Maricel who Kevin was chatting with, but Rohan. Alone. His suit rumpled, his tie loosened, a big bowl of beef noodle soup in front of him, and a bright-green boba tea.

Rohan.

Why was he here? He was clearly as surprised to see Kamila as she was to see him, because they were staring at each other.

How many days had it been? Only four. It felt like so much longer. His hair wasn't its usual combed with precision, and there were faint circles under his eyes. Well, she probably didn't look too hot, either. She'd skipped her whole blow-dry routine on her last wash day so her hair was limp and stringy. She was wearing a dress, but it was kind of a boring solid thing. Deep magenta, but still much less…Kamila than normal. She couldn't take her eyes off Rohan's face, though, both relieved to see it again and weirdly uncomfortable about how much seeing him made her feel better.

See? Awkwardness. This was why anything between her and Rohan was a monumentally terrible idea. That face meant too much to her. She couldn't risk losing him. She might already have.

"Rohan!" Tim said, startling her. She'd forgotten she had anyone with her. "I didn't know you hung out in tiny noodle joints. This place is a bit quirky for someone like you."

Rohan chuckled, standing. "Kam introduced me to this soup and I've grown a bit addicted."

"Best in town," Kevin said with a grin. "Y'all sitting with him? I can get three more place settings."

Rohan was nothing but polite and generous, so, of course he insisted they join him at his table. Kamila assumed he didn't really want her there, so she ensured there was a comfortable amount of space between them by sitting neither next to him, nor across from him. Diagonal was best. No chance of eye contact or worse—physical contact.

"Here." Rohan handed Kevin a business card after Kevin put soup spoons and chopsticks on the table. "We can talk more later, but I think I have just the opportunity for you."

"Dude, this rocks," Kevin said, taking Rohan's card. "I'll be around to get your order in a few." He headed to the front of the restaurant.

"What were you talking about?" Asha asked.

"He's looking at changing his university major and was asking me about accounting and law designations."

Kamila frowned. "He's a student?" Kamila didn't know why that surprised her. Why wouldn't Kevin be in school?

"Yup. Part-time. He's a good kid. I told him to apply for an internship at HNS—he can get a feel for both business law and accounting with us. He was concerned because he can't afford to take an unpaid internship. But we pay our interns."

Of course they did. Rohan was a conscientious employer. Kamila hid behind the menu, which was really unnecessary because she knew she wanted a mango-matcha boba tea and a beef noodle soup. But wait. That's what Rohan had in front of him. She didn't want to order the same thing as him. What would he think? That she was obsessed with him? She needed to order something else.

When Kevin returned, she reluctantly ordered a brown sugar oolong milk tea and Taiwanese popcorn chicken on rice. The soup was better than the chicken, but sacrifices had to be made.

But maybe she was imagining weirdness that wasn't even there. Because as soon as their orders were in, Rohan smiled a normal, casual, not-at-all-awkward-because-they-had-kissed-and-not-talked-about-it smile. "It's handy I bumped into you, Kam. I was planning to call you later tonight."

Call her. At night. Why? Omg, was he going to FaceTime her again?

Kamila tried to ask why, but when she opened her mouth, no noise came out. *Smooth, Kamila.*

Thankfully, Rohan was so unaffected he just kept talking. "We need to talk about food for the Aim High party. The caterer needs the final menu by Friday. I'd been hoping we could pop into their restaurant to try some of their food, but I don't think there's time. Maybe if you have some availability tonight, we can look over the menus and pick the food? I'm heading for a workout after this, but I can put it off. Or do you need to get home to your dad?"

He wanted to speak to her alone. Did he actually want to talk about kissing and not menus? Or, holy crustaceans, did he not want to talk about the kissing and actually do more of it?

Kamila bit her lip as she felt her panic rising. Why was she reacting this way? She didn't normally overthink things. She needed to get over this. She couldn't think straight.

"Maybe we can have a drink or"—he chuckled, looking at the bright tea in front of him—"more tea and discuss?"

Asha's foot kicked her under the table. Her friend was clearly noticing Kamila's little panic attack and was offering a little footsie support. Kamila was grateful. "Oh, I mean, yeah," Kamila said. "I guess we need to do that. I've got a lot going on right now... You know how it is, with the prom, and Dad—"

"I get it, Kam," Rohan said. "If you don't think you have time, I can handle this. You need to look out for yourself and your father first. I'm sure Anil would understand."

"No, no, I'm fine," Kamila said. "I'm not backing out. It's just tonight..." She needed an excuse right away. "I was planning to take Darcy to the dog park. The floral backpack I ordered for her came in, and I need some pictures for her Instagram." Okay, that excuse didn't do much to make Kamila seem like a normal, well-adjusted person. But it was the truth. She shrugged. "Darcy always looks great at dusk."

He smiled warmly, that same caring and slightly amused smile he always had for her. But for some reason that same old Rohan smile only turned her stomach upside down this time. "I can squeeze in a quick workout and meet you at the dog park afterward. Eight thirty work for you?"

Kamila nodded. Then her stomach flipped again.

Troubling, to say the least.

CHAPTER 19

Kamila didn't want to meet Rohan at the dog park. She couldn't seem to think in a straight line since she'd first slid her lips over his early Saturday morning. And clearly, being around him just made it worse. But she knew the only chance of getting back to the way they were supposed to be was to talk to him. So even though she really wanted to go home and eat ice cream, she had no choice but to keep the date. Kissing him had been impulsive—now it was time to deal with it.

As was becoming the norm, Dad was watching a food reality show when she got home, this time with Rashida Aunty. After kissing both of them on the cheek, Kamila found Darcy in the dog bed.

"Hey, girl." She picked up her sleepy dog. Darcy, of course, immediately smelled puppies on Kamila and looked at her like she was some sort of cheating charlatan. "Sorry, baby. I'll make sure to check with you next time I have a play date with Potato." She scratched Darcy's ear and turned back to Dad and Rashida Aunty. "How was dinner?"

"Rashida brought eggplant and rotlis, and I made an omelet."

"Dad! You should have had a salad with it!"

"We had salad, too," Rashida Aunty said. "His omelet was so fluffy!"

"This man on TV showed how to make proper French-style eggs and I wanted to try it. Did you know eating eggs doesn't increase cholesterol? It's all the butter we usually cook them in. For years we all avoided eggs, but really, they're fine. I'll make you an omelet on Saturday. Rohan will be here for breakfast, right?"

"I don't know."

"You joining us for the show?" Rashida asked, heading toward the kitchen. "It's patisserie week. I'm making some chai. I brought whole-wheat nankhatai for your father. I made it with less butter and added extra bran. Of course, I made the regular ones, too. Chocolate, because Jana will only eat chocolate cookies." Rashida stuck her hand out the kitchen door with the plate of nankhatai.

"I'm sorry—I can't stay," Kamila said, taking one of the Indian cookies and eating it in two bites. She needed to leave soon before more talk of Jana put her on edge. She grabbed Darcy's new backpack and her denim jacket, then switched her own cardigan for a matching denim jacket and added lipstick in the exact color of her dress. Her hair was a bit disappointing for Instagram selfies with Darcy, but whatever. She chose the purple leash to finish the look. "I'm meeting Rohan at the dog park to go over some of the details for the Aim High party."

"I don't know how he finds the time," Rashida Aunty said as she put the kettle on. "He works such long hours. At dinner last night he said he—"

Kamila stepped into the kitchen. "You had dinner with Rohan last night?"

Rashida Aunty spooned some chai masala into a pot of water for tea. "He was taking Jana out for coffee, and I insisted he have dinner with us first. I don't think he eats when he's alone. It's so great you three are still so close. If only Shelina and Zayan lived in Toronto, too! Who would have thought when we used to go on vacations all together that you would still be friends twenty years later?"

Dad called out from the living room that a baker was laminating dough, whatever that meant, so Rashida rushed back to finish watching British people make fancy French pastries with him.

Kamila stood near the door, watching them a moment, irritated that she was so rattled about Rohan seeing Jana alone the night before. There was nothing going on between them. Kamila knew that. She had no right to object to their friendship. She took a deep breath and headed to the door. "Okay, I'm leaving. Call me if you need anything."

"Have fun, beti," Dad said.

Kamila didn't see Rohan when she got to the park. He was probably still at his climbing gym, which was fine. She was in no hurry to have this conversation. Might as well get some pictures of Darcy before he got there.

But she was a bit too anxious to get any decent shots. Or maybe Darcy wasn't being accommodating. Every picture ended up being Darcy's backside—which might have been workable since the point here was pictures of her backpack, but it would have been nice to get Darcy's sweet face, too. Ah well. She shouldn't try to force it. She could come back another day.

She left Darcy to wander alone in the off-leash and sat on one of the benches—now was a good time to plan what she would say to Rohan. She needed a script so she wouldn't freeze up again.

After sitting quietly for a few minutes working through the best way to say *I'm sorry I kissed you* without making it seem like there was any reason why anyone wouldn't be thrilled to be kissing someone like Rohan, someone sat beside her. Someone who wasn't Rohan.

"Hi, Kamila!"

"Oh. Hey, Dane."

"Great to see you here tonight. Alone. You usually have so many friends with you," he said.

Kamila frowned. To be perfectly honest, while she was still holding out for a match between Maricel and Dane, she wasn't really in the mood for his brand of butt kissing right now.

She ran her hand through her hair. "I'm actually meeting someone."

He wagged his eyebrows for a reason Kamila couldn't decipher. He was sitting a little closer than she'd have liked, and he smelled like beer. Alone at the park on a Wednesday night smelling like a brewery? She frowned again. Had she been wrong in thinking Dane was an upstanding potential boyfriend for her friend?

"A date?" he asked.

"No, not a date." She didn't want to mention she was meeting Rohan, because then she'd hear more brownnosing about Rohan's brilliance. "Just a planning meeting for some work I'm doing for a nonprofit. What are you up to?"

"Nothing. I still don't have a lot of friends in the neighborhood. My nights are pretty lonely. I assumed meeting you would mean I would have a more active social life."

Okay, that was rude. Kamila had been inviting this man to her Bollywood parties for weeks and had introduced him to all her friends. What more did he want from her? "You could have called Maricel—she's working days at the shelter this week. You could have gone to a movie or something."

He inched closer. "Or I could have called you," he said.

Her nose wrinkled as she tried to inch away. "I've been really busy lately…"

He only inched closer again. His hand landed on her knee. "Did I mention how great it is to see your gorgeous face alone, without your whole squad…finally?"

Holy shoe leather…Dane was totally coming on to her. She removed his hand from her knee. This was because he was drunk. She should divert his attention back to where it belonged. "I mean, I'm not bad, but nowhere close to Maricel. Didn't she look stunning on Friday night? You love her in pink, right?"

He jerked back. "Really—*Maricel*? Why would I notice a Maricel when there is a Kamila in the room?" He smiled and leaned close, his hand finding her knee again. Ugh. He wasn't even good at this.

Kamila's mind jumbled as she froze, panicked. She had to stop this—now. "Maricel! You printed a picture of her!"

"I printed a picture of *you*. C'mon, Kamila, I know you're into me, too. You keep inviting me over. I'm fine with going slow, but this is getting ridiculous. Enough of this hard-to-get bullshit. I know you want this." His hand slid up her knee.

Kamila pushed his hand off as she stood quickly. "You're mistaken, Dane. I only invited you over because you were into my friend Maricel."

His face contorted as if he'd smelled Limburger. "*Maricel*. She what—cleans up after dogs for a living? I was only talking to her because I need a dog trainer." He stood and reached for her.

She jumped out of the way of his embrace. Yuck. Tech bros were the worst. She knew how to deal with this—firm, with no room for misinterpretation. "I'm *not* available. Let me be clear, Dane—I'm not interested in anything romantic here. With you, or with anyone else. Please step away from me."

Now he looked angry, but he took a step forward again. "Be serious, Kamila. You're going to regret this. I'm going to be a huge deal soon..."

"You heard her. Leave her alone," another voice said behind her. Rohan. She wasn't happy to have him rescuing her. She didn't need him—she'd already put this fire out.

Dane put his hands in front of him. "Rohan, my man, no worries. Kamila and I were just chilling."

"She asked you to step away from her. Do it. Now." Rohan's voice was a clear warning. She'd never heard him so...forceful.

Dane looked at Kamila, venom in his eyes. "This is bullshit. I was so nice to you...fucking tease." He waved his hands at Rohan as he walked away. "Have at the frigid bitch. She's just like all the others. C'mon, Byte, we're leaving."

Kamila kept her eyes on Dane as he left the enclosure, not relaxing until the gate was closed behind him and his dog.

She fell back on the bench and covered her face with her hands. "I really want to swear," she mumbled.

Rohan sat next to her. "Are you all right?"

She rubbed her face, then put her hands in her lap. "I'm fine, I'm fine. Pissed off, but fine."

He took her hand in his. "Are you sure? He didn't—"

Kamila snapped her hand back. "I'm *fine*, Rohan. I'm not a child, you know. I can handle handsy men. I don't need you to sweep to my rescue."

"I never said you were a child."

"Well, you act like it sometimes. Everyone does. *Oh, that Kamila, getting herself into trouble again.*"

"Kam, why are you mad at me here?"

She exhaled. "I'm not. I'm just…angry. I totally misjudged Dane. You understood his character way better than I did. I'm such an idiot. I have no idea what I'm going to tell Maricel." Ugh…she'd made such a mess of this.

Rohan reached for her as if he wanted to hug her. "Kam, you shouldn't—"

She put her hands up, stopping him. "Don't even say it. Yes, my puppeteering with my friends' lives backfired spectacularly. But this is going to hurt Maricel, so maybe now isn't the time to rub this in my face."

Rohan blinked a few times, looking at Kamila. Finally, he looked straight in front of him. "I don't know what to say to you right now."

Kamila closed her eyes, refusing to acknowledge her tears. This week had already been so hard. So very, very hard. Now to add to it? Hurting Maricel and disappointing Rohan.

After several long moments of silence, she sighed. "I…Can we just not?" she asked softly, watching her dog in the distance so she wouldn't have to look at his face.

"Not what?"

"Not any of it," she said quietly. "Not fight. Not be awkward and weird. Not talk about what happened on Saturday morning. Not *not* talk about it. Not anything. Can we just go back to being best friends?"

From the corner of her eyes, she saw him rub his chin. He hadn't changed out of his workout clothes—short sleeves and athletic pants. So much forearm out—and biceps, too. "Isn't Asha your best friend?" he asked.

She was jolted out of her forearm admiration and looked at his face. She had only just realized it—but it was true. He *was* her best friend. She valued him as much as Asha. Maybe even more lately. She'd been a complete wreck for weeks because she was terrified of losing him. "A girl can have two, can't she?"

"A girl like Kamila can have whatever she wants," he said. "Except…we can't both talk about and not talk about what happened Saturday morning. The laws of temporal physics don't work that way."

She sighed, exasperated. "But if we don't talk about it, then we'll be thinking about it and wondering how the other feels about it, and it will make things different between us. If we talk about it, then we might find out that yes, we don't feel the same way about it and it will make things hard, too. We're in a pickle, Rohan."

He chuckled. "Well, when you put it that way. We have no choice but to turn back time. I'll get started on a time machine. I don't think I can get a DeLorean. Hopefully my Audi will work."

She smiled. Destruction of their friendship aside, Kamila didn't actually want to go back in time, either. Because she'd needed him that night, and he was there, and she wouldn't give that up for anything. But if she said that out loud, she was also exposing something she wasn't sure she wanted said.

"We should probably put a name to it, don't you think?" she asked. "Be mature adults. Make sure we're both talking about the same thing."

Rohan narrowed one eye, smirking. "You mean we should stop calling it *it*?"

Kamila nodded.

"Okay, fine. I'm sorry I kissed you," he said. "We were both tired and emotional, and it doesn't have to change anything."

"*I* kissed *you*."

He rubbed his beard. "You did?"

"You don't remember?"

His forehead wrinkled. "Actually, I don't. I was sleeping, and then I was kissing you. I don't remember how it happened."

Kamila bit her lip. "I guess it doesn't matter who started it." But it *did* matter. She knew without a doubt in her mind that she'd started it. Both times they'd kissed, it had been her. "Do you remember what happened after the kiss?" she asked.

He frowned. "More kissing?"

Yeah that, plus his tongue on her nipples, but that wasn't the part messing with her emotions. Although the tongue thing *was* nice.

"We fell asleep in each other's arms," Kamila said.

He turned to look at her. "We're close friends, Kam. This doesn't need to be complicated. I know you're going through a lot right now, and if this is causing you stress, we can put it behind us."

"Just like that? Put it behind us?"

"Is that what you need?"

Yes, she needed to put this behind her. But that wasn't all she needed. Maybe she should take Asha's advice and tell him. "It *is* what I need. But...actually, I need more from you." She paused. "When I'm worried about Dad, or when Dad is freaking out and not listening to me or his doctors, you're the only one who can help us. I...I need to know you'll still be here when we need you. Even when I act impulsively."

"Of course I'll be here, Kam."

"Even when I'm self-absorbed?"

He cringed. "I regret saying that on Friday. I'm sorry. I was angry and frustrated. I don't think either of us were in top form that night."

Kamila frowned, remembering what she'd said to Jana at the party. She had regrets about bringing up the past in front of everyone. Especially considering later that night Jana took Dad to the hospital. "I know I wasn't."

His eyes were determined. "I *will* be there for you, Kam. No matter what. I meant what I said before. You... you make my life interesting. You won't be free of me that easily. We're friends."

"Even if... something changes in your personal life? Or mine?"

"You don't have to worry about that. We're family, too, right?"

She looked down at her hands. Yep. *Friends. Family.* "Thank you."

"Consider the matter discussed and resolved. We are officially back to where we were before. If you're okay, should we get to the catering plan now? Actually, wait... I have one question first."

"What?"

"What exactly is your dog wearing?"

Kamila laughed. "A designer backpack and a stone-washed denim jacket. It's her eighties look. Now, how about that menu?"

"Right." He pulled out his phone. "We can look over it online."

They spent the next hour ironing out food plans for the party. Working together, like they were supposed to. Things were objectively fine between them.

Fine, but maybe not normal. Maybe things felt normal to him, but not for her.

But all she could hope for was that with time, she'd go back to not noticing that no one had forearms better than Rohan's. Or that his rare, full-face smile had enough brightness to easily light up a room.

Maybe in time, she'd forget the feeling of waking up surrounded by his warmth. She could hope, at least.

CHAPTER 20

Kamila had, of course, canceled Bollywood night that week. It just felt wrong to celebrate only a week after Dad's medical incident. She ended up just watching cooking shows with him on Friday night after making Thai rice bowls together.

Getting into bed at a reasonable hour on a Friday night felt weird, though. Not talking to any of her friends all day felt weirder. She'd half expected Rohan to show up around dinnertime anyway, but she hadn't heard from him since that night at the dog park. Maybe she should call him. They'd agreed that everything was back to normal between them, and it was normal for Kamila to see Rohan on Friday nights. She sat up in bed and opened a video call with him. Ten seconds later, his face was on her screen.

"Kam, what's wrong?" He looked concerned.

She smiled playfully to put him at ease. If she acted completely normal, maybe this would feel normal. He was in bed, too. In his pajamas, and again, not the fancy plaid ones he wore when he slept over here. But there was a difference from the last time she saw his bed in a video call. "You tzhujed!" The pillows she had bought him were behind him, adding the much-needed splash of color to his bed. But it looked like there was more color there, too.

He lowered his chin and chuckled. "Is that why you called? To check on my bedroom decor?"

"No, I had something to ask you, but let me enjoy this view first. Show me the rest of the bed."

He moved his phone farther so she could have a wide shot of his headboard.

"You have more pillows! Not just the ones I bought you!" There were two other decorative pillows there, in a deep green with a mitered gray stripe around them. Kamila would have preferred them brighter, but they were still a huge improvement. "Hey," she said as she made a realization. "Your new pillows are the exact color of my head scarf." She'd tied a green-and-gray scarf around her hair to sleep instead of the bonnet tonight.

"Great minds and all that," he said, grinning. He brought the camera closer to his face again and leaned back. "So, what did you need to ask me?"

"Oh, right." She hesitated. "Are...are you coming for breakfast tomorrow morning?"

He blinked. "I don't know. Am I invited?"

Kamila bit her lip. "I mean, yeah, you're always invited. And Dad didn't get his business talk last week. He'd love to see you. But I know it's far...and...you know, to come all this way just for—"

"I'll be there. Can I pick up breakfast? How about Montreal-style bagels? I can get whole wheat for your dad."

Kamila grinned. "Clearly you know that carbs are the way to a girl's heart."

He laughed. "You didn't have to FaceTime me to ask that, though. You could have texted."

She leaned back against her headboard. "I could have, but then I wouldn't know about your new pillows. So, my impulsivity was fortuitous. I knew you'd be up."

He settled back in his bed, too. "I was about to turn off my lights. How's your dad doing?"

"He's good. Quite good, actually. Would you believe he's learning to cook?" She paused. "Everyone keeps asking me how Dad is."

"And not enough people are asking how you are?"

"Oh, no! I didn't mean it that way!" For once, that wasn't a hint for people to pay more attention to her. "I meant I'm lucky. Everyone is looking out for Dad. He's blessed. I am, too."

"He's lucky to have you. Can I ask *you* something, Kam?"

"Go ahead."

He looked at her a few seconds before speaking. He felt so…present. Like he was really here in her room. It didn't feel like they were talking through phone screens. Finally, a small smile slid onto his face.

"How are *you* doing, Kamila?"

She smiled wide. "How nice of you to ask, Rohan. I am well, all things considered. I'm feeling a little stressed about how much stuff I have going on right now, but I'm managing, thanks to the help of my amazing friends, present company included. Did I tell you I haven't had a cooking disaster in weeks?"

"A Toronto miracle! How many virgins have you sacrificed?"

"Shush, you." She told him about the Malaysian noodles, the Thai rice bowls, then they talked about what kind of biryani they should get for next Friday's Bollywood night, since she wasn't canceling again. Even though that was the same weekend as the Aim High party and the Dogapalooza.

She probably should have been more stressed about the Aim High party, since their board meeting was the week after it. If Kamila wanted them to vote to put Emerald on retainer for all their financial needs going forward, she really needed to impress everyone at that party. And she still wanted that retainer. Eventually, Dad was going to be returning to work, and securing the Aim High account was the way to prove to him, and everyone else, that she could manage Emerald if he only worked part-time. But she was fine. Everything had been going so well with Anil, and the party was shaping up perfectly, too. Kamila was not worried.

"Fine," Rohan said. "We'll do your rom-com next week—even though we had a comedy last time, too. But then, classic Bollywood drama. Maybe even black-and-white."

"You know I'll change your mind later. You can never say no to me." She smiled and bit her lip, batting her eyelashes.

He laughed. "Kam, you are, as always, trouble."

"Yeah, but I'm your trouble. Now I need my beauty sleep. Good night, Rohan. See you tomorrow."

"Good night, Kam. Sleep well."

Kamila disconnected the call and turned off her light with a huge face-splitting grin.

This. This was exactly where they were supposed to be.

CHAPTER 21

On the Thursday before the double-party weekend (triple if she counted Bollywood night), Kamila had a final meeting with the puppy prom committee at the shelter to go over a list of preparations.

"The caterer emailed asking if the dogs can be kept out of the food-prep area," Tim said.

"Isn't it all preprepared food?" Kamila asked. Seeing as the theme was Bollywoof, they had hired an Indian food caterer and ordered samosas, pakoras, and at Kamila's insistence, masala momos. Rohan promised he'd come to the prom, and she was looking forward to him confirming that the Rohan-and-Kamila-made momos were better than any restaurant ones.

"Yeah, but they'll have to warm the food and plate it on site. They're using the church kitchen," Asha said.

"The church kitchen has a door," Kamila said. "Shouldn't be a problem to keep the dogs out. Just let Maricel know." She checked her list of who was doing what. "Where is she? We can talk to her now."

Asha shook her head. "I told her about this meeting, but she left for the day. The girl has been so distracted lately. Did you know she's seeing someone?"

Kamila frowned. She hadn't seen Maricel since the handsy-Dane incident. She did text her briefly... to tell her that Dane wasn't coming to Bollywood nights anymore, but Maricel hadn't said much. She hadn't seemed all too upset. Maybe because she was secretly dating? "Who?"

"Maricel won't say. She says it's too early to talk about it. But she's walking around like a lovesick puppy, and she's constantly texting someone."

Huh. "What's next on the list?" Kamila asked, changing the subject so she wouldn't dwell on this. She really needed to stop meddling in her friends' lives.

"The adoption team is asking if there is a sectioned-off area for the adoptable dogs. They don't want them mixing with the guest dogs. Apparently, the puppies aren't quite used to big crowds yet."

Kamila's ears perked up. "Puppies? Are Potato and his siblings ready to be adopted?" Potato, who was currently on Kamila's lap where she preferred him to be during meetings, poked his head up at the mention of his name.

"Oh my god," Asha said. "He's *answering* to Potato now. Heaven help the family who adopts him. They might want to give him, you know, a *normal* name."

"There is nothing more normal than a potato." She scratched under his chin. "So, will he be making his society debut at the ball?"

"Apparently. The litter's last checkup was great. They're ready."

"Did you hear that, Potato? You're going to be a debutante! Who's a good little boy? You'll get to meet Darcy, Lizzy, Luke, and Leia." Excited by Kamila's enthusiasm, Potato started wagging his tail and hopping around on Kamila's lap.

"We can probably put the puppies in a separate room. Like one of the old classrooms or something," Tim said.

"Perfect," Asha said. "I think that's it. Can we meet on site at three o'clock?"

"I'll be there." Kamila squeezed Potato. If he was going to be put on the adoption block on Sunday, her days of snuggling her favorite puppy were numbered. But it was fine. She was used to seeing dogs she loved getting homes. It was the circle of a shelter dog's life.

"Kamila," Asha said, looking at her clipboard. "Danielle told me to tell you she needs you backstage at three forty-five on Saturday for the canine couture fashion show."

"What? Why? The Aim High party is on Saturday night." Saturday was day one of the Dogapalooza festival, but Kamila was only planning to drop by for a little while. She'd need time to get ready and head downtown to set up the room for the cocktail party.

Tim gave Kamila a pointed look. "You're emceeing, remember?"

Barnacles. She *had* volunteered for that.

"What time is the Aim High thing?" Asha asked.

"Seven. But I'm meeting Rohan there to set up at six."

"You can tell Danielle that something came up."

Kamila sighed. She couldn't do that. She made a commitment. "It's fine. It will be an excuse to wear my dalmatian dress again." She did some timing calculations in her head. She could probably just make it on time if she left right after the fashion show. She could quickly change into the little black dress she'd bought for the Aim High party and take an Uber downtown instead of the subway.

"You don't have to say yes to everything," Asha said. "And you're still doing Bollywood night, too?"

"I have to do Bollywood night. Everyone expects it, and I canceled last week."

Asha shook her head. "Everyone expects you to take care of *yourself*, not just them."

Kamila waved her hand. She could do this. Plus, it wasn't like she was working alone. Tim was helping with the prom, and Rohan was working with her on the Aim High party. Kamila stood and gently put Potato down with the other puppies. "I should go. It's getting late."

Tim checked his watch. "Ack! Yes, I have to get the chosen ones from the groomers!"

After Tim rushed out, Kamila was packing up her things when Dad called.

"Don't forget I'm cooking dinner tonight," he said as soon as she answered. "I'm making the broccoli pasta the young English-man on TV makes. Sorry, no. Not broccoli. *Broccolini*. Did you know it's a completely different vegetable?"

"I'm just leaving the shelter now."

"Okay, beti. Maybe you can pick up that bubbly wine you like? I have news to celebrate. Rohan will be over at six."

Rohan was coming for dinner? Why? He hadn't mentioned it when he'd texted her earlier today with some details for the Aim High party. "What kind of news, Dad?"

"A special surprise for you. I'm making Caesar salad, too. If my friends could see me now!"

Frowning, Kamila disconnected the call.

"What was that about?" Asha asked, looking at Kamila with concern.

"Dad has some secret big news for me. He wants me to pick up prosecco, and Rohan is coming for dinner."

"What's the news about?"

"I have no idea." It was too early to make any decisions about going permanently part-time—the Aim High board meeting wasn't until next week. A realization hit her, and her heart sank. "Actually, I think I do know. It's probably about estate planning. Dad's been finalizing his will for the last few weeks and Rohan is the executor."

"Oh wow. That's weird."

Kamila sighed. "I know. *Ugh.* It can't be healthy for him to think about his death so much right now."

"I wonder if that's why he's been in such a good mood lately, though," Asha said. "It probably helps him to know you guys will be taken care of."

Kamila bent to rub Potato's belly. She just couldn't keep her hands off him. "Yeah, maybe. What kind of family drinks bubbly when they talk about estate planning?"

Asha laughed. "The Hussains never do anything without style." She checked her watch. "I need to run, too—I have to pick up Nicole. Her car's in the shop."

Kamila's phone vibrated in her pocket. She checked it—it was a funny meme about nonprofits from Anil. She laughed and showed it to Asha.

"That's hilarious. Anil sends you memes?"

Kamila smiled. "Yeah, he's great. We're thinking of taking a drive to that gallery up north next week. You know, the one with—"

Asha's phone sounded loudly with a text. She pulled it out of her pocket and looked at the message. "Nicole wants me to pick up dinner, too. Talk soon?"

"No worries, Asha. Later."

Like a dutiful daughter, Kamila picked up a bottle of prosecco on her way home, even though she didn't want to have whatever this conversation was going to be. She also grabbed a bottle of red wine, in case she needed to keep drinking after their "talk." And a bottle of craft beer aged in bourbon barrels that she knew Rohan liked.

There was loud music playing when she got home—looked like Dad had pulled out his old qawwali CDs. Either that or Rohan finally was able to show him how music streaming worked. Rohan was at the table with his back to her, tossing a salad in her big wooden bowl. He didn't notice her come in, so she picked up Darcy and watched him for a moment.

He'd clearly been wearing a jacket and had taken it off. Probably came straight from work. Unfortunately, his shirtsleeves were rolled up again, showing off his forearms. Those things were a danger to humanity. The way he was leaned over the table meant she could also see solid thighs and a very cute bum, too. Rohan was so…nice to look at. His face was even nicer. She honestly didn't think she'd ever met anyone she liked looking at as much as him.

This was ridiculous. Kamila didn't understand where this physical attraction came from. She'd been fine the handful of other times she'd seen him since that evening at the dog park. Kamila blamed the forearms. When those things were on full display, the effects were near lethal.

He shifted, putting the salad servers on either side of the bowl, and Kamila was overcome with an undeniable urge to walk up behind him and put her arms around his waist. What would he feel like? Warm. Would she feel muscles through the thin cotton of his shirt? Would it feel as cozy as falling asleep on him?

Kamila literally had to clutch Darcy to her chest to prevent herself from embracing Rohan. What was wrong with her?

This impulse to be closer to him, and not necessarily for sex…this was new. And troubling. She'd never felt like this before…for anyone. And she couldn't feel this way for Rohan, of all people. She needed to put some distance between them. Maybe their close friendship was a bad idea.

He turned. "Oh, Kam, hi. I didn't know you were there. Your dad is on the phone with Shelina upstairs."

Kamila actually had to steady herself so her knees would hold after hearing his voice. Great. Now she was practically swooning. She put Darcy down and turned around to put the volume down on the speaker, mostly so Rohan wouldn't see how red her face probably was. She closed her eyes a moment, and willed her body to turn off this errant response it was having.

Turning back to Rohan and smiling normally, she hoped, she put the bottle of prosecco on the dining table. "So, what's Dad's big secret, anyway?"

Now that she could see his face…Rohan looked uncomfortable. Clearly this whole estate-planning-over-champagne idea didn't sit well with him, either. "This is just the final paperwork—"

"Kamila, beti, you're home!" Dad came down the stairs. "Excellent. Shelina just called. She was supposed to be here for this because it involves her, too, but she couldn't get away from the boys." Dad went into the kitchen and poured a box of pasta into a pot of boiling water.

This wasn't a conversation Kamila wanted to have right now. She didn't want to talk about Dad dying. Not when he was doing so well.

But watching Dad stir his pasta, Kamila could see his lightness. He'd been like this since coming back from the hospital. His blood pressure was lower—he'd been testing it himself every morning. And he was happier than she'd seen him in a long time. Maybe Asha was right, and it was this estate planning that was making him feel better. Less anxious. If this was putting his mind at ease, then Kamila should be excited for him, not dreading the conversation. She was being selfish.

"You okay, Kam?" Rohan asked.

She could do this. Keep Dad from seeing how much she didn't want to talk about this and keep Rohan from knowing that minutes ago she'd almost been knocked to the ground by a wave of intense attraction to him. Easy peasy lemon squeezy.

"I'm absolutely fine." She smiled, putting on her same old Kamila face. She breezed by to get champagne flutes out of the sideboard. She even did her trademark lip bite and swept her fingers over Rohan's forearm as she passed him. Yeah, that was a mistake. Inappropriate flirting was her modus operandi, but she should probably not be touching his forearms when she was so inconveniently obsessed with them right now. His skin was cooler today but still soft. Solid. Rohan was so solid, and she was on the verge of falling apart because of it.

She exhaled a shaky breath and poured two glasses of prosecco.

Dad put the big pasta bowl on the table. "Okay, let's eat."

The pasta was pretty good. The noodles might have been a touch overcooked—but the bitterness of the broccolini and the rich saltiness of the cheese went well with the dryness of the wine. The conversation was great, too. Dad didn't bring up his news yet. Instead, they talked about the Aim High party in two days. Kamila had received confirmation today that two reporters from newspapers and one from a news website would be coming, and the guest list was shaping up to include an impressive list of important names in Toronto.

"You've done a wonderful job, Kamila," Dad said. "I'm very proud of how well you're doing on Anil's team."

Kamila smiled. She'd enjoyed working on Aim High more than she thought she would. She'd still ensured Anil only saw the respectable and professional side of her, but he was a lot more fun than she thought he would be. And inconvenient attraction aside, she and Rohan worked well together planning this party. But the point of all this was to show Dad, and Rohan, too, that she could be "fancy accountant" enough to take more complicated clients. And she knew she'd succeeded there. Anil had no issues with the opening balance statements or the articles of incorporation she'd drafted. She had no doubt that when the board met next week, they would agree to retain Emerald as their financial partner. She even thought she had that Marlene lady's vote.

"It's been great," Kamila said. "I've found the case to be straightforward, and Anil already signed off on all the documents I prepared. Hopefully, you'll see that clients like this are no problem for—" Her text tone rang. It was Asha, saying she needed to talk to her. "Hang on." She texted Asha back telling her she was having dinner, and she'd call her later.

"It's been a lot of work for you, though, beti," Dad said.

"It's been fine! But yeah, I've been busy. After the prom is done, I'll be a lot freer—at least until we plan next year's event.

Did I tell you Tim wants to do an eighties-and-nineties theme next? I don't know—"

"Ah, but maybe I can ease some of your burden now…" Dad interrupted, a wide smile on his face. He looked at Rohan. "I think it's time to tell her."

Kamila smiled, but she could feel her hands clam up. "Tell me what?"

Dad got up and grabbed a file folder from his briefcase and sat back down. "Now, beti, I know you worry about me very much—and I'm blessed that you care so much." He smiled. "I feel like you've been a different Kamila lately. I have never seen you work so hard—at Emerald, at the shelter, and now with Anil and the incubator project. You've grown so much. But you've sacrificed too much for me."

"No, Dad, I—"

"Just listen, Kamila. I know why you've become who you are." His voice gentled. "The way your mother treated you was wrong, but I didn't know how much it was hurting you until it was too late. I've told you so many times, and you'll hear it again—I'm sorry I wasn't there for you more. I was so busy with Hussain, Nasser, and Suleiman that I neglected my family. I failed you. But now I can make things right."

"Dad, you haven't failed me. I—"

"Ah! Let me finish. Look what all that focus on my work got me… health problems in my body." He tapped his head. "Health problems in my head. Sometimes I feel I haven't had one moment when I wasn't worried or sad since your mother passed on. But these past weeks… my outlook has changed. My new drugs are working well. Did I tell you I even saw a new psychiatrist? On video call! What is the world coming to!"

Kamila hadn't heard that he'd had an appointment with the psychiatrist. Why hadn't he told her? She tried to ask him more about this doctor, but Dad but his hand up to stop her.

"You've been right the whole time, beti," he said. "I need to take care of myself. I need to step away from so many responsibilities."

Tonight was about good news! He was agreeing to go part-time even before the board met! This was exactly what she wanted. Kamila grinned and turned to Rohan, but he wasn't smiling. Or, he was, but she could see it wasn't a real smile.

She felt a chill go through her. "So, what exactly are you saying?" she asked slowly.

Dad grinned. "It's time to give all this up. I'm retiring. I purchased a unit in the same condo as the Nassers. I'm going to spend my winters in Florida."

Kamila blinked. So...it wasn't estate planning? Dad was retiring? In Florida?

Dad continued. "I'm selling my HNS shares to Rohan and Zayan. And I'm giving you and Shelina the money from the sale now! Why wait until I'm dead? I want to watch my girls enjoy their life. Now you'll have more free time. You can focus on your volunteer work or do whatever you want to do in your heart! Maybe find a job as an event planner, since you're so good at it. Or work with animals. You can follow your dreams instead of working for mine. You can be your own Kamila."

Did Dad really think she wasn't being her own Kamila? That she wasn't doing exactly what she wanted with her life?

But wait...if he was selling his HNS shares, what would happen to Emerald? Her Emerald?

Kamila would have blinked again, but instead she dropped her fork.

"But...what about Emerald?" She looked at Rohan. He'd known Dad was doing this?

"You can continue to work with your Emerald clients at HNS if you'd like," Rohan said. "We plan to absorb all the operations into HNS and close the Emerald office. But I've been telling you that for a while now—you're always welcome at HNS."

But she wasn't welcome. Or at least she hadn't been when she'd worked there before. And Rohan knew that. When she'd worked at HNS, the other accountants would speak over her. She was never given any real clients. There were comments about her clothes. About her makeup. And there was that guy who used to look at her breasts instead of her face when talking to her. She'd even managed to acquire the nickname "I-Don't-Like-Math Barbie" among the junior associates.

Dad smiled and put his hand on Kamila's. "You don't need to work there if you don't want to. I know you got your accounting degree to continue in my footsteps, but your mother never worked. And your sister doesn't, either. The house is paid for...and I'll only be here half the year anyway. Maybe less. You could get a roommate. Maybe that lovely girl Maricel. The money from the sale will be plenty to support you until you decide what you really want to do. You can be yourself now."

Patriarchy. That's what this was. Because a woman who loves parties and pretty clothes shouldn't have to be bothered with a pesky office job. In finance, no less.

Kamila loved her father, but she'd never been so betrayed by him in her life.

"So Emerald is closing. I won't have a job."

Rohan shook his head. "We're not closing it. We're keeping

it as a separate division specializing in small businesses, but we'll be operating it out of the HNS office."

Kamila looked down at her plate, not being able to bear the look on Rohan's face a moment longer.

So that was it. She was effectively losing Emerald and getting a trust fund instead. A third of HNS—even split with her sister, it would be a lot of money.

She looked at Dad. He was happy. Almost deliriously giddy. His stress was lower. She actually liked the idea of him retiring and spending his winters in Florida with his close friends. It would be good for him. He could watch food reality shows and play cards all day, and she'd still get to see him all summer.

For a lot of people, this bombshell would be great news. He was giving her financial security—something most millennials would kill for. A gorgeous house. Kamila wouldn't have work stress anymore. A dream come true, right?

He didn't see how much she loved her work at Emerald. He thought poor Kamila shouldn't be encumbered with business details. Even as he watched her hustle to bring in new clients and work night and day for them while maintaining a demanding volunteer job and taking care of his needs, too. Not to mention this deal they had for the last month. She'd taken on Aim High so he could go part-time, and she'd even volunteered to throw a cocktail party for the client to impress them.

Dad saw all that and decided that she didn't really care about Emerald, that she was only doing all this out of gratitude to him. And he made a major decision affecting her life without even mentioning it to her.

Dad didn't really know her at all. He only saw the superficial person on the surface. Which was exactly all Mom saw, too.

Only difference was, to Dad Kamila needed to be coddled and protected from big discussions, instead of Mom's strategy of shame and name-calling.

Her father meant the world to her and he didn't know her at all. She looked at Rohan. How long had he known this?

"When did you make this decision?" she asked, more to Rohan than Dad.

"We'd been talking about it for a while, but your father solidly agreed to it that morning at the hospital." He didn't meet her eyes.

Hours after he'd left her bed, Rohan had made plans to take her company. Her job.

He also didn't know her. He thought she was ridiculous. Trouble. That she should be humored and indulged to turn her office into a dollhouse and dress up her friends, but that she couldn't play in the big leagues and be involved in big decisions. To Rohan, Kamila was just a flighty flirt who spent more energy on her dog's fame than anything else.

She'd called him her best friend. She'd thought no one knew her like he did. But all she was to him was parties, signature drinks, matching outfits for her dog, and casual sex. Not a person to take seriously.

Kamila felt a prickle behind her eyes. She shut them quickly, not wanting Dad to see her upset. He was happy. That was what mattered. She could put on her mask.

Why did this feel like she was losing so much more than a job?

When she opened her eyes, Rohan was looking at her. Looking through her. He appeared apologetic, at least. But if he were really sorry, then he wouldn't have kept this from her in the first place. Letting Dad effectively shut down Emerald from under her, and hiding it from her, meant he didn't care about her as much as she cared about him.

But she already knew that, didn't she? She knew, without a doubt, that *she* had kissed him both times. He didn't feel anything more than friendship. He'd even said so at the dog park that night.

And how did she feel? Kamila was finally willing…*able*…to admit the truth to herself. She'd been pushing down this knowledge for weeks. She'd fallen in love with Rohan.

Completely and hopelessly in love.

She exhaled—and took a bite of pasta. She had no idea how she would do it, but she needed to get through this meal.

CHAPTER 22

Kamila managed to get through the rest of dinner while listening to Dad go on about his new place in Florida and how excited he was to never see snow, all while she averted Rohan's eyes. Barely. But thankfully her text tone rang as she was swallowing the last heavy bite. Asha again.

Asha: I really don't want to alarm you, but I need to speak to you before someone else tells you. Can you come over?

She texted back right away.

Kamila: Is everyone okay? Nicole? Lizzy?

After this terrible night, the last thing she needed was more bad news.

Asha: Yes, yes. We're all fine. It's just... Can you come over?

From the sound of it, Asha's news wasn't good, but honestly, she was glad for the save to get out of there.

Kamila: I'll come over soon—I need to talk to you, too.

Her escape was easy—she told Dad that Asha needed her for a personal talk. Dad patted Kamila's shoulder. "You're so good to your friends. Give her my best. I'll put the rest of the pasta away for your lunch tomorrow. And I'll take Darcy for her walk."

Kamila called an Uber since she'd had that prosecco. As she was waiting for the car outside, Rohan came out onto the front porch. "How are you feeling about this, Kam?"

She shook her head. "Why didn't you tell me?" she asked, hearing the hurt in her voice.

He reached for her hand, and she immediately pulled it away. She didn't want to touch him. Not now.

"I'm sorry," he said. "I hated keeping this from you. But your father was insistent. He wanted to surprise you. But I can see you're upset. You didn't deserve being blindsided like this. I owe you a huge apology."

She snorted. "Yeah, I'm upset. But you don't owe me anything. We're just friends, right? Or...business associates?" A realization hit her. "You didn't tell me this because you were afraid I would talk Dad out of it. You wanted his HNS shares, didn't you?"

Rohan stepped closer to her. "Kam, no! You can't possibly think that about me!"

She shook her head. "I don't know what to think. I thought I knew you. And I thought you knew me. But if you really knew me"—her voice cracked—"you'd have known that this is the last thing I'd want. I've told you I can't work at HNS. I've told you how much I love Emerald. But apparently you weren't listening."

"Kam, no, I really—"

"I don't know why I'm surprised. This isn't a friendship. I'm just...entertainment for you."

He didn't say anything. That was all the answer Kamila needed. She saw the car pull up.

"You know what? Fuck you, Rohan Nasser. Friends don't keep secrets this big. Don't tell Dad I'm pissed off. At least *he* gets to be happy about this."

She got into the car and didn't turn back.

☂

The second Asha opened the door after Kamila knocked, Potato ran out. Thankfully, Asha was holding the other end of his leash.

"Potato!" Kamila said, reaching for the puppy. "What are you doing here?" She looked up at Asha. "Oh my god, is Potato okay? Is the bad news about him?"

"No, he's fine. We're trying to get the puppies used to homes before they're adopted. And I thought you might need him tonight, so I went and grabbed him."

Kamila hugged Potato close as she walked in and kicked off her shoes. Asha was right, as always. She did need Potato tonight.

Asha gave Kamila a once-over after taking her coat. "You look terrible. What happened? Oh my god—you already know."

"Know what?"

"The reason I called you over."

Kamila had literally forgotten it was Asha who asked her to come over. Her mind had been racing the whole way over with five words...*I'm in love with Rohan.* She hadn't thought of much else.

Kamila frowned. "Oh my god, you *also* knew about Emerald?"

"What? No. What happened to Emerald? Oh my god, is your Dad okay?"

"Ladies," Nicole called from the other room. "You're going to give each other whiplash. Ease up with the *oh my god*s. I made mulled wine."

Smart woman, that Nicole. It was handy to have someone so levelheaded in her circle of friends. Kamila took a breath to steady herself and followed Asha to the living room. The fire was lit, and after Potato greeted Lizzy, he came back and flopped on Kamila's foot to chew on a rope toy. Kamila picked the puppy up.

Nicole raised a brow as she placed a mug near Kamila's seat. "You look like you've been crying." She handed her a box of tissues, too.

"Yeah...I just..." She put the puppy next to her so she could take a tissue. "I've had a massive realization...and...fu..." Her voice trailed off as she looked at Asha, eyes welling again.

Asha took her hand. "Holy crap—this is big, Kamila. You almost swore there."

"Actually, I just said *duck you* to someone. Except I didn't say *duck*, but instead a word that rhymes with it."

"Whoa. What the hell happened?" Asha asked.

She blinked, looking into her friend's big eyes for strength. "I think...I..." She trembled. "I'm sorry," she said, sniffling. "I think I've fallen in love with my friend."

The room was silent. Except for the low hum of Lizzy snoring.

Asha's eyes comically darted toward Nicole and back to Kamila. Her hand tightened on Kamila's. "*Shit*. So...I didn't know you felt this way. You know you mean a lot to me, right? But I'm married. In fact, you set me up."

Kamila blinked, realizing what Asha was thinking. "Holy Jesus on a cracker, Asha!" She snorted a laugh, which was an unfortunate reaction while sniffling from crying. A snot bubble landed on her sweater, which made her laugh more. "Not you! I'm not in love with you, you nitwit!" She dabbed her sweater with a tissue.

Asha burst out laughing as well. "Obviously! I made you laugh, though, didn't I?" Soon, Asha and Kamila were both giggling while Potato barked at the commotion. Lizzy even raised his head up to see what the heck was going on.

"Are you sure you're not in love with her?" Nicole said loudly. "Because you two might be made for each other."

Still laughing, Asha stood and went to Nicole, kissing her soundly on the lips and telling her wife exactly who was made for who in this room. She sat back down, took Kamila's hand again, and squeezed. "But seriously, what's going on, Kamila?"

Kamila put her head back on the sofa. "I'm...I don't know. I thought we were friends. I've been spending a lot of time with him lately, and we've become so close...but he's been lying to me."

"Hold up, Kamila," Asha said. "Before you say anything else..." She looked nervously at her wife. "I have a feeling I know who you're talking about, but just in case it's this other person...will you let us tell you our news first?"

Kamila scratched Potato's ear. "Okaaay..."

Asha smiled uncomfortably, then looked at Nicole. "I think it's best coming from you."

Nicole nodded. "You understand doctor-patient privilege, right?"

"Of course." Kamila frowned. What did that have to do with anything?

"Okay," Nicole said. "There is something I've known for a while, but I haven't told anyone because of doctor-patient privilege. This isn't about an actual patient of mine, but of a colleague. Today Asha picked me up from the clinic because my car was being serviced, and a person we all know was there waiting for an ultrasound."

"Who's pregnant?" Kamila asked.

Asha put her hand out. "Just to make sure you know this, she, the pregnant person, knows we're telling you this. She actually asked us to tell you. She's showing pretty obviously, and she said she was planning to announce it soon anyway."

"Asha, who is pregnant?"

"Jana Suleiman."

Kamila's hand shot to her mouth. Jana was pregnant! That's why she'd been so cranky and irritable!

Kamila said the first thought that came to her mind. "That is going to be one gorgeous baby." Then a second realization hit her. "She left her fancy job in Central Asia because she was knocked up? This is Anil's friend's baby, right? Her boss at the aid agency. That's why she left."

"Actually"—Nicole looked at Asha—"I *did* know she was pregnant, but I didn't know who the father was until today. Like I said, not my patient, not my business. But the father was with her at the clinic this afternoon for their four-month scan. It's not her old boss—it's someone we all also know well. Someone you have spent a lot of time with lately…"

Kamila blinked, in shock. *Rohan.*

Impossible. It couldn't be him. This couldn't be happening. Then again, she'd learned, tonight actually, that Rohan Nasser wasn't who she thought he was. He was more than willing to keep things from Kamila.

He'd been so protective of Jana lately. Mysterious chats.

Spending time with her. Dinners. He knew things only Jana could have told him. Jana had been in his apartment—somewhere even Kamila had never even been.

Would Rohan kiss Kamila when he knew Jana was pregnant with his child? Earlier today she wouldn't have thought he was capable of that. But the last hour had given her a proper education on the limits of men's terribleness.

Kamila felt like throwing up. "No..." she whispered.

Asha cringed. "I'm sorry. I'm not sure what's been going on between you two since—"

"I...think I'm going to be sick," Kamila said. "Rohan and Jana are having a child."

Asha recoiled. "What? Did I say Rohan? Wasn't he at your house for dinner? How could he be at the clinic at the same time?"

Kamila frowned. Right. "My brain hadn't gone that far yet." It wasn't Rohan. She exhaled, relief washing over her. She was still incredibly angry with him, and she had no intention of being friends with him anymore. But she wouldn't have been able to deal with him having a child with Jana. That would have been too much. "So, who *is* the father?"

"Anil," Nicole said. "Anil Malek is the father."

Kamila's jaw dropped. That was...monumentally unexpected. "*Anil?* Are you serious?"

Asha nodded. "I'm sorry, Kamila. I mean, I know things have been weird for you lately, and maybe you thought you and Anil could have something after that whole mess with Rohan."

Of course. Kamila wasn't really into Anil...but how would anyone know that? Especially since she'd been flirting with the man so much at Bollywood nights.

Kamila felt like a fool. Anil had flirted back. Was he playing her?

"This sucks," Kamila said, lifting the puppy back up. Potato promptly starting eating the tissue in her lap.

"I'm so sorry," Asha said.

That snapped Kamila out of it. "Asha, no. Don't worry—I'm not, like, heartbroken or anything over Anil. I'm not interested in him like that." She frowned. "Did you think I was talking about him when I got here? I've only known Anil for a few weeks."

"I thought there was a chance, and...So there is nothing going on between you two?"

Kamila shook her head. "I was flattered by his attention, and maybe I was subconsciously trying to make Rohan jealous..." *Whoa*—make Rohan jealous? Where did that come from...? Kamila put it aside to examine later and got back to this bombshell. "I shouldn't have flirted with him so much in front of everyone. Him, too. I could tell that Anil never wanted more, and neither did I. But we are...*were* friends. Also, *holy carrot cake*, Anil and Jana are *together*? Like *secretly having a baby together* together?"

Nicole shook her head. "No, I don't think they are. I don't actually think they're on great terms. We'll have to wait for details if we want more information on how this all happened."

Asha turned to her wife, smirking. "Nicole, I know you've never been with a man, but as an obstetrician, you should know this. When a man and a woman really like each other, they have this special kind of hug—"

Nicole threw a pillow at her wife.

"Anil is married," Kamila remembered, trying to work through timelines. "It's only been a few months since he separated."

Asha cringed. "I don't want to speculate or gossip, but I'd bet there was overlap."

"You literally just speculated and gossiped, Asha," Nicole said. Asha waved her hand.

"This is so messed up," Kamila said, getting angrier as she thought about all their interactions over the last few weeks. "The things he said to Jana! That stupid game of Never Have I Ever! And he drew me into it, too. I need to apologize to her. He was using me to get back at her or something. Ugh. Here we were for weeks thinking we were all friends...Poor Jana. Anil is the same as the rest of them. I don't want to do that big party for his incubator thing on Saturday anymore. Or take his organization as a long-term Emerald client."

Kamila bit her lip. That didn't matter anyway. Emerald, as it was now, wasn't going to exist much longer.

"I'm profoundly disappointed in them both," Asha said.

"No, not Jana." Kamila shook her head. "I mean, she's the same old Jana—snooty, condescending, and kinda crabby—but I have no doubt Anil manipulated her. He *wanted* me to think Jana had an affair with her boss, when it was him the whole time! What a complete dingus! How could he say those things to the mother of his child? He's the utter worst...He makes Octopus Dane seem like a saint." Kamila slouched in her seat. "I'm so done with men right now. All of them." She took a gulp of her drink.

"You're welcome to join our team," Nicole offered.

"I tried that in college. It was quite lovely, but it didn't take." She took another gulp. A long one. She looked at Potato playing next to her. Why couldn't people be more like dogs? Dogs never had secrets or ulterior motives. Nothing but complete, earnest devotion. She wiped an errant tear that had escaped.

Asha said softly, "Kamila, what happened earlier tonight?"

Kamila exhaled. "Other men have been lying to me, too."

"Rohan?"

Asha knew her. She knew few people could upset her this much.

Kamila sighed. "Not just Rohan. Dad too. I don't even know how to think about what they told me tonight."

She told Asha and Nicole everything. The fact that Dad had been planning for months to sell his HNS shares and close Emerald. The fact that this plan was already in the works when Kamila made the deal with him to take on Anil's account so Dad would go part-time. All that had been just a "placate Kamila" project—they didn't care if she could secure the Aim High project or not. They just wanted to shut her up so they could continue to close Emerald without telling her. And they assumed she would be happy about it.

They hadn't trusted her to know what she wanted with her own life.

Asha was as shocked as Kamila had been. "I've seen how dedicated you are to Emerald! To everything you do."

"Yeah, well, apparently the men in my life think I'm a flighty, frivolous, worthless nothing." She exhaled. "I get it, sort of. Dad has a lot of guilt over how Mom treated me when I was a teenager. He thinks everything I do for Emerald is out of loyalty to him. And now he thinks he's releasing me from that burden. The worst part…" Kamila sniffled. "The worst part is Dad is *happy*. He's really happy. He's healthy, and his stress is low. I wanted him to go part-time, but maybe an early retirement is even better. I never imagined he'd be willing to do this, but it could be great for him. How can I be upset?"

"Kamila, you have every right to be upset. They should have discussed this with you. They should have asked you what you wanted," Nicole said.

Kamila shrugged.

"This is just like men of his generation," Asha said. "Always underestimating their daughters. It's why I barely speak to my own father. Your dad should be giving Emerald to you, not closing it. Are you sure you don't want to work at HNS?"

Kamila shook her head. "Absolutely sure. I hated it when I worked there before. Not all the associates there are men, but most are. I'm just not interested in working in a vat of testosterone...I'd rather *not* have to fight to be heard every moment of my day. And I love Emerald. I just helped Ink Girls secure that loan to open a new location, and Maricel and I are ready to start submitting grant applications for her puppy school." Ugh. She couldn't imagine Maricel or any of her clients going downtown to the financial district to meet with their accountants. "The worst part is Rohan. He..." She looked down at her hands. "Maybe everything he did for me and Dad was just so he could get Dad's HNS shares."

"I don't think that's true, Kamila. Rohan's the person you were talking about earlier, right?"

Kamila nodded.

"And that kiss a few weeks ago wasn't as meaningless as you claimed it was?" Asha asked softly.

"Wow, wait," Nicole said, eyes wide. "You and Rohan kissed. Like, *kissed* kissed?"

Kamila snorted through her tears. Man was she glad she'd come here. She looked at Asha. "Do you and your wife ever talk when you're alone?"

Asha shrugged. "We're newlyweds. We mostly have sex when we're alone. So, you finally admit you have feelings for Rohan?"

Kamila sighed. "Yes. But...it's one-sided. Even if he cared about me, he doesn't *see* me, not really, or he wouldn't have done this. He was just tolerating whatever 'kooky Kamila' did next. *I* kissed him...twice...He's never initiated anything. I call him more than he calls me. He's never even invited me to his condo. Jana has been there, but not me. He doesn't care, not like I do." She wiped her eyes and took another sip of her wine.

"And what about you?" Asha said. "Are you sure? Are you really in love with him?"

Kamila closed her eyes. She remembered a few hours ago, when she'd wanted nothing more than to wrap her arms around him. She remembered the way she could just look at his face and be three hundred times happier. How hard she worked to get him to smile. How comfortable she was sleeping wrapped in his arms. She remembered his forearms, and his low chuckles while they made momos together. Her delight at seeing him in his bed when she'd video called late at night. And she remembered his mouth all over her body.

This wasn't a new thing. She'd always loved him. But something changed in the last month. She'd *fallen in love* with him. And Kamila didn't know what to do with that.

"I'm sure," she said quietly. "I love him." She wiped her tears. Only, he didn't really see her at all.

"Oh, Kamila," Asha said as she put her arms around her. Kamila gave in and cried properly.

CHAPTER 23

I t went without saying that Kamila wasn't really feeling Bollywood night on Friday. Face all her friends and pretend
everything was fine? Who would come anyway? Now that Jana's
pregnancy was out in the open, maybe she wouldn't want to pretend everything was normal by socializing with people she
clearly didn't like. And Anil? Kamila had no intention of letting
that snake into her house. Not that he'd come anyway, since
there was no longer any reason for him to be charming and make
Jana jealous.

And what about Rohan? She made it clear yesterday she was
done with his so-called friendship.

Wow—she'd lost a lot of friends in one day. She called Asha.

"Negative," Asha said after Kamila suggested canceling.

"What?"

"You're not canceling Bollywood night. Not an option. We'll
watch a tearjerker. It will take your mind off everything."

"I'm not having Tim and Jerome and Maricel and everyone
over to see me cry because I'm an idiot."

"You're not an idiot. You're in love."

"Same thing."

"Fine, tell everyone you're not feeling it. But Nicole and I are still coming over. We'll bring the food. I'm not leaving you alone. We're renaming it 'Bollywood Heartbreak Recovery by Eating Ice Cream' for one night only."

"What about Rohan? Is he invited?" Kamila didn't want to see him. Probably.

"Kamila, I know you usually do casual over serious relationships, but when a girl invites her friends over to help her get over a failed romance, it's normally not customary to invite the object of her affections, too. No matter how bad she has it."

"I know, I know. I'm just...He'll be upset." Despite everything, she just wasn't used to upsetting Rohan.

"Who cares how he feels! He was fine threatening your friendship by lying. If you don't want him to know that your feelings have...evolved, that's fine. But now isn't the time to be more concerned about *his* feelings than yours."

Asha was right. Kamila sent out a group email, telling her friends that because she had such a busy weekend, she was canceling movie night this week.

And exactly as expected, Rohan texted her minutes after she sent the email.

Rohan: Can I still come over? I was hoping we could talk.

She wanted to say yes. She wanted to gloss over their problems, to not hold a grudge, and make sure he was okay. Because that's what she'd always done—made sure others were comfortable.

She knew she did that. She knew she was doing it with Dad right now. Asha was right—she was a people pleaser down to her core. All she wanted was for everyone to be happy to have her in their lives.

Kamila: I'm not actually canceling Bollywood night. I'm significantly reducing the guest list. Only my closest friends tonight.

He didn't write back right away. Finally, the text came.

Rohan: And I'm not included.

Kamila took a deep breath before writing back.

Kamila: No.

Rohan: Kam, I'm sorry. You have to understand I'm only doing what your father wanted.

Kamila: I get why you did it. But I'm allowed to be upset that neither of you consulted me.

Rohan: Can I call you at least?

Kamila: No. I depended on you to help me with Dad, and I am grateful. But he's doing well. I don't need you anymore, Rohan.

Kamila squeezed her eyes shut as she sent those words. They were true. She *wanted* him...or at least she wanted who she thought he was. But she didn't *need* him.

Rohan: Don't do this, Kam. Please.

She didn't text back. She put her phone aside and went back to drying her hair. After a few minutes, he texted again.

Rohan: Kamila, I'm sorry. I really, really am. I hope you'll talk to me at the Aim High party tomorrow.

Kamila tossed her phone aside and turned her hair dryer back on. How was she going to face Rohan at that blasted cocktail party anyway? And not just Rohan—Anil, too. And all those irritating Aim High board members. Maybe she should skip the whole thing and spend the day at the Dogapalooza where her real friends were.

But she wouldn't. She'd made a commitment. And even though she didn't want to be anywhere near Rohan Nasser or

Anil Malek, this was still a good cause. And a part of her wanted to prove that she *could* be the fancy accountant they thought she couldn't be—not to anyone else, but to herself.

Bollywood Heartbreak Recovery by Eating Ice Cream night turned out to be just what the doctor ordered. Specifically, in this case, an ob-gyn who had wonderful taste in ice cream. They ate take-out palak paneer, dal makhani, and naan, then sampled from the several hand-packed gourmet pints Nicole had brought. Kamila couldn't decide if the orange cardamom or the London fog was better. The milk tea boba flavor would have been her top choice, but it reminded her of Rohan, so she'd only had one taste. And as for movies, at the last minute, she'd chosen a frothy rom-com because she didn't think she could handle a tearjerker.

"Why the heck did I pick a friends-to-lovers movie? This is cruel and unusual punishment," Kamila said grumpily. The movie was billed as a Bollywood *When Harry Met Sally*. Two people finding love after years of friendship.

Asha shrugged. "I think your subconscious has been affecting your movie choices."

Kamila clutched a cushion. "Humph."

During a long song, the hero and heroine emerged wearing new outfits. "I always wondered if when the couple had a clothing change midsong, it was meant to imply they'd had sex," Kamila said.

Asha laughed. "I used to think Indians didn't have sex or even kiss because it never happened in movies. I was shocked when I caught my brother making out with my babysitter when I was nine."

Another clothing and set change in the song made Kamila

sad. "Rohan would have loved this one. There's nothing that turns him on more than a singing-in-the-rain song. Wet saris always crank his shaft." The actor and actress were dancing so close that Kamila really hoped they'd been tested for STIs. She fanned herself with her hand. "This is so hot." She sank down in her seat. "I miss sex. Maybe I need a rebound."

Nicole looked at Kamila. "I don't really understand what went down with you and Rohan. You claim he never saw you that way, but yet he told you what cranked his shaft, so to speak?"

"He doesn't see me that way."

"Sure, he does," Asha said. "Did you forget the second-base incident?"

"What's second base again?" Nicole asked. "I haven't been sixteen in a long time."

Asha giggled. "Remember this morning when we woke up and you—"

"Can we *not* right now?" Kamila said, pointing to the movie. "Oh. I think these two just found second base."

The scraps of sari still wrapped around the actress were now completely plastered to her wet body, and the actor's lips seemed to be enjoying her damp skin. Kamila wondered if she'd ever see Rohan turn pink watching a wet sari again.

There was a knock on the door. "That had better not be him," Kamila said.

"I'll get it." Asha stood. "Want me to get rid of him if it's Rohan?"

"Yes, please." The rain scene was over anyway, so there was nothing for him here. "Anil too. And Dane. No male-identifying humans allowed! Dogs are okay."

Asha opened the door.

It was a pretty small house, so Kamila could hear what sounded like a feminine voice. Kamila shouted out to Asha. "If it's a woman or a nonbinary person, invite them in! There's plenty of ice cream! There's wine somewhere, too!"

The person who walked into the living room really shouldn't be drinking wine, though. Jana Suleiman.

Kamila tried not to narrow her eyes menacingly, but old habits died hard. "Hello, Jana."

"My mother saw me sneaking out of the house, so she insisted I bring you some biryani on my way," Jana said, holding out a Saran-wrapped plate.

"Oh." Kamila said, eyeing it. "We weren't supposed to be doing the biryani thing tonight." Homemade was better than store-bought, though. And biryani was probably the only food that Kamila could never get tired of eating. She took the plate. "Too bad there's no biryani ice cream. That would have worked with tonight's theme."

Asha cringed. "Ew. I hate fusion biryani."

Kamila put the biryani on the dining table and looked at Jana. This was the first time Kamila had seen Jana since finding out she was pregnant, and to be honest, Kamila couldn't believe she hadn't figured it out earlier. Jana had been wearing baggy pants and tops since coming back to town, and she had ridiculously glowing skin. Because of course perfect Jana would even do pregnancy perfectly.

"Where were you sneaking out to?" Maybe to see her baby's father?

"Just a café. Mom's having her card party, and I needed to escape the judging aunties and uncles."

Asha gave Kamila a look. She knew what her friend meant—

she was telling Kamila to be nice. That it must be terrible to be an unwed, pregnant Indian woman at a party full of aunties and uncles. Well, Asha didn't have to say it. Or imply it in this case. Kamila totally sympathized.

"Don't go to a café," Kamila said, sitting back on the sofa. "Hang with us—we've retitled tonight's party Bollywood Heartbreak Recovery by Eating Ice Cream night. The only rule is we're not allowing male members of the human species in tonight, because we plan to bash them pretty harshly."

Jana chuckled, then rubbed her belly. "Well, it's a good thing this is a girl, then. I'll stay if you really don't mind."

Kamila grinned, patting the spot next to her on the sofa. "You're having a girl? Can you even imagine how stunning this child will be?"

Jana raised a brow.

"Did you eat?" Nicole asked. "Let me make you a plate."

Once they were all satisfied Jana had food and drink, Kamila looked at her. "So…" Jana hadn't mentioned Anil yet, and Kamila wasn't sure she wanted to be the first to say something, but she really wanted to know the details of how Jana came to be carrying his child. "So…" she tried again. "Pregnant, eh?"

Jana sighed. "Yes, I'm pregnant. Four months along. Yes, Anil Malek is the father. Yes, I'm keeping the baby, but no, I'm not marrying Anil. And finally, yes, he asked me, but I said no."

Kamila's eyes widened. "Were those the questions the judging aunties asked?"

"Yes, but they were accompanied by disapproving tsks and scowls."

"Well, I'm not judging you." Kamila took a spoonful of toasted marshmallow before clarifying that statement. "Well, I am, because I always judge you and probably always will, but not for this situation specifically. I don't think less of you for having a baby. Personally, I prefer dogs, but to each their own."

Jana narrowed her eyes, looking at the melting pints on the table. "How much ice cream do you guys have?"

Kamila frowned, collecting a few of the pints and taking them to the freezer. Not all, though. She still needed some. "Doctor's orders. It's the primary treatment plan for Bollywood Heartbreak Recovery by Eating Ice Cream."

Jana scowled. "I hope this heartbreak is not over Anil. He is *not* worth a sugar crash. And I warned you about him."

"Oh my god, no." Kamila sat back down and shook her head vigorously. "No, it's not Anil I'm heartbroken over." She sighed. "I'm sorry, Jana. I let Anil manipulate me to get to you."

"So, he's not the reason you're upset?"

"No. We didn't have anything going on, honest. We were friends. Tell her, Asha. My heartbreak is because of . . . someone else."

Asha nodded. "Yeah, what she said. Someone else."

Kamila sat up straight, deciding this conversation was straying too close to Rohan, and she didn't want to be close to Rohan, even though she very much did want to be close to Rohan.

"Okay, not judging—honestly—but curious," Kamila said. "What happened with you and Anil? He asked you to marry him?"

"He did the gentlemanly thing when I told him I was pregnant—I only told him yesterday so he could come to that ultrasound. We had a thing . . . an affair." The word made Jana cringe. "I'm not proud of it. My birth control failed because I was on antibiotics for a sinus infection and I didn't think."

"He was married."

"Yeah. But he told me he was separated at the time. He failed to tell his wife that, though. He was very...charming. I moved back to Toronto to have the baby, and I had no intention of telling him I was pregnant. But when he heard I was moving here, he changed his plans to come here, too—lord only knows why. To torture me, I think."

"I thought he came to start the incubator."

Jana shook her head. "Technically, yes. But the original plan was to do it in Washington. He moved it to Toronto because I would be here."

Kamila took another spoonful of ice cream. "You sure you don't want any of this? It's working wonders."

Jana frowned. "Maybe later."

"Why are you having the baby?"

Asha glared at Kamila for asking such a personal question. But what Asha didn't get was that this was Jana. They may not have ever been friends, but they weren't strangers, either.

Jana rubbed her belly. "I'm having her because I want her. Kamila, you ever feel like people only see you as one thing?" She looked at the ceiling a moment. "That you aren't allowed to be anyone other than what they expect you to be? *Jana Suleiman can't be an unwed mother! Unthinkable!*"

Boy, did Kamila ever understand that. Too well. But she had no idea that Jana ever felt stifled by her image of perfection.

"But to have a child just to rebel against their expectations?"

Jana shrugged. "She's mine. I get to raise this person. To nurture and shape her and help her be whoever she wants to be. I'm having her because I want her, not because it's expected of me."

"You're raising her alone?"

"I was planning to. But it's only fair to give Anil a chance to be a parent. We'll see. But I'm also getting my custody arrangements and child support sorted out, too. Rohan's been a big help with legal advice."

Kamila couldn't help it—she yelped. Darcy, concerned her owner might be in distress, was at Kamila's feet immediately. "Oh my god, *that's* why you've been meeting with Rohan!" She looked at Asha. "Asha, Rohan knew! That's why Jana was in his condo! That's why he was so concerned about her!"

Jana raised one brow. "Um, yeah. He's the only person in Toronto I told until yesterday. I needed him to help me find a family-law lawyer and... Wait—did you think there was something going on between me and Rohan? Holy shit, I think I figured out who you're heartbroken over. It's Rohan, isn't it?"

Kamila frowned, picking up Darcy and hugging her. "No comment."

"It is!" Jana smiled widely. "*Finally*! You're in love with Rohan! You don't have to worry there. Rohan and I are just friends. I've known him forever."

"I've known all of you forever," Kamila said.

Nicole put her hand up. "Not us... we're new here. But please carry on. This is better than a Bollywood drama."

"I did once wonder if we could be more, though," Jana said. "I mean, Rohan is such a great guy—handsome, kind, really quite annoyingly perfect."

"You are way more annoying with your perfection," Kamila said.

"Thank you," Jana said. "Anyway, a while ago I thought maybe I should, you know, see if there was anything there... Then I realized he would never look at me the way he looked at you, and I didn't want to put myself through that."

"I don't know what you're talking about," Kamila said.

"Oh, come on, Kamila. Don't give me that fake modesty. I see right through it all. Anyone could see, even when we were kids, that he was completely fascinated with you. But since I got back to Toronto? It's so obvious he has it really bad. He's *obsessed* with you."

That was impossible. It just wasn't true. "Did he tell you that?" Kamila asked.

"No, but I can tell. He cares about you a lot."

"That's what I've been telling her," Asha said.

Kamila shook her head. "Well, if Rohan freaking Nasser cares about me so much, then why the heck has he been keeping something huge from me? Something that directly affects me and my life. Why wouldn't he have faith in my ability to know what I want?"

"Wow, you almost swore there, Kamila Husscin. Seems you have it bad, too," Jana said smugly. Kamila remembered why she'd never liked this woman.

Kamila crossed her arms on her chest. "Everyone sees me as a flighty, frivolous, superficial pixie. I work my butt off at Emerald and in my volunteer jobs, and everyone assumes I'd rather be dressing up my dog. I can care about pretty clothes and designer furniture *and* about my clients. I thought Rohan understood that. I thought Dad did, too, but they wouldn't have done this if they had."

"What exactly did they do?" Jana asked.

Should she tell Jana Suleiman about her troubles? About her insecurities, about her family's betrayal? This was her nemesis, right?

But whatever was in this ice cream took away her filter. She told Jana everything.

"Wow," Jana said when Kamila was done. "I'd be angry, too. They're closing your business. Can't you just tell them not to?"

"I mean, I could...but Dad is doing well. Retirement is a good idea. He'd be devastated if he found out I wasn't happy. I mean, if he owned Emerald outright, I would tell him to peace out and I'll keep the office going, but it's owned by HNS. And I do *not* want to work with HNS."

Jana sank down in her seat. "I don't blame you. That place is a total sausage fest."

Huh. Kamila wouldn't have imagined that Jana would use the term *sausage fest*. Also, she seemed to understand Kamila. Maybe she'd underestimated her nemesis.

"And Rohan knew I didn't want to work at HNS."

Jana shook her head. "I take back what I said about him. He's as bad as the rest. Stupid men."

"Let's start a women's commune," Asha said.

"Ooh, yes—let's!" Nicole agreed.

Kamila chuckled. "Of course that's what the lesbians want." She got up to get another pint of ice cream, since she'd finished the one she was working on. "I'm unfortunately not willing to give up men altogether. But I'm going back to casual only. Feelings aren't worth it."

She hadn't been on any dating apps since Ernesto left, but it was time to switch her status back to "looking."

CHAPTER 24

The two-day Dogapalooza was part carnival, part festival, and a celebration of all things dogs. It had been one of Kamila's favorite community festivals long before she even started volunteering at the shelter. This year's event was going to be even more epic than usual, with bigger and better vendors, dog obstacle courses, a large ball pit, silent auctions, and more. All ending with her baby—the puppy prom on Sunday. It all should have been more than enough to keep Kamila's mind off everything, but there was just way too much going on, and she found it hard to look forward to the event.

She tried to be light and breezy with Dad at breakfast. She still didn't want him knowing how upset she was about his news on Thursday. He was so giddy, eating his yogurt parfait and drinking his green tea while showing her pictures of the activities area of his new condo in Florida. She was pretty sure he didn't notice her foul mood. After finishing her breakfast, she dressed, packed up the outfit to wear to the canine couture fashion show, put Darcy in her yellow sundress, and kissed Dad on the forehead. She headed for the festival.

Kamila wandered the green space behind the shelter where

the event was being held. She did some shopping, let Darcy play in the dog ball pit, and chatted with a few friends. After having a hot dog with Tim and Jerome, she found Maricel at the dog-and-car wash. Maricel's clothes were completely soaked, but she looked thrilled to be helping unruly, and wet, dogs clean cars.

"Hi, Kamila! I'm glad I found you!"

Darcy pulled on her leash to try and hop into the tub of soapy water, but Kamila wasn't having that. She held her dog tight.

"I meant to call you last night," Maricel continued, leaning down to greet Darcy. "But I was here so late making decorations for today. The Dogapalooza is packed! Did you see my email?"

Kamila frowned, pulling out her phone. She hadn't checked her email this morning, mostly because she assumed Rohan would choose that format to send her a long, drawn-out rationale for why he'd done what he'd done. She owed Rohan a lot and fully intended to listen to his side of things, but not quite yet. She needed to get through this weekend first. Opening her mail app, she saw that, yup—there was an email from Rohan. She didn't open it. She opened the one from Maricel instead and skimmed it briefly, but she couldn't make sense of it. Probably because Darcy was still pulling on her harness, so Kamila couldn't keep her phone steady.

"What's this about, Maricel?"

"That lady we talked to last week at East End New Business Development called me yesterday. She remembered me and really liked my business plan. They have an unexpected opening for a start-up in a co-op space, and it comes with a new business grant. The deadline for the application is Monday. She even said she'd look over my application for me if I applied. But I'd need a business license and I'd have to be willing to open in a month."

Kamila grinned. "That's awesome! Send in the application! Opportunities like this are rare!"

Maricel shook her head. "I can't get a business license in two days. We need more time, don't we?"

"You can't get a license in two days, but you *can* in a month. Call her back—see if you can still get the grant as long as the business license comes through before the grand opening."

A very wet, very large Bernese mountain dog charged at Maricel then. Kamila took a step back so she wouldn't get wet.

After Maricel subdued the beast-like dog (Maricel was just so good at dog obedience), she agreed to call the woman about the grant and let Kamila know what she said.

"By the way," Kamila said, "I heard you're dating."

"Oh." Maricel blushed, then let out a bashful giggle. "It's just starting. I...I don't want to talk about it and jinx it yet. But I'm hoping he'll come to the puppy prom tomorrow. He's having a lot of family problems right now, though, so I don't know."

Kamila grinned. "I hope he can come, too. But I won't pry. I'm really happy for you."

It was almost time for the fashion show by then, so Kamila left Darcy with Asha and headed inside the shelter to change into her emceeing dress.

As she was touching up her makeup, her phone rang. She checked the screen. Rohan.

Reluctantly, she answered it.

"You didn't read my email, did you?" His voice was clipped. Annoyed? Still, though, it made her shiver.

"Hello to you, too." She had to force the deadpan tone in her voice.

"Kamila, I know you hate me, but I really need to speak to you. Can we meet before the party tonight?"

She exhaled slowly. "I don't hate you, Rohan." She didn't. She loved him. But she was so angry. Hopefully the anger would help the pesky being-in-love-with-him thing to go away soon. "And I can't come early. I'm emceeing the canine couture show in ten minutes."

"The what?"

"The dog fashion show? It's one of those silly Kamila things that I do. I'll have a ton more time to do things like this soon, thanks to you."

"Kamila..." She heard him sigh. He sounded...wounded. He clearly wanted to explain himself. To fix things. Because that was his nature. This was just guilt. He was a stand-up guy.

But there was no way to fix this. Not now, with Dad so happy.

"Look, I need to go, Rohan."

"Are you coming to the Aim High party at all?" he asked.

"Of course I'm coming. I made a commitment. I'll be there to help set up the room with you at six." As much as she didn't want to, she'd be at that damn party. Then she wouldn't have to see Anil, or the rest of the Aim High team, ever again. That was one benefit of Emerald being absorbed into HNS.

It hit her again. Emerald, as she knew it, wouldn't exist anymore. She shook her head—she just did her makeup. She couldn't cry again.

"Okay. We'll talk while we set up the room. If you get a chance before, take a look at the email, okay?"

"Fine. If I get the chance. Bye, Rohan."

Kamila touched up her eyes, put on a bold-red lipstick, and headed back outside to emcee the fashion show.

Because the show must go on.

After the dogs all finished walking the catwalk (dogwalk?), Kamila rushed out to her car in the shelter parking lot. She had to get home and change as quick as possible to make it downtown by six.

"Kamila!" A voice behind her said. Kamila turned and saw Maricel running toward her.

"The woman said I should apply!" Maricel said breathlessly when she reached her. "It's due Monday morning, but she said that if I send her my application tomorrow, she'll look over it before submitting it to the board by the deadline. She's really nice! She loves dogs! Are you free to go over it now? It's kind of confusing."

Kamila checked the time. She really needed to get home, like, five minutes ago. "How about tomorrow morning? The prom's not till three—I'm completely free before that."

Maricel shook her head. "I won't be free. I'm working the Dogapalooza all morning until the prom. Thankfully, I'm on photo booth duty instead of the dog wash, so I'll be drier. It's okay—I'll try to figure it out myself."

Kamila knew these grant applications were complicated. She almost offered to come by after the Aim High party to help Maricel...but she stopped herself.

Why?

Why was she still busting her butt doing what everyone wanted her to do? This fancy cocktail party for an Emerald client didn't even matter anymore, did it? She was tired of pretending to be someone she wasn't to impress Anil and the rest of the Aim

High board. And for what? To help an adulterous philanthropist look good and show her family she could be serious, even though they would never change how they saw her anyway.

Because no matter how hard she worked for people, people would only see her as Kamila. And clearly for some, Kamila wasn't enough.

But Kamila *was* enough for her own clients. For people like Maricel who trusted her to make her dream come true.

Kamila relocked her car with the key fob. "Let's do it now, Maricel. My party can wait. Let's get you your business grant." They headed back into the shelter so they could use Asha's computer to fill out the grant application. She texted Rohan from there, telling him that she'd been held up with a client, and hopefully he could manage setting up without her. She didn't get a response.

☂

It was past six by the time they finished the application. Kamila was sure it would be approved—the puppy academy was a fantastic concept and absolutely perfect for the cooperative space and for the neighborhood it was in. Kamila didn't stick around to celebrate with Maricel, though. She may have bailed on setting up the party room, but it wasn't in her to just skip the party altogether. Maricel agreed to take Darcy home for her, and Kamila drove straight to the Aim High cocktail party downtown.

It was after seven when she finally walked into the already-pretty-full party room. She lingered in the doorway—she could see most of the board of directors, including Anil and that insufferable Marlene. It took her a bit longer, but she eventually spotted Rohan.

He was staring intently at his phone on the other side of the room. She'd last seen him two days ago—and in those two days she'd realized both that he meant more to her than anyone who wasn't a blood relative, and that despite saying he didn't underestimate her, he did exactly that.

Of course, he looked *good*, though. No one wore a suit like Rohan. She tilted her head and looked carefully. But lately his look was different. He was a bit less…severe. The new beard. Slightly more casual clothes. More modern tailoring to his suits. Even more color. Today's suit was charcoal, but his shirt was pale yellow. Yellow! On Rohan! And he wasn't even wearing a tie.

She wanted to go to him. She always wanted to be closer to him. Whether it was to straighten his tie, smooth his hair, or squeeze his arms, she'd constantly find reasons to let her skin come into contact with his. Being near him had always cheered her up, but considering her distress right now was because of him, he probably wasn't the right person to comfort her.

He looked up suddenly, noticing her. She half expected that wide, rare Rohan smile. Or even the small, secret Kamila-you're-incorrigible smile. But no. He stared a few moments, looking at her, his expression in its unreadable "corporate" mask.

What was he thinking, anyway? Maybe disapproving of her choice of attire for the party? She'd, of course, not changed into the respectable little black dress and was still wearing the dress she'd worn to the fashion show. In a rich glossy satin, the dress had a black off-the-shoulder and backless bodice and a full skirt. The skirt was printed in a bold floral with red, blue, and purple flowers, and if anyone looked closely, they'd see little dalmatian puppies peeking from behind the flowers. She was wearing it with a full black-lace crinoline and red patent T-strap heels. And instead of slicked back and "professional," her hair was open and curly, with nothing but a comb holding it back on one side. This was *not* how she'd intended to dress for this party, but she just didn't care anymore. She was going to be herself—the real Kamila. If anyone didn't approve, it was their issue, not hers.

Rohan slipped his phone into his pocket as he walked toward her.

"Kam, you're finally here."

"Is that a crack at me being late? I had a client crisis." She looked around the room. It looked great—or as great as a boring corporate party room could look. "You seem to have done fine without me."

He shook his head quickly. "No. It wasn't a crack. I'm glad you're here. Can we talk now?" He glanced around. The room was filling up. They'd need to schmooze soon. "Can we step into the lobby for five minutes?"

Kamila bit her lip, annoyed. "Why?"

"Hi, Kamila!" someone very perky said. Kamila turned around...and the perky person was Jana Suleiman? What? Why was Jana even here? And why was she being so...bubbly?

She looked radiant, as usual. She was wearing a slim red shift dress that did nothing to hide her emerging baby bump. And she had the perfect red lipstick to match. She kissed both of Kamila's cheeks—*weird*—then looked at Rohan.

"Rohan, good to see you," Jana said.

"I'm surprised to see you," he responded.

"Just here to support one of my oldest friends." She looped her arm through Kamila's. Was it normal to become a completely different person in the fourth month of pregnancy? Maybe it was the prenatal vitamins. "C'mon, Kamila. I see some people I know from the aid community here—I'll introduce you." And she pulled Kamila away from Rohan.

"What are you doing here?" Kamila asked after Rohan was a fair distance away.

"I asked Anil if I could come. I thought you might need an advocate. I knew you'd have no friends here."

Kamila frowned. "Are we friends?"

Jana shrugged. "We're comrades in arms right now."

"But Anil is here. And your colleagues. Aren't you worried about gossip?"

Jana smiled. "I'm not worried about gossip—I'm *expecting* it. People want me to hide away like a fallen, shamed woman. He's the one who was married, not me. I'm flipping the script on their expectations."

Kamila nodded, impressed. "You're a renegade. I like it."

"Thank you." Jana cringed. "Are those dogs on your dress? I'll never understand how you manage to pull off clothes like that."

Kamila laughed.

With Jana by her side, Kamila mingled with the crowd. The food was perfect. Anil's impassioned speech about the good work the incubator would do was probably effective, even if Jana rolled her eyes through it. Judging by the numerous donation forms being filled out in the room, it looked like the evening was a financial success, too.

It actually made Kamila feel good. As much as she didn't respect Anil anymore, and as much as she had discovered that all this work she'd done was useless for her, hearing Anil talk about the project gave her the warm fuzzies about the small part she'd played in raising the money. Helping people with their small businesses was Kamila's passion, and she loved that Aim High's mandate was to help refugees and newcomers make their dreams come true. Her bitterness about being here started to wash away. A little bit.

And to add to the night's positives, Rohan didn't approach her again. He seemed busy with his corporate buddies. Marlene did, though. Annoyingly.

"I'm surprised to see you," she said primly to Kamila. "You should thank me for arriving early enough to help Mr. Nasser deal with the caterers. Weren't you supposed to be here to let them know where to set up the food?"

She didn't understand why this woman called Rohan Mr. Nasser. And as if he weren't capable of telling a caterer where to put veggie platters. "I did let him know I had a work crisis."

"I was under the impression you were at a pet festival? What was the crisis...a flea outbreak?" She laughed at her own joke, then eyed the lower half of Kamila's dress. "Your skirt has dogs on it."

"So?" Kamila asked.

Marlene shook her head. "We're voting on whether or not to put your little firm on retainer for our financial needs at next week's board meeting. Personally, I believe it would be better for Aim High to work with a more reputable accounting agency. And now that I see that you're not truly dedicated to the cause of helping immigrants and refugees start their own businesses, I am sure it won't be hard to convince the rest of the board to look elsewhere for our financial administration needs."

Kamila thought about defending herself. After all, helping an immigrant start a new business was literally the reason Kamila was late tonight. But unlike Marlene, Kamila wasn't looking to earn a medal for doing it. This was just a party, and contrary to what Marlene believed, telling a caterer where to put food did not put them on par with Mother Teresa.

Kamila decided to be straight with Marlene instead of getting defensive.

"I know you don't like me, Marlene. And do you know what? I don't really care. I know I'm good at what I do. I don't need a judgmental wannabe socialite philanthropist with cat hair all over her pantsuit to validate my self-worth. Vote to retain Emerald, or don't vote for my firm. It won't make a difference to me, so there is no use holding it over my head. C'mon, Jana. Let's find someone more interesting to talk to."

Jana laughed as soon as they were out of earshot of Marlene. "You have to teach me to do that, Kamila."

Chin held high, she looped her arm through Jana's. "Stick with me, Suleiman. We'll tell off all our haters together."

Later, at a rare moment when Jana wasn't at her side, Anil found Kamila. There were too many people around for Kamila to throw her soda in his face, so she had to be nice, for the sake of Aim High.

"Kamila. You look beautiful as always."

She snorted. She'd worked so hard to impress him with sophisticated clothes, and he was just as complimentary with her in a dog-print dress with a frilly crinoline. "Anil. Looks like the evening's a success."

"Yes, thanks to you. I, um, I see you're here with Jana."

"I am. She looks great tonight, doesn't she?"

"She's always stunning," he said. "But...she'd probably not like me saying that."

Kamila tilted her head. "Really? I remember a time when you said she left her glow behind in Central Asia. Now she's *stunning*?"

He cringed, rubbing his hand on his bald head. Kamila realized it wasn't actually very sexy after all. "Yes, well..."

Kamila shook her head. "You know, you're a terrible person. I don't even know why I'm talking to you. Why did you say those things about her? At Rohan's party?"

He nodded. "I know, I know. I was a complete ass. It doesn't do much to redeem me, but I didn't know she was pregnant back then." He sighed. "But I was still terrible. I fell for her so hard. I came to Toronto to try to win her back. But I couldn't let anyone know about our past involvement. And...I was trying to make her jealous. It was a bad strategy."

"It was a revolting strategy. You used me."

He nodded sadly. At least he looked contrite. "I know. I'm so sorry. Forgive me, Kamila? I'd like it if we could stay friends."

"You need *her* forgiveness, not mine."

"I'm trying." He looked over and watched Jana across the room. Here was her proof Anil had *never* been into Kamila— she'd never seen him look at Kamila like she hung the moon. How had no one noticed this? He suddenly chuckled. "She's so beautiful. She has me completely under a spell. I...Would you believe me if I said I'm so stupidly in love I can't seem to act in a rational manner?"

Kamila shook her head. "I admire your earnestness, but you don't treat people you love very well. This is concerning, considering you're about to be a father."

He looked at Kamila. "You're a wise woman, Kamila. But don't worry—I have accepted I screwed up too badly to even hope to get her back. I *am* determined to be a good father, though. I'm working on my flaws. I'm even starting therapy soon. Jana and I are in agreement that she gets to call the shots for a while…maybe forever. Which is fine with me as long as I get to be a father. I *will* be there for my daughter."

"Well, from the bottom of my heart, I honestly wish you all the best. For Jana and the baby's sake."

"I guess that's the most I can ask. I hope you'll be in the baby's life?"

Kamila snorted. "Of course I'm going to be in that baby's life! Jana doesn't have siblings, so someone has to be the baby's fabulous aunty."

Jana joined them then and gave Anil an irritated look. "I hate the fact that I'm impressed with what you've done here," she said, indicating the big banners that outlined the mandate and goals for the incubator. "You executed our plan better than I could have."

"I had a great team," Anil said.

"This incubator was *your* plan?" Kamila asked Jana.

"Ours. We thought of this idea together. And when I saw him in D.C. earlier this year, we started the process. That's where we…" She rubbed her belly, then glared at Anil. "You need to stop calling this an incubator."

Anil nodded. "Noted. To be fair, I didn't know you were expecting."

Kamila suddenly laughed. "Now I get why you were crabby any time anyone mentioned Anil's incubator! Because you're incubating his baby."

Jana's eyes narrowed, apparently still irritated.

"Well, whatever you call it, it's still a great idea," Kamila said.

"She's quite brilliant," Anil agreed, looking at Jana with that expression again. How had Kamila not noticed how much of a devoted puppy this man was?

Later, when Kamila was getting herself another soda water, Rohan cornered her again. The party was wrapping up and there were few people left to be a buffer. "Kam, there you are. Now will you talk to me?"

"Oh," Jana said, rushing to Kamila's side. "Kamila and I had…um…plans. For a late dinner. Girl talk, you know, about the baby."

Kamila couldn't help it—she giggled. Jana Suleiman was a trip tonight.

"Ten minutes, Kam," Rohan pleaded.

Kamila had been okay today, thanks, in no small part, to Jana making sure they stayed far, far from Rohan. She'd socialized, met people, and mostly forgot how miserable she was.

But he was close now, and he looked so…sad. She knew if she got even an inch closer, she'd give in. She'd accept his apologies, she'd forgive him. She'd be back to batting her eyelashes to coax a smile out of him, knowing he'd never feel about her the way she felt about him.

She would continue to be the Kamila that Dad and Rohan expected. Throw a party, flirt a bit, dance with her dog, be Rohan's friend.

But she didn't *want* to be just that anymore. Kamila knew herself now better than she ever had. It wasn't only the realization that she loved him, but also that she was worth more than what he, and everyone else, thought she was worth.

But maybe she owed him ten minutes—after all, this was still Rohan. He'd done so much for her and Dad—and she *was* grateful.

She looked at Jana. "Can you give me ten, and then we'll get dinner?"

Jana watched Kamila's face carefully, clearly wanting to make sure she was okay. Kamila could have hugged her for that. Except—no. She wasn't going to hug Jana Suleiman.

"It's fine," she reassured Jana.

"I'll be around." Jana flipped her hair and walked away. Kamila didn't miss that she walked in the direction of Anil, but she wasn't going to make any assumptions.

"Okay, talk," she said to Rohan.

"Come. We can go to the lobby."

After following him out to the coatroom, where he'd fetched his briefcase, they went to the lobby sitting area. It was pretty secluded and empty since most people had left the party. Kamila perched on a chair, while Rohan sat on the ottoman in front of her and took a folder out of his bag.

He ran his hand through his hair, messing up the style a bit. Kamila squeezed her hands together, resisting the urge to smooth it.

"Did you read my email?"

She shook her head. She was intentionally avoiding it, which, yeah, probably wasn't healthy.

"Okay. I'll explain, then. First, again, I'm sorry we blindsided you on Thursday. I told your father I didn't like keeping you out of the loop on these plans, but he was insistent he wanted to surprise you. He's been thinking of closing Emerald for a while but made his final decision in the hospital that morning when Shelina and Zayan were here."

Kamila's fists balled. "So, my sister and brother-in-law knew, but no one had the courtesy to actually tell the person who Dad lives with. The person who works at Emerald."

"That was a mistake. Like I said, he was so excited to surprise you. He thought you'd be ecstatic. You'd been telling him to reduce his hours for so long."

"Reduce his hours. Not close the office where I work. Did *you* think I'd be happy about this?"

He looked at her. Deep into her eyes, and Kamila saw his mask chink away. He was very upset about hurting her. He did care—that was true.

"I didn't know what you'd think. I...I knew you were dedicated at Emerald, but...maybe I didn't think it was what you truly wanted with your life? You teased me for being in finance all the time, and you showed no interest in working at HNS."

"Because I was *happy* at Emerald. You thought I was just playing there? Working my butt off just to kill time?"

"I knew you worked hard. I admired you for what you did there. But...your father said you only studied accounting because of him. And you only worked at Emerald for him, too. You do so much for your father—I didn't see that it was something you were doing for yourself, too." He exhaled, looking down. "I should have asked you. I shouldn't have assumed."

"You've always assumed with me," she said. "Everyone has. You assumed I didn't love being an accountant as much as you and your HNS crew because I don't work ridiculously long hours or wear a suit to work. You think I redesigned Emerald just because I wanted to post it on Instagram—it never occurred to you I wanted to make the space more welcoming to the type of clientele I wanted to attract. You think because I'm excited to bring in hairstylists, tattoo artists, and dog trainers I must not care as much as if I were trying to get more...respectable clients. You think because I care so much about my hair, my clothes, my parties, and my dog, that I can't possibly have serious thoughts about building my future in this head at the same time."

He shook his head. "Kamila, that's not true. I've told you so many times that I think people should stop underestimating you."

Kamila clasped her hands together, frustrated. "It's a little bit true, though, isn't it? I'm not an idiot, Rohan. I know it's what everyone thinks of me."

He said nothing.

"Loving fashion, or my hair, or dressing up my dog doesn't mean I'm shallow. It doesn't mean I'm not entitled to have a say in decisions that affect my life. I'm not surprised Dad thought this way. Disappointed, but not surprised. He sees what he wants to see in his daughters. But you...you doing this is what kills me. Everyone else said you were uptight and shrewd, but I saw..." Her voice cracked. She closed her eyes a moment, then looked into Rohan's. "I saw the Rohan no one else saw. The warm, generous, *alive* man who would ride the same roller coaster six times in a day and hide his tears during the sad parts of Bollywood movies. The man who wouldn't think twice about rolling up his sleeves to make momos in a polka-dot apron. I *saw* you, but you didn't see me."

She was crying, and she hated that. She hated all of this. She picked up her bag. "Your ten minutes are up. I—"

"Wait, Kam." He held her arm so she wouldn't leave. "I didn't get to tell you my idea." He sighed, opening the folder. "I'm sorry. I...want to fix this. I don't know what you want, but we have options. I think…Maybe…" He rubbed his hands on his legs. She'd honestly never seen Rohan so unsure. "My first idea is you can start your own accounting firm that's all yours. I can help. I'm sure many of your Emerald clients would come with you. I can assist with the start-up capital if you need it or help with the process. Anything you need, I commit to. You can recreate your own Emerald. Even call it what you want."

She had considered this, the option of starting her own practice. She had a feeling Rohan was right—she could probably take most of her clients with her. Definitely the ones worth keeping. It was scary, but it could be great. She was always helping others start their own businesses. She could do it for herself.

"Before you say anything, there is another option I'd like you to consider." He took a breath. "I know you don't want to come to HNS as a CPA…and you said you didn't get any respect when you worked there before, but I think you *would* get respect if you were an owner."

Kamila froze. "What?"

"Your father's shares in HNS…you could buy them instead of Zayan and me. Then you could come and work at HNS as a *partner*."

CHAPTER 25

Kamila was speechless. Literally, there were no words in her entire body, possibly for the first time in her existence.

Her? A partner in Hussain, Nasser, and Suleiman? Was that even a possibility?

She found something to say. "You would be willing to give up Dad's shares?"

He nodded. "I would. Our fathers built the company. It would be pretty amazing if we continued it together. Zayan is on board with this idea, too. We'd need to convince your dad."

"Seriously? *Me?* This isn't the small firm our fathers built anymore. It's the third largest accounting firm in the province. It's massive." She frowned. "How would I pay for the shares?" Dad was only planning to give her part of the money from the sale, not all of it.

He pulled out a printed spreadsheet. "I ran the numbers—your father would technically loan you the money to buy him out, which you would pay back gradually from profits. It wouldn't even take long, especially if we increase the client load in your division."

She raised a brow. "Division?"

"Zayan and I have been impressed with Emerald's growth. The original plan was to absorb Emerald into HNS, but what if instead we grew it? We're proposing starting a whole line of small neighborhood-based offices geared toward financial literacy and services for millennials and Gen Zers. This is a perfect project for someone with your skills and talent."

"Rohan, we'd be working together."

He nodded. "We did well with the momos—we could do well here, too."

Kamila blinked, not sure what to say about this. She'd meant it when she claimed HNS wasn't for her. Rohan, Zayan, and their father, when he was still active there, had grown the small accounting firm into a sterile, massive organization. She preferred a small grassroots practice like Emerald.

But maybe Rohan was offering her the best of both worlds—the security and wealth of the large firm, and the opportunity to continue to do what she was doing at Emerald. Actually, she had the opportunity to do more—to grow Emerald.

"I don't know what to say."

"You don't have to say anything. Just think about it, Kam."

She looked at him. Warm eyes, soft hair. He was sacrificing a lot by making this offer—literally sacrificing one-third of his company.

He wouldn't have done that if he didn't have faith in her, or if he didn't think she could bring value to HNS. Rohan was generous, yes, but he was a businessman, too. He would never do anything to put HNS at any risk. This offer meant he trusted her.

He also wouldn't be doing this if his feelings for her went

anywhere beyond friendship. What was it he said to her weeks ago? *Work isn't living... I'm never getting involved with a colleague again. It distorts the relationship.*

Kamila had admitted to herself that she loved him, but she wasn't exactly sure what that meant for her. Did she want a relationship with Rohan? A future?

If he wanted to be business partners, that meant he didn't want that.

This offer proved Rohan cared about her. He valued her. He respected her. He had faith in her. But he didn't love her.

She exhaled. "Okay. I'll think about it."

Jana was at a small table inside the now-empty party room when Kamila went back to look for her. Surprisingly, she was sitting with Anil. Kamila tried to give them a wide berth, not sure how personal their conversation was, but as soon as Jana noticed her, she motioned her over.

"Are you ready for dinner now? I'm starving," Jana said, standing. "I think this is the hungry part of the pregnancy."

So apparently Jana actually did intend to eat a meal with Kamila. She hadn't said it just to save her from Rohan? Remarkable.

Anil stood, too. He put out his hand for Kamila to shake. "Thanks for everything. The party was even better than I had hoped."

Kamila shook his hand. "It's a good cause."

"I'll be in touch about what we need from your firm. I think this is the beginning of a great working relationship."

Ha! Marlene must not have spoken to him. She decided not to mention the issues with Emerald's future right now. "Thanks," Kamila said.

Anil looked at Jana. "You'll think about my offer?"

Jana nodded. "All I'm committing to right now is thinking about it."

He smiled, but it wasn't the overly charming, confident smile of his. This was insecure but hopeful. "It's all I can ask. Stay in touch, though. Take care, both of you."

Kamila and Jana ended up going to a lively Japanese izakaya for a late dinner. Kamila was surprised at Jana's choice—she had assumed Jana would have wanted somewhere quieter and more...boring. Not a rowdy bar with rich fried foods.

"I've just discovered this place," Jana said as they slid into a booth. "I like that you can sit alone at the bar and not stand out. They do really interesting nonalcoholic cocktails. If the baby wants fried tofu and octopus balls, who am I to say no?"

Apparently, prim-and-proper Jana had an adventurous side. At least when it came to her culinary choices. That *alone* comment was a bit sad, though—Kamila would have had a meal with Jana (despite not even liking her) if she'd known Jana was lonely since she'd come to town. After they'd ordered several small plates and adventurous fresh juice concoctions, Kamila settled back and looked at Jana.

This was supposed to be her enemy—her *nemesis*. But in the last two days, Jana had seemed to know exactly what Kamila needed before Kamila even did. Actually, even longer. She hadn't forgotten Jana's support in the hospital.

Despite knowing Jana all her life, she knew very little about the woman. She'd noticed the perfect grades, the scholarships, and the great jobs. Kamila had only seen the surface of Jana. And apparently, Jana felt as stifled by people's assumptions about her as Kamila did.

"Thank you, by the way," Kamila said, after the food arrived. "For coming to the party. Not sure I could have done that alone."

Jana shrugged. "I came for you, but also a bit for me. This project was supposed to be mine, and I wanted to see it come to fruition."

"I hope it wasn't too hard for you to see it all without being involved."

"Actually, that's what Anil asked me just now. He wants me to be the managing director of Aim High."

Kamila's eyes went wide. "Holy crucifix, he offered you a *job*?"

She shrugged. "It's actually my area of expertise. That app idea I had never got off the ground. I've picked up some contract work lecturing, but work in this field in Toronto is scarce. This job is a dream."

"But would you work with Anil? After everything he did?"

"I don't know." She pushed her hair behind her ear. "He totally lied to me, but it takes two, right? There were signs he wasn't being honest about his marriage. I believed what I wanted to believe. He was very charming." She tapped her belly. "If this baby is as persuasive as her father, then I'm in trouble."

"But what about everything he did here in Toronto? The goading and trying to make you jealous by flirting with me."

Jana nodded. "He's not forgiven for that. He's been groveling, but it's not enough. Part of me wants to have nothing to do with Anil. But..." She looked off into the distance. "I'm having this baby. I think she deserves two parents, and a mother with a good job."

"Sounds like you've already decided."

"I haven't. But I'm going to think seriously about it."

"Be careful, though. He's only known he's going to be a father for what—three days? I hope he doesn't burn out from all this groveling."

Jana gave her smug shrug. "What about Rohan? How was his grovel?"

Kamila exhaled deeply. "He said all the right things. He apologized profusely. I'm still in shock over what he offered me, though."

"What did he offer you?"

"One-third of HNS."

"Holy shit."

"Yeah." Kamila nodded. "That was my reaction. I probably would have forgiven him if he had given me a puppy, but instead he offered me partnership in a multimillion-dollar company."

Jana snorted. "Rohan has always been a bit extra, don't you think?"

Kamila nodded and explained the details of Rohan's offer.

"What about...you know...I was under the impression you developed feelings for him?" Jana asked.

"I'm in love with him."

Jana chuckled. "Yeah, that. Maybe he feels the same way and he's doing this to be closer to you."

Kamila picked at her agedashi tofu, watching the bonito flakes sway in the steam. "Actually, it's the opposite. I don't know if you remember, but Lisa, his ex-wife, was a lawyer in the same firm as him. He told me he'd never want a relationship with someone he worked with again. It's too much stress on the relationship and on the business. He doesn't mix business and pleasure...and he asked me to be a business partner."

"Damn."

Jana said nothing for a while, and Kamila silently ate her tofu. Damn was right.

Jana looked up from her food. "So, you're giving up on him, then?"

"I mean, there is nothing to give up. I'm hoping my feelings will die out. But I can't do this to myself. Work at HNS? It would be torture."

"How can you not, though? This is HNS, Kamila! The company our fathers built. Zayan and Rohan are doing great with it, but can you imagine if a woman was a partner, too? You'd get your own division. Here's your chance to put your stamp on it."

Kamila wasn't convinced. It sounded like a whole lot of heartache to work with Rohan and a headache dealing with people who she didn't see eye to eye with. "You don't actually think I could do this, though, do you? This is high-powered finance stuff—not hairstyling and Bollywood gossip."

Jana looked at Kamila for a few seconds, blinking. Then she looked down at her bowl of noodles. "You think I'm a bitch," she said.

Kamila didn't think that. At least not since…Thursday. But the fact was, this was *Jana*. It was all good to be buddy-buddy now, but there was too much history between them to take this advice at face value. "Like I said before, I'm not sure I would have gotten through tonight without you…or that night at the hospital. But I can't exactly forget everything else." Even if Kamila were to let ancient history, and the whole Bronx Bennet thing, go, Jana had been pretty nasty in the last few weeks, too. Also? Now that Asha had reminded her of how ridiculous it was,

Kamila chuckled to herself whenever she thought of the name Bronx Bennet.

Jana twirled her noodles with her chopsticks. "I'm thinking an apology isn't going to mean much to you, but...I am sorry. You always brought out the worst in me. I mean, it's no wonder— after so many years of everyone telling me I should be more like you."

Kamila was very glad she wasn't drinking her yuzu-lychee fizz at that moment, because she would have spit it all over Jana's face and possibly ruined that perfect red lipstick (she made a mental note to ask Jana the shade when they weren't in the midst of repairing a twenty-seven-year-old relationship). "You're kidding," Kamila said. "Why would anyone tell *you* to be more like me? You are the very definition of a perfect Indian daughter."

"Did you forget about the unwed-mother part, Kamila?"

"Okay, but that's a new development. For my entire life people asked me why I couldn't be smart and respectable like Jana Suleiman."

"And people asked me why I couldn't be fun and easygoing like Kamila Hussain."

Kamila glared at Jana, eyes narrowed. Finally, she sighed. "But I had more than just petty comparison as reason to dislike you...I mean, you *did* hook up with the guy I was seeing when we were eighteen, and you *didn't* tell the nosy aunties that it was you, not me, fogging up his windows outside your house."

Jana frowned. "This is all because of Bronx? Didn't he hook up with every brown girl in the neighborhood?"

Kamila raised a brow. Was that supposed to make her feel better?

"Fine, fine. You're right. I shouldn't have done that. I knew you were seeing him. I didn't think you were exclusive, though. He lured me with his Rumi poetry."

Kamila snorted. "Really? Rumi?" Kamila and Bronx *weren't* exclusive—it was casual. But him fooling around with Jana stung a little more than if it had been anyone else.

Jana shrugged. "Honestly, I wasn't used to guys paying any attention to me. Especially guys who'd shown an interest in you first. I kind of wanted to see what it would be like to be you for a moment. Anyway, that guy had a major South Asian fetish."

"Well, yeah, duh." That NAMASTE shirt he always wore gave that away. But Kamila was young and stupid back then and thought he was soooo respectful of her culture. "It wasn't Bronx Bennet that pissed me off. It was the fact that you didn't come clean when I was accused of being the one in his car. Even after my mom gave you my graduation party because of it."

Jana froze. "She gave me what?"

"The party my mom threw for you for getting into Oxford, that was supposed to be my graduation party. Giving it to you was my punishment for being parked with Mr. Kama Sutra after I'd been forbidden to see him. Except it wasn't me. And no one believed me when I told them that." It was such a silly thing to get in trouble for—just one of many silly things that proved that no one trusted or respected Kamila. Ever.

Jana shook her head. "I'm sorry, Kamila. I didn't know that. They told me you didn't want a party. I didn't realize that was all supposed to be for you."

Kamila just blinked. It was no surprise her parents had lied to everyone. "If you'd known, what would you have done?"

Jana looked down. "I would have taken your party anyway. I

didn't like you. Mostly because you were what everyone wanted me to be."

"I didn't like you for the same reason." Kamila sighed. "They pitted us against each other. I think maybe we didn't have a chance."

They were both silent for a while. Kamila couldn't help but wonder if they had a chance now.

Finally, Jana spoke. "Hey, you know I've never even seen your office? It's nearby, isn't it? Maybe we can pop in next."

Kamila frowned. "It's not far. But why would you want to go there now?"

"Because I want to see it. I want to see the place that you say means so much to you."

Kamila shrugged. "Sure. Why not?"

They didn't mention the past again as they finished their dinner. And after a quick stop at Boba Noodle (weirdly, Kevin wasn't there) to get teas, they headed to Emerald. Walking in for the first time since she'd learned she was most likely going to lose it, Kamila was immediately overcome with sadness, despite the calm that came whenever she walked into her office. The pale flooring. The pink, green, and lavender geometric feature wall. The plants on every surface. All it needed was the sunlight that normally streamed in from the large window in the lobby area. She really loved this place. She couldn't believe Dad and Rohan were closing it.

"Wow," Jana said. "It's stunning in here. I'd heard you re-decorated, but…" Jana walked into the waiting area, running her hands over the glossy white end table. "Wow."

"It's really great, isn't it?"

"I was expecting it to look more like your house. Bright and quirky is more your aesthetic. Not this."

"Yeah, I like bright at home. But I wanted to go with pale and soothing here—financial talk is stressful, and a calming palette seemed a better fit."

"I can't believe this is an accounting office. It's so...feminine. But modern, too. Show me around."

Kamila did. First the boardroom. "We don't use this room much, so I didn't do a lot here. Just a coat of paint."

"It looks a bit like a classroom," Jana said, looking at the whiteboard on one wall.

"It used to be one. This office used to be a tutoring business." She took her to Dad's office next. "We didn't do anything here. Dad insisted he liked his box-store desk. I did change the artwork, though." The pale landscapes were a far cry from the weird motivational posters that used to hang here.

"And finally, my office."

Of course, since she had designed the whole space, Kamila's own office was her favorite. A glass desk and pale-pink leather office chair. Succulents in white ceramic pots. Beautiful butter-yellow armchairs for clients. A teal filing cabinet. Brass and brushed-gold accessories, and a window that let in lots of natural light during the day.

Jana immediately sat on one of the armchairs, deep in thought. Kamila sat at her desk. While she was here, she might as well grab the Ink Girls file so she could work on their balance sheets after the prom tomorrow. She'd wanted to do it yesterday, but her broken-heart situation prevented her from coming into the office. She opened the file and started flipping through the paperwork inside, making sure it was all there.

"This is impressive," Jana said finally. "I had a motive for bringing you here—I thought I could convince you to join HNS and grow Emerald while you were in your office. But...honestly? I love it here, too. You look like you belong here. Don't let them turn this place into a corporate cookie-cutter chain. Don't give up on what you're doing here, either. Don't let them close it, Kamila."

Kamila looked up at Jana. She was right. Being here, at Emerald, it was so clear—she couldn't give it up. Restarting somewhere else wasn't an option. And Emerald would lose its personality if it was expanded into a chain.

"I can't work at HNS. Even with Emerald as my own division, even keeping this space, a giant firm is the opposite of what I want."

"What would be your perfect solution?" Jana asked.

"Keeping things the way they are."

"But you said yourself that your father retiring is a good thing."

"It is a good thing." She sighed. "There is no happy solution. I can't run Emerald alone, and I don't want to work with HNS."

"Why can't you run it alone?"

Kamila looked at Jana, blinking. "I can't because..."

"Because people like that Marlene lady think you can't?" Jana asked.

"Yeah, people like her, and my mom, and even my dad. And probably Rohan, and definitely *you* don't think I could do it."

"Okay, but Kamila, why the hell do you care what any of us say? Do *you* think you could do it?"

Kamila didn't have an answer to that.

"The Kamila I've never liked always got what she wanted," Jana said. "From anyone."

"*A girl like Kamila can have whatever she wants,*" Kamila whispered.

"Who said that?"

"Rohan." Kamila put her hand on the desk, the cool glass giving her strength. "You're right. Why can't I do it alone? Let Dad sell his HNS shares—I don't want them. But why can't I buy Emerald from HNS? The clients, the space, the name. I could do this." It would be a lot of work—even more than she was already doing—but it was doable.

Jana grinned. "Exactly."

"Actually"—Kamila couldn't believe she was about to say this—"I can grow it alone. Offer more services. Financial literacy classes, estate planning. Hey, maybe partner with Aim High to teach classes to the incubator clients. Turn the boardroom into a classroom. Sorry, not incubator. What are you calling it now?"

Jana frowned. "You'd want to work with me?"

"I would. Our fathers created something from nothing years ago—maybe it's our turn."

Jana snorted. "Now who's a renegade? But how are you going to convince Rohan to sell it to you? Now he's talking of expanding Emerald."

Kamila bit her lip, thinking. Then she smiled. "It's not Rohan I have to convince. It's Dad. What are you doing tomorrow, Jana?"

Jana grinned. "I'm there if you need me." She paused. "By the way, did you know that Bronx Bennet is now a professor of South Asian religions?"

Kamila blinked, then laughed loud and long with Jana Suleiman for the first time in her life.

CHAPTER 26

Kamila had been looking forward to the puppy prom for months, and she really needed to be rested for the big day, but with everything going on, she simply could not quiet her brain enough to fall asleep. Instead of tossing and turning in her room, though, she went downstairs, made some tea, and pulled her computer onto her lap to do some research. If she was going to make a case to Dad for keeping Emerald for herself, she needed to have all her ducks in a row.

After a bit of market research, she drafted a business-expansion plan and target-income statements. It all came together easily. She could see growing Emerald to offer more financial services, like classes for sole proprietors on basic bookkeeping and budgeting, plus debt-reduction strategies. And classes for new business owners, both for Aim High as well as for her own prospective clients. She could even do more personal finance work, like offering workshops for new couples on how to deal with the money bits of a relationship. And add seminars on non-profit governance. This was an exciting idea. In fact, she wished she had taken more control of Emerald's future before now.

After finishing the business plan, she knew she still wouldn't be able to sleep, so she put on the next Bollywood movie in her queue and snuggled Darcy on the couch. The movie was *Dear Zindagi*, and she had originally put it in her queue because Alia Bhatt was so luminous in it. But watching it now was eye-opening. The story was about an impulsive but driven young filmmaker who sees a psychologist to help her come to terms with how her abusive upbringing was affecting her life and her choices. Add a stunning beach in Goa, and Shah Rukh Khan with a beard, and it was no wonder it resonated with Kamila tonight. Clearly Asha was right that her subconscious was being a bit nefarious in its movie choices.

The movie made Kamila think about her own past. Her mother had been emotionally abusive and overly critical and called her a lazy, irresponsible harlot. And, while Mom was alive, Kamila's rebellion was to be exactly what her mother expected—there was no point in being anything else. But everything changed when Mom died and Dad's depression got so bad. Kamila did a one-eighty.

Her mother had called her irresponsible and lazy, so she reenrolled in college to follow in her father's footsteps in accounting. And she volunteered for everything under the sun.

Her mother had called her selfish and self-centered, so she threw lavish parties for her friends and made photoshopped portraits of their pets to make them happy. And she constantly tried to matchmake for them, wanting them to have their happily ever afters *because* of Kamila. She wanted everyone to be grateful they had Kamila in their lives.

Even the way she dressed was because of Mom's disapproval. Her mother had said she dressed like trash, so Kamila became interested in fashion, so she could be the most fabulous in any room.

She even decided to stop swearing one day, and she hadn't since—save for telling Rohan to eff off a few days ago.

And wow, what did that mean? The first person she'd used profanity in anger on in at least six years was someone she was in love with? She should analyze that—another time, though.

Her therapist had said she changed to prove her mother was wrong about her. But Kamila thought it was also to become the person Dad *needed* her to be when his mental health took a nose dive. Because Dad deserved it—he was the only one who made Kamila feel like she was more than a useless burden on her family.

And changing had been good for Kamila. She discovered how much she loved helping people. She found volunteering incredibly rewarding. She loved having a welcoming home for her friends and family. And she really loved discovering her own signature style.

But getting addicted to that positive attention meant sometimes she meddled. And she wasn't always authentic. She put too much focus on what others thought of her and not enough on figuring out what was really important to her. What she valued. What she loved. Who she loved.

And whenever Rohan saw her deeply—saw that her parties and clothes and her social media *didn't* mean she was frivolous or unworthy—she brushed him off. Flirted a bit and kept things playful.

Maybe because *she* didn't think she was worthy. Not good enough to run Emerald. And definitely not good enough for anything serious with Rohan.

She hadn't overcome all the things her mother had said, at least not as well as she'd thought she had. Kamila rubbed her hands over her face. Good thing she'd already made an appointment with her therapist for next week. She had a lot to talk to her about.

But right now…this decision to keep Emerald and grow it into her dream accounting firm was the first big thing Kamila remembered doing that felt like it was just for *her*. Not to prove Mom wrong or make Dad proud. Not to impress Rohan or her friends. She was doing this because she loved Emerald, and helping her clients, present and future, was incredibly important to her.

She was doing it because she thought she *could* do it, and she knew she should.

☂

Eventually Kamila did get some sleep that night, but she woke up with major stomach butterflies about the day in front of her. This wasn't fair—she'd planned everything for the puppy prom meticulously so she could really enjoy herself on the day of the party. But of course, fate had other plans, and instead, she was a nervous wreck over talking to her father this morning about keeping Emerald.

But in the words of the wise Freddie Mercury, the show must go on. She got out of bed and did a run-through of Darcy's routine a few times. After practicing, she took a shower and laid out her sari so she could easily slip it on before leaving for the prom. She'd had the sari, a deep-turquoise-and-gold georgette, stitched for easy wear and had the tailor put more fullness in the skirt to accommodate the musical canine freestyle routine. And she'd had a matching ruffled skirt thing made for Darcy to wear. The doorbell rang as Kamila was setting out her costume jewelry.

It was Jana, with treats from Dad's favorite Indian bakery in one hand and an umbrella in the other.

"Shoot," Kamila said, peeking out after Jana came into the house. "It's raining. It wasn't supposed to rain today. My hair..."

Jana raised a brow. "Your hair looks fine."

"Yeah, but it won't if I get caught in the rain. I can't have frizzy hair for Darcy's dance."

Jana shook her head as she put the paper bag on the dining table. "I can't believe you're going to dance with your dog. In public."

Kamila shrugged as she started taking parathas, samosas, and sweet rolls out of the bag. This was all way off Dad's diet. Kamila would serve it with fresh fruit. "Hey, if we're going to try to be friends, you're going to have to accept me as I am."

Jana raised a brow. "Are we going to be friends?"

With all her other self-discoveries last night, she hadn't really thought about the talk she'd had with Jana yesterday. But she gave it a few seconds now and realized that none of her epiphanies last night would have even happened without Jana. And Kamila much preferred having a friend than a nemesis, anyway. "Yes," Kamila said. "We should give it a shot long-term. Because you desperately need a girlfriend in town right now, and I need someone to call me out when my ridiculousness goes too far."

Jana huffed a laugh. "That, I can do."

"Jana!" Dad said from the stairs. "That smells delicious."

"Look at the treats she brought!" Kamila said. "I need to talk to you about something, and Jana came for brunch to help me convince you."

"Ooh, mysterious." Dad checked his watch. "Rohan asked to meet with me to go over some details for the sale in an hour. I can eat quickly, and maybe we can talk this afternoon?"

Kamila shook her head. "I need to be at the prom then—can you call Rohan to push your meeting back a little bit?"

Dad checked with Rohan while Kamila cut up some fruit. She tried very hard not to pay attention to Dad's call or to speculate about Rohan's mental state. She was pretty sure he wouldn't be happy about her plan. But she wasn't doing it for him. And she didn't want to get sucked back into her people-pleasing habit. Even if she was inconveniently in love with that person.

After they were all at the table digging into the breakfast goodies, Kamila started her plea.

"Okay, Dad, I have a proposal for you, and I hope you'll hear me out before you make any more decisions."

"A proposal? What is it? Have you thought about what you want to do after leaving Emerald?"

"No, that's not it." Kamila took a breath. "First of all, I'm honestly very happy you've decided to retire. You've seemed so much...lighter since you stopped working a few weeks ago. I'm going to miss you loads and loads when you're in Florida, but I think you're doing a good thing to reduce your stress for your health."

Dad squeezed Kamila's hand. "I'm doing this for both of us."

Kamila smiled. "I know you are. And...I'm happy you made a choice for your own health, but I..." She looked at Jana, who sent her a small, reassuring smile. "I don't want to lose Emerald."

"But, beti! You won't need to take care of me anymore! You can do what you want with your life."

"But that's just it, Dad—I *am* doing what I want. Yeah, when I started working there, it was for you. But I love what we've turned Emerald into. I love my clients. I love the work I'm doing. And now I want to take it further."

Dad blinked, obviously surprised. Kamila knew she should have told him before today how much the company meant to her. Maybe then he wouldn't have done this. She made a silent vow to herself that from this moment on, she'd make sure everyone knew what she valued.

Kamila exhaled, again looking to Jana for strength. "Rohan offered to let me buy your HNS shares instead of him and Zayan buying them. I'm pretty sure that's what he's going to talk to you about today. They want me to be a partner in HNS, and together we'd grow Emerald into a chain of small regional offices."

"What? That's not something we'd ever—"

"Wait, Dad. I haven't given him an answer yet, but I'm going to say no. I don't want that. Selling your HNS shares to Rohan and Zayan makes more sense. They know what they're doing there. I just want Emerald."

"What?"

"You can make it a condition of the sale of your shares that they must first sell Emerald to me. We can even set the price now."

Dad paused, thinking about it. "You want Emerald alone?"

Kamila nodded. "I mean, I'm not really alone. I have friends"— she looked at Jana—"who can support me. Maybe...Rohan for guidance. I have ideas. I don't want to make it a chain of shops or anything but instead grow the services we provide. Even partner with Aim High to teach finances to newcomer businesses. Let me show you."

She showed him the printouts of the plans she worked through late last night. Even though Jana hadn't seen them, she elaborated on Kamila's ideas, seeming to understand completely what Kamila was trying to do with Emerald.

Huh. Jana Suleiman understood her. That was pretty cool.

Dad exhaled. "Kamila, I didn't know you wanted this."

"Do you think she can do it?" Jana asked.

"Of course she can do it. I have faith in Kamila, but this will be a lot of work. Kamila, do you *want* to do this? What about all the other things you do? Your volunteer work, your parties, your friends, your videos with Darcy. Running a business is a big commitment with a lot of risk."

"I know, Dad." She exhaled. "I've been unfocused. And maybe too concerned with what people think of me, and I didn't stop to really think about what I wanted." Or who she loved, either. She looked down. "I didn't see my potential, but I do now."

Dad didn't say anything for a while. Finally, he sighed. "Your mother underestimated you."

Kamila snorted. "That's an understatement."

"I'm so sorry, Kamila. I should have asked you what you wanted. I assumed you were only at Emerald for me. Not for you." He frowned, looking over Kamila's printouts. "I'll worry about you, beti, working alone."

"That's how I know you love me. Let me try, Dad."

He exhaled. "Okay. I'll tell Rohan. Let's see what you can do with Emerald."

Kamila smiled widely and hugged Dad from behind. That

was all easier than she'd thought it would be. "Yay! Thank you, Dad! Amazing!"

Truly the sweetest man in existence.

"I'm proud of you, Kamila. I always was, but today, I'm extra proud."

Kamila sent Jana home after brunch, but not before giving her a free ticket to the puppy prom. "If we're going to try to be friends, you're going to have to learn to love dogs."

Jana chuckled, taking the ticket. "Fine. I'm curious about this dog-dancing thing anyway."

"We can do a duet next year."

Jana snorted as she left.

As soon as Jana left, Kamila called Asha to tell her everything that had happened since she last saw her at the Dogapalooza. She knew they wouldn't have much time to chat at the prom, and she couldn't exactly not talk to her best friend when so much was going on. But she kept it brief, and after the call, Kamila started getting ready for the prom. Thousands of thoughts swirled through her mind as she put on her sari and did her hair and makeup, but she felt really good about how the conversation with Dad went. He listened—really listened. And best of all, he agreed.

But knowing Dad was now telling Rohan about her plan brought her stomach butterflies back at full speed. There was no question Rohan would be upset. Both because she was taking Emerald from him, and because she went to Dad with her proposal instead of him. But Kamila wanted her own future more than she wanted to please Rohan. Especially since Rohan had made it clear he didn't see her as anything more than a friend.

Kamila and Darcy headed to the old church an hour before the party was to start. Thankfully, it had stopped raining, so Kamila was less worried about her hair. Tim and Asha were already there, setting up the decorations with some of the shelter staff.

Asha kissed Kamila's cheek. "That sari is to die for. I can't believe you can dance in it."

"Darcy does most of the work. My role is just walking with style," Kamila said, putting Darcy down then patting the top of Lizzy's head. Lizzy was decked out for the occasion, too, fully clean and poufy, and with an Indian-print scarf around his neck. Asha herself was wearing an elaborate lehenga in a deep purple. "You look awesome, too."

Asha shrugged. "Nice to get some use out of our wedding clothes. Nicole's wearing the salwar kameez she wore at my mehndi ceremony."

Looking around the space, Kamila could see that there was very little left to do. Jewel-tone streamers had been hung on the walls, along with huge arrangements of colorful roses donated from a local florist. The food was being laid out on wide copper-and-brass platters. Bollywood music was already being piped through the old church's PA system.

"It looks fantastic in here. What can I do?"

"Not much. Rest up before your dance. How are you doing?" Asha tilted her head sympathetically.

Kamila sighed. "I'm emotionally…exhausted." She'd been pretty giddy and optimistic earlier, but everything happening at once felt like too much now.

"Probably physically, too. You didn't get much sleep last night."

Kamila sighed. "Yeah. I'll put my happy face on again in a minute. I'll manage today."

"Of course you will, sweetheart." Asha rubbed Kamila's back. "But...you're going through a lot. Your dad moving. Running a business alone. Rohan. It's okay to be overwhelmed. You need time to process it all." She looked around. "Tim can handle things here for a bit. I think we need to visit the puppy sanctuary."

Kamila raised a brow. "Puppy sanctuary?"

"C'mon." After asking Tim to keep an eye on Lizzy and Darcy, Asha led Kamila down a small hallway off the back of the main room. "That's what we're calling the adoption room."

Asha opened the door, and Potato immediately looked up from his spot resting near the window and bolted to Kamila. She reached down and picked him up quickly before the puppy's claws could ruin her sari.

"Potato!" she squealed as the puppy desperately tried to lick her face. She put her hand near his mouth to spare her makeup. "Look at you!" Potato had obviously been cleaned and groomed, and was wearing a regal purple-and-gold-print bow tie. Kamila nuzzled her face on his soft head. "Aw, my sweet baby is all grown. You look so dapper." Her shoulders slumped. There was no question someone was going to fall in love with this puppy and put in an application to adopt him today. A few days ago, that was fine with Kamila. But now it only made her sad.

"So, have you heard how your dad's meeting with Rohan went?" Asha asked.

Kamila shrugged. "They're probably still together."

"What do you think Rohan will say?"

That was the million-dollar question, right? "I don't know. If he's considering the bottom line only, I think he'll refuse to give up Emerald. Or at least renegotiate for some ownership in it."

"But this is Rohan—he's not going to only think about the bottom line. I think he'll agree."

"He's probably going to be annoyed I didn't tell him myself and just made Dad do it."

"Why didn't you tell him?"

"I dunno." She scratched Potato's ear.

"Kamila, Rohan doesn't want a relationship with someone he works with. Your plan means you won't be working with him."

Kamila shook her head. "That isn't why I'm doing this."

"I know. But this is still an opportunity."

"No, Asha, it's not. The fact…" She gulped. "The fact that he offered me that partnership in his firm in the first place means he doesn't see me that way. I'm not going to push for something that isn't there. Not with someone so connected to my family. I can't risk it."

"So, that's it, then?"

Kamila nodded, then put her head down, burying it in Potato's fur. "How am I going to survive without him?"

"Rohan or Potato?"

Kamila exhaled. "Potato. Actually…Rohan. Both."

"Kamila." Asha shook her head in wonder. "I honestly never thought it was possible that *you* could fall so hard. I should have known the queen of casual was actually the biggest, most romantic, feeling-y person around. I mean, you're a hopeless romantic with your friends and in your movie choices. I've just never seen it in your relationships before."

Kamila frowned. "Feeling-y? Is that a word?"

"Shush. Let it be known I think you should tell him how

you feel. But I get it. This is your *family*. If you think it would be too destructive, I'll respect that and leave you be. Three or four more Bollywood Heartbreak Recovery by Eating Ice Cream nights and you'll be good as new."

Kamila doubted it would be that easy to get over him. This was Rohan Nasser.

After a few more Potato snuggles, Kamila left him with the attendant. She had an idea as they were making their way back to the main hall. There was no reason she had to lose both Rohan and Potato at the same time.

"Asha, what if *I* adopted Potato?"

"You want another dog?"

Kamila smiled. This was a perfect idea. "Why not? Dad is moving. Darcy and I will be lonely at home. Maybe 'Heartbreak Recovery by Getting a Puppy' is the answer."

Asha grinned. "I think it's a wonderful idea." She pulled out her phone. "Derek, the adoption coordinator, isn't here yet, but I'm telling him to put a hold on the beige puppy for you. I know your application will go through fine."

Kamila smiled. This going after what she wanted was easier than she thought it would be.

CHAPTER 27

The puppy prom started out as a rousing success. The lively Bollywood dance hits accompanied by a cacophony of barking and howling dogs were the perfect soundtrack to the boisterous canine activities and delicious food for both humans and dogs. The pups loved the dog dance lessons, and the humans especially appreciated the photo booth made to look like a mehndi tent with Indian accessory photo props for both people and pets. Asha proclaimed it to be the best puppy prom yet, outshining even last year's fancy tea party.

But all through it, Kamila was on edge. It was harder to put on her happy, not-an-emotional-wreck face than it was yesterday. Probably because all she could think about was Dad's meeting with Rohan. She was looking, probably forlornly, at the plate of momos, when someone tapped her arm. She grinned when she saw who it was. "Jana! You made it! And you brought...Anil?"

"I wanted to see the famous dog prom in person," he said.

Kamila raised a brow at Jana. Jana bringing Anil to the prom meant she'd spoken to him in the few hours since she'd left Kamila's house. Jana gave Kamila a look that said, *This doesn't mean what you think it does*. Meanwhile, Anil was sporting his happy-puppy look again. At least he fit in.

"Well, I'm glad you came. Let me show you guys around. Jana, you especially—I need to show you the adoption room."

As she was trying to convince Jana and Anil that they absolutely needed to get a picture in the photo booth wearing basset hound ears, Asha approached them, Darcy in her arms. She handed Kamila her dog. "You're on in ten."

Kamila kissed Darcy on the head. "Let's get your costume on. Your fans await. Don't forget, Asha—I need you to film the whole thing so I can get some footage for TikTok."

"I know. Tim and I are both going to record it so you have two angles."

The performance started well. Darcy skipped, spun, and twirled to the Bollywood dance song, while Kamila gave her hand and voice commands. The tricky bits, like when Darcy wove figure eights through Kamila's legs—no easy feat, considering Kamila was wearing a sari—or when she jumped through the golden hula hoop, were executed flawlessly. Darcy kept in time to the music, her four little feet tapping enthusiastically as she danced around the stage.

Kamila wished she could feed off the audience's energy during the song because she herself had little energy reserves. But she had to maintain eye contact with her dog the whole time so Darcy would understand this was obedience time, not playtime. Kamila had no idea if the crowd was enjoying the performance or looking incredulous because she was dancing with a dog—in public.

But it seemed to be going okay, until Darcy lost her focus at the worst possible time—right at the bridge of the song when Darcy was supposed to be weaving figure eights again, but this time, while Kamila stomped across the stage, the belled ghungroo anklets she'd tied to her feet chiming to the beat. Darcy let out an excited little yelp at something in the direction of the back of the church, and Kamila tripped over the dog, her sari-clad bottom landing on the wooden stage. The commotion only excited Darcy more and concerned poor Lizzy, who was watching from the front row. The anxious corgi hopped onto the stage to make sure his doggie best friend was okay. That opened the floodgates, and several other dogs in the audience assumed the stage was now a free-for-all and rushed up to join in the fun, many of them batting at Kamila's belled anklets. This all happened in seconds. Asha climbed onto the stage to help calm the dogs and break Kamila free of the mob of excited pups.

Ugh. What a disaster. Kamila was going to be teased and laughed at all year for this. She looked at the audience to see if they were already laughing at her. Over in the direction of whatever distracted Darcy, standing alone and watching her, was Rohan.

Rohan was here.

Their eyes met. His expression was, as usual, unreadable. Maybe a little concerned.

He was wearing a pale-green linen shirt with a casual charcoal jacket over it, along with dark-blue jeans and an expensive-looking messenger bag over his shoulder. They stared at each other for a few seconds as the song Kamila was supposed to be dancing to ended, then he smiled slightly and waved. That was the secret smile. The one just for her.

That broke Kamila's spell. She waved back, then picked up

Darcy and stepped to the front of the stage and bowed, ignoring the half dozen dogs biting at her ankles.

Laughing, Asha joined Kamila at the front of the stage.

"Thank you, thank you, Kamila and Darcy! They sure know how to end an event with a bang, don't they? And that brings this year's Dogapalooza events to a close! Thank you so much, everyone, for supporting the shelter and all it does for animals in this community! Please stay, mingle, shop, and eat! And thank you all for coming!"

Kamila looked back at Rohan, who was still watching her— until he turned to speak to someone who Kamila couldn't see.

"Let's go, Kamila," Asha whispered, pulling gently on Kamila's arm. Asha guided Kamila to an office room they had been using as a backstage area. As Kamila bent to take the sari skirt off of Darcy, Asha frowned.

"Are you okay?" Asha asked. "That was an epic fall."

"I'm fine, I'm fine. Embarrassed." She scratched behind Darcy's ear. "I blame you, by the way," she said to her dog.

Darcy licked Kamila's hand while wagging her tail, and Kamila remembered that she couldn't be mad at her sweet dog.

"I have bad news, Kamila," Asha said.

Kamila shook her head. "Please, no. I can't take more."

"Just got a text from Derek. Someone put in an application for Potato today—before you."

Kamila's face fell, "Fudgsicle. But I can still put in an application, too, right?"

"Yeah, but you know we process them in the order we get them. No preferential treatment for people who work, or volunteer, at the shelter. So, you can only hope the other applicant is, like, a slob, or owns eight bearded dragons, or is a pet anti-vaxxer."

"Oh my god, are there pet anti-vaxxers?"

"Human intelligence comes at all levels. I'm sorry, Kamila."

Kamila sat on the floor and scooped Darcy into her arms. "It's just you and me, then, girl. We're in this alone," she said with a shaky voice.

"No, Kamila." Asha joined her on the floor. "You're not alone. *Ever*. You have me, Nicole, and Lizzy. Even Jana is your friend now, right? We're all going to be here for you through all this."

Kamila nodded, still rubbing Darcy's sweet little head and trying not to break down in tears. "I know, I know. I'm being ridiculous. I should be happy, right? I have Emerald. Dad is healthy. It's just…" She sniffled loudly. "I don't like being feeling-y."

"He's here, you know."

"I know. He's who distracted Darcy. It doesn't mean anything."

"Of course it means something! He didn't have to come. He's not mad at you."

Kamila shrugged. He came because he was Rohan, and he'd always be there for his friends. She had her friend back.

All she had to do was figure out how to stop loving him.

"Hey, there," Tim said, walking into the room and frowning at the three of them sitting on the floor. "Whatcha doing down there?"

"Oh, you know," Kamila said, wiping a tear. "Bit of dog therapy. You're supposed to cry at proms, aren't you?"

"I spent most of mine making out in the coatroom," Tim said.

Kamila sniffled. "Parking lot for me."

Tim put his hand out to help Kamila stand up. "People are starting to leave, but they want to say goodbye to the amazing dance team first. You and Darcy caused quite a splash, you know. Someone asked if you perform at private dog parties, too."

Kamila blew out a puff of air as she stood. Time to put on the happy face again. If Rohan was still there, she was going to have to face him. Pretend to be normal. "Okay. Let's do this."

They started walking back to the main hall when someone stopped Asha to ask her something. Tim and Kamila continued toward the front of the church where most of the people were gathered.

"Jerome put the dogs in their raincoats for their turn about the park for their business," Tim said. "Thank god we brought them. You do not want to see wet, matted Afghans. Last time they got caught in the rain, I used two bottles of conditioner on them. Each."

Kamila cringed. "It's raining?"

Tim nodded. "Yep. Rohan even brought his car closer for Maricel. Hey, is something going on between those two? They came together. And Maricel is positively glowing." He leaned close to Kamila as they reached the crowd near the door. "This is your doing, isn't it? It's not a couple I would have considered, but you, Ms. Matchmaker, always know best."

Kamila froze. "What did you say?"

But Tim hadn't frozen and was still walking to the door. Maricel and Rohan? Was that possible? Rohan couldn't be the secret man Maricel was seeing, could he?

Kamila felt her stomach drop as she scanned the room. There was chaos—dogs everywhere... including the ones from the adoption room. Staff members were chasing the puppies, trying to get them into crates.

She didn't see Rohan or Maricel. That was good. But Kamila still wanted to throw up.

It was probably fine. So what if they came together? They were friends.

She finally spotted Maricel, trying to get a leash on a golden retriever. Tim was right—she was positively glowing. Laughing. Happy.

Then Kamila saw Rohan. He also looked happy. He leaned in close to Maricel and said something in her ear. Whatever he said made Maricel blush and smile.

It was true.

But just as Kamila's heart began the first stages of shattering into thousands of pieces, the door to the church swung open, revealing Jerome wearing a long gray raincoat, and the Afghans, who were wearing very strange, futuristic, full-body hooded red jumpsuits. "It's really coming down out there. Everyone have a safe—"

While he was talking, Potato came out of nowhere (or, more likely, from the puppy sanctuary) and squeezed between the Afghans, bolting out the door without Jerome or the dogs noticing.

Kamila didn't think, and just acted. She ran to the door, pushed a confused Jerome out of the way, and bolted after Potato. The church was at one end of the park, but a busy road was right there. Visibility was terrible, thanks to the heavy rain, and Potato was a very light-colored dog.

"Potato!" she screamed, chasing him across the field. Running in a sari wasn't ideal, but she was grateful for the extra-wide skirt. And grateful she was wearing the sari with blue sneakers instead of sari slippers.

But it was cold and wet, and the Bollywood movies were wrong. There was nothing sexy about wet georgette fabric.

Potato kept running across the grassy field, thankfully away from the road, but the park was big, and Potato was fast.

"Potato!" she screamed again. The dog finally heard and stopped. He turned, cocking his head.

Kamila was afraid to move, knowing enough about puppies to realize that if she continued the chase, he'd only think this was a super-fun game and run faster.

She crouched down, accepting the sari was ruined anyway. "Come here, boy. Come…Who's a good Potato? Come on, love."

After Potato stared for a few seconds, he opened his mouth, wagged his tail, and started running full speed toward Kamila. Thank god.

The moment Potato jumped into her arms, large hands reached down and clipped a leash onto the dog's bow-tie collar. Kamila looked up to see who it was.

Rohan.

"I figured you didn't have a leash." He patted the messenger bag he was still wearing. "Lucky I had one right here."

"No…I…" She stood and immediately understood the appeal of Bollywood rain scenes. She might not feel sexy in a sopping-wet sari, but wow, did he ever look…wow. That linen shirt was plastered to his chest. His hair was in wet clumps on his forehead. His lips were glistening and full.

And his eyes, sparkling in the low light. Concerned. Raindrops clinging to his long lashes.

He was so, so beautiful.

She quickly looked down at Potato, who was looking up at them with his goofy puppy grin. "Thanks," she said. "I guess...I wasn't really thinking when I ran after him. Now you're all wet."

"It's just water. Look, Kam, can we talk? Dinner tonight? Maybe..." He gazed down at her wet clothes. "After we go home and change?"

She wrapped her arms around herself. "Why?"

"You know why. About what your dad asked me today...I accepted his proposal, of course. I'm only sorry I didn't think of this solution yesterday. If you want Emerald, it's yours. I think it will be amazing. But I don't understand why you didn't ask me yourself."

Of course he was okay with her taking Emerald. He was so good. She looked away.

She couldn't do this. She'd thought—hoped—she could eventually move on. Be *just friends* with the best person she knew. But Kamila was all about learning about herself lately, and she'd discovered that she wasn't the type to secretly pine for someone. She needed to either tell him or avoid him. Neither option was good for their friendship. She could feel tears well up in her eyes again. At least the rain would mask them.

"I can't tonight," she said, hearing the hurt in her voice. "Anyway, don't you have plans with Maricel?"

"What?" A gust of wind blew more rain in his face. He looked around. "Here—come." Still holding Potato's leash, he grabbed Kamila's hand and rushed toward the gazebo a few feet away. Kamila had no choice but to go with him. The gazebo wasn't in great condition, and the old roof was letting lots of rain hit the concrete floor. Rohan guided her to a dryish corner. She leaned back against the wide railing.

"What was that about?" he said, confusion evident in his voice.

"What?"

"That look you gave me over there. Asking about Maricel. What was that about?"

"It was about nothing, Rohan. Just a question. I know you guys came to the prom together. It's your life. If you have a thing with someone, then whatever. It's just . . . to rub it in my face like that after you yelled at me about setting her up with Dane—" She couldn't bear it. She covered her face with her hands.

"Don't hide from me," Rohan said, taking her hands off her face as a big drop of water fell onto her cheek. He wiped the water running down her skin with the back of his hand. "I did bring Maricel here today. But that was because she spent the night at Kevin's, and he knew I was coming here, so he asked if I would drive her. He'd be here, too, but he's working at Boba Noodle today, because his aunt's daughter had a baby."

Kamila froze. Kevin? Boba tea guy? OMG, Maricel was dating boba tea guy! How utterly perfect!

"Why would he call you to drive her? You barely know him," Kamila said.

"I'm mentoring him for his law school application. We've become friends. I encouraged him to ask Maricel out when she kept coming to the shop for his tea. She's a sweet girl—I think they're well suited."

Kamila smiled a little. "You match-made?"

Rohan pushed his hair off his face and let out an exasperated breath. "Yes."

"Then you only came here today because Maricel needed a ride?"

"No! Of course not!"

"Then why are you here?"

He shook his head. "We need to talk . . . not only about the business, though." He rustled in his bag and pulled out a plastic bag. He handed it to Kamila. "This is for you."

Confused, she took the bag, shifting a bit so whatever was in it wouldn't get rained on as she pulled it out. It was a picture frame. And the picture in it made Kamila bark an inelegant laugh when she saw it.

It was a photo of a small, run-down food cart on a rickshaw, probably taken somewhere in India. The sign on the cart said SIZZLING MOMOS—BEST IN TOWN. On either side of the cart, wearing bright T-shirts that said SIZZLING MOMOS, were Rohan and Kamila, clearly photoshopped. Rohan's hair was graying, but Kamila's hair was in big, voluminous curls. Sitting on the bicycle seat of the rickshaw was Darcy.

"*Oh my god.* Who did this?" Kamila asked. She didn't know whether to laugh or cry. This was the most amazing piece of art she'd ever seen.

"Last night I learned that you can hire someone online to manipulate a photograph at any hour of the day."

Kamila shook her head, still in awe of the picture. This, with its surrealism and bright colors, would look amazing in her house. She was going to get it printed on canvas. But she didn't understand why Rohan had commissioned it. "Why did you do this?"

He ran his hand through his wet hair. "I needed a way to show you how sorry I am. I know I apologized about everything with Emerald. Kam, I don't want to lose this friendship." He shrugged and pointed at the picture. "You said we were going to retire and run a momo cart together one day. I'm hoping I haven't destroyed our retirement plan. We're still friends, right?"

Kamila exhaled. "Friends. Like, tell-each-other-everything kind of friends?"

Rohan looked at her intensely. He'd always done that. Looked at her like he wasn't sure what to make of her. Finally, he spoke quietly. "Yes. Exactly that kind of friends."

They stared at each other for several seconds. Kamila didn't know what he was thinking. She knew what she was thinking, though. She was thinking that it would be utterly impossible for her to look at that face, the face of her friend, and not tell him everything she felt for him. And she knew that telling him would be the end of the friendship.

Unless... that look in his eyes. He was still staring at her. Could she be wrong about his feelings? She'd had a lot of friends. None of them had photoshopped a picture of the two of them in their retirement together. That didn't sound like a friend thing.

Could it be possible? She didn't know how to ask.

She exhaled. "Okay, then. Let's be the kind of friends who tell each other everything. Would you tell me if you developed feelings for someone? Like... strong feelings?"

He stared at her even longer. Eyes still unreadable. The rain pelted loudly in her ears.

"I would tell you," he finally said. "I wanted to recently. But... the current situation made it hard to say anything."

She waited for him to say more. Because she wasn't completely sure what he meant. Or... *who*.

Eventually, he looked away. "Kamila, don't pretend you don't know it's *you*. I've developed feelings for *you*."

Kamila blinked, staring at the side of his face. He'd said the words. It was *her*.

"How can you not see it?" he asked, turning back to her. "Almost everything I do is for you."

"No," she said, shaking her head and looking down at the

photograph. "You tolerate me. You think I'm troublesome. You humor me. You're fond of me, but that's it."

"I'm in love with you."

"What did you say?" she whispered, looking up at him.

"I love you," he said, intense eyes boring into hers. He wiped the wet hair off his forehead and took a step back. "I wasn't planning to say that today. I had the picture made because I wanted to show you that we could still be friends, still be a team, no matter what. But then after what your father told me today, that you were determined to run Emerald alone... I saw your plan and, Kam, I... am so proud of you. I fell in love with you even more. I've been a fool. Everyone underestimated you, especially me. You had a huge setback and were let down by me and your father, and you decided to create something amazing out of it. Call me names, Kam. Call me a dirty old man, tell me you don't want anyone to feel this way for you, to grow too attached to you. Tell me off, and then maybe I'll be able to stop thinking about you like this. But don't stop being my friend. *Please*."

Was this a dream? Could it be real? "But... this... this isn't possible. You can't... How long..." Her voice trailed. She didn't know what to say.

He looked away, into the rainy sky. "It's been a long time. Maybe a year? I don't know. I was too far gone by the time I knew what was happening."

"But you kept all that from me. About Emerald and Dad retiring."

He leaned against the railing next to her, still not looking at her. "Your father told me that's what you would have wanted. And I told myself I didn't have the right to interfere in your relationship with him. I hated keeping that information from you. I should have asked you what *you* wanted."

"But...I..." She honestly had no words.

"After that night, when your father was hospitalized...when we kissed—"

"We did a lot more than kissing, Rohan."

He finally looked at her, pink tingeing his cheeks. It was adorable. "Yeah, I remember. I thought maybe that was our time. I know you were just tired and emotional that night, but I was going to say something to you the next day. Formally ask you on a proper date. But then your dad told us his final decision to retire, and if you came to work at HNS, it would be too complicated. And then in the dog park, you were adamant to that guy that you weren't looking for a relationship." He sighed. "I know I screwed up and I wish I could make it make sense, Kamila, but you know me. You know me like no one else does. If I loved you less, I'd be able to explain myself better. If you wanted a part of HNS, you could have it. If you wanted to never work another day in your life, I'd make that happen. If you want Emerald, it's yours. Just tell me what you want, and you can have it. Even if you don't want me." He looked out into the rain.

This was real. Not a dream. She slowly put the photograph back in the plastic bag and put it on the railing behind her. She took Rohan's hand in hers. "What if what I want is you?"

His head whipped around, and he looked at her. Such a lovely face. When had she not loved it?

He smiled ever so slightly. "Say that again."

"Literally all I want is you. I love you. So much. But I...I couldn't imagine you felt the same way. Rohan, I'm *Kamila*. I don't fit in your world."

He shook his head and squeezed her hand. "Fuck fitting in my *world*. I want you in my *life*."

She closed her eyes for a second, overwhelmed. But when she opened them, he was still there. Looking at her like that.

Biting her lip, she stepped in front of him and lifted his hand. She slowly unbuttoned his shirt cuff. Pushing the wet fabric up his arm, she leaned down and kissed his forearm, the skin wet and cool against her lips. He shivered. There was a look of complete wonder in his eyes, so she did it again, letting her lips linger on the arm that she'd been so obsessed with, even letting her tongue reach out to lick a drop of rain off his skin.

"Kam," he said, voice thick. His other hand landed on the inches of bare skin between her sari skirt and blouse. "You..." he whispered, right before lowering his lips on hers.

A simple kiss. A gentle kiss. It wasn't their first, but it was the first one he initiated, which meant a lot. It was the first one in the rain, with their clothes sopping wet, and a cold wind chilling them in the damp gazebo.

It was their first kiss after she told him how she felt.

And it was everything.

The kiss didn't stay sweet for long. Just like their other two kisses, he deepened it. His hand was on her cheek, the other still clutching her side. She wrapped her arms around his neck, pulling him as close as she could get him. They fit together perfectly. She belonged here—always. Screw the rain and the cold wind— she was going to stay here, kissing the man she loved, and who loved her back, forever.

Something tugged at her waist and Rohan pulled back, looking a bit shell-shocked with swollen lips. He looked down, and Kamila remembered he was still holding Potato's leash.

Potato was fine, though. He'd positioned himself on the gazebo floor under one of the bigger roof leaks, head up, lapping happily at the water dripping from the gazebo ceiling.

Kamila giggled, letting her forehead fall to Rohan's chest.

"He's a bit of a goof," Kamila said.

Rohan chuckled, kissing the top of Kamila's head.

She tilted to look at him. "What happens now?"

He smiled. "First of all, as stunning as you are in that sari, I think we should go home and change. Then we can talk."

She playfully slapped his chest. "Oh my god, it was the sari, wasn't it? That's why you said you loved me. I'm in a soaking-wet sari."

He tightened his arm around her. "I said I love you because I do. But…" He pulled her in against him. "Maybe the wet sari motivated me to say something today, though." He started kissing her neck and down her shoulder. "And it's probably why I'm reluctant to let you go."

She shivered. It was mostly because Rohan was kissing her neck, but also…it *was* cold. She was barely dressed. October wasn't the best time of year for the whole wet-sari-love-scene thing in Canada.

"Let's go home, Rohan."

He put the framed photograph back in his bag, and they walked hand in hand back toward the church. This was really happening. Rohan and her. He loved her, too. She couldn't stop smiling.

"Question," she said as they crossed the field. "Why were you the only one with the gray hair in the momo picture?"

He snorted. "Like Kamila Hussain would ever go gray naturally."

Good point. She grinned. "The photo was an excellent groveling gift. Five stars—would recommend to friends. Much better than offering me a third of HNS." She looked at Potato. "A puppy would have worked, too."

Without pausing, he reached down and picked up Potato and put him in Kamila's arms. She hugged the puppy close. Her sari was ruined anyway, and Potato was the best. He licked her face.

"There," Rohan said. "I just happen to have a puppy for you, too."

"You can't just give me this puppy. Someone put in an application to adopt Potato. He belongs to someone else."

Rohan frowned. "Sure, I can. He belongs to me. I put in the application."

Kamila laughed as she hugged the squirming dog. "*What*? Potato is *yours*? You're not a dog person! Since when do you want a puppy?"

He looked affronted. "Of course I'm a dog person! You've seen me spoil Darcy. I thought I'd be lonely since on Thursday I assumed I'd lost my best friend. So, I went to the Dogapalooza today while waiting for your father, and I put in an application for this puppy. I didn't know you were acquainted with him. Why do you keep calling him Potato?"

"Because that's his name."

"I was thinking of calling him Duke or Max."

"Those are great names for a dog, but he already has a name. Potato." She put Potato down so she could keep walking. "Also, you have amazing taste in dogs. Because Darcy and Potato are my favorite dogs in the world. And you can't give him to me—you have to promise not to give the dog away when you adopt from the shelter."

He handed the leash to Kamila anyway. "Well, you can have visitation, then."

"Careful. I'll be over to visit him a lot. In person, too. No FaceTime calls."

He smiled as he touched her cheek. "Then I'm definitely keeping the dog." He kissed her again. In the rain, while she was in a sari and a small puppy wearing a bow tie was trying to drink the water falling from the sky.

It was the most perfect moment of Kamila's life.

CHAPTER 28

There were a fair number of suspicious looks and smirks when Kamila, Rohan, and Potato finally made it back to the puppy prom soaking wet and grinning ear to ear, but Kamila put off any speculation and gossip and happily went to the bathroom to change into the jeans and sweatshirt she'd thankfully brought to clean up in. A few minutes later, while maneuvering the adoption dogs into carriers, Kamila cornered Maricel.

"I heard you were with Kevin last night."

Maricel's eyes widened as she blushed and stammered. "I was going to tell you...I mean...I wasn't hiding but...I wasn't sure you'd approve."

"Nonsense. I'm very happy for you, Maricel."

Maricel grinned. "I really, really like him. He likes me, too, for real."

"Of course he does. You're *you*."

Asha gave Kamila a knowing smile from across the room while Kamila was putting Darcy's leash on. Kamila grinned back, knowing her friend would understand. She expected Asha would call her as soon as they were all out of this church to get a play-by-play of what happened when she and Rohan chased Potato out the door.

After they were done cleaning, Rohan walked Kamila out to her car. They decided not to have dinner together, or even meet up later that night. Kamila was exhausted, and she desperately needed to go home and shower. Rohan said the same. They agreed they had all the time in the world, and kissed goodbye. But of course, Kamila regretted the decision the second her hair was dry and safely tucked into her sleeping bonnet.

What if he changed his mind about her? Also, what if she misinterpreted what he wanted for their future? Maybe none of it was real and that soggy gazebo was some magical portal place where Kamila could have everything she wanted, but then it disappeared once she was dry.

She should call him. She picked up her phone just as a video call flashed on her screen. Of course, it was Rohan—she didn't know why she doubted him.

She answered with a big smile. "Hey, old man."

He was clearly already in bed—he wasn't kidding about being tired. She wanted to be in that bed with him. He raised a brow. "You're still going to call me old man?"

Holding the phone in front of her, she climbed into her bed. "I wouldn't have agreed to this whole being-in-love thing if I thought it would change things between us. Didn't I tell you that I wanted to keep my best friend?"

He grinned. "I'm actually hoping things *will* change between us."

She was intrigued. She pulled her duvet cover over her. "Really? Elaborate. How would you like things to change between us?"

His eyes narrowed as he settled against his headboard. "Well, we've already had conversations in bed at night, but hear me out...What if we were in the same bed?"

"So, you're hoping we'll share a bed again?"

"I'm counting on it. I'm hoping you'll fall asleep in my arms often."

"Just sleep?"

He chuckled that low, rumbling laugh that went straight to her core. She was very much hoping for a lot more than just sleep, too. A sudden thought snapped her out of her arousal, though. She sat up straight. "Rohan, do you think it will be weird?"

"What will be weird?"

"You know. You and me. Sex."

"I can't believe you just asked me that."

"Um, have you met me? You do remember I've never been shy or demure when it comes to conversations about sex, right? I used to give you details about my hookups all the time. Oh wait." She cringed. "I probably shouldn't have done that. You were pining for me and I was telling you my favorite positions."

"I wasn't pining."

"You said you were pining! You said you had feelings for me for a while. That's pining, Mr. Nasser."

"Kam, you're incorrigible."

She smiled impishly. "And yet you love me anyway. It's okay. I was pining, too. That's why I haven't had a hookup since Ernesto. You're the reason I've been so sexually frustrated. Anyway, do you think sex will be weird between us? I mean, we've known each other, like, *forever*, and maybe we weren't always tight, but...did you ever see the *Friends* episode where Rachel laughed every time Ross touched her butt?"

"Kam, I've touched your butt before. Just a few weeks ago, remember? I don't recall you laughing."

She remembered a lot about their spare-room shenanigans. She hadn't been able to look at her tattoo without shivering since. But she didn't remember any rear-end groping. She wrinkled her nose. "How is it you remember touching my butt but don't remember who initiated that kiss? Is my butt that memorable?"

He snorted a laugh. "Actually, yes, it is. You know what, Kam? I've been pining, as you call it, over you for a year. I didn't expect this would be the conversation we'd have on the day we finally come together."

She waggled her brows. "Oh, believe me, Rohan, when we finally *come* together, there won't be any conversation. I plan to leave you speechless. Also, tell me more about this pining…You've known me for twenty-seven years, and you've only pined for one year? Was there no pining the year you finished law school?" The moment she asked the question, she wished she could take it back. Bringing up the past didn't fit this light-and-playful conversation.

"Kam, I—"

"No, never mind, Rohan. It was a long time ago. We can continue to pretend it didn't happen."

"No. You asked the question. We're going to be honest with each other, remember? We should have talked about that day a long time ago. I didn't have…these kinds of feelings for you back then. I thought you were sexy, and we had fun that summer, but I wasn't looking for more. I didn't think you were, either. I'm sorry if I misinterpreted you."

She shook her head. "You didn't misinterpret me. I mean, I

had a small crush on you, but who didn't? And let's face it—I hooked up with a lot of people back then. It's just after..." Could she tell him about the cascade effect that little kiss (and a butt grope that she *did* remember) had on her life? "You remember that my parents found us making out on the couch, right?"

"Yeah, of course. They never said anything to me about it, though."

"Well, they did say something to me. Mom screamed that I'd ruin your life, and that you were way too good for me, and she basically reminded me how worthless she thought I was. Dad defended me, and they got into this massive fight. We were in the car and we got into an accident."

"Oh my god, Kam. Is that why you refused to speak to me?"

"What? I didn't refuse to speak to you."

"I called you the night after your accident to see how you were doing. Your mother said you didn't want to talk to me again. I believed her. So, I let it go. I thought...well...we didn't need tension between our families. My brother and your sister were dating, and our fathers were business partners. I should have been there for you."

Kamila exhaled. "It's fine. My mother was wrong about me, anyway. I was in therapy for a while to help me understand that. And..." How could she explain this? "I want to make this work with you, Rohan. I do. But the thing is, that memory of you and me back then is kind of attached to a very bad memory for me. Lately, my brain has been getting it all jumbled and I've been feeling a lot of insecurity come back for...reasons. I'm going to start therapy again soon. Just so you know."

He smiled small. "Thank you for being honest with me. We can go slow. Whatever you need."

Kamila frowned. "Not too slow, I hope."

He smiled. "And Kam? I think your mother *was* wrong." He paused, looking deeply at her. This was a big mistake. She wanted to see him for real, not through a phone screen. "You were different back then," he said. "You were a kid, and you were a ton of fun. No one took you seriously. But we talked a lot that summer—"

"Like we do now."

"Yeah, like we do now. I saw something else in there during those talks. You were empathetic, and you understood people so well. You were so deeply kind and conscientious, and much smarter than people realized. We were in different stages of life, and maybe we both needed to grow up, but...I don't think you would have ruined my life. I was definitely not too good for you—probably the opposite. Because the Kamila I fell in love with was in there, and I saw her back then."

Kamila blinked. He saw her. She was twenty years old—a college dropout with no future and a giant chip on her shoulder. Everyone saw a delinquent, and he saw the best in her. She didn't know what to say. She looked at him through the tiny screen on her phone.

"Say something, Kam. Are you crying?"

"Yes," she said, sniffling. "I love you."

"I love you, too, Kam. Now, tell me more about this frustration of yours."

☂

The Aim High board of directors met on Monday, and much to Marlene's disappointment (Kamila assumed), they voted to retain Emerald for all their finance needs. Kamila came very close to saying no, and not taking the client—she didn't much like the idea of continuing to work with Anil. But Jana convinced her otherwise. If Jana accepted the job at Aim High, then she would be Kamila's contact person, not the sperm donor (as Jana had taken to calling Anil). Plus, Rohan was on that board. Not that Kamila needed excuses to see him anymore, but still. She liked the idea of him sort of being a client of hers.

And about seeing Rohan, it turned out getting a new boyfriend at the same time as putting in an offer to purchase a company wasn't ideal for finding the time to actually see that boyfriend. The fact that the boyfriend was the one she was buying the company from, all while he was purchasing shares of his company from her father, only exacerbated their free-time scarcity. Kamila was in meetings with clients all week, both hers and her father's, and in the evenings she and Dad worked on getting Emerald's business valuation sorted and putting together the paperwork for her offer to purchase. Rohan was working long hours ironing out the legal details for both sales. Although they had several business conversations during the week, they still kept their nightly video chats before sleeping. Playful, loving, teasing. Just like it had always been with Rohan. Kamila had her best friend back.

Most of their friends and family were thrilled about the upgrade to Kamila and Rohan's relationship. Shelina seemed to think this meant her sons were finally getting cousins—and double cousins at that. Kamila didn't have the heart to tell her sister that she didn't really want kids. Dad didn't believe Kamila at first when she told him she and Rohan were seeing each other, but then he surprisingly gave his blessing. He said he'd worry less about Kamila while he was in Florida if he knew Rohan was there to take care of her. Kamila rolled her eyes at that—she didn't *need* to be taken care of. But yes. She dreaded Dad leaving less now that she knew Rohan would be around even more.

She'd decided to officially shift Bollywood night from weekly to monthly, since she'd be busy running her own business, and she no longer needed to use it as an excuse to see Rohan each week. On Friday morning, they got word that Potato was ready to be released from the shelter, so Kamila decided enough was enough. Dad was spending the weekend with Shelina and the boys, so it was time to see her boyfriend's home for the first time.

After leaving the office early, she went home to pick up Darcy, then went to the shelter to get Potato. Kamila then drove downtown to Rohan's condo. After the man at the security desk let her up, she took the elevator to the sixteenth floor.

She knocked once, and then he was there. Dressed casually, in jeans and a faded gray sweatshirt that brought out his pale-brown eyes and the silver strands in his beard. He was so...handsome. Dignified looking, even in his sweatshirt. She suddenly felt awkward and shy, which were not sensations she was accustomed to feeling, especially with Rohan. She was glad she had two excited dogs to manage right now.

"Hi!" She walked into the door. "Did Potato's crate and food get here? Look at him! They gave him a bath and put a new bow tie on him and—"

"I'm going to need more than just a hi, Kam," he said, locking the door and enveloping her in his arms. She dropped the dogs' leashes, trusting Rohan had puppy proofed, and wrapped her arms around him.

After a few seconds of hugging, the awkwardness was gone and she looked up at him. "And I'm going to need more than just a hug." She wrapped her hands around his neck and pulled him down for a kiss. He took control again, deepening the kiss and pressing her up against the wall near his door. His hand was straying very close to her butt.

When he finally pulled free, he lowered his head to touch hers. "Why haven't we seen each other since Sunday?"

"Let's not do that again," she said.

He nodded and gave her another quick kiss. "No. Let's not."

"I think Potato is peeing on your kitchen cabinet."

Potato was, in fact, not peeing on the cabinet but was clearly considering it. It was time to get the puppy acclimated. They could make out later.

After puppy pads, toys, water bowls, and the crate were all positioned, they were inspected, inventoried, and played with by both Potato and Darcy before Potato passed out in the middle of the kitchen floor and Darcy fell asleep in Potato's crate. Kamila performed a sleepy switch, putting Potato in the crate and setting Darcy's blanket nearby so she could keep an eye on her new puppy brother.

Exhausted, Kamila and Rohan fell on the sofa. She finally took a look around the place.

Rohan's condo was pretty posh, as she expected. Huge picture windows, high-end appliances, gleaming quartz countertops. But what she didn't expect was that it was also pretty...lively. Homey. Not the sterile corporate man cave she expected. Lots of family pictures, Indian-inspired art, a stunning Aegean blue-and-gray area rug that looked like an abstract Japanese wave painting, and to her utter shock, decorative throw cushions. Not a lot of color, but the place had a lot more Kamila-esque details than she had expected. And yes, he had a print of their momo cart on a shelf in the dining room.

"You didn't do all this tzhujing for me, did you?"

He chuckled, burying his nose into her neck. "No. This is how my place has always looked." He nipped her skin lightly with his teeth. Rohan appeared to be quite orally inclined. Nice.

"Huh. Looks nothing like your office."

"Did you expect my home to look like my work?"

"No, I mean, I like it here. I still don't understand why I've never been here before."

He shrugged. "I . . . I was always at your place anyway."

"I'm not sure that's a good excuse."

He raised his head from her neck and looked at her. "Fine. I didn't invite you over because I thought . . . Kam, I never expected to get this far with you. *Ever.* I assumed I was destined to spend the rest of my life loving you from afar. It was easier for me not to have any memories of you in my own home."

She smiled and pulled him on top of her. "Well, now that that train has left the station, we may as well make lots of memories."

"Mmm . . . yes, brilliant idea," he murmured before leaning to kiss her.

This wasn't like their other kisses. Not like the soggy-sari one in the rain. Not like the one just now in the doorway. This was a whole-body kiss. He pressed himself on her, kissing her powerfully. This was *her* Rohan. His hand was on her butt, and there was no weirdness in sight.

"Fuck," he said when he pulled back, sounding overwhelmed.

"Language, Mr. Nasser."

He chuckled, sliding his hand to her belly.

"I don't want to go too fast," he whispered into her neck.

"You're not. I'm okay. We have time to go fast, then slow, and then everything in between. I brought condoms. A big box." She smiled, then arched her back to press his erection into her.

His pupils widened, then he laughed. "Trouble as always, Kam."

"The dogs will probably be sleeping for a while," she said, pushing his shirt up. "I'd love to see how the bolster pillows I bought match your room in person."

He kissed her neck. "Whatever you want, Kamila, you can have."

She didn't even look at the bedroom when she got to it. She didn't have the chance to, since he immediately backed her onto his dark-gray bedding and started peeling off her clothes.

Sex with Mr. Perfect was, in a word, perfect. He'd clearly been paying attention when she'd told him her favorite positions, and she was delightfully correct about his oral fixation. She'd honestly never fit so well with anyone. As she slowly drifted back down to earth after a mind-blowing orgasm, she lay on his chest. He tightened his arms around her. "That was..." he said, voice trailing off.

She leaned up onto her elbow and grinned. "I told you you'd be speechless."

"You weren't kidding. That exceeded my expectations. By a very large margin. Here's your merit increase." He pinched her bottom.

She yelped and then tickled him in retribution. After a few minutes of scuffle, she decided it was probably a good idea to get off him so they could clean up in the bathroom.

She settled back onto his chest afterward and yawned. "I could fall asleep here, but we should really go see what kind of destruction Potato has unleashed in his crate."

He nodded. "There'll be plenty of time for you to fall asleep on me later." He paused. "You know, I held you in my arms when you were three days old."

"I'm not sure where you're going with this, Rohan, but it's kind of gross so far. I was an *infant*."

He laughed, tightening his arms. "What I was *going* to say is, you cried too much, and I didn't want to hold you, but our parents forced me to. Then you fell asleep and I was stuck there on the sofa because the adults didn't want to move you. Life takes strange turns, because now I want to hold you here forever. You're the only one I want to hold like this."

"And Potato."

"Right. You and Potato."

"Darcy will get jealous."

"Okay, you, Potato, and Darcy."

"Also, I mean, I'm pretty sure I don't want kids, but we have nephews, you know. I think Shelina is trying for another one. Plus, Tim and Jerome are talking about—"

"You are trouble, Kamila Hussain."

"I'm your trouble."

He squeezed her tighter. "Yes, my trouble." He kissed her gently. "Forever and—"

"Always." She let herself get lost in his kiss again.

RECIPES

Author Farah Heron shares two great recipes for your own Bollywood party night.

CHICKEN BIRYANI FOR BEGINNERS

Serves 6–8

There are a lot of ingredients and many steps to a good biryani—and this is a good biryani. It's not particularly difficult to make, but I do recommend reading through all the steps before starting. Get your rice soaking first, then chop, dice, and prepare all your ingredients before cooking. Believe me—all this work will be worth it. With patience, you will have a dish worthy of your own Bollywood-and-biryani party.

INGREDIENTS

- 3 cups basmati rice
- 3 tbsp cooking oil or ghee

- 4 onions, sliced thin
- 2 tbsp ginger garlic paste (or 2 garlic cloves, crushed, and 1½ tsp grated ginger)
- 2 lb bone-in chicken pieces, skin removed (Thighs and drumsticks work well; if using breasts, cut them in half. Boneless chicken is fine, too—cut in bite-sized pieces and reduce the cooking time.)
- About 2–3 tbsp ready-made biryani masala (*see note*)
- 4 medium tomatoes, diced
- 2 green chilies, slit down one side (omit or reduce if you want it less spicy—the biryani masala is quite spicy on its own)
- ½ cup plain yogurt
- 3 medium-sized potatoes, peeled and cut into quarters
- 1 cup cilantro leaves, chopped (set aside ¼ of this for garnish)
- 1 cup mint leaves, chopped (set aside ¼ of this to layer with rice)
- 3 pods green cardamom
- 4 whole cloves
- 1 stick cinnamon
- 1 bay leaf
- 2 tsp salt
- 10 cups water
- 3 hard-boiled eggs (Optional. These can be boiled while the chicken is simmering.)
- ½ cup crispy fried onions (Optional, and available from an Indian store. If not available, fry 2 sliced onions in ghee or vegetable oil until dark and starting to crisp.)

DIRECTIONS

Cook chicken:

1. First, rinse and soak the rice: cover rice with water in a large bowl, swish around, then drain the water. Repeat twice more for a total of three rinses. The water should be mostly clear by the third rinse. Cover with water a fourth time and let soak for 30 minutes. Drain rice and set aside until you need it.
2. Heat oil or ghee in a large pot with a lid.
3. Add the sliced onions and fry on high heat for around 12 minutes until the onions are light brown.
4. Add the ginger garlic paste and fry on low heat for 2 minutes.
5. Add the chicken pieces, mix and fry on high heat for 2–3 minutes.
6. Add the ready-made biryani masala, mix and fry on medium heat for 3 minutes. Add a splash of water if things stick to the bottom of the pan.
7. Add the diced tomatoes and chilis if using. Mix well and cook on medium heat for 4–5 minutes until the tomatoes are soft.
8. Keep the heat on medium and add the yogurt and potatoes. Give a mix and then add the ¾ cup each of chopped cilantro and mint leaves.
9. Once it boils, lower the temperature to medium-low and cook uncovered for 2 minutes until the oil separates (you will see the oil or ghee rise to the top at the edges of the sauce).
10. Cover the pot and simmer on medium-low heat for around

20–25 minutes until the chicken is tender and the potatoes are cooked through (10 minutes if using boneless chicken pieces). Stir several times while the chicken is simmering.

11. Uncover and increase heat to high. Boil about 5–10 minutes to thicken the sauce. You want it to be a rich, thick sauce that coats the chicken, not watery.

Parboil the rice (while the chicken is simmering):

1. In a second large pot, bring 10 cups of water to a boil over high heat.
2. Add the cardamom, cloves, cinnamon stick, bay leaf, and salt to the boiling water. Then add the rinsed, strained rice.
3. Boil for 5 minutes over medium heat until the rice is almost cooked (a grain of rice should break when you pinch it).
4. Strain the partially cooked rice with a fine mesh strainer (keep the spices with the rice). Set aside until the chicken is cooked through.

Layer the chicken and rice:

1. In a large, wide, heavy-bottom pot with a lid, spread half the partially cooked rice across the bottom.
2. Spread the cooked chicken with sauce and potatoes over the rice uniformly.
3. Spread the remaining rice over the chicken.
4. Sprinkle with reserved ¼ cup of chopped mint leaves and a handful of crispy fried onions (optional).
5. Cover and cook over low heat for 7–8 minutes.

6. Remove from heat and let the biryani rest for 10 minutes.

7. Open the lid and very gently mix the chicken and rice. Empty onto a platter and garnish with quartered hard-boiled eggs (optional), cilantro leaves, and crispy fried onions (optional).

Biryani masala note: I use about half of one box of **Shan** biryani seasoning mix for this recipe (available in Indian stores or online). My favorite is the Shan Sindhi biryani mix, but the Bombay biryani or the regular biryani mixes are great, too. If you can't get the Shan mix, there are other brands and even homemade biryani masala recipes online. Note that the Shan mixes contain salt, so there is no need to add salt to the chicken. If you are using a mix without salt, you will have to add salt to taste when you add the biryani masala.

STARRY FUZZY FIZZ

This nonalcoholic cocktail is heavily scented with star anise and is amazing chilled. Perfect for brunch or late-night movie parties with friends.

INGREDIENTS

Star anise simple syrup:

- 1 cup water
- 1 cup white sugar
- 12 star anise
- 2 cinnamon sticks
- 1 long length of orange peel (orange part only—not the white pith)

Drink:

- 3 ounces peach nectar
- Soda water or prosecco
- Lemon wedge
- Mint leaves

DIRECTIONS

To make the syrup:

1. Boil one cup of water with the sugar, spices, and orange peel for 5 minutes. Turn off the heat.
2. Remove the cinnamon sticks and orange peel.
3. Cool the syrup (with the star anise still in it) in the fridge until chilled.

To make the drink:

1. Mix one ounce of syrup, 3 ounces of peach nectar, and the juice of one lemon wedge (about a teaspoon of lemon juice) in a wineglass.
2. Top with soda water (or prosecco) and ice cubes.
3. Garnish with a star anise from the syrup and fresh mint. Enjoy!

ACKNOWLEDGMENTS

I have many people to thank for helping me with *Kamila Knows Best*: My agent, Rachel Brooks, who is the best partner in this business that I could ask for. My editor at Forever, Leah Hultenschmidt, whose editorial insight strengthened this book immensely. The rest of the team at Forever, including copy editor Kristin Nappier, editorial assistant Sabrina Flemming, production editor Luria Rittenberg, art director Daniela Medina, publicist Estelle Hallick, and everyone else who had a hand in bringing *Kamila Knows Best* to readers. I am always grateful to have such an amazing publishing team behind me. And my beta readers for this book, Lily Chu and Laura Heffernan, who helped me polish my messy early draft into something that better resembled the story I wanted to tell.

I drafted most of this book in the first months of the global pandemic. Like so many people around the world, I was struggling. I would go back and forth between extreme anxiety and sadness about the unknown future, and it was hard to immerse myself in Kamila's world of biryani parties, rambunctious puppies, and extravagant dresses. For the first time, I had to write with my entire family here in my small house, while my husband transitioned to working from home, and my kids learned to navigate online school.

It was one of the hardest periods of all our lives, and I'm grateful that I have this book as a positive memory of those early days of the pandemic. I always say that I couldn't be a writer without my family supporting me—my husband, Tony, and my kids, Khalil and Anissa—but they were even more instrumental for this book. I'm grateful for their patience, their understanding, and for always being around (especially lately) to inspire me, to motivate me, and to make me laugh. They are my everything.

AUTHOR'S NOTE

Jane Austen famously said about her book *Emma* while writing it, "I'm going to take a heroine whom no one but myself will much like." But of course, Jane was completely wrong about Emma. So many people loved the character when the book was released. And the popularity of Emma has only grown in the years since then. *Pride and Prejudice* may be my favorite Austen novel, but Emma has always been my favorite character.

Like so many romance readers and romance writers, I've been an Austen fan forever. I still have my first copy of *Pride and Prejudice* that my mother gave me when I was thirteen, and I completely wore out the VHS tapes of the 1995 *Pride and Prejudice* miniseries. And I wore out another VHS tape, too—the 1996 BBC production of *Emma*, with Kate Beckinsale in the titular role and the charming Mark Strong as Mr. Knightley. To this day, that is my favorite *Emma* adaptation (followed very closely behind by the modern, teen adaptation of *Emma*, *Clueless*, mostly for the clothes and Paul Rudd).

When I started writing romance, it was inevitable that I would eventually tackle an Austen retelling. I chose Emma because of, well... Emma. Headstrong and fiercely loving of her friends and family, Emma always wanted everyone around her to be as happy as she was. And she was always up for a party. True, she was a touch clueless, and maybe a bit self-satisfied, but Emma had the biggest heart under all that extra-ness. And Mr. Knightley...sigh. Wise, respectable, powerful. And quietly loving Emma, despite all her faults. I loved bringing my interpretation of one of my favorite literary couples to life. With her touch of Bollywood flair, and her enviable social calendar, I hope you will love my Kamila as much as the beloved Emma.

ABOUT THE AUTHOR

After a childhood raised on Bollywood, Monty Python, and Jane Austen, **Farah Heron** wove complicated story arcs and uplifting happily-ever-afters in her daydreams while pursuing careers in human resources and psychology. She started writing those stories down a few years ago and never looked back. She writes romantic comedies and women's fiction full of huge South Asian families, delectable food, and most importantly, brown people falling stupidly in love. She lives in Toronto with her husband, two children, and a rabbit named Strawberry. She recently adopted two cats, one of which is named Mr. Darcy.

To learn more, visit:
FarahHeron.com
Twitter: @FarahHeron
Instagram: @FarahHeronAuthor